Prai

"Funny and original, extremely revealing about Sri Lanka. . . . Brilliant."
—*The Times* (London)

"A crazy ambidextrous delight. A drunk and totally unreliable narrator runs alongside the reader insisting him or her into the great fictional possibilities of cricket."
—Michael Ondaatje

"There's much to enjoy in Wije's garrulously meandering narrative—in the grouchy humor, the laconic observations on Sri Lanka's political tribulations, the pathos of coming to the end of your life only to realize that maybe life does matter and you might have let people down. . . . A debut bristling with energy and confidence, a quixotic novel that is both an elegy to lost ambitions and a paean to madcap dreams."
—*The Sunday Times* (London)

"A delightful novel: reading it feels like a long dilatory conversation with an agreeable drunk companion at a Press Club somewhere, with assertions made and defended by diagrams penciled on paper napkins. . . . A baggy Test match of a novel. It charms because of its grouchiness, its open-heartedness, its humor and its honesty, obvious most of all when it comes to the obsessive, possessive passion that particularly centers on cricket."
—*The Times Literary Supplement* (London)

"Karunatilaka has a real lightness of touch. He mixes humor and violence with the same deftness with which his protagonist mixes drinks. . . . He allows memory to be distilled through the filters of age and arrack, illustrating what the best fiction always does: show that there is never just one truth, one reality. . . . A great novel."
—*The Guardian* (London)

"[*The Legend of Pradeep Mathew*'s] free-wheeling, zany tempo is part of its charm too. Its picaresque action . . . gives a vibrant comic pulse to Sri Lankan life, even though Karunatilaka's portrait of the country is scathing. . . . It confirms that cricket, a game that is largely played in the head and inhabits a bizarrely detailed parallel world to our own, is ideally suited to the purposes of fiction."
—*Financial Times* (London)

"A Great Cricket Novel. For a game without much great fiction, that's a reason to applaud with drums—and forget the rules the marshals impose at Lord's."
—*The Independent* (London)

"The first genuine contender for the title of Great Sri Lankan Novel has entered the lists." —Richard Simon, *Sunday Times* (Sri Lanka)

"The best cricket novel I have ever read. Shehan's love for the game is matched by his flair for storytelling. As spellbinding as an India-Pakistan one-day match. I felt like shouting Howzat on every other page. If you love cricket read this, if you love novels read this, and if you love both, you know this one is for you." —Mohammed Hanif

"This is one of the most astonishing novels I've read in a long, long while. *The Legend of Pradeep Mathew* transcends fiction archetypes and takes on a rhythmic, breathing, life force of its own. Just when you think you've got the story pegged, it refracts in a direction you didn't expect towards a conclusion that doesn't seem possible. Yes, there is cricket in this novel, but there is much, much more. To refer to *The Legend of Pradeep Mathew* as a book about cricket is a sin tantamount to calling *Moby-Dick* a book about a whale. I have not felt that tingle at the back of my neck since my first experiences with Murakami and Bolaño."

—Jamil Zaidi, The Elliott Bay Book Company

THE LEGEND OF PRADEEP MATHEW

THE LEGEND OF PRADEEP MATHEW

A Novel

SHEHAN KARUNATILAKA

Graywolf Press

First published by Jonathan Cape, a division of Random House Group Ltd, London, as *Chinaman*

This publication is made possible in part by a grant provided by the Minnesota State Arts Board, through an appropriation by the Minnesota State Legislature from the Minnesota general fund and its arts and cultural heritage fund with money from the vote of the people of Minnesota on November 4, 2008, and a grant from the Wells Fargo Foundation Minnesota. Significant support has also been provided by the National Endowment for the Arts; Target; the McKnight Foundation; and other generous contributions from foundations, corporations, and individuals. To these organizations and individuals we offer our heartfelt thanks.

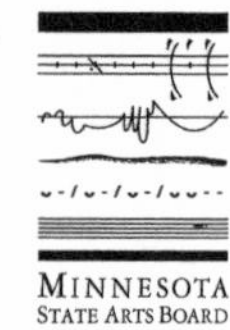

Published by Graywolf Press
250 Third Avenue North, Suite 600
Minneapolis, Minnesota 55401

www.graywolfpress.org

Published in the United States of America

ISBN 978-1-55597-611-8

2 4 6 8 9 7 5 3 1
First Graywolf Printing, 2012

Library of Congress Control Number: 2012931911

Cover design: Kapo Ng

For
Suranjan, Dilo, Ranil,
Mani and Percy

THE LEGEND OF PRADEEP MATHEW

Contents

If a liar tells you he is lying,
is he telling the truth?

First Innings

'I think the word 'great' is overused. It should only be used for the real legends of the game. We keep saying, 'It's a great goal', 'It's a great save', 'It's a great shot through the covers', when we are talking about orthodox, normal things that happen in every game. I think it denigrates the word.'

Geoff Boycott, England batsman (1964–82)

Pradeep Who?

Begin with a question. An obvious one. So obvious it has already crossed your mind. Why have I not heard of this so-called Pradeep Mathew?

This subject has been researched lengthwise and breadthwise. I have analysed every match our man has played in. Why, you ask, has no one heard of our nation's greatest cricketer?

Here, in no particular order. Wrong place, wrong time, money and laziness. Politics, racism, power cuts, and plain bad luck. If you are unwilling to follow me on the next God-knows-how-many pages, re-read the last two sentences. They are as good a summary as I can give from this side of the bottle.

Deadline

I made my decision after the 1996 World Cup. The last years of my worthless life would be dedicated to a worthy cause. Not world peace or cancer cures or saving whales. God, if he exists, can look into those. No. In my humble opinion, what the world needs most is a halfway decent documentary on Sri Lankan cricket.

No one knows about this visit to Nawasiri Hospital. Not Sheila, who has begun to notice my falling hair, my swollen fingers and the rings under my eyes. Not Ari, who has remarked on how my hand shakes as I pour. Not even Kusuma, the servant, who wakes up every other morning to clean up my acidic, bloodstained vomit.

The doctor is younger than my son and has a put-on smile that does not soften the blow. 'Mr Karunasena, your liver is being destroyed. And it will get worse.'

'At least I have my heart.'

My giggle is as pathetic as my attempt at humour. He ignores it and begins scribbling.

'Can't you give me pills?'

'I can give you pills for the nausea and the fever. I can also refer you to our alcohol counsellor.' The doctor tears off a chit branded by a pharmaceutical company I have not heard of. 'The rest, Uncle, is up to you.'

'How much time?' I keep my tone even and my eyes fixed, hoping the pup won't see that the old dog is ruffled.

'If you stop drinking and start eating, exercising, Uncle can bat on for another ten, twenty years.'

The things they don't teach you at school. How to love. How to die. How to stage a dramatic comeback.

Is it possible to hammer 3 goals in extra time after trailing 2–0 ? Or to land a knockout punch at the end of the 12th? Is it too late to score a 10 an over and turn a paltry 170 into a magnificent 300?

In my life I have seen beauty only twice. I'm not talking *Tharuniya* magazine front-cover beauty. I'm talking staggering beauty. Something so beautiful it can make you cry. Sixty-four years, two things of beauty. One I have failed to cherish, the other I may yet be able to.

Sheila at the Galle Face Hotel, 31st Nite Dinner Dance, 1963.

PS Mathew vs New Zealand, at Asgiriya, 1987.

'What if I cut down to two drinks a day?'

He doesn't look surprised. But at least he lets go of the smile. 'A year or two. Maybe more.'

Thus it was settled. I would attempt to do a halfway decent documentary on Sri Lankan cricket. There is nothing more inspiring than a solid deadline.

Sheila

'I don't mind you writing as long as you don't depress people.'

My beloved wife is making me sweep the kitchen. The last time I held a broom, Diego Maradona was a thin, teetotalling teenager.

'You used to be a poet, Gamini. Now you're just a grumpus.'

She says I cannot spend my retirement in my room reading about cricket and drinking. So I have chores, which at sixty-four, I find abominable. But as long as I am helping around the house, we are not talking about my drinking, and in my retirement such mercies are welcome.

'Don't talk rot, Sheila. When we were young anger was fashionable. Angry young man and all. Now I'm a grumpus?'

'That's not a cricket bat, Gamini. Sweep properly.'

It is true. The world has changed and I have not. As with everything, my fault entirely.

'Heard from Garfield?'

'Just go, men.' Sheila is cutting onions and not crying. She keeps jabbering. 'He's doing well. You better stop this business and talk to him. He's calling tonight.'

'Tonight I will be writing.'

'Do whatever the hell you want.'

She adds the red chilli to the dry fish.

I say nothing, keep sweeping, and decide to do just that.

Pradeep Why?

Another question. Why am I chasing a man who played only four test matches for Sri Lanka? A man who denied me interviews, delighted me on occasion, disappointed those he played with, and disappeared three years ago. A man whose name is remembered by a minority smaller than our tribal Veddah population.

I ask myself this right after my bath and my morning tea. My tea is taken milk-less with three teaspoons of sugar and five tablespoons of Old Reserve. As you will soon see, I take arrack with a lot of things.

So when did Pradeep Mathew stop being just another Lankan spinner of the 1980s? When did he become something worth obsessing over? A cause I would champion? To answer that I will take you to a boxing match between two men in dinner jackets. One was my dearest friend; the other, my oldest enemy.

Wicket

The word wicket can refer to the three stumps that the bowler attempts to hit. 'The ball almost hit the wicket there.'

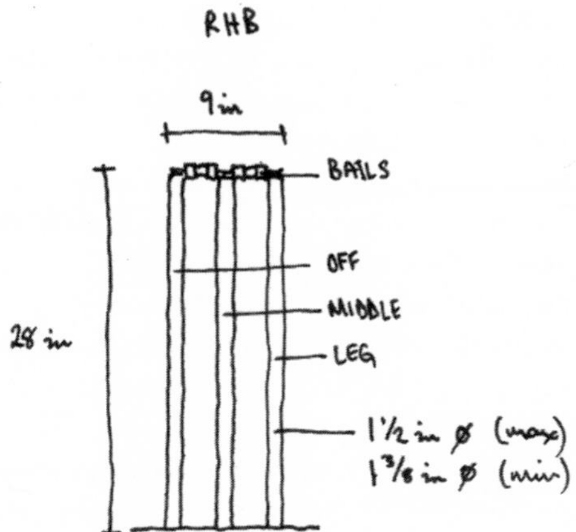

The surface they are playing on. 'The Eden Gardens wicket is dry and difficult to bat on.'

The bowler's performance. 'Laker's taken 7 wickets in this match so far.'

The batting line-up's mortality. 'South Africa lose 5 quick wickets.'

Its versatility is bettered only by a four-letter word that serves as noun, verb, adjective, adverb, and expletive.

Clean Bowled

The simplest dismissal is when the bowler knocks over the batsman's wickets. Mathew did this with most of his victims. He sent left-arm chinamen, googlies, armballs and darters through pads and feet. Here is a not-so-random sample of batsmen whose bails he dislodged. Border. Chappell. Crowe. Gatting. Gavaskar. Gower. Greenidge. Hadlee. Imran. Kapil. Lloyd. Miandad.

You are shaking your head. You are closing the book and frowning at the cover. Rereading the blurb at the back. Wondering if a refund is out of the question.

Punch-up at a Wedding

In the buffet corner, weighing over 100 kilos, from the bridegroom's hometown of Matara, sports journo, talent broker, amateur coach: Newton 'I came to eat, not to be insulted' Rodrigo.

In the champagne corner, weighing under 180 lbs, teacher, preacher, video fixer, uninvited guest: Ariyaratne 'I have watched every test match since 1948' Byrd.

Ari is my neighbour and my drinking partner. I have smuggled him in and he has smuggled in a bottle. The Oberoi wasn't Ari's usual watering hole. He has tanked up already at somewhere far less plush. I should have expected trouble.

We are at the wedding of the Great Lankan Opening Batsman, or the GLOB as we shall call him. The GLOB is a man of the people and has invited to his wedding members of the press, ground staff, and a sprinkling of international cricketing celebrities.

Thirty tables away, Graham Snow and Mohinder Binny are swooning over a gaggle of girls. Both were former players who became commentators and then became players. The buffet table has seven types of buriyani. Next to vats of chicken, Tyronne Cooray, the Minister for Sports and Recreation, is laughing with Tom Whatmore, the then coach of the Sri Lanka cricket team.

And this is where it begins. At the Lanka Oberoi in 1994. With Ari Byrd, Thomian blazer torn along the creases, pressing a chicken drumstick into the face of Newton, shrieking, 'You came to eat, no? Ithing kaapang! Eat!'

I have seen many fights. Boxing bouts in Kurunegala, barroom brawls in Maradana. Never have the combatants been less skilled, more drunk, or better dressed.

A waiter guards the buffet table as the men in torn suits roll against empty chairs.

Newton takes a hard bite on the chicken, chomping down on two of Ari's fingers.

'Ah-wa!'

Ari's scream is high and girlish. Our table, composed of inebriated journalists like myself, chuckles, sips and gazes around with pleasure at sari-clad women, exotic dancers and international celebrities, who, thanks to Ari's scream, are gazing back, though perhaps not with as much pleasure.

Most observe from the dance floor. Disapproving aunties and jolly uncles push through the has-beens and never-will-bes. Hand on mouth in mock shock. 'This is what happens when you invite the riff-raff,' cackles a crow in a sari. No one for a moment considers stopping the fight just then. Not even us.

Two reasons: (a) Sports journalists rarely see anything in the way of entertainment, especially these days, especially on the cricket field. (b) We all dislike Newton and feel he deserved this bludgeoning with buriyani chicken.

Newton has made a lot more money than any of us. 'For me, of course, journalism is a hobby. A calling. Pocket money.' Newton brings young cricketers to Colombo and sells them to clubs; he also studies race sheets, politically and literally backing the right horses always. I know this pudgy man as well as I know the gentleman who was dousing him in gravy.

'Shall we do something?' asks Brian Gomez, TV presenter and prankster. Brian once typed a letter on Oxford stationery asking Newton to visit the British High Commission to receive his Queen's scholarship. The next day Newton wore a suit to work.

'Let them be,' says Renganathan, Tamil cricket writer. Renga is a good bugger, but unhealthily obsessed with Roy Dias. When he was editor at the *Weekend*, he ran one issue with seventeen articles on this wristy batsman of the 1980s.

Newton gains the upper hand. He smears rice in Ari's eyes and crawls under the table. Elmo Tawfeeq of the *Daily News* tries to separate them, gets elbowed twice, and decides to sit down. Elmo once told us that he hit Imran Khan for a 6. In actuality, he played club cricket with a Bangladeshi who Imran once hammered for 6.

These are the men I have spent my years with and they are all drunk. Failed artists, scholars and idealists who now hate all artists, scholars and idealists. The band has stopped playing and I hear raised voices in the distance. Newton and Ari knock into veteran scribes Palitha Epasekera and Rex Palipane and I decide to intervene.

I gulp down the last of my rum, but before I can offer my services, the bride of the GLOB enters, shining under yellow lights. A delicate petal, bouquet in hands, tears in eyes.

In the distance, her husband advances with concern smeared across his brow, thinking what I am thinking: that these animals would tear his flower apart. The flower drops her bouquet and screams in an accent that sounds like Sydney but could be Melbourne, in a voice that is anything but petal-like: 'Get the fuck out of my wedding! You fucking arseholes!'

We can take a fist from a brute, but not a curse from a bride. The waiters assist us in packing up the fight. Released from Ari's gin-powered grip, Newton picks up a mutton curry with intent.

'Put that down!' The GLOB descends on the scene. 'Yanawa methaning! Get out!' Both Newton and Ari heed the great man. With the GLOB is Ravi de Mel, has-been fast bowler. He looks for the softest target, finds it, and snarls. 'Ah, Karunasena. Who else? Kindly take your friends and bugger off.'

Fearing unfavourable press, the GLOB puts on his man-of-the-people smile and pats me on the back. 'Don't get angry, Mr Karuna. Wife is bit upset. Don't you know?'

As we are led out, I see a dark man with a crew cut. He is leaning on table 151, surrounded by sycophants. Indian captain Azharuddin is chatting to him, though the man doesn't appear to be listening. Our eyes meet and he raises his hand. I return the wave, but he has already averted his gaze.

That may or may not have been the moment that started what you are about to read. But it was most certainly the last time I ever saw Pradeep Sivanathan Mathew.

Slide Show

Today Newton looks like a hippo, those days he was more like a rhino. Mathew may have caused the fight, but it was started by Newton. He had issues with me that went beyond cricket and provoked me knowing I would not respond. He didn't count on noble, smashed-on-stolen-gin Ari leaping, quite literally, to my defence.

The ballroom smells of flowers, buriyani and thousands of clashing perfumes. Strategic buffet tables separate cricket refugees from social parasites. The deluxe section features the national team, some minor celebs film stars, models and people wealthy enough to own film stars and models.

The middle section is filled with aunties and uncles, media and business types. They have the best view of the dance floor and the band, neither of which seemed to interest them. And then there are us. The journalists, coaches, ground staff, B-grade cricketers, C-grade friends.

Our table sits ten: me, Ari, Newton, Brian, Renga, Elmo, a Pakistani from the Associated Press, his friend and a young couple who look lost. At the other end of the room, there is a bar serving scotch, vodka and champagne. Our table has a bottle of arrack and several glasses of passion fruit cordial. We are men of simple tastes: anything, or even with nothing, with arrack will do.

'I should be drinking Chivas with Snow and Sobers,' says Newton. 'They must've misprinted my ticket.'

'So go, will you,' says Ari. 'Maybe Mohinder Binny will ask you to dance.'

The band plays a synthetic love song and the happy couple hold each other and move from side to side. We make quick work of the booze. Everyone whacks two shots, Ari and I whack four. The Pakistanis, Allah be praised, do not drink. As the lights dim, I explore unoccupied tables for bottles to steal. When I return with gin, the conversation has turned to cricket.

Brian Gomez, ever the patriot, proclaims that this Sri Lankan team could be our greatest. Ari says they are OK, but nowhere near the true greats like Lloyd's Windies or Bradman's Invincibles. 'Clive Lloyd's team is the best I've ever seen,' proclaims Renga. We hide our smirks. Every time Renga sees a film or witnesses a cover drive, he proclaims it to be 'the best he's ever seen'.

The Pakistani journalist talks of an all-time football XI featuring Zico, Best and Maradona. We sip stolen booze and begin fantasising.

What if Ali fought Tyson? Or Navratilova played Billie Jean? It's a good way to pass the time. Better than staring at the dance floor, pretending to grin.

We agree that Lloyd's team were literally head and shoulders above the rest. Elmo offers that Bradman's Invincibles were invincible only because of Bradman. 'You eliminate him, good team. Invincible? That I don't know.' We all drink a toast to Clive Lloyd. The young couple slink off to another table.

Newton is petulant throughout. 'Our team couldn't even draw a two-day match with Bradman.'

'Don't say that,' says Brian. 'We beat New Zealand.'

The dance floor writhes with famous names and dolled-up women who do not belong to them. From the roar of the house band and the machinations of the dancers, it is evident that the alcohol denied to our table has been flowing freely on the other side of the room. Understandable. Dolled-up women prefer to have their bottoms pinched by international cricketers and not by those who write about them.

The Pakistani journalist begins scribbling on napkins. As the only man at the table with an education outside of Asia, he convinces us with diagrams and eloquence that the perfect cricket team should be composed as such:

Two solid openers
Three aggressive batsmen
Two genuine all-rounders
One agile wicketkeeper
Two unplayable fast bowlers
One genius spinner

Seduced by his Parthan lilt and logical arguments, we nod collectively. The Windies were great, but not perfect. No spinner. No all-rounder. Lloyd had four types of hurricanes at his disposal: the elegant Holding, the belligerent Roberts, the towering Garner and the fiery Marshall. Who needs spinners, counters an argumentative Newton.

Booze flows and conversation splinters. Graham Snow toasts the GLOB and his bride, who begin doing the rounds of the ballroom. Ari and the Pakistani journalist whisper and scribble on napkins. The rest of us charge our glasses and clap as the band switches to traditional baila and a bald man with a moustache commandeers the mic from a bearded man in a hat. Both are middle-aged, potbellied and wearing leather trousers.

Ari and the Pakistani journo silence the table with an announcement. Elmo, Brian and Renga listen while wiggling their bellies to the bajaw beat.

'Gentlemen. We have constructed the world's greatest cricket team.'

Ari and the Pakistani have prepared a slide show of napkins. Dinner arrives at the table, but is pushed aside for the presentation. 'Of course, I don't agree with some choices,' says the Pakistani.

First slide:
Openers

- Jack Hobbs (Eng-20s)
- Sunil Gavaskar (Ind-80s)

Newton raises his glass. There is much nodding. 'The masters,' says Elmo.

Next slide:
Middle Order

- Don Bradman (Aus-40s)
- Viv Richards (WI-80s)
- Allan Border (Aus-80s)

There is applause. We grin at each other with appreciation. 'How about Zaheer Abbas?' says the quiet friend of the Pakistani journo. We all glare at him and he pipes down into his passion fruit.

Next slide:
All-rounders

- Garfield Sobers (WI-60s)
- Wasim Akram (Pak-90s)

I mention the word Hadlee. Ari and the Pakistani inform me that sadly there are no New Zealanders on this team. 'What about Sri Lankans?' asks Brian and we all snigger. This was 1994. We were drunk, but not stupid.

Next slide:
Wicketkeeper

- Denis Lindsay (SA-60s)

And here the group erupts. Denis Lindsay over Tallon? Knott? Bari? Madness. Newton calls the list pathetic. The rest of the critics hurl their knives. Not me.

I saw Lindsay tour Sri Lanka as part of a Commonwealth side in the 1960s and keep wickets to the fire of Wes Hall and Freddie Trueman and the wiles of Chandrasekhar and Prasanna. I have never seen that level of agility in anyone outside of a cartoon film. Apartheid was responsible for many tragedies. Somewhere at the bottom of a long list would be the short careers of Graeme Pollock, Barry Richards and Denis Lindsay.

Next slide:
Fast Bowlers

- Sidney Barnes (Eng-10s)
- Dennis Lillee (Aus-70s)

Some say ooh. Some say aah. Some say Sidney who? I mention that the great Lillee took all his wickets in England, Australia, and New Zealand. That over a twelve-year career he never took a wicket in India or the West Indies. No one listens to me.

The clatter of plates and chatter of guests replace baila as the dominant noise. Across the ballroom everyone digs into the roast chicken and richly flavoured rice. But our table is undivided in its attention.

Who could the genius spinner be? A leggie like Grimmet or Qadir? An offie like Laker or Gibbs? A left-armer like Bedi or Underwood?

Final slide:
Spinner

- Pradeep Mathew (SL-80s)

And pandemonium begins. The Pakistani shakes his head and says he had nothing to do with it. Renga, Brian and Elmo hoot with laughter.

'Y'all are cocked, ah?' Newton launches into a tirade. 'If you want to put a Lankan, put Aravinda or Duleep. Pradeep Mathew? How can you call yourselves sports journalists? Bloody fools.'

Ari puts up his hand. 'This list is based on stats and natural ability. Both Mathew and Lindsay have strike rates and averages that rank them with the greats.'

I step in. 'I saw Lindsay in '63. Maara reflexes. Jonty Rhodes is nowhere. He jumped in front of the batsman to take a catch at silly mid-off.'

'You bloody drunkard, it was '66,' says Newton. 'Y'all are idiots. Mathew can't even make the current side.'

And in the economy section of the crystal ballroom, gobbling chicken buriyani amidst famous acquaintances, Ari and I begin telling them. About the multiple variations, the prize scalps, the balls that defied physics, and that legendary spell at Asgiriya. No one believes us.

Newton calls me a drunk a few more times. I call him a bribe-taking pimp. The rest of the table retreat, while Ari begins slurring.

And as the temperature rises, I look around and see the man himself in a circle of people, looking lost. At his side is a pretty girl, whispering in his ear is the Indian skipper, hanging on each syllable are career reserve Charith Silva and Sri Lankan cheerleader Reggie Ranwala.

Mathew is glaring at me, as if he knows his name is about to cause a brawl. As if he knows I will spend the next five years searching for him. As if he knows he will never be found.

And then, Newton calls me a talentless illiterate who should be writing women's features. And then, Ari stuffs a chicken into Newton's open mouth. And then, all is noise.

Willow and Leather

The ball is made of leather with a hard seam running its circumference. The bat is made of willow. The sound of one hitting the other is music.

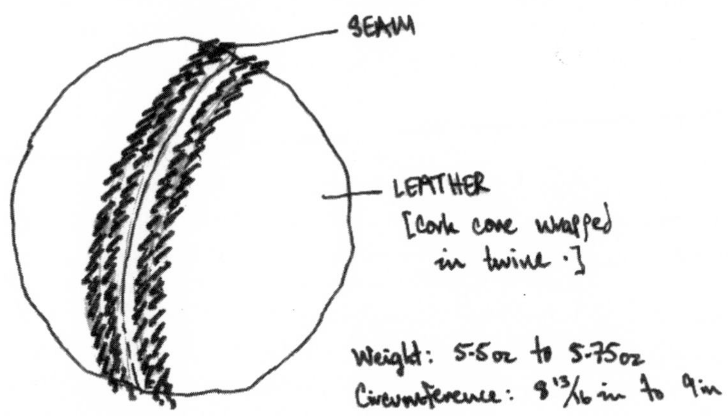

Birds

Today I cannot write. There are birds outside my window. They are being shrill. People, mainly birdwatchers, think birds are treasures of Lanka and their songs more melodious than the collected works of Boney M and Shakin' Stevens.

I find a fish market more melodic. These sparrows and parrots remind me of parliament during my reporting days. I cannot write. I cannot think. There are birds outside my window. So I will drink.

Spinners or Plumbers?

The GLOB once claimed that just because he could hit a ball with a bat it didn't make him better than anyone else. Was he being falsely modest or genuinely humble? Like many of our local umpires and selectors over the years, I will give him the benefit of the doubt.

But there is some truth to what he says. Does Sri Lanka need more schoolteachers, more soldiers, or more wicketkeepers? What's more useful to society? A middle order batsman or a bank manager? A specialist gully fieldsman or a civil engineer? A left-arm spinner or a plumber?

I have been told by members of my own family that there is no use or value in sports. I only agree with the first part.

I may be drunk, but I am not stupid. Of course there is little point to sports. But, at the risk of depressing you, let me add two more cents. *There is little point to anything.* In a thousand years, grass will have grown over all our cities. Nothing of anything will matter.

Left-arm spinners cannot unclog your drains, teach your children or cure you of disease. But once in a while, the very best of them will bowl a ball that will bring an entire nation to its feet. And while there may be no practical use in that, there is most certainly value.

Pitch

The battleground. 22 yards, punctuated at either end by three stumps. If the pitch is grassy and moist, the ball whizzes through. If it is wet or bone dry, the ball will spin. The pitch serves as a scapegoat for many failures, though it is seldom referred to by those celebrating success.

The Articles

Inspired by napkins and wedding punch-ups, I decide to write short articles on the ten greatest Sri Lankan cricketers of all time. I will not tell you who are on my list. I am already sick to death of lists.

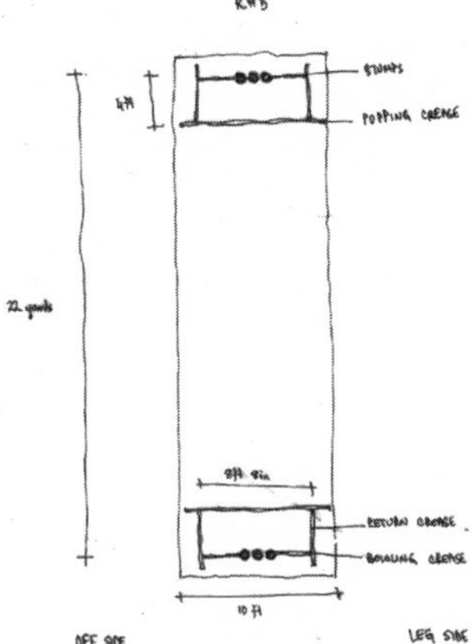

At the risk of sounding like Renga, I will say that the articles are the best things I have written in forty-one years of wielding a pen. Despite this, or perhaps because of this, the *Observer* refuses to publish them.

The *Observer* and I have a history. I was there from '58 to '71, winning Ceylon Sportswriter of the Year in 1969. I left to find my way in the world. I then lost my way in the world, and returned a prodigal in '91. In between I had won a few more awards, done a stint in radio, been sacked twice from reputed newspapers and acquired a reputation as a belligerent drunk.

I'm not sure why the editor of the *Observer* despised me. It could have been my debonair, devil-may-care swagger. Or it could be the fact that I spilled brandy on his wife at a Christmas party in '79. He could not sack me before I was pensionable, for fear of labour courts. So, sadist that he was, he kept me away from the sports pages and put me on parliament duty, the role of a glorified stenographer.

He refuses to publish my articles, claiming, maliciously, that they are poorly written. The *Weekend* doesn't think so. They publish three before going bankrupt. Or more specifically, before going bankrupt due to their printing presses being set on fire by men with gold jewellery and cans of petrol a week after publishing a story involving the government and an address that was too accurate for its own good.

Kreeda, a magazine I helped start, publishes all ten, but has the circulation of an illustrated porn rag. Palitha Epasekera agrees to translate the articles for *Ravaya*, but that never happens. But then in '95, over a year after they are written, *Sportstar* say they are interested in three: Aravinda, Sathasivam and Mathew. *Sportstar* pays handsomely, which is just as well, because the *Observer* is in the process of terminating my employment for freelancing for other publications.

This too is just as well. I am tired of sitting in parliament, watching fat men braying like mules and squabbling like infants. I send a letter to the company accountant on 26 April, the day of my birth, informing him of my recent elevation to the age of pensionability. I now never have to work or worry about drink money ever again. There are some perks of ageing.

There are also some perks of working forty-one years in journalism. Free buffets, free booze, free hotel rooms, free invites to functions, free tickets to matches. In exchange for no pay, no respect, and the very real possibility of being bludgeoned to death by a government-sponsored thug.

Cheerio to the lot of you. You will not be missed.

Sales Pitch

If you've never seen a cricket match; if you have and it has made you snore; if you can't understand why anyone would watch, let alone obsess over this dull game, then this is the book for you.

Definitely

Ari Byrd is my next-door neighbour. He teaches maths at Science College in Mount Lavinia and lectures at the University of Moratuwa. He calls himself a fixer of gadgets, but I would describe him as more of a breaker. His front room and his garage are littered with carcasses of video players, walkmans, spool machines and Polaroid cameras. He buys these gadgets through the *Sunday Observer* classifieds, obsolete technology with broken parts at a cut price.

'Wije, God has given you a gift that you are wasting,' he says. 'You must write a book.'

This was many years before the stomach pains.

'Yes. Yes,' I reply. 'One day, the stories I will tell... Definitely.'

Promises uttered by Sri Lankans ending in the word definitely have a high likelihood of being broken. We use the word as the Mexicanos would say mañana.

My friend Jonny Gilhooley likes the articles and is not a man given to insincerity. He says, 'WeeGee, me bonnie lad, you should write for

Wisden.' Renganathan calls me and says 'Karu, those were the best articles I have ever read.'

Of course, there are the critics. My sweet, darling Sheila in her kind, gentle way says, 'What, Gamini? Those three were hopeless, no? Your Duleep and Arjuna ones were better.'

Thankfully, the years have given me the maturity to deal with criticism.

I bump into my nemesis Newton Rodrigo at a club game.

'Heard you got sacked from the *Observer*?'

'I retired. Unlike some, I know when to quit,' I parry.

'If that was the case, you would've quit in the 1970s,' he chuckles.

'When I was at the top. True,' I muse. 'As I recall, even in those days you were feeding at the bottom, no?'

He stops laughing. 'I don't have time to talk baila with you. Why are you obsessed with that Mathew? Your articles were OK. In the hands of a better writer, they could've been good.'

I submit the articles to *Wisden*, and receive no response. So in the early months of retirement, I spend my minutes hidden in my cluttered room, trying to write more words for syndication. I end up wasting afternoons arguing with Sheila about our son, Garfield. The boy is just out of his teens and shows no interest in anything other than listening to noise in his room and pretending not to smoke.

My favourite waste of time is daydreaming unanswerables about Mathew. Who did he get his talent from? Why did he not play regularly? Where did he disappear to?

I haven't yet told you about the Asgiriya test. I'm hoping there will be world enough and time.

The phone rings. The phone is always for Garfield. Giggly girls and boys shouting swear words. I have ways of dealing with them.

'Could I speak with DubLew Gee Karoonasayna, please?'

'Speaking.'

'You been writing for the *Sportstar* on Shree Lankan cricketers?'

'That is correct. To whom am I…'

'Great stuff. Especially that piece on the spinner Mathew. I saw him, you know, in the '87 World Cup…um…hold on, please.'

I hear the same voice barking in the distance. 'Oh, for fuck's sake… I thought we weren't going live. OK. OK. Now piss off.'

'Hello, Mr Karoonasayna…'

'Call me Gamini…'

'Mate, I've to go on air. Can you make it to the Presidential Suite at the Taj at 10?'

'Of course.'

'Oh, and come alone.'

'Definitely.'

And that was how I got to meet Mr Graham Snow.

Presidential Suite

It has its own entrance and its own lift. Both are carpeted and plated in silver, shined to the point of reflection. The lift is as big as my office room, designed, presumably, to transport bodyguards and entourages to the seventeenth floor in one go.

We aren't the only ones heading to the Taj Renaissance Presidential Suite. We share the lift with Hashan Mahanama and career reserve Charith Silva, both a year away from being immortalised as members of the '96 world-conquering squad. They are flanked by no less than five young lasses. All with straightened hair, knee-length skirts and varying degrees of make-up.

The security guards body-search me and Ari, and leer at the display of thigh and cleavage that they are forbidden to touch. Silva and Mahanama, knowing that they know me from somewhere, give me the tiniest of nods before shepherding their harem from the lift.

'You bugger,' says Ari as we enter the darkened room. 'This is a bloody opium den.'

'Just go, men,' I say, walking past supine bodies and crimson lampshades. The air is filled with smoke and desperation and the thump of something resembling music. Ari is prone to melodrama.

'If I didn't know better, Wije, I'd say we were at a party. As my daughters would say, we are crashing the gate. Are you sure this is…'

'Fellow told me 10 at Taj Presidential Suite,' I say, pasting a smile on my face to mask my terror at being surrounded by women in various states of undress. We elbow our way through the corridor, glancing at the populated rooms. In some, people are sitting on rugs and puffing on teapots made of glass. In others, strobe lights are flashing reds and pinks and a man with headphones is scraping a table.

'You wan tequila?' She is Chinese and blonde and wearing boots and shorts. Her friend looks East European and is wearing no bra.

'Tequila. Tequila. Gimme. Gimme,' says the Russian. She looks at us.

'Uncle. Ko-he-ma-da?'

'Kohee-meedi…' mimics Marilyn Ming-Roe. They both giggle.

Ari and I down the shots.

'You no take lime and salt?'

Unsure what to do in these situations, I look her square in the breast and grin like a goon.

Ari takes charge. 'Is Graham Snow here?'

'Ah, you friend of Graham? We take you,' says the Russian.

'Graham is not in good mood,' says her companion, sucking on a lime.

We pass through rooms where expensive bottles of vodka are being emptied down unappreciative throats. Where young men and younger women wiggle to bone-rattling noise. I fancy I spy some famous faces, many, like me, much too old to be here. The Russian leads us up a spiral stairway to a garden on the roof.

Gusts of cool breeze take the sweat from our shirts. To our left is the open space of Galle Face Green with the Indian Ocean curling at its feet. To our right, a troubled city of lights and silence. A more spectacular view of Colombo I am yet to see.

Perched alone next to a table of bottles, puffing on a crumpled cigarette, is Gatsby himself, Mr Graham Robin Snow. He raises a solitary eyebrow.

'Oh right.' He rises. A giant in a batik shirt and a straw hat.

'Sirisena! Bring another chair.'

He squeezes our hands and avoids our eyes. He motions for us to sit and looks down at his slippered feet. 'Didn't know there'd be two of you.'

'This is Ari Byrd. My statistician.'

Unimpressed, Snow begins pouring vodka. 'Drink?'

A man with muscles in a white T-shirt enters carrying chairs.

'Siri, bring some ice, will ya?' Snow's voice rises with each sentence. 'Siri, I can smell fucking dope. I caught two of them having it off in these bushes. Tell Upul no fucking dope and no fucking fucking! I'll kick everyone out.'

Rambo scrambles down and barks orders at an unseen security guard.

We sit with our drinks, next to one of the greatest English cricketers of the 1970s.

'Are you married?' he asks. We both nod.

'Happily married?' Ari nods slightly more vigorously than I do.

'It's easy for you chaps. No offence. But you don't have women throwing themselves at you all around the world.'

I look at Ari, who looks at me.

'I just didn't think she'd leave.'

And then the man who demolished Kim Hughes's Australians in '81 begins sobbing into his vodka tonic.

Nineteen Eighty-five

The very first time I see him bowl is on Jonny's massive TV during the 1985 Benson & Hedges World Series. That's when Pradeep gets me sacked from the *Island*.

I can blame it on the stakes.

On Jonny's coffee table stands a bottle of Chivas, a bottle of Gordon's and a bottle of Old Reserve. The winner gets all three, certainly a prize worth fighting for, but perhaps not worth losing one's job over.

Jonny Gilhooley, Cultural Attaché at Colombo's British High Commission, receives his stipend in pounds. He donates the Chivas. Ari receives rupees like I do, and a meagre sum at that. But he does not wish to appear ungracious and pledges an expensive gin. I have little money and less grace. The arrack is my contribution.

Jonny refuses to discuss his life before Sri Lanka. We secretly suspect he may be a Cold War spy in hiding.

'Jonny, are you a Cold War spy in hiding?'

After four pints of ale, Ari tends to forget what is secret and what isn't.

'Aye, bonnie lad,' says Jonny. 'And I'm also the bastard who's gonna take home ya bottles!'

The bet is not on who will win. In 1985, there is only one answer to that. The team that isn't Sri Lanka.

'Absholutely shuperb delivery.'

We stop our chatter and gawk at the TV. Is Richie Benaud saying something nice about Sri Lanka?

'P.S. Mathew's figures are not flattering. 7 overs. None for 51. But thish over hash been as good as I've sheen from a left-arm chinaman bowler.'

I will no longer reproduce the quirks of Benaud's speech. I wouldn't want to offend the great all-rounder. Ari, on the other hand, has no such qualms.

'This pious bugger gets on my nerves.'

On the giant TV in this air-conditioned room, Sri Lanka is suffering its seventh successive thrashing of the year. We will go on to be soundly beaten five times by Border's Australians and five times by Lloyd's West Indies. But never more soundly than the match that day.

The TV is the size of half a cinema. When Jonny got promoted from press officer, he insisted on a cinema room, pointing out at high-flown meetings, in hifalutin tones, that screenings of French new wave and German expressionist films at the Alliance Française and the Goethe Institute were popular with middle-class Sri Lankans.

A sports fan like us, Jonny rigged the screen to the MI6 satellite and got live feeds of cricket, football, rugby and tennis. Taking advantage of unspent budgets and absent high commissioners, he equipped the room with soundproofing, a well-stocked bar and plush sofas.

Jonny always invited me and Ari over to the High Commission to watch live games and let us booze and shout abuse at the large screen.

And in 1985, Ari and I do both in abundance. We also play silly games. Like the Seamless Paki, a contest of who could construct the longest sequence of overlapping Pakistani cricketers' names. At the time of writing, Ari is reigning champ for 'Saqlain Mushtaq Mohammad Wasim Akram Raza'.

Today's bet has to do with our favourite commentator, Graham Snow. The only one who has nice things to say about Sri Lanka.

'I'm with ya, Aree mate. Benaud's a tosser,' says Jonny. Jonny's accent is a mixture of Geordie and Punjabi, two very similar dialects spoken by two very dissimilar people. On screen, with Australia 262–1 off 37 overs, Richie Benaud does not respond.

Black and white photographs adorn the lime walls. Lord Mountbatten, Sir Oliver Goonatileke, Queen Elizabeth, Sir Richard Attenborough, the current High Commissioner. The air conditioner is set to just right.

'I say wicket this over,' says Ari. 'Loser serves drinks.'

The *Island* editor had insisted I hand in my match report by midnight. I make a mental note to depart early. And then Mathew bowls a perfect googly.

Anticipating the off break, Dean Jones dances down the pitch, his sunglasses glinting. The ball pitches on middle and leg and cuts sharply into the gloves of keeper Amal Silva, who whips off the bails. Jones out for 99.

'What did I tell you?' squeals Ari. 'OK. Jonny, for calling the great Richie a tosser. Gin for me, arrack for Wije and make yourself something nice.'

Ari turns his thinning head of hair towards me. 'I say, who is this fellow?'

'Pradeep Mathew. Our latest partner for DS.'

The veteran leg spinner D.S. de Silva was in his forties when Sri Lanka gained test status. The 1985 series was his swansong. It would be ten years before Sri Lanka had a regular wicket-taking spinner in the side. In the decade in between, we experimented with seventeen different ones.

When Mathew removes Allan Border's leg stump with what can only be described as a slow, reverse-swinging yorker, the three of us scream. The ball, curling in the air from off to leg and snaking under Border's bat, causes Richie Benaud to launch into uncharacteristic hyperbole.

'That'sh one of the mosht amazing deliveries I've sheen.'

Inside the soundproof cinema room there is the din of three men cheering lustily. A change in commentary: Benaud is replaced by Bill Lawry and former England captain Graham Snow.

I cast the first stone. 'For this session, three.'

Jonny chuckles. 'You must be barmy. If this spinner takes another wicket, he'll do at least seven.'

Ari has a notepad ready. 'OK, gentlemen. Round 4. How many times will Graham Snow say 'these little Sri Lankans'? Wije three? Jonny seven? I'll say five. Starting now.'

'Morning, Graham. Morning, all,' says Bill Lawry.

We wait with bated breath.

'Morning, Bill,' says Graham.

'Interesting passage of play here. Can Australia make it to 300?'

'I tell you what. These little Shree Lankans are finally putting up a fight.'

We clink our glasses and growl.

'And it's all thanks to this young man, Mathew. He's bowled a blinder.'

David Boon misjudges the flight of a wayward chinaman and spoons a catch to Madugalle. Australia 277–5. We gape at the screen.

'Another one! That's his third. Look at these figures. First spell, nothing to write home about. But this spell. 3 overs. 3 for 4.'

'Well, not being unkind, Graham, but till the last hour, this Sri Lankan team has been nothing to write home about. Comprehensively beaten in seven matches.'

Ari takes a swig of his scotch and then winces, realising Jonny has forgotten the ice and the soda.

'Blow it out your arse, Bill,' sneers Jonny. 'How boring was he? Worse than bloody Boycott.'

'You're talking rot,' I say. 'I saw Lawry stand up to a blitz from Trueman and Statham at Lord's. He was class.'

'You applying for an Aussie visa, WeeGee?' Jonny winks at Ari.

'I have no intention of leaving this miserable isle.'

'Wije. Stop bullshitting, men,' says Ari. 'Bill Lawry was a corpse with pads.'

At that moment, with the score on 290, the corpse bursts to life. 'GOT HIM! What a ball! Young Mathew traps Simon O'Donnell leg before.'

'That was a top spinner,' Graham Snow observes. 'I tell you what. This boy has them all. Chinaman, googly, top spinner and that amazing arm ball that got rid of the Aussie captain.'

Australia end up on 323 for 7. Snow says the phrase seven times during that session and twenty-three times for the whole game. Jonny wins the round, but I win the three bottles. Ari's scoring system is as mystical as the Duckworth–Lewis. I will not even attempt an explanation.

Mathew adds Kepler Wessels to his 5 scalps for 65 runs, but Sri Lanka can only muster a paltry 91, with only two batsmen reaching double figures. It is Sri Lanka's heaviest defeat.

The next day's newspapers lament our dismal batting. None mention Mathew's 5–65. The *Island*'s match report would have, had its writer handed in his copy on time.

The Shrink

All credit should go to Ari. While I pour the vodka, he sits with his arm around our host, sharing a cigarette and his secrets to happiness.

'Graham, I have always admired your grit.'

When Ari says it, it doesn't sound like brown-nosing.

'You weren't the most talented, but you were the toughest. The only fellow to stand up to that Lillee and Thompson.'

As I gaze at Colombo's rooftops, from the corner of my eye I spy Graham burying his head in his palms. How drunk is he and why is he discussing his marital problems with two strangers?

'Glenda has left. My boys ignore me. SevenSports may not renew my contract. That's it, I suppose,' he sobs.

'Stop this nonsense, Graham. Don't become a spectacle.' Ari is strict. 'Who are these people downstairs?'

'The Indians paid for the party.'

'What Indians?' I ask.

'From NSPN. A sponsorship deal for the World Cup.'

I decide to join the group therapy session. 'See, Mr Snow. NSPN! What is SevenSports? People respect you. Make cricket the centre of your life. And everything will follow.'

Ari glares at me. 'Wije. Don't talk crap. Make God and your family the centre. What is cricket?'

'Good advice,' I say. 'Except for two things. His family hate him. And God doesn't exist.'

White T-shirt Rambo interrupts what could have escalated into World War III. With him is a middle-aged man wearing a tie and a just-been-dragged-out-of-bed expression. 'Mr Graham. Dr Nalaka is here.'

The man blushes, scratches the back of his head, and then extends a limp wrist. 'You called for a psychiatrist. I am Dr Nalaka. Sri Jayawardenapura Hospital. I don't usually do night calls…'

'You're the shrink?' Graham Snow looks at me and Ari. 'Then who are these jokers?'

I flash my old press pass like a cop with a badge. 'W.G. Karunasena, *Sportstar* magazine.'

Ari bows. 'Ari Byrd. Scientist. Statistician.' He extends his hands like a preacher.

And then the man who had been sobbing just ten minutes earlier bursts into uncontrollable laughter.

Till the Ship Sails

6 balls make an over. 50 overs, or 300 balls, give or take, make a one-day game innings.

In a test match, each team bats twice. An innings ends when ten batsmen are out or when the batting captain declares the innings closed. This is not measured in overs, but in days.

From the dawn of cricket till the late 1930s, when yours truly was still a toddler chasing lizards in Kurunegala, test matches were timeless, played till both sides were bowled out twice. At first, games did not last longer than seventy-two hours, but then, as the sciences of batting and pitch making developed, matches began to stretch to four, five, sometimes six days.

In 1938 a test between South Africa and England went on for nine days and remained unfinished. Pursuing 696, England had to stop their run chase at 654–5 as their ship back to Blighty was ready to leave.

After that, test matches were restricted to five days. Some say they are still too long; I think they are just right.

These Little Shree Lankans

'I'll tell you what I love about you Shree Lankans?'

The shrink has been paid a consultancy fee and sent home while we do his job for him. We help Graham through the first bottle and most of his depression. His wife had caught him with a barmaid in the West Indies and left, leaving a hole in his life that no amount of parties in presidential suites or sponsorship deals could fill.

'You're passionate about the game, but you're also easy-going. The Indians and the Pakis have gone absolutely bananas.'

It is November of 1995. Little do we all know that in less than six months Sri Lanka would also be going bananas. In the preceding year, Sri Lanka had won their first series overseas, humbling Craig Turner's New Zealanders, and had become the first team to beat Pakistan at home in fifteen years. Later this year they would travel to Australia, where Darrell Hair would no-ball Murali for chucking, setting in motion a chain of events that would climax at a World Cup final in Lahore in March 1996.

'I read all of your articles,' says Graham. 'The *Times* could do with writers like you.'

I hope he means the *Times* of London.

'England it's all Cantona and Mansell. No one gives a flying fuck about cricket. But suddenly these little Shree Lankans are capturing the imagination of the world.'

Ari and I chuckle quietly. We decide against telling Graham Snow about our silly game. 'Sir Richard Hadlee reckons they might grab the Cup. Not sure I'm sure about that...'

'Graham, please.' I begin counting down my fingers. 'Look at our batting. Sanath, Kalu, Guru, Aravinda, Arjuna, Roshan, Hashan...'

'Flair at the top, maturity in the middle, discipline lower down,' Ari says with gusto. 'And our bowling and fielding are much more focused.'

'For the first time,' I say, 'we are real contenders for the Cup.'

'Hmm. You may well be right,' says Graham. 'This fella Mathew. Will he play?'

Ari and I exchange glances. Pradeep Mathew had not played a test since the 1994 Zimbabwe tour. He was a surprise selection for the tour to New Zealand, but did not play a single game. I attempted to contact him when researching the *Sportstar* article, but the Sri Lanka Board of Control for Cricket, SLBCC, refused to give me his details. He did not play in that year's domestic season. There were murmurings of a serious injury.

'You know that boy holds the record for best bowling in a one-dayer,' says Graham.

'You are mistaken,' says Ari. 'That is Aaqib Javed with 7 for…'

'7 for 37. Right. Mathew got 8 for 17.'

'Impossible,' says Ari.

'Wanna bet?'

'You don't want to bet with me, Mr Graham.'

'Listen,' says the great man. 'There are two reasons I called you here. One is for a business proposition. The other is to show you this…'

He pulls an envelope from his shirt pocket. And right then, the Russian brunette, formerly bra-less, now topless, runs into the garden, chased by Rambo – and Mohinder Binny who is wearing nothing but boxer shorts. Ari and I look on in disbelief. The Russian is rolling on the tiles while Binny tries to hold her down. We are unsure if she is laughing or crying.

'This is not an opium den,' says Ari. 'It's a bloody orgy house.'

We both shrug, clink our glasses and stare at the envelope while Graham Snow yells raw expletives at Rambo.

All-rounders

An all-rounder is a player who can bat and bowl. A genuine all-rounder should be able to make the team on either skill alone. A genuine one is as rare as a punctual Sri Lankan.

There are plenty of bowlers who can bat a bit, and plenty of batsmen who roll their arm over occasionally. Such players are patronisingly described as 'useful'. The New Zealand team once comprised eleven such 'useful' players, prompting the Turbaned Indian Commentator, or TIC, to remark, 'I bet even the sheep in New Zealand can bowl medium pace and bat number 7.'

Nineteen Eighty-seven

The 1987 World Cup was the first to be held outside of Blighty. It was the beginning of the eastward march of cricket's power base. A move that would be completed by the time Sri Lanka held the trophy aloft nine years later.

In '87, the number of overs per innings was reduced from 60 to 50, giving Lady Luck a greater hand in close games. Spin replaced pace as the dominant force, and for the first time neutral umpires stood in the middle.

Games were closer. Here is a random sample of results: Australia beat India by 1 run, NZ beat Zimbabwe by 3, Pakistan beat us by 15, but lost to the West Indies by 1 wicket. For the first time ever the Windies failed to reach the semis, despite Viv Richards plundering a then record 181 against, who else, Sri Lanka. It was the beginning of the end for them. The baton of supremacy would soon be wrested from their ebony fingers.

The curry-phobic West came well prepared. New Zealand shipped tins of beans and bottled water and had to book two extra rooms in Hyderabad to store provisions. England brought an expert in tropical diseases and a microwave oven, but sadly not too many batsmen who could score over a run a ball.

Nevertheless, the land that invented the game overcame hosts India to reach the final, while Allan Border's Aussies, fired up by Zaheer Abbas calling them 'a bunch of club cricketers', outplayed the favoured Pakistanis at Lahore.

Sri Lanka had an awful tournament. Even Zimbabwe looked more competitive. Our team was shunted from Peshawar to Kanpur to Faisalabad to Pune: two-day journeys each way, with more hours spent in transit lounges than in the nets.

Sri Lanka toured with three spinners: Sridharan Jeganathan, Don Anurasiri and Pradeep Mathew. Mathew played only one game against Pakistan, which we lost by 113 runs. He picked up the scalps of Imran Khan, bowled by an angling googly, and Javed Miandad, yorked by a darter, causing some to question why he was not used till our fifth game.

In 1987, my son Garfield played Under-13 for Wesley. He began the season as an opening batsman and a left-arm spinner. He ended the season as a reserve in the B-team. I told him not to worry. That we would work on his game. That next season he would be a regular player and in three years he could try for the 1st XI. What happened was nothing of the sort.

Graham Snow remembers 1987 as the first rock-and-roll World Cup. A masala of noise and colour. 'The fireworks, the magic shows, the armed escorts and, we didn't know it at the time, the bookies. I tell you, this was a far cry from the members' stand at Lord's.'

I tell him I do not remember Mathew playing more than one game in that tournament.

'Oh, Mathew was rubbish. So were Shree Lanka. Forget the World Cup. I'm talking about the qualifying games. Me and Bill did the commentary.'

In 1987, Sri Lanka had been a test nation for five years, but were, statistically at least, a disappointment. 25 tests: 2 wins. 61 one-dayers: 41 losses.

NZ took twenty-six years to post their first test victory, we took just three. Yet in 1987, Sri Lanka, five-year-old test nation, suffered the indignity of having to qualify by playing third-string sides like Zimbabwe, Bangladesh, Denmark, Argentina, Israel and Gibraltar. Yes, Israel has a cricket team.

'Against Gibraltar, Pradeep Mathew took 9 wickets. 9 for 40-odd. Gibraltans were all out for 120, your men Mendis and Dias belted those runs in 20 overs.'

This is news to us.

'9 wickets? Can't be. In '87, the record belonged to Winston Davis, 7 for 51,' says Ari the show-off. 'Are you sure, Graham?'

'No one reported it, because Gibraltar were not a recognised side.'

'Fair enough,' I say, winking at Ari.

It is another of our recurring arguments. Do records count if they are against weak opposition, at home, or in favourable conditions? To this day Ari argues that Sri Lanka are still not a great side, since we win all our matches at home. Like our record-breaking 398 against Kenya in Kandy. I argue that he is talking through his rectum.

'Against Bermuda, in the semi-final, he takes 8 for 17,' says Graham. 'Now Bermuda were losing finalists in the '82 ICC qualifiers, which gave them temporary one-day status, which meant...'

'...that Mathew's figures were official,' I say. 'Which means a Sri Lankan holds the record for best one-day bowling.'

'Not officially,' says Graham. 'But yes.'

Ari starts laughing. Sri Lankans deal with injustice in different ways. I grumble and moan, Ari laughs.

Who Wins?

Batsmen score, bowlers try and get them out, fielders catch and stem the runs. Whoever is left standing on the most runs at the end, wins.

In test cricket, unless four innings are completed, a draw is declared. If teams bowl defensively or if batsmen play too slowly, no one wins. Least of all the poor buggers who wasted five days watching.

Andy Ganteaume

I no longer feel the roof vibrate under my feet. The party has quietened and the vodka has wrapped a fluffy blanket across our mood. We are joined by Mohinder Binny, still in boxer shorts, sans the topless Russian. He sits down, toasts the memory of 1983 and passes out.

Hashan Mahanama and a hard-hitting Sinhalese Sports Club, SSC, batsman whose name I forget smoke cigarettes at the other end of the balcony.

'Buggers shouldn't smoke,' says Ari. 'They are professional sportsmen.'

'Hogwash. We lived on beer and fags and steak and pies,' says Graham Snow. 'Would Gower have been more elegant if he'd been raised on isotonic drinks? Nonsense.'

Graham lets us read and reread the letter he obtained from the International Cricket Council's Sri Lanka file. 'After I read your article, I got my PA to do some digging around. She came up with this a few weeks ago. Convinced me of two things. That Shree Lanka is filled with passion for the game. And that I should do everything I can to help you guys.'

Flat 7C/123 Cotta Road
Colombo 8
Sri Lanka

To: Lord Colin Dexter, President International Cricketing Council
Re: Humble suggestions

Dear Sir
Pardon for intruson.
I play for small country torn by war, a poor relation of cricket world. I write you becauce game in my country is controlled by PUPPETS. I am dropped from the national side due to refusing to cheat during Pakistan series and due to my race which is Tamil. In Sri Lnka, if Captain or Coach or Minister likes you, you are in team.
I do not wish to waste lordship's time with personal issue. Instead to offer suggestions for your kind perusal. Here are ways we can remove corruption in Sri Lanka and improving the game.

1. Umpiring—Neutral umpiring is very essential. Bad umpiring is ruining cricket
2. Technology—Use television cameras for run outs and to look at player discipline. There is TOO MUCH SLEDGING on field. Old friend of mine, David Hawkins has developed technology to judge LBW. Contact him at Hampshire University.
3. Change structure of cricket in developing nation. Encourage Sri Lanka cricket board to select from all over the island and FROM ALL RACES. Not just Colombo school Sinhala Budhist.
4. Local coaches too much politics. Give Sri Lanka foreign coaches, fitness trainers and more home tours. We need coaches who can analys game. Give us chance to host next world cup. Only then we will learn.
5. I am earning less than $50 per test match. Last 3 years Sri Lanka has played 4 test matches. All of us have to work for full time jobs. We play becauce we have passion and talent. But talent will leave game if there is no money.

If you put reforms and promote cricket in Sri Lanka, we will for sure produce teams like the great West Indies. Please make no mention of this letter to my cricket board or fellow countrymen.

Yours faithfully
Pradeep Mathew
14/4/87

'Typical sour grapes letter,' says Ari.

In my time I have heard many such whinges from players on the fringes. Captain favours certain schools. So-and-so bribed his way into the squad. Some even attempt to pass them off as autobiographies.

'Mate, this was the letter that got the third umpire agenda on the ICC table. Dexter consulted with Sri Lanka cricket a few years later. You now have foreign coaches and are about to host a World Cup.'

I feel the cheap paper between my fingertips. How did a man who could barely speak English write the blueprint for Sri Lankan cricket reforms?

'I wasn't talented. There've been players more gifted than me who never reached their potential. Do you know who has the highest test average?'

I step to the wicket. 'Most people think Bradman. But not so. Andy Ganteaume. Played one test and scored 112. Never played again.'

Andy Ganteaume was blamed for scoring too slowly and turning a possible victory into a draw. He never did manage to break back into a strong post-war Windies side featuring the three Ws, Sobers, Kanhai and Stollmeyer. His average sits at 112 for all eternity, 13 above the great Don.

Graham applauds and the game begins. The names come thick and fast.

Ray 'The Goat' Manigault, described by Jordan and Magic as the greatest street basketball player there ever was, succumbed to crack addiction and failed to make the NBA.

Laxman Sivaramakrishnan, India's leg-spinning boy wonder, with three gods in his surname, exploded on the international stage with 6-wicket hauls in his first three innings and then lost form permanently. Bob Massie and Narendra Hirwani took 16 wickets on debut and faded into obscurity.

Everyone tells the story of the fiery pace bowler from Jaffna who bowled at 110 mph during an SSC trial, returned to the war zone to gather his belongings and was never heard of again.

'Wasting talent is a crime,' says Graham.

'A sin,' concurs Ari.

I think of Pradeep Mathew, the great unsung bowler. I think of Sri Lanka, the great underachieving nation. I think of W.G. Karunasena, the great unfulfilled writer. I think of all these ghosts and I can't help but agree.

De Saram Road

We shake hands as Graham leads us to the lift. All that is left of the party are empty bottles, fallen ashtrays and broken furniture.

'You know, WeeJay, when I asked you to come at 10, I meant tomorrow morning,' smiles Graham.

'What do you mean?'

'I never drink with the press or let them see me drunk.'

'But you said come at 10…'

'Doesn't matter.' Graham lifts his hand. 'Was a pleasure meeting you both. Can I trust you not to write about my personal life?'

'Definitely.'

Ari looks smitten and does not let go of Graham's hand. I wonder if I should leave them alone for a goodnight kiss.

'We didn't get to talk business. Will you be at home tomorrow?'

Ari and I say yes at the same time.

'Where do you live?'

This time I let Ari say it by himself. '17/5 de Saram Road, Mount Lavinia.'

'Shall we say 10?' says Graham to the closing lift doors.

While drinking and talking cricket till 2 a.m. may offer the illusion of friendship, I was not expecting to hear from Graham Snow ever again. Many people have promised the world over bottles and delivered little more than nothing. I am one of them, and they are one of you.

The next morning I'm arguing with the urchins playing cricket on my road. It is the second ball to hit my windows and I'm in the process of confiscating it.

'Let them play,' calls out Ari from the next-door balcony. 'We must nurture cricket at street level.'

When Graham Snow's 4WD pulls up, the urchins gaze in awe. Graham rolls down the window. He is wearing a suit and a frown.

'Sorry, chaps,' he mutters. 'Just got called to the airport, problem with NSPN, need to be in Mumbai.'

He hands me a huge purple file. It is filled with legal documents with Snow's signature. Ari has run down in his sarong and shouts for the whole neighbourhood to hear. 'Ah. My good friend. Mr Graham Snow. How? How?'

'Hello, Aree. Gotta rush. No time to explain. You're the blokes I've been looking for. I'm recommending you for the Graham Snow Commonwealth Cricket Grant.'

The urchins have stopped their game. Housewives are peeping from balconies. A crow drops a watery turd on my gate.

'Go to the Sri Lanka Cricket Board and speak to Danila Guneratne. She'll give you the details. Tell her I have picked you and Aree for the grant.'

'How much is the grant?' asks Ari.

Graham's driver revs his engine. 'Gotta go. See ya. My card's there.'

'How much is the grant?'

'Speak to Danila. Good luck.'

His jeep speeds off, leaving me and Ari with a purple file and a requisition for…

'Seven lakhs!' gasps Ari.

The number is scrawled in a fancy font on a certificate that carries the Queen's seal.

The urchins resist the urge to chase after the jeep, and, sensing gossip, walk towards us. I throw them their ball and pull Ari to the veranda. 'It says here we have to make five half-hour documentaries.'

'So? Let's do it. I saw this video camera for sale in the *Observer*…'

'But what do you know about making documentary films?'

'How many documentaries I have seen. How hard can it be?'

Harder than we thought. It was three years before those documentaries aired. By that time, kingdoms had been won and lost. The bubble of Sri Lankan cricket had ballooned and burst. And sadly, so had W.G. Karunasena.

Strange Ways to Die

91 per cent of all dismissals are caused by bowlers hitting wickets, fielders taking catches, batsmen obstructing stumps and runners falling short of their ground. Bowled, caught, LBW and run-out are to cricket what cancer, heart disease, stroke and road accidents are to life.

But there are more unusual ways of surrendering your wicket. You can be out for handling the ball, hitting the ball twice, obstructing the field, not coming out on time, or falling on your wicket. All of these occurred in the 1994 Sri Lanka vs Zimbabwe series. You-know-who featured prominently.

The First Meeting

At the first meeting, everyone is late. Ari and I are the first to arrive at 00.15 Sri Lankan Time. That is, fifteen minutes after the scheduled start. By 01.23 SLT, everyone is gathered around a table in an air-conditioned room.

Representing the SLBCC are Miss Yasmin Alles, giggly and girly, looking just out of school uniform; and Ms Danila Guneratne, older, fair and flawless, could have been a model, probably was. Representing Independent Television Limited, ITL, are programming director Dr Rakwana Somawardena, sports editor Mr Abdul Cassim and Mrs Kolombage, stenographer. Representing us is just us. We are wearing ties. I have even combed my hair and polished my shoes.

'What experience do you have, Mr Karunasena, in creating television?' Rakwana, specs on nose, scrutinising our proposal, his eye darting towards Miss Alles leaning over her notebook.

I feel like asking this bearded bureaucrat in national dress the very same question.

Ari speaks. 'I lectured in filmmaking in the UK, I have studied it and taught it for over thirty years.' Ari always smiles, but he only shows his teeth when he is lying. In truth, he attended a workshop in filmmaking at the British Council in '79 and has been master-in-charge of the Science College AV Club since the late 1980s.

'You have showreel?' Danila sounds like a vatti amma selling veggies on the street, even though she looks like a Parisian model. Fair skin, dark eyes, a beauty spot below her nose, a smile that could stop traffic and a voice like a car crash.

Fluorescent light falls from tubes on the ceiling and bounces off Ari's exposed teeth. 'My showreel is on Kodachrome Color Reversal film stock. It has deteriorated over the years. It is currently being restored in Singapore.'

'Graham Snow recommends you highly. We like your articles, but we'll need a script to approve budget.'

'Script is essential,' says Cassim, more for his boss to hear than for us.

'Must have script,' nods Mrs Kolombage.

'Directing documentary is no joke,' says Rakwana to us.

'Not a joke,' nods Mrs Kolombage, closing her notebook.

Secret Weapons

A week later, we bounce back, but this time with some secret weapons. We unveil our first.

'Danila, meet Brian Gomez, sports presenter for…'

'We know Brian,' smiles Danila.

'Aren't you contracted to RupaVision?' asks Cassim.

'No, my dear,' grins Brian. 'I'm a free agent. Doing some NSPN work. Behind the scenes. Presented a few shows for Sirasa. Now I'm at your service.'

Brian's off-screen persona is much more charismatic than what we see on television. Though he is prone to bouts of toe-curling corniness.

'Dhani, how to say no to Wije and Ari? These men are encyclopaedias of cricket.'

I interrupt. 'I will script, Ari will produce, Brian will direct and present.'

'Sha. Brian, you can direct?' Today is a casual Friday and she is wearing a shawl and beads.

'Why not? Why not?' smiles Brian.

Brian picks up a transparency that I helped type and places it on the projector. The square of blinding light on the opposite wall fills up with text. 'This is our list.'

First slide:

Aravinda de Silva	Batsman 80s/90s
Sanath Jayasuriya	All-rounder 90s
Gamini Goonesena	All-rounder 50s
Sidath Wettimuny	Batsman 80s
Mahadevan Sathasivam	Batsman 40s
Duleep Mendis	Captain. Batsman 80s
Pradeep Mathew	Bowler 80s
Arjuna Ranatunga	Captain. Batsman 90s
Muttiah Muralitharan	Bowler 90s
Rumesh Ratnayake	Bowler 80s

'Pradeep Mathew?' says Danila. 'Was he that good?'

I spy Mr Cassim stealing glances at her low neckline. The mousey girl takes notes. Brian jumps in, as rehearsed.

'Dhani, let us go through the concept and then we will debate content.'

God bless him. While Ari and I can bullshit with the best, it helps to know the lingo.

Second slide:

Aravinda	The Artist
Sanath	The Punisher

Goonesena	The Gentleman
Sidath	The Stylist
Satha	The Genius
Mendis	The Strongman
Mathew	The Mystery
Arjuna	The Warrior
Murali	The Magician
Rumesh	The Fighter

'We will give each cricketer a persona,' says Ari, 'and do ten-minute segments on each, using themes and music appropriate to…'

'Warrior and Fighter are the same thing,' says Cassim with relish.

'Not necessarily…' I begin.

'This is mainly the concept.' Ari has had many battles on semantics with me and knows that things can get violent. 'We will tweak where necessary.'

'I'm not sure my boss Mr Jayantha Punchipala will be happy about including Pradeep Mathew,' says Danila. 'Otherwise, very nice concept.'

And then just before Christmas, in Jonny Gilhooley's room, watching Sri Lanka beat the West Indies at Adelaide in the first match of the legendary 1995/96 World Series, we receive a phone call.

Graham Snow is commentating with, who else, Bill Lawry. 'This Shree Lankan batting line-up has developed over the years. Flair at the top. Maturity in the middle. Discipline at the bottom.'

'Heard that? Heard that?' exclaims Ari. 'I only said that! Fellow is quoting me.'

'For the first time they are real contenders for the World Cup,' continues Snow as if the words are his own. 'And real contenders here.'

'How's your documentary, lads?' asks Jonny.

The years have been good to our friend. We no longer camp out at the High Commission. By the mid-1990s, he had built a villa by Bolgoda Lake and moved his TV room there. We make the trip whenever an important match is on. Though less often than we used to.

I shake my head and wave my hand. It is not a topic I wish to discuss while watching Sri Lanka beating West Indies, a feat unthinkable a mere ten years earlier.

And then I hear a series of Morse code-like squeaks and I feel the drinks table vibrate. Ari has purchased a cellulite phone, a brick-like contraption that sucks batteries and weighs a ton.

'Ari, it's the mothership,' says Jonny.

Ari picks up the block and walks towards the veranda by the lake. He returns moments later, wiggling his hips like a hula girl and waving his arms. 'Bring out the Chivas, Jonny boy. They approved original concept. MD wants to meet us.'

And then captain Ranatunga late-cuts a 4 as Sri Lanka inch closer to the improbable. And I'm thinking that if there is a God, he too may be watching the cricket with his feet up and a big smile on his face.

The List

Aravinda, Sanath, Gamini, Sidath, Satha, Duleep, Mathew, Arjuna, Murali, Rumesh.

Consensus reached between me and Ari and Brian Gomez on 9 December 1995. This is a list of bitter compromise. One player is there because he is fourteenth on all our lists. Two of my top five are not even present. But it has taken much statistical analysis, pleading of cases and arrack to arrive at this final decision. And as this is the Gibraltar on which our documentary is to be built, we all agree to stand by it and desist from criticism.

I will say three last words on the subject and then be forever silent. Guru? No? Why?

The Wall that I Stare at

I cannot face a window when I write. I cannot begin the writing of anything on a Friday. I cannot write without liquid passing my lips. I have learned over the years that it pays to nurture your idiosyncrasies. Even a hack must respect his muse.

I begin my assignment on Monday, 4 January 1996. I am asked to stay at home and manufacture scripts that are everything to everybody. Ari and Brian will haggle, renegotiate, coordinate, source and organise. I am grateful to be excused from the tedium of production meetings.

Before we are given the equipment and the budget, we are given the deadline. We must be ready to shoot straight after the World Cup. 'In case we get to the semis,' suggests Rakwana.

'In case we whack the Cup,' says Brian.

I spend the first two weeks drinking stout and going through my library. Throughout my life, even when times were tough, I never stopped buying books. Or, come to think of it, booze. My library is dusty and well stocked. My liver is well worn. I skim through my cricket collection and delve into my favourite wastes of time. Byron, F. Scott and the Bible.

To me, the Bible is perhaps the greatest book ever written. Not as a step-by-step guide to life or as a travel brochure for the afterlife. In that respect, it is positively dangerous. But as a tightly written work of fiction, it is magnificent.

There is a knock on my door and then a turning of the handle. I see the unruly hair before I see the ungrateful lad.

'Thaathi. Busy?'

'A bit. Why?'

My office is strewn with paper cuttings and books. Garfield looks about and nods. 'Ammi says you and Ari Uncle are doing a TV show?'

'With Graham Snow and Brian Gomez,' I say nonchalantly. 'When are your results coming?'

'Next month.'

'What do you want?'

'Need to discuss…things.'

'Bit busy. After lunch?' I say, knowing that I take my lunch when others take their tea.

He is gone.

That was our first conversation in three weeks. He had caught me off guard. I usually prepare for my meetings with Garfield by making my heart into a fist.

Our fights began shortly after his fifteenth birthday. First he joined a rocker band. Then he was suspended for smoking. Then he was dropped from the Wesley College 2nd XI cricket team. Sheila broke the news and I accidentally broke one of her vases. That conversation ended badly.

'He is playing in a band, smoking, running with girls, of course he will be dropped. What do you expect?'

Sheila spoke quietly. 'Gamini. This is good in a way. Now he can concentrate on studies.'

'This fool? Concentrate on anything?'

The boy never talks back to me. At least I have taught him something.

Our last argument had been over his choice of A-level subjects. I recommended he study commerce or science and he went behind my back and enrolled in history, Japanese and logic.

The reason he was now breaking the silence was obvious. Money. But what for? To travel to Japan and study Confucius? To marry some girl he'd impregnated? To buy guitar strings for his rocker band?

I turn to Ari's notebooks. I have borrowed his collection of 1985–95. The blue ones include scorecards and written summaries for each match he has seen. And Ari claims to have seen them all. The yellow ones are the fattest. Scrapbooks of paper cuttings. The pink ones contain undecipherable diagrams and formulae.

With our combined libraries, I have enough data to hammer short films on each cricketer. Except for one. I appear to be the only person to have written about Pradeep Sivanathan Mathew in the last ten years. By the time I am ready to meet Garfield, it is five in the evening and he has left for tuition class.

I spend weeks scribbling and pasting notes on walls. For inspiration I have a mess of books, a window overlooking flowerpots and a wall that I stare at. The wall gazes down on my flimsy table and my flimsier typewriter. It is a 1971 Jinadasa, gifted to me by my sister, the only relative not to file me under lost causes. The keys are as brittle as my bones, but the ribbon is fresh and the ink is wet.

I type career summaries for my top ten and paste them on the wall. I draw up a list of potential interviewees and a list of potential questions. I compile a list of memorable footage to be sourced. Mendis's twin centuries vs India in '82, Ratnayake's catch in our first test win in '85, Aravinda's 267 vs the Aussies in '88 and Mathew's '94 Zimbabwe tour. I then type random sentences and paste them on the wall. Pretentious stuff that I may never use.

'Goonesena, a gentleman to his fingertips, placed etiquette above aggression.'

'Ranatunga was a fox in a grizzly bear's clothing.'

And then, with three days to deadline, with the wall I stare at full of scribblings, I sit in my banian and sarong before my 1971 Jinadasa and daydream as hard as I can. It is the compulsory procrastination before each assignment. I think of Garfield and of our history of silences. I think about opportunities squandered. I think about Sathasivam. And then I start typing.

I quickly realise that everything – Satha, Garfield, even this Jinadasa typewriter – is a product of its era. The Jinadasa company was propped up by the Sri Lanka Freedom Party, under the assonant slogan 'Stationers to the Nation'. The products were hardy and underpriced. But after just three months of free market capitalism under the United National Party, the company collapsed spectacularly in 1978.

They say countries with the word democratic in them usually aren't. Throughout the 1970s, the SLFP's policies involved the culling of economic freedoms. For most of the 1990s, the UNP have been hopelessly divided.

Back to Satha. He was perhaps the most elegant cricketer of them all. A gentleman drunk, a playboy who could play. Notorious for turning up at games minutes before the first ball, attired in the previous night's evening dress, smelling of alcohol and someone else's wife, Satha would order eggs and bacon at the clubhouse, shower, knock back a hair-of-the-dog scotch and score a scintillating double century.

Writing at the speed of arrack, turning article to voice-over is easier than I thought. Then we pick out as many friendly commentators, coaches, has-beens and current players as we can think of, and post them questionnaires for interviews. The rest would be up to Brian and Ari.

When Garfield barges in, I have finished the questionnaire and written eight profiles. I am also pretty tanked up. He brings Sheila and I know I can no longer avoid this. I stop jabbing at the Jinadasa and remove my glasses.

'Sorry to disturb, Gamini,' says my darling wife. 'Juices are flowing today, no?'

She looks at the typewritten sheets on the table and thankfully, not at the empty bottle by my chair. 'Garfield wants to talk to you.'

They sit on the cane chairs by the window. I swivel around and light myself a cigarette.

'I thought you gave up?'

'Writing, no?' I grin.

Smoking history of W.G. Karunasena:

- Years 0–16: 0 cigarettes.
- 17–48: 12 a day, sometimes 25.
- 49–59: 0 cigarettes.
- As of last year: 2 a day. Before writing and after.

Sheila shakes her head and says nothing. She points her chin towards our son. 'So. Tell, tell.'

Garfield doesn't look me in the eye. His eyes dart along the books on the floor and rest on the empty bottle of Old Reserve. 'I want to do an engineering course in India.'

It takes all the muscles in my lower body to stop me from falling off my chair. 'Without science subjects?'

'They need good A-level marks. They don't care what subjects.'

'So will you get good marks?'

Garfield looks at me for the first time and nods.

'You can study Japanese and become an engineer?'

Sheila butts in. 'He wants to study sound engineering.'

'Sound engineering? Like Sony Walkmans? That's why you need Japanese?'

I only mean to smile kindly. I end up letting out a high-pitched giggle.

My son gives me a look. A look I recognise instantly as one I gave my teachers and elder siblings. A look I frequently got slapped for.

'Putha, go and check if the kettle has boiled,' says Sheila, as our son exits. She stares at me. Despite my behaviour, I'm in a good mood. Good booze, a good day's work, my son having not impregnated a Japanese teenager.

'OK. OK. How much?'

'Airfare and fees will come to three–four lakhs. Then accommodation…'

'Sheila, I don't have anything. We sold the family plot to buy this house.'

'What about the leftovers?'

'Nothing's left over.'

'I have a bit I saved up.'

'Where money for you?'

She puts her hands in her lap. There is no raising of voices. She has obviously prepared for battle. 'I saved, Gamini, I didn't waste.'

Sheila didn't like me going overseas on assignments, unless the newspaper or the sponsor paid my expenses. Sadly, the per diem I received was not enough to enter a homeless shelter and obtain a bowl of soup. I always returned in debt.

'You must ask your Loku Aiya.'

My cigarette over, I pour myself the last drink of the day. I have no desire to talk to my eldest brother.

'Now why are you drinking? How many times have they offered? If we say for Garfield's education, they will give.'

I shake my head. 'You know what Loku Aiya said about me, no?'

Sheila says nothing.

'No need of borrowing from anyone, I will give.' I squeeze her arm. 'Write down the amount and give. I will somehow get it.'

That night, the three of us eat at the table, though we keep the TV on. Sri Lanka, invited to make up the numbers at the 95/96 World Series, look about to beat Australia and perhaps even book a place in the final.

Garfield doesn't say a word, but his face has something resembling a smile. Sheila is happy and has cooked kiribath, the only dish she can make better than anyone else in the world. I'm having my third last drink of the day.

And even though I have no idea how I am to raise nine lakhs, I decide to put off worrying till tomorrow. Another day, another bottle. Procrastination is as much a group activity as watching cricket.

Old School Tie

School cricket is what feeds the Sri Lankan national side. We have no counties or Sheffields or shields and earlier, had no academies or strong first-class tournaments. Before the 1990s, two schools in particular fed Sri Lankan cricket, fed Sri Lankan politics and fed themselves from the fat of the land.

All of our male prime ministers and presidents have been from Royal College, Colombo, or St Thomas' College, Mount Lavinia, except for the Rt Honourable Mr StopGap in the 1960s and His Excellency Mr BenevolentDictator in the 1980s.

It's funny how legacies are passed on. They say in a mixed marriage children are beautiful. This is true if you get a pleasing combination of white features and black complexion. Not so, if vice versa. With age, I have realised that we are doomed to be parodies of our parents and that if there are virtues and vices to inherit, we will get a fraction of the former and a multiplication of the latter.

Nations are prey to my genetic Murphy's Law. Ideally, we Sri Lankans should have retained our friendly, childlike nature and combined it with the inventiveness of our colonisers. Instead, we inherit Portuguese lethargy, Dutch hedonism and British snobbery. We inherit the power lust of our conquerors, but none of their vision.

The old school tie is one such trait. Ari tells me that its influence is on the wane. 'Look at our World Cup squad. Ananda, Nalanda, Richmond, Mahinda, St Servatius, St Sebastian's. One Josephian. Royal–Thora no show. Same with all the top jobs.'

The unwritten school hierarchy is as follows. The top table is occupied by Royal, STC, St Joseph's, St Peter's, Ananda, Nalanda, Trinity. The next table would seat Thurstan, Isipathana, St Sebastian's, Prince of Wales, DS, Wesley and Bens.

'So this means the cream is rising to the top and replacing the cherries.'

'Nonsense,' says Ari. 'The cherries have all gone to London, Washington and Sydney. The dregs at the bottom are rising to the top.'

'I wouldn't call Sanath and Kalu dregs, my friend.'

'Maybe so. But I tell you, Wije, they are intentionally keeping us Thomians out. The Ananda–Nalanda brigade. Payback for the Brown Sahib treatment.'

Legend has it that when teenager Arjuna Ranatunga, an Ananda boy, first arrived at the Sinhalese Sports Club and addressed stalwart F.C. de Saram, a proud Royalist, the latter smirked, 'It speaks English, does it?'

Ari is an old Thomian who played for College in the 1940s and secretly believes that because he went to one of the Royal-Tho-Jo-Pete, he is somewhat less of a savage. I grew up in Kurunegala and attended Maliyadeva College. The old school tie bullshit neither benefits nor impresses me.

Like my office, Ariyaratne Byrd's front room is littered with paper cuttings. He has lived down the road from me since Sri Lanka got test status. His office room is as dusty and dingy as mine. But it is neat. Cobwebs hang on alphabetised shelves, teacups with fossilised cockroaches are stacked in symmetrical towers. Another important difference: air conditioning.

Both the front room and neighbouring garage are AC-ed. Ari managed to tap into a roadside power cable and make sure that Mr Marzooq from No. 17 got the bill. Don't ask me how. In the garage are a beat-up 1979 Ford Capri and dozens of broken gadgets. In the front room are the shelves of notebooks that deal with two broad subjects: electronics and cricket.

The electronics books are orange, the cricket books are blue, yellow, pink, grey and purple. Each has articles under various headings culled from the *Cricketer*, *Sportstar*, *Kreeda*, the *Island*, the *Weekend*, the *Observer* and *Wisden Cricket Monthly*. We stumble upon Pradeep Mathew's 1987 World Cup profile from the *Daily News*:

Pradeep Sivanathan Mathew
Left-arm chinaman. Right-hand batsman

Born:	19 February 1965, Colombo
Test debut:	vs India, Colombo, 1985
ODI debut:	vs West Indies, Hobart, 1985
School:	Thurstan College
Club:	Bloomfield CC

> Pradeep Mathew is a spinner of some promise who has excelled for Bloomfield this season, becoming the second highest wicket taker in the 1986 Lakspray Trophy. He made his debut in Sri Lanka's inaugural test victory against India. He has played mainly as a test bowler despite good performances in the 1985/86 World Series, including two 5-wicket bags against Australia and the Windies. This is his first World Cup.

Ari has even collected school cricket reports. We dig out three mentions of Mathew. This time playing U-15 and then U-17 for Thurstan. 'Here, my dear. Thurstan vs DS, Astra Margarine U-15 trophy 1979. Thurstan takes first innings lead, P. Mathew takes 4 for 17.'

'Ariya-pala-rala…'

My voice is slurring and my motor skills are waning.

Ari frowns. 'I think it's time for your nap, Putha. And I think Sheila knows that you're boozing during the day.'

'She said something?'

'Manouri saw her throwing out bottles. How much are you whacking?'

Ariyaratne uses his three-year head start in life and the size of his brood to put the fatherly act on me. Like any brat worth his salt, I know how to change the subject.

'We have no records of Mathew playing 1st XI cricket? Here. Thurstan team profiles for '82 and '83. No Mathew.'

'That is the thing. I know the Thurstan coach, Lucky Nanayakkara. Maybe I can put a call to see if he's still around. Now kindly go wash your face before Sheila gets back. I will only help you if you behave.'

I make the Scout's honour sign and promise.

Classified Ad

The good news is I have finished most of the scripts and the questionnaires and both Ari and Brian are pleased with the results. I explain that my Mathew piece is incomplete and that I need more time.

I call up the accountant at the *Observer* to check if I have any outstanding pension or gratuity. I am informed that after all deductions have been made, the *Observer* owes me Rs 695.63. I ask him what I could do with that princely sum and he tells me I can buy a bottle of arrack or take out a classified ad in that Sunday's issue.

So that's exactly what I do. The latter.

W.G.

I wish I was known by my initials. Like F.C. de Saram and C.I. Gunasekera, Lanka's first great batsmen. Or D.S. de Silva, Lanka's last great spinner. Like T.S. Eliot. D.H. Lawrence. Even O.J. Simpson.

My name is Wijedasa Gamini Karunasena. My mother and sister call me Sudu; my three brothers no longer call me. Strangers call me Karunasena; friends call me Wije. My wife calls me Gamini dear when she wants money and unprintable things when I don't give it to her. But, regrettably and unfortunately, no one calls me by my initials.

If they did, I would share my name with the greatest cricketer of the nineteenth century, Dr W.G. Grace, undoubtedly the game's first hero, and perhaps, something of an arse. 'They came to see me bat, not to watch you umpire.' It's an old joke. Sobers never was sober. W.G. did not have any grace.

Dr Grace toured Ceylon in 1891 and in an after-dinner speech at the Grand Orient Hotel expressed the hope that the island would some day send a mixed team of Ceylonese and Europeans to play at Lord's. The good doctor's wishes took eighty-three years to come true, though by this time the island was no longer Ceylon and the team no longer had room for Europeans.

W.G. may not roll off the tongue, but I like how it sounds. Come W.G., let's put a drink. W.G. at your service, madam. I'm sorry, Mr W.G., but we cannot refund your bet.

Sadly, the only place my initials appear is where I place them myself. At the tail end of my articles. And at the end of the ad that I put in the *Sunday Observer* classifieds:

> **Information** on Pradeep Sivanathan Mathew. Cricketer.
> Played Thurstan 1977–83.
> Bloomfield/NCC 1986–94.
> Sri Lanka 1985–95.
> Any information, call 724520. W.G. A friend and admirer.

This ad runs in January of 1996. There is a response, though not perhaps the desired one. I rerun it a year later with one amendment. At the end I add the line: Callers will receive payment.

The pressing question of the moment is not what the ad did. It is how the hell did the self-proclaimed W.G., unable to foot the bill for his son's education, manage to pay for months of advertising and for cash rewards? How could I do all this and finance an arrack habit on just my humble pension? Sheila has come in to sweep the room. I will tell you later.

Fielding Practice

'Buck up. Buck up!'

Lucky Nanayakkara's voice is a shade of ebony. It is as polished as the pipe he puffs and as rich as the tobacco he burns. The boy who spilled the catch looks at his feet. 'Dodanwela! Third one today, no? Go practise with Dixon Sir.'

The youngster shuffles to the seventh circle of fielders, to join his butterfingered brothers.

'See,' says Nanayakkara. 'Every season I get forty ten-year-olds. Every season I get exactly five natural cricketers and nine who can't catch. Every year.'

We are sitting in the Royal College pavilion watching a Thurstan U-11 fielding practice. It is a sweaty afternoon and I am offered Lanka Lime from the nearby canteen. I have not had alcohol in over fourteen hours, but my hand does not shake.

Lucky Sir teaches religious studies and is master-in-charge of cricket at Thurstan College. From the scorer's desk, we have a good view of the nets and the seven circles of fielders.

'Nothing like the start of the season. If I'm lucky I can pick the future stars.'

The boys have switched from high catches to ground fielding. The sun beats down hard. Another boy misses a catch. Lucky Sir puffs gusts of smoke and clears his throat. 'This year looks like pickings are slim.'

A troupe of cubs dressed like the Hitler Youth march the boundary lines, chanting nonsense. Mild traffic passes by on Reid Avenue. Lucky Sir presents me with scorebooks from the 1976/77 to 1980/81 seasons. They are fat and rectangular and look like faded canvases. We run our fingers along the creases and skim over smudged dots and dashes of ink.

'I remember this fellow Mathew. Very good talent. He went on to play for Sri Lanka also.'

He gives me a did-you-know-that look and I give him a yes-I-did nod. According to the books, Mathew was a regular in the Thurstan U-15 and U-17 A-teams, appearing to open both the bowling and the batting. His batting average rarely rose above his age, but his bowling figures showed him to be a strike bowler, expensive, yet effective. A best of 8–120 vs Zahira and no less than seven 5-wicket bags.

'Lucky Sir, I'm writing about great cricketers who played for Lanka. It says here that Mathew opened the bowling. You opened with a spinner?'

Mr Lucius pats down his parted white hair and rubs his pencil-thin mousto. I like this man; he is, like me, a gentle lover of cricket. Since 1996 the game has attracted a mass market of dabblers and dilettantes who are very vocal on the obvious points and not very knowledgeable on the finer ones. Sadly, some of them sit in the commentary box.

'No. No. He used to bowl pace. Actually he could bowl swing, off break and leg spin. Anything. Not medium pace, mind you, full dum pace. Like Waqar.'

He tells me that P. Sivanathan was one of seven Tamil boys in a school of 2,500 pupils. According to Lucky Sir's astonishing memory, during the late 1970s there were seventeen Muslims, two Burghers and one Chinese at Thurstan College. These pupils were excused from Buddhist prayers and occasionally bullied on the playground.

'He was about Grade 3. Crying away. Unfortunately, Thurstan gets some rough types. A bunch of them were throwing fruit at him, calling him Tamil kotiya. This is a good school, but things can happen.'

The bullies had been asking him if he was Tamil or Burgher. Pradeep's reply had been, 'Amma Sinhala.' My mother is Sinhala.

'He couldn't even speak proper Tamil. I punished all the fellows. Told Sivanathan to get his parents to complain. They never did. Next time I saw him was at the U-11 trials. Mousey fellow. Took the ball and...my God.'

Lucky Sir drafted the boy into the U-13 squad. Pradeep could not catch, neither was he a natural athlete. But he was certainly a star.

'He could imitate any action, no? After the boys saw him bowl, the bullying stopped.'

After Grade 5, as classes were shuffled to accommodate scholarship children, on Lucky Sir's advice P. Sivanathan was enrolled as Pradeep Mathew in a parallel class.

'We can't change the world, no? I told him to stay out of trouble. To concentrate on hard work, doing the basics. Sometimes, fellow would listen.'

Pradeep began deflecting tormentors by imitating their bowling actions. He became the first to be picked during interval cricket, but remained the last to be invited to parties.

'Sir Garfield Sobers came and coached our youngsters for a week. He said this boy will play for Sri Lanka.'

The mention of Sir Garfield reminds me of a son who bats like a girl and can barely bowl slow.

'What a waste. If Pradeepan played our Big Match we would've won.'

The Thurstan–Isipathana Big Match has not had a result in twenty-three years.

'Why didn't he?'

When Pradeep failed his O-levels, his Sinhala mother and Tamil father visited the school for the first time.

'Father was quiet. Mother said no way. No more cricket. He was sent for tuition, but I don't think he went.'

'What did he bowl? Left-arm spin or left-arm pace?'

Mr Lucius puts down his Portello and shakes his head. Our drinks are fresh from cool storage; they begin sweating on arrival.

'You will not believe me, Mr Karunasena, you will think I am bowling you a googly. Ha. But when he was at Thurstan, he bowled right-arm.'

For the first time that day, I stop thinking about the half-bottle of Mendis rum stuffed in my almirah.

'Ah?'

'I know he played for All-Ceylon as a left-arm spinner, but for us he was a right-arm fast bowler. He was pretty quick and accurate, but not much stamina. Fellow gets tired, bowls spin. Right-arm leg spin and googlies. Gets hammered sometimes, but picks up wickets also.'

While it is possible to be competent with both hands in a given activity, ambidexterity works on the jack-of-all-trades, master-of-jack principle.

If you teach yourself to write left-handed your right-handed writing will deteriorate. If you practise both regularly, neither will attain excellence.

It may be possible to roll over the arm without being no-balled and hit a point on a pitch. But to hurl a cricket ball at speed or to spin it across its axis with either arm to a level sufficient to dismiss a Sri Lanka school batsman would require near-super powers.

My Lanka Lime tastes like chilled food colouring. Lucky Sir offers me biscuits and I decline. I do not understand why biscuits are considered good things to put in your mouth. The sun lowers the heat and the boys come in for tea.

'Adihetty. Very poor. Buck up. Buck up!' Lucky Sir gets into master-in-charge mode.

'Did you meet him when he played for Sri Lanka?'

'Sometimes. In the early days he would drop in. I said, son you have a talent, work every day at it. Fellow was lazy.'

Lucky Sir's rich ebony voice blends well with the fading light. The boys who missed catches begin running their laps of penance along the boundary ropes.

'I would advise him on variations. He listened, same expression, like he's not listening. Then he'd bowl a brilliant ball, but not the ball I asked him to bowl.'

I close the tattered scorebooks, they have nothing more to tell.

'So how did he go from U-17 to playing for Sri Lanka without 1st XI cricket?'

Lucky Sir gathers the scorebook and looks around.

'He might have unofficially played for the Royal 1st XI.' He pats down his hair and winks. 'But I did not tell you that.'

Nineteen Eighty-three

Consider these facts:

- In 1983, a team of West Indian rebels toured apartheid South Africa.
- In 1983, Pradeep Mathew may or may not have played 1st XI cricket for Royal.

- In 1983, the Tamil Tigers sank a Sri Lankan army boat. The ensuing riots by Sinhalese mobs ensured that over the next decade (a) 80,000 lives would be lost and (b) Sri Lanka would only play ten home test matches.
- In 1983, Royal won the Royal–Thomian cricket match for the first time in fifteen years.
- After seven years of Grand Slam glory, Björn Borg lost his confidence and retired aged twenty-six.
- In 1983, India snatched the World Cup from Clive Lloyd's invincible Windies in classic underdog fashion.
- That year, I wrote an uncomplimentary article about Indian cricket and Kapil Dev refused to be interviewed by me.

Millennium Bug

My phone starts ringing at 6 a.m. I hear it as if in another room, my conscious mind misted by the fumes of evaporated rum. My body aches and my head is nailed to my pillow. The phone keeps ringing. I hear Sheila mumbling, asking, replying, snapping, screaming, shrieking. I pick out random words. 'Y2K...Millennium Bug...Y2Komputers... Pradeep Mathew...'

I turn over, cover my ears and part my eyelids. Sheila is lying on her side snarling into the phone. It rings as soon as she puts it down.

'Listen. You...you...f...f...fellow. I told you no Millennium bugging.'

Next caller.

'Who is this...There is no b...blooming Pradeep Sivanathan... Kindly stop calling.'

She slams down the phone and I jolt awake. She glares. She is in her nightdress and even though she is shaped more like an alarm clock than an hourglass, I see beauty in her. When she glares, her eyes shine and her skin glows, and the girl who I followed on a bus to Kotahena in '64 barks at me in her sweet voice. 'Did you put some ad in the papers about Y2K or Millennium something?'

The memory of the Burgher girl at Galle Face Hotel Dinner Dance 1963, the girl on the bus to Kotahena, takes what little blood I have in my brain and sends it elsewhere. I barely manage a grunt.

'From morning...ringing...ringing...Y2K...Millennium...Sivanathan ...Mathew...'

I first saw her on the night of 31 December at Galle Face, when my friend asked her to dance, while I sulked at the bar. She was going steady with a trainee reporter, apprenticed with me at the *Daily News* under Mr Herbert Hulugalle. For six months, I pretended to live in Kotahena, even though I was boarded in Nugegoda on the other side of town.

Once, we both happened to be standing in a packed bus. Every time her bosom brushed my arm, she apologised, politely and sweetly.

After six months of buses to Kotahena, I gave the fair girl a letter. A poem by the Lord Byron which I passed off as my own. I then plundered the Lords Keats, Blake and Shelley, typed them on scented paper, and signed as Gamini Karuna.

After five letters, she replied. 'I may betray my boyfriend for someone at some point, but it won't be today and it won't be you.' She was only right about the first part. After seventeen more letters, she agreed to go to the film hall with me.

The phone rings again. Sheila picks up and sits up.

'Hello…No…Y2Komputers…Mr Mathew…is…is…mathewing… your mother.'

She pulls the phone out of the socket.

'Gamini. Are you sure this isn't one of your things? I know you've been drinking again. What did the doctor say last check-up?'

After the film, the fair girl with the polite bosom told me she liked my letters but that I should find my own style and stop stealing from the *MD Gunasena Treasury of English Verse*. I married her a year later. My friend screamed to the world that I had stolen Sheila from him, and he was right.

I begin replugging the phone and deflecting the question.

'What did you say about Mathew?'

'I knew it was you. What are you up to, Gamini? Do you know this Mathew Pradeep fellow?'

The phone rings as soon as I plug it in. I am saved by Lanka Bell.

'Is that Y2Komputers?'

A man's voice. A man who sounds too wide awake for 6.37 a.m. on a Sunday.

'No. Sorry. Wrong number.'

'Is Mr Mathew there?'

'Who?'

'Mr Pradeep Sivanathan Mathew. You see, I run a small import–export company…'

'What do you want with Pradeep Mathew?'

'My operations are fully computerised. Do you install the software as well…'

An hour and twenty-seven calls later, I unplug the phone and open the *Sunday Observer* classifieds. Amidst cars and houses and brides for sale is the personal section and the ad I have placed.

All morning I get enquiries for Mathew and millennium bugs. Sheila goes next door to Ari's to escape the din. After lunch I pick up the newspaper and I see an ad spilling over from the electronics section.

R U Y2K ready?
Protect your business from the Millennium worldwide system crash. Y2Komputers Millennium Bug Debugging System. Install before too late. Less than 40 months till new millennium. Call for more Information on Pradeep Sivanathan Mathew. Cricketer. Played Thurstan/Royal 1977–83. Bloomfield 1986–94. Sri Lanka 1985–95. Any information or anecdotes, call 724520. WG. A friend and admirer.

I receive close to 200 calls that Sunday. And a further 200 during the week. Each wanting Sri Lanka's greatest left-arm spinner to debug their office networks. And then on Thursday:

'Hello. Mr W.G., please.'

'Speaking.'

'I call about ad about Pradeep…'

'Sorry. That was a mistake. We do not do Y2K viruses.'

'I call…'

'Sorry for the inconvenience.'

'I call…because I coach him at Royal in '82 and '83…'

Seven Lakhs

'That is absurd,' screams Brian. 'Production has begun. We have done the script, built the sets.'

'Here, don't bullshit, Brian.' Danila's boss, Jayantha Punchipala, MD of the SLBCC, has invited us for a fight. 'You haven't built any sets.'

Punchipala's office looks nothing like the dingy ITL meeting rooms. After the death of Minister Tyronne Cooray in a suicide attack in 1994, the post of Cricket Board chief attracted many pretenders. Punchipala's betting empire financed his successful bid over more qualified candidates. Within a year he would be replaced by an interim committee, but that afternoon, he was very much in control.

Most Sri Lankans smile when they are angry or ill at ease. The MD grins with his whole face. He is a thickset man, dark as a West Indian, with Elvis hair and shiny cufflinks. He directs the tea boy towards us.

'I like the concept. But what is the meaning of this production cost?' says Punchipala. 'Y'all are hiring Spielberg?'

He laughs at his own joke.

'Also, the script needs to be revised.' He looks at me. 'Am I right?'

'Revised, how?' I ask, as if I am a drunk in a bar wielding a bottle.

'Pradeep Mathew,' says Danila, shaking her head.

'That fool was a troublemaker,' says the MD, smiling at his cufflinks. 'Also, he left debts to the Cricket Board.'

'What sort of debts?'

'Bigger than all your annual salaries put together, Uncle. Broke his contract and left loans. The SLBCC does not wish to promote such a character.'

'Where is he now?' asks Ari.

The MD shrugs. 'Ask Dhani, Pradeep was her friend, no?'

Danila smiles and says nothing.

'If I knew where he was, I would personally break his face,' says the MD with a smile.

Brian has been seething in a corner for some time. He controls his voice. 'If you like we will remove the Mathew segment. But you cannot cancel funding. Graham Snow promised these gentlemen…'

'No offence, Brian,' says Danila. 'Graham Snow makes a lot of promises when he's drunk. If we funded every one of them, we'd be bankrupt.'

'Seven lakhs, no, Wije? We have it in writing.'

The MD pours himself some coffee. 'There are many sports shows wanting grants. We cannot put all our eggs in one basket.'

The walls have photos of great cricketers of eras past and a few bats with signatures on them. On the antique desk is a photo of Punchipala's wife and two sons. Next to it is a giant TV screen showing the highlights of Sri Lanka's surprise win over Australia in the Benson and Hedges World Series. This is the reason for the meeting starting thirty-nine minutes late or at 0.39 SLT.

Under a framed photo of Madam President, the TV replays Kalu belting Glenn McGrath. It distracts us for a moment. I breathe in air that has been conditioned and freshened, listen to the low hum of the TV, and speak. 'I suggest we call Graham Snow. It's his money. We have invested time into this project. If anyone is to pull the plug, it should be him.'

At first there is resistance. Danila places her hand on Punchipala's forearm and suggests this may be a wise course of action. He calls his secretary. A toy is placed on the table, black with flashing red lights. We are told that it may take a while to get Graham Snow on the line.

'Bugger must be full busy. NSPN have extended his contract,' says Brian, not without envy.

'How are our boys? You think they will get into finals?' The MD turns up the TV and steers us in the direction of all Sri Lankan conversations this holiday season.

Despite the future of our documentary being in tatters, Ari cannot resist. 'MD. This is only our second win. We have to win all remaining games to get to the finals.'

Neither can I. 'No. No. We will win. Our team is pumped up. They are playing for Murali.'

'Now they have cleared Murali, no?' says Rakwana.

'Real umpires haven't no-balled him,' says Mrs Kolombage. 'Only that fellow Hair. Must cut that hair. Hee. Hee. You saw that, Doctor? Watch. Watch. McGrath is shouting at our Kalu. Next three balls, Kalu whacks him for fours.'

It is more words than she has spoken in all previous meetings combined.

'Hello. Graham Snow speaking.'

His voice crackles from the toy on the table. The static is worse than my Samyo radio, which gives me perfect reception from Lord's, Barbados and Cape Town, but can only offer broken signals from neighbouring Mumbai. Danila reaches for the remote and kills the TV.

'Hi, Graham. This is Jayantha Punchipala. Sri Lanka Cricket Board.'

'Hi, Jayantha.'

'We have your friends, Karunasena and Byrd.'

'Hello, chaps. Sorry for being out of touch. My schedule's been mental. Love those scripts. Magnificent work. Can't wait to see the films.'

'We have my advertising manager, Danila…'

'Hi, Dhani.'

'My accounts manager, Yasmin…'

'Look, Jayantha, could we skip the roll call? I'm really busy.'

The MD drops his accent. 'Graham. I am sorry but the Cricket Board cannot approve a script with Pradeep Mathew.'

'Why not?'

The MD explains. Graham responds.

'I don't understand what you're saying. Look. Let's shoot all ten. We can choose which ones we run.'

'I'm sorry, Graham, but that is not advantageous.'

'Look here. I'm providing funding. Either you give the money to W.G. and Ari or I donate it to the Bangladeshis.'

Danila winks at me and places her hand on the MD's shoulder. He brushes it off. Brian, Ari and I resist the urge to punch the air.

The call is ended. The MD looks like he's just been run-out without facing a ball. He snatches a chequebook from Danila and begins scribbling.

'We are washing our hands of this. OK? From now on you deal direct with Graham.'

Brian lets out a yelp. 'Excuse me, sir. The agreed fee was seven lakhs.'

'Who agreed on seven lakhs?' asks Danila.

I am more worried by the familiarity with which she handles the MD's briefcase than with her changing allegiance.

'This is an insult,' yelps Brian, getting to his feet. 'We have written proof.'

Ari extracts the signed requisition from our files and passes it to Brian.

Brian bangs it on the table. 'See.'

And we do.

Rs 100,000 Only

'Is that a 7?' asks the mousey girl.

Ari grabs it. 'My dear, it is quite clearly a…' He narrows his eyes and looks at me.

The MD has donned his suit jacket. Danila is holding his briefcase. They are evidently departing together. He shoos us from his office. 'Sort it out with your good friend Graham.'

Chinese Rolls

We are back to meeting at ITL. We are served Chinese rolls and tea with floating lumps of milk powder. I have stopped wearing polished shoes and combing my hair. Brian has stopped calling us names. Ari has stopped cursing Graham Snow.

'Bottom line,' says Cassim. 'ITL will require at least four and a half lakhs to shoot ten shows.'

Rakwana no longer attends meetings.

'Also, if you are using footage,' says Mrs Kolombage, 'there is a fee.'

'What about sponsors?' asks Ari, trying to look hopeful.

'If you can find, of course, why not?' says Cassim.

'Can you help?' I ask.

'ITL is only contracted for production,' says Mrs Kolombage.

I liked her better when she was a parrot. How could two wretched old men find sponsors? How many logos would Brian need to wear on his undies? Brian no longer talks at meetings. He is typing on his mobile phone and shaking his head. He has sulked all afternoon. He still blames Ari and me for not checking the cheque.

At Ari's insistence, we fork out Rs 49,750 for the footage. The sight of two boxes of videotapes is more than he can resist. The long walk to the ITL cashier's is done to the soundtrack of Brian bitching.

'You can't even shoot a hand-held porn film with Rs 50,000. That's it, Uncles. I'm done with this.'

'Just wait, Brian. I think W.G. should write to Graham,' says Ari. 'Tell him the budget.'

'Why me?'

'You're the writer.'

At the cashier's we are told that the government no longer subsidises ITL's refreshment expenses. We are required to fork out a further Rs 50 each for the tea and short eats. Brian is livid.

He refuses to carry the two dusty boxes and will not allow us to transport them in his Datsun. He waits while we negotiate with a three-wheeler and says he is thinking of going back to radio. He also tells me that Jayantha Punchipala's wife stormed into the Cricket Board office last week and called Danila Guneratne many unsavoury names.

'Call me when you find sponsors,' he says.

'You will also look?' I ask.

He puts the car into gear and avoids my eye. 'Definitely,' he says and drives off.

Yellow Card

These days I only smoke when I write. Drink, however, is a different story. If I could I would drink in my sleep. I know men younger and healthier who have suffered the inconvenience of multiple bypasses. I know drinkers whose bodies were unable to keep up. Who exchanged the bottle for sobriety and the permanent frown it brings.

I have watched drinking acquaintances find solace in religion and family. I have seen men go from being life-and-soul-of-the-party to disagreeable old teetotaller. I have seen diabetic thirty-year-olds convinced that they were cursed.

I, on the other hand, have been blessed. For the mornings and afternoons of my working life, I have treated myself to a compulsory shot, and have treated breakfast and lunch as optional extravagances. And, contrary to chemistry and biology, for sixty years my bill of health has been clean.

And while Sheila and Ari argue that alcohol cost me jobs at the *Daily News* and the *Island*, they do not know of what they speak. Alcohol has enhanced my life and the world I inhabit. It has given me insight, jocularity and escape. I would not be who I am without it.

It begins with the swellings around my stomach and legs. Then I am unable to sleep. Then I shit droplets of blood. I tell no one about my visit to Nawasiri or the tests that I took or how much they cost. I take it as a warning. A yellow card. If I behave myself, I may not have to miss any games.

Ambarella Juice

We have almost given up on sponsors and of ever getting through to Graham. I return home empty-handed and Garfield stops talking to me.

Unfortunately, Sheila doesn't. I have to convince her that I am working even when I am staring out of the window. My morning hangover muffles her shrieks. Unable to fight back, I let the moment pass and it always does. I wonder if cricketers have money troubles or screeching wives.

Saturday night is spent like most Saturday nights. On Ari's balcony with bottles. Ari's balcony is the only one on de Saram Road with a clear view of the sea. We watch stray cats negotiate the tiles of rooftops. There is barely enough room to swing one of them on this ledge with parapets. I am drinking my usual and Ari has a glass of what looks like urine.

'Ambarella juice. Rochelle gave Manouri a blender. Have some. Good for your insides, Wije.'

I sip some through the straw. The type a drowning man would clutch at.

The drink is not as putrid as I thought. I want to tell Ari that my insides are rotting, and even though this is the place, it is perhaps not the time.

'Rochelle is getting married, no? Do you Burgher buggers have to give dowry?'

'Nope,' says Ari, pouring the urine-coloured ambarella into the glass-coloured glass. 'We just put on booze and fry cutlets.'

Cushioned in sea breeze, Ari and I discuss the possibility of an ambidextrous bowler. Ari thinks the idea is nonsense and even though I argue, I secretly agree. We reminisce about 1983, the year Sheila and I and little Garfield moved to Mount Lavinia, next door to Ari, his first wife Norma, and the girls.

We talk about the riots. Our friends Krish and Nathan who fled to Canada. We talk about Kapil Dev's high catch to dismiss the great Viv Richards, how he plucked the World Cup seemingly out of the air. I tell him how Kapil refused me a one-on-one because I wrote India off in my preview of the final. We savour the warm air and toast to memories.

'Some fellow has called you?'

'Satyakumar Gokulanath. Old Tamil gentleman. Former Royal fielding coach. Can we chat with him at your place?'

'Why?'

'Sheila doesn't like me drinking at home.'

'But you still do.'

'Not that. Were you at the '83 Royal–Thomian?'

'Of course. I had liver problems that year. Remember?'

Ari is now pouring arrack and I am swimming in my thoughts.

'I didn't know you then. We only met in July when they came to burn Nathan's house.'

'Ah. Right. Right. The Royal–Tho was in March...obviously. My first sober Big Match since 1952.' He grins. ''52 I got cockered. Thora won. '53 I got even more cockered and we won by an innings!'

The pre-poya moon casts a white glow on Ari's balcony and reflects off his bald spot. In the distance, the sea snores.

'I got cockered every year for the next thirty years, but only two more results. We won in '64, they won in '69. Then in '83 I had my hepatitis scare. Must look after the liver, no? You lose your liver, you can't live.'

Ari is so engrossed in his chatter he fails to notice the look on my face.

'So in 1983 I stay sober. And the year I am sober those beggars thrash us.'

Ari grins.

'Now I realise that in life and in cricket, whether I booze or not, what will be, will be.'

We croak a few refrains of 'Que Sera' and I lift my glass to the being of what will be.

Ari's eyes narrow. 'You know that Royal cheated?'

I roll my eyes.

'Listen to this. The whole Royal team were wearing blue and yellow caps when they were bowling. Who does that?'

'Blue and gold.'

'Yellow. If that is gold, I'm a Chinaman with a ponytail. Wije, do you know what I saw?'

'The Royalists raping your little girls in style?'

'Apart from that. Everyone said I am sour grapes, that I was drunk. Bullshit. I was fully sober. I saw what I saw.'

'What, so?'

'There were five bowlers in the Royal team. Their spinner took 5 wickets, their pacey took 3. According to the records, that is.'

'So?'

'I swear to this day. On Norma's grave, rest her soul.' He crosses himself. 'In the second innings, there was a sixth bowler on that field. He took all the wickets. No one noticed except me.'

Satyakumar Gokulanath

When he tramples Manouri's flowerpots, I know there is going to be trouble. Ari, not noticing, leads us up his garden path to the chairs on the lawn. We take seats around a formica table, sheltered by araliya trees. It is the place where Ari sees guests he doesn't want his wife to see.

With Satyakumar Gokulanath, there is plenty not to see. He mumbles and shakes. His face is all jowls and his hair is dyed oily black. He wears a faded Chinese collar shirt adorned with multiple food stains. His slacks are tented over his twig legs and his sandals are covered in Manouri's compost. He looks like he has spent his whole life painting houses without ever bothering to change clothes.

I have seen him before at the Visible Bar in Katubedda and at the Kaanuwa in Moratumulla. He is one of those drunks who stand at the bar talking to no one. At the Kaanuwa, everyone stands – the carpenters, the trishaw drivers, the sportswriters who miss their buses.

I have seen Gokulanath bare his beedi-stained teeth at four-finger widths of neat gal arrack and knock it back in one gulp. Gal is a close relative of turpentine and just as tasty. Strange for this creature to be coaching a Colombo 7 school.

The day is pleasant. Drinks cool, sunshine bright, grass green, company peculiar. Ari has put on a spread of rambutan, shelled and deseeded so as not to offend our fragile teeth. I could not think of a worse hell than living in a house with six ladies, but I see it has its advantages. Our guest has arrived drunk and is demanding more. Before we begin, he wants to finalise the fee.

Mr S. Gokulanath was the assistant coach of the Royal 2nd XI from 1968 to 1997. He taught PT and environmental studies at Royal to Forms 2–3. When the government changed in '70, he taught PE and social studies to Grades 7–8. When the government changed again in '77, he was teaching saramba and parisaraya to Years 8–9. There is a Sinhalese phrase which translated reads: 'The changing of the pillow will not cure the headache.'

Gokulanath is a skeletal man with bad posture. He is a Jaffna Tamil who speaks impeccable Sinhalese, but shaky English. I have translated, paraphrased and attempted to replicate.

He spends a full hour tanking up on booze while Ari ribs me about Sunday's classified debacle. Gokulanath tells us the reason he was reading the Sunday classifieds that day was to look for work. After twenty-nine years of service, he was sacked from Royal College on a false allegation and was not given his thirty-year bonus or his pension.

We voice our sympathy and Ari talks about what snakes the Royalists are.

We discuss Lanka's prospects for the World Cup, followed by the Murali saga. This topic does a couple of rounds and then Gokul speaks. 'Y'all are Thomians, no?'

Ari nods his head. I shake mine. 'Maliyadeva.'

'What I'm telling, please write to papers. And to Thomian magazine. Royal is not good. It is changed. Thirty years and they throw me out, because I am Tamil. Can you believe?'

I decide to get down to business, before he repeats the story for the third time. 'Did Pradeep Mathew play for Royal?'

'Pradeepan? Yes, yes. But not in legal way.'

Ari puts away the bottle and asks, 'So in what way?'

And then he tells us.

Sunscreen

The story begins in Soysapura Flats in Moratuwa and is punctuated by coughs. The narrator sticks beedis into the gaps in his teeth and draws phlegm from his soul. 'He told me he went to Royal…urrrgg…so I told him to come for practice.'

Gokulanath coached six-a-side tennis-ball cricket at the Soysapura grounds, surrounded by balconies of dirty laundry and flats filled with gangsters like Moratu Sumith, Maiyya and Goo Cheena.

The Soysapura scene was known for its hard-hitting batsmen and bowlers of questionable action. Both Gokul and Pradeep hailed from the flats, though they didn't meet till Gokul's Katubedda Kings took on young Pradeep's Rawatawatte Fingara Club.

Gokul was immediately impressed. 'Left-arm seam. Ammataudu. You should've seen. Every ball pitching off stump, then doing different things. Cutting in, cutting out, keeping low. Whole afternoon, one spot. Then he bowls right-hand. I couldn't believe. I have never seen bowling like that.'

In six-a-side tennis-ball cricket, there really is nowhere for a bowler to hide, but Pradeep ended up getting bounce, turn, and, most importantly, wickets. 'So I ask him…urrg…why he never come for Royal practice? He tells me his parents send him for tuition.'

Gokul didn't realise Mathew was from Thurstan till he had played him in four games for the 2nd XI. 'But how to sack best bowler I have coached?'

The boy had put in solid performances as the first change bowler. In the last game before he was found out, Mathew opened the bowling and took 5–39 against St Sylvesters.

'Ari darling. Me and Melissa are going, OK?' It is the shrill voice of Manouri Byrd. She is peering over round spectacles from the balcony and pretends not to see me. Ari leaves us to go to church. Before he goes, he drags me into his workshop. The fluorescent bulb lights up the rust and the dust, the broken machines and the grounded Ford. He hands me a cassette recorder.

'Here, Wije. This fellow is mad. But in case he says something useful, press that and keep. And don't give him too much drink. I'm off.'

'What's that?' I ask, pointing to a clunky contraption, shaped like a miniature washing machine.

'A 1965 Polaroid 20 Series Swinger. Just 200 bucks from some aachchi in Dehiwela.'

Only Ari would be proud of robbing old ladies.

'Does it work?'

He snaps a shot of me placing the tape recorder before Gokul below a darkening sky. The picture that comes out is blank. Ari begins flapping it, then Manouri shouts from the balcony and he runs off. I'm left alone with Gokul.

I ask what he did when he found out Mathew was a Thurstan boy. 'I told head coach, there is boy who can be BATA Schoolboy Cricketer of the Year, if we get him to Royal. For once head coach listens to me.'

Gokulanath then drops ash onto his lap and topples his drink into the rambutan.

Mathew could not be admitted to Royal due to class overcrowding. The head coach and Gokul set up a Tamil scholarship programme that would…the details fly over my head as Gokul rambles on and clears phlegm from his throat. Suffice to say that it began in October 1982 and was concluded in February 1984, four months after Mathew had passed his London A-levels and was too old to play school cricket.

Nevertheless, the boy practised with the Royal 1st team squad and our man Gokul got a promotion to 1st XI fielding coach for his find of the season. He claims to have helped Mathew develop his unusual deliveries.

'Tamils have to be twice as good as Sinhalese to be recognised. I played for Jaffna St John's. I bowled googly. Look at these fingers. I could spin the ball on water. Pradeepan's were even longer.'

He wraps his spider-like fingers around his glass and coughs into his other hand. 'Pradeepan…urrg…no discipline, no control. I told he must empty his head of thoughts. Let the ball come to him. To think of nothing when he lets go.'

The '82 season passed without incident. Mathew attended practice, played a few friendlies, worked on his bowling and his fielding, helped along by Mr Gokul. The head coach wouldn't put him in the side till the deal with Thurstan College, the Royal Admissions Secretariat and the Royal College Scholarship Fund was finalised. The boy told his family he was going to Royal for tuition class. To keep up the façade, Gokul would help him with his homework after practice.

The '83 Royal side was captained by Chulaka Algama and was top-heavy with quality all-rounders like Sandesh Jayawardena, Malik Malalasekera and Rochana Amarasinghe. They had three coaches, two specialist trainers and a fitness instructor. The Sri Lankan national team at the time barely had a manager.

The results were plain to see. The team, overflowing with experience and variety, notched up six consecutive wins against the likes of Isipathana, Richmond and Prince of Wales. Mathew meanwhile had developed the stamina to play as a fast bowler and had perfected the actions of Bob Willis, Mohinder Binny and the entire Royal 1st and 2nd side squads.

But the fitness instructor's regimen was starting to reveal cracks. 'That fitness coach was a pandithaya. Instead of Nihal Sir, we had to call him Sir Nihal. Like he's some English lord. What fitness? Bugger couldn't even jog.' Wrist fractures, ankle injuries, hamstring and groin strains spread through the team like influenza. And in desperation, the head coach turned to Pradeep.

Ari returns from church just as the story enters the realm of fantasy. 'Did you pass any holy water, Father Byrd?' Religion is one of the many topics Ari and I argue over.

'Wije, I told you I don't like you blaspheming in my garden. Just wait till you're close to your death, only then you'll realise the value of God.'

Poor Ari. I really should tell him.

As Gokul stumbles to the toilet, Ari points to his nose and waves away a smell. 'Looks like a bittter bugger. Bittter with three ts. And I don't accept this right-hand, left-hand bullshit.'

Mathew featured in four games before the Big Match. Around that time, it was compulsory for every Royal cricketer to wear a large sunhat, cover their face in sunscreen and wear Dean Jones-style shades. The sunglasses offended the visiting Nalanda College coach, who complained to the Sri Lanka Schools Cricket Board, SLSCB. They agreed that sunglasses were unsuitable accessories for school cricket. The sunscreen escaped scrutiny.

Listen carefully. This is what a drunken bitter ex-schoolmaster is having us believe. Pradeep Mathew appeared for Royal, but *not as himself.*

In the first match he wore a double T-shirt and played the role of burly pacey Nalliah de Silva. Against Nalanda, he wore a gold chain and mimicked Chanaka Devarajan, de Silva's new ball partner. He took four wickets and ripped the spine out of a Nalanda batting line-up featuring future international stars Roshan Gurusinha and Hashan Mahanama.

In the St Josephs match, he masqueraded as star spinner Rochana Amarasinghe, while his namesake recuperated from an ankle sprain. His spell of 6–72 livened up an otherwise drab game.

It is now night and Manouri and two of the Byrd girls bring dinner. Manouri smiles at me, the two girls are too busy arguing over some nonsense to notice us. One is tall, the other is plump and I remember neither of their names.

As we tear into the paratha and prawn curry, I keep grilling our guest.

'Come on, Mr Gokul…surely the opposition can tell if you're playing an unregistered player.'

Gokul coughs rice back into his spoon. 'We had so-called Closed Pavilion Policy. Sir Nihal's idea, what else? Outsiders can't speak with team. Only master-in-charge, head coach and Sir Nihal could enter dressing room. Sir Nihal said it was for the preparing of the mental… urrg…I knew fishy things were going on.'

'Surely, Mr Gokul…in a Royal–Thomian? The players know each other. They will notice if Gihan Dandeniya is suddenly someone else.'

The question is mine. Ari, the sceptic, is strangely silent. He has been like this all through dinner. I poke him. 'Oi. Mr Silent Partner. How?'

'That's what it was.' Ari looks me square in the face. 'They all looked alike. Now I know why. Sunscreen. Bloody sunscreen. Every one of those jokers was covered in that crap…'

Closed Pavilion Policy

On the eve of the Royal–Thomian Big Match, six of Royal's nine coloursmen had injuries. Several all-rounders could only play as batsmen. Some bowlers could hardly play at all. What follows is conjecture, as even Mr Gokulanath was left out of the Closed Pavilion Policy.

The policy was raising a few eyebrows. The Royalists even asked for a separate entrance to the SSC so as not to fraternise outside of the closed circle.

'There were thirteen players, which included our man Mathew. Then the coach, the manager and Sir Nihal. Everyone thought it was arrogant, but no one questioned. Royal was winning, no?'

'No one else had access to the players?'

Gokul shakes his head.

Night descends on de Saram Road and plates are cleared. Gokul is hunched forward and asleep. Every part of him is asleep, except for his mouth. He is muttering.

'Don't think…bowl. You don't think…you bowl.'

'Can you bowl the double bounce ball, Mr Gokul?'

Mr Gokul is not fit to bowl anything. He keeps muttering. I shake my head at Ari. 'If you believe this story, you're a bigger fool than you look.'

The hand that holds the glass looks positively deformed, as does its owner. His knuckles are twisted at improbable angles. He tries to convince us that Mathew took the field under various guises. Before lunch, he was the fast bowler, after lunch he bowled spin, in the last session he bowled medium pace. And while he did this, three Royal players rested in the closed confines of the dressing room.

He tells us that in the first innings, Pradeep took 3 wickets. '2 as the pacey, 1 as the spinner.' But he cannot claim all the credit.

'The Royal fielding…sha! Like eleven Gus Logies, diving, throwing, catching,' recalls Ari. 'Plus the Thora batsmen played like mutts.'

Trailing by 160, the Thomians turned on their grit and dug in. By the end of the second day they were 104–4 needing to bat an entire day.

Mathew did not feature in that session.

'The third day was pathetic,' says Ari. 'They bowled like emperors, those pacemen, that all-rounder, that left-arm spinner…'

'Same person, same same,' snorts Gokul. He is beginning to nod off again, though his mouth is still working. 'All Pradeepan… That whole match I knew. Team arrive. Straight to dressing room. Straight to field. Straight to dressing room. For three days… And they win the game.'

He tells us that when Sarinda Jurangpathy, the left-arm spinner, came on to bowl, he knew beyond doubt. The action was immaculate, but the bowler's arms were four shades lighter than his face.

'That's why they never took off the blue and yellow caps. Bloody Royal cheaters,' says Ari.

By Gokul's count, Pradeep finished the game with a match bag of 13 wickets, though credit was shared by the legitimate Royal bowlers.

Ari is staring into space and for the first time in years, I'm smoking a cigarette outside of my writing table. Mr Gokulanath says he and all the Royal staff involved in cricket received a Rs 5,000 bonus for delivering the first Royal victory in sixteen years. He starts rocking forward with his eyes closed and mutters. 'We did nothing…said nothing…and that is why…they pay us.'

Then he leans over his chair, wiry limbs flailing, and vomits prawn curry and arrack into Manouri's anthurium plant. Ari runs out swearing and returns with a garden hose and a schoolteacher expression.

My bonus to Gokul is not as generous as Rs 5,000, but factoring in the free food and the bottle of Old, he hasn't done too shabbily. Gokul hisses to Ari about contacting the Thomian Old Boys Association with this information. Ari hisses back.

That weekend, after being sent by Sheila to buy new flowerpots for Manouri, I call every person connected to the 1983 Royal–Thomian I can find. Coaches, teachers, spectators, Royalists, Thomians.

Administrators at Royal College inform me that Mr Satyakumar Gokulanath was dismissed after twenty-nine years of service for misconduct and disgraceful behaviour. Six hundred rupees and much coaxing later, I find the incident involved stolen money from the school sports coffers.

My attempts at contacting Sir Nihal and the head coach are blocked when I foolishly mention that I want to interview them about the 1983 Big Match. I speak to old boys who played in that game, including the vice captain Sarinda Jurangpathy and first reserve Heshan Unamboowe. Both vehemently deny any conspiracy in the '83 match, and then look at their wrists and excuse themselves a minute after the question is posed.

The only people to verify that Royal used questionable methods are the Thomians I speak with. But none mention sunscreen or a bowler of a thousand actions. Seven claim food poisoning, nine claim ball tampering and four claim that the umpires were bribed with arrack and prostitutes.

Iceberg

Consider these stats:

- 7 tests, 47 wickets
- 27 one-dayers, 44 wickets
- Best test bowling, 10 for 51 (vs NZ, 1987)
- Best one-day bowling, 8 for 17 (1987 World Cup qualifier vs Bermuda)

Bowling is all about how many wickets you take. Your strike rate is how many balls you need to get them. Your average is how many runs each cost. P.S. Mathew's average was abysmal. He conceded many runs en route to his 91 international wickets.

He once told Charith Silva, when they were sharing a room on tour, 'An over is six bullets in a gun. I don't mind firing some into the sky if one hits the target.'

But when it came to the taking of wickets, he was unmatched. Let me illustrate by using one of Ariyaratne's invented stats. Wickets per match. Number of wickets divided by number of matches. Not rocket science.

Bowler	*Wickets*	*Matches*	*WPM*
Mathew (Tests)	47	7	**6.71**

My Jinadasa comes equipped with a darker setting. There is a reason that figure is in bold. Here are the greatest all-rounders of the 1980s. Perhaps even some of the greatest cricketers to walk the earth. Here are their wickets per match in tests:

Bowler	*Wickets*	*Matches*	*WPM*
Botham	383	102	3.75
Hadlee	431	86	5.01
Imran	362	88	4.11
Kapil	434	131	3.31

The greatest bowlers of yester-decade, no one within spitting distance of 6.71 wickets per match. This, you will find, is the tip of a chunk of ice at least twice as big as that which sank the *Titanic*.

The Sister

At first, she is suspicious. She walks around my room, glancing at my cricket books while tightly clutching her bag and umbrella.

'Please take a seat, Mrs Sabi,' says Ari, with a bow and a sweeping hand.

'Who are y'all?' she asks, not sitting down.

'We are great admirers of your brother.'

'Y'all are with that fellow Kuga?'

'Who?'

'Kuga. Are you with him?'

'Who is Kuga?'

Ari raises his eyebrows and I watch her watch us. She does so for some time.

Sabeetha Amirthalingam nee Sivanathan looks very much a woman who wears the shalwar pants and controls the remote. She is plump, with gold rings on her painted toes. Her hair seems permanently wet, her wrists imprison bangles, and her square glasses hang like picture frames from her red pottu.

She surveys my shelves, my Samyo radio and the stacks of newspaper clippings on my desk. She picks up my article titled 'Pradeep Mathew. Unsung Hero'. The one with the grainy picture and the purple prose. She still does not sit.

'My brother passed away last year.'

My heart sinks to my stomach and my stomach sinks to my bowels. I glance at Ari and catch Mrs Sabi glaring at me.

'How did he…?'

She stares at the picture. The one with the short-lived headband. 'I hated this long hair. He nicely cut it once. Last time I saw him, he was bald.'

'When was that?'

'Five years ago.'

I try to pick the resemblance. Pradeep had a pinocchio nose; she has an eggplant honk. He had tiny squints; she has bulging eyes. He was skinny, dark; she is russet-coloured, chubby.

'Are you sure your brother is dead?'

She nods. Not without sadness. Then, finally, she sits. A few sips of

Sheila's ginger tea softens her leather handbag exterior. Her speech gathers speed. 'Don't know much about Pradeepan's cricket. Tell you frankly, I didn't have much contact with our family those days.'

Mrs Sabi gives us the Wuthering Heights of it all. Aided by a loan from Sampath National Bank, the very firm that would later employ his son, Muhundan Sivanathan became part owner of Malinda Bakers in Moratuwa and was able to move the Sivanathan family from the Soysapura Flats to a respectable part of Angulana.

'Appa said, "Hard work never killed anyone." In the end it killed him. Pradeepan was a very quiet child, used to cry for the slightest thing.'

Overbearing Sinhala mother and workaholic Tamil father raised two children who did not know what race they were. That was till 1983.

'Our bus went past the flats. Fridges and TVs being thrown from the windows. Vehicles burning. Tamils being beaten on the street. We were terrified.'

The men with clubs and knives stormed the bus and asked passengers to speak Sinhala, to say words that Tamils found tricky to pronounce, like baaldiya. Irangani and Sabi passed the test, an elderly gentleman in front did not. He was dragged out and set on fire.

Mrs Sabi curls her lips and shakes her head. She pushes her glasses along her nose and looks at the wall that I stare at and the numerous pieces of paper bearing her brother's name.

Pradeep was rescued from Thurstan by the driver of Muhundan's silent partner, Bharatha Malinda Dasanayake. Muhundan had wisely let the local mudalali put his name on the bakery he ran. The mob, who feared Dasanayake, kept their kerosene cans away from the Sivanathan home, but proceeded to burn down three houses on Daham Road.

Had Malinda Bakers been named Sivanathan Bakeries, the owner-operator and the baker's assistants would have been hurled into the ovens. Had Muhundan not been delivering steady profits, Dasanayake would not have sent his driver to pick up young Pradeep.

'Pradeepan wouldn't tell us what he saw on the drive from Thurstan, but I know it affected him. Appa was worried he'd become political, so they sent him away, for studies.'

Remembering his Thurstan mentor's advice, Pradeepan Mathew Sivanathan dropped his surname when enrolling at the University of Hampshire in the UK in 1984. He then dropped his studies a year later to join the touring Sri Lankan cricket team. Both events caused a storm at home and for a while Pradeep was *persona non grata*.

All this was overshadowed when Sabi Sivanathan ran away with Indrakrishnan Amirthalingam, the baker's assistant.

'I thought, no problem, nice, hard-working Tamil boy. But Amma wanted me to marry a Kandyan. Appa didn't want me marrying a low caste. They themselves had a mixed marriage. Still they threw me out.'

She had no contact with the family for most of the 1980s. While this may explain why Mrs Sabi knew little of her brother's cricketing career, it does not clarify why a mother of four would travel all the way from Angulana for a badly typeset newspaper ad. Nor why she would volunteer her life story to strangers.

'Pradeepan visited when the children were born. Didn't talk about his cricket.'

Ari administers the questions and I watch her and try to ascertain why my gut tells me that she is lying through her teeth.

'When did Pradeep start playing cricket?'

Mrs Sabi has an uncanny knack of relating any answer to the story of her mother and her.

'One Christmas, Appa got him a bat and a ball. I got a Yamaha keyboard. Amma never learned music when she was a girl. So I had to go for piano classes.'

'Did anyone coach him?'

She bares her palms and shrugs. 'He was always playing with those thugs from the flats, or the street kids. He was never home. Neither was I. Ballet, sewing and elocution classes…'

I look at her deportment, her dress and hear her uneven accent. Ari pours tea and the woman keeps jabbering.

She hardly saw Pradeep but was aware that he had secured a job at Sampath National Bank and played occasionally for Sri Lanka. Appa was right; hard work didn't kill him, it just left him paralysed. The stroke came in 1991 and drained the family coffers. Pradeep had no money of his own, so Sabi, emboldened by funds sent by her husband from Dubai, came to the rescue.

'Amma and Appa were against my marriage and my husband. In the end it was Indi's money that looked after them,' she says. Not without triumph.

'Later Pradeepan also made money and he would send us, but I hardly saw him. I was busy with the children. Every time Indi came from Dubai, he would leave me with a bump.' She rubs her tummy and allows herself a chuckle.

'Did Pradeepan take loans from the Cricket Board?'

The grin freezes on her face. The eyes hold their expression. The change in manner is switch-like. 'Is that what this is about?'

'I beg your pardon?' says Ari.

'Are you with Kuga or with the SLBCC?'

'Who is…' I begin.

'We're with Kuga,' says Ari and puffs his chest out.

I attempt damage control. 'No. No. We're doing a documentary on your brother.'

'I know my brother wasn't so famous to do a documentary on.' She shuffles to her feet.

'If only you knew, Mrs Sabi,' I say. 'My colleague and I believe he was the greatest Sri Lankan cricketer ever.'

'I am not a Chinaman with a ponytail.' She is someone whose voice lowers when they are angry.

She walks to the table with all our cuttings and waves a wand-like finger. 'This is documentary? My brother is dead. You better leave him alone.'

'Kuga is willing to leave him alone, Mrs Sabi.' I shake my head at Ari.

But the buffoon has already begun strutting like Perry Mason. 'Mrs Sabi. How did Pradeep die?'

She hands me an envelope and pulls a yellow umbrella from her handbag. 'Mr Karunasena. Please tell your boss to tell *their* boss that Pradeepan Sivanathan has nothing left to give.'

She walks past stacks of newspapers that are waiting to be scrapped. She barks at the puzzled-looking Ari leaning by the doorway. 'We're not scared of your Kuga. Or your Cricket Board. We also have connections.'

Perhaps she expected a fight or at least a show of machismo. Anything but two scared old men. Suddenly there is a flash of light. I blink to find Ari holding his miniature washing machine. A piece of paper comes out of it. This is the sort of bravery that garners Victoria Crosses.

'Give me that,' shouts Mrs Sabi.

'See. See. It is blank,' shows Ari. This time he does not flap it.

She storms off to the veranda and looks at the sunbeams scorching my driveway. She opens her umbrella, considers, then lowers her voice to a whisper. 'The Moratuwa Police DIG and the Mayor of Panadura are both old customers at our bakery. Our partner Bharatha Malinda is a powerful man. If your people come near my family, you be careful.'

She walks onto de Saram Road, flags down a three-wheeler as yellow as her umbrella, casts us one last scowl and disappears in a huff of exhaust fumes.

The cardboard in Ari's hand has broken out in spots of brown.

'Does that thing take proper pictures?'

'This is Ali McGraw's Polaroid Swinger,' says Ari, as if that means something. 'Look.'

He stops flapping it and I see a shadowy blotch of a plump lady attempting to block a camera.

'Good photo,' I say. 'If you like abstract art.'

'Not that,' says Ari. 'What's in the envelope?'

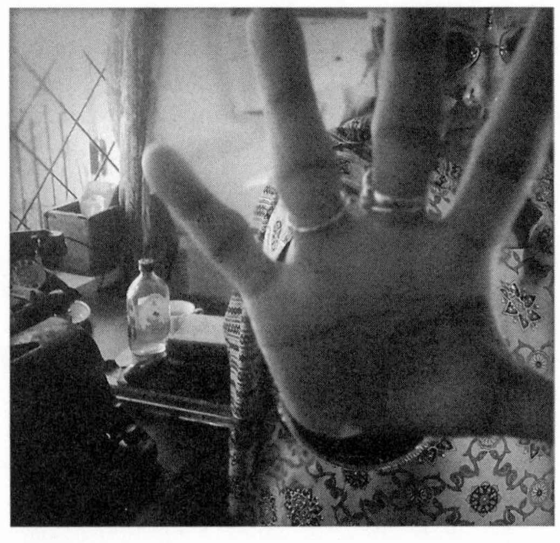

The Envelope

This is what is in Sabi Amirthalingam's envelope. Typewritten on official pastel stationery. If it's a forgery, it is a pretty decent one.

Melbourne City Council
37 Jellicoe Avenue
Selwyn Circus
Melbourne

Dear Mrs S Amitringham,
It is with deep regret that we inform you that your brother, Pradeep Sinavathan Mathew, succumbed to injuries following a car crash on

July 13, 1995, at the Melbourne General Hospital. His remains have been cremated and interred at the City South Cemetery as per request. State insurance has borne the cost of these services. Please find attached death certificate.

We are truly sorry for your loss.

Julia Bedford
Director of Services

'I don't think this letter is real,' I say.
Ari shrugs. 'Why would anyone make it up?'

Women's Cricket

Graham Snow, alas, was proving to be unreachable. We missed two of his calls and he missed seventeen of Ari's. After three letters outlining our financial woes, we receive a postcard from Cape Town promising to send more money.

Ari wails like a jilted lover, but I understand. A Graham Snow has an Ari Byrd in every port. Wherever he goes there are clones of us, wanting to talk about the 1971 Ashes or the underarm incident. He can't be expected to keep up with every one of us.

Meanwhile, Garfield and Sheila are leaving sound engineering course leaflets on my desk. A not-so-subtle hint for me to call my eldest brother.

The Loku Aiya who called me a parasite. Sheila tells me it is because I got drunk and was rude to him, but I do not recall this.

I have one other option. That too requires a sizeable loss of dignity. Newton Rodrigo, the rotund gentleman whom Ari once assaulted, now coaches the Sri Lanka women's cricket team. The kindest thing I can say about women's cricket is that it's better than women's rugby. Newton had received the appointment a month earlier; there was an announcement in his old paper, the *Lankadeepa*.

I stand outside the Colts Cricket Club, telling myself to resist. No jibe or barb or smart alec comment. No matter how strong the compulsion. I am here on business.

He sees me and raises his hand. 'Wije. Kindly bugger off.'

I approach him with a friendly smile. 'Newton, old chap, shall we put a drink?'

'Daughter is here, have to go.' A skinny girl in a blue tracksuit approaches Newton's Mercedes Benz. Coaching obviously pays far more than journalism.

'Your daughter is in the national team?' I ask. Making conversation.

He speaks to me from behind the car door. He appears to be holding in his stomach. 'Wije. Do not provoke me. So what? I am coaching the women's national squad. What are you doing?'

His daughter hurls her cricket bag into the back seat and averts her eyes. 'Thaathi, let's go.'

They leave without a goodbye.

The Art of Cricket

The next day I am better organised. My press pass and cock-and-bull story get me into the Colts ground. Newton is hitting catches to women in baggy tracksuit bottoms with ponytails. His free hand wears a wicketkeeping glove that he uses like a baseball glove. He scoops up the wayward throws from the ladies, spoons the ball and hits gently, but with pinpoint precision.

While Newton's torso is pear-shaped, his limbs are twigs. The glove looks monstrous next to his wrist. I am carrying a book and wearing a humble smile. I accost him on his way to the changing rooms.

'Wije, I'm busy.'

'I came to give you this.' I hold a first edition of Sir Donald Bradman's *The Art of Cricket*. He knows exactly what it is. I turn to the page with the words *Best Wishes Donald Bradman* written in black felt pen in the great man's own hand. I now have his attention.

'Autographed? I thought you were bullshitting.'

I hand it to him; he strokes it as if it were a kitten. He beckons me to the pavilion. 'Come. Sit.'

'Newton. I have more. All first editions. Sobers' *Coaching Manual*. With handwritten notes by the man himself. Douglas Jardine's *Bodyline Diaries*. I'm getting a new book about the apartheid tours.'

Newton thumbs through the honestly written, well-diagrammed bible of insight from the world's greatest batsman. It is unclear whether he hears me.

'Wije. Why are you selling this?'

No longer caring about dignity, I opt for honesty. 'I need to pay for my son's studies.'

'I heard you and Brian and all were trying to make a documentary.' He laughs.

'You have big ears.'

'And a big brain.'

'I know. And big keeping gloves.'

Newton and I were friends in the 1950s, rivals in the 1960s, enemies in the 1970s. Long story. Over the last twenty years, our paths hardly crossed, except for the occasional incident with weddings and buriyani.

'I cannot accept this.'

'Accept it. I have no use for those. It is all in here.' I point to my grey scalp.

'Wije. Be a man, will you? How can you do this? How much money do you have?'

'Not much. SLBCC advanced hundred. We may get another fifty.'

'Have you seen my car?'

I nod and sigh. He was going to give me a lecture on how he rose from the sewers of Panadura to become a cricket entrepreneur. I mentally buckle up.

'You think twenty years at *Lankadeepa* paid for that?'

'Look, I don't want to talk about this, Newton.'

'No. Talk. Talk. I know what they say. Newton took kickbacks. He made money off players. He brought outstation boys to Colombo and sold them to cricket clubs. He was a cricket pimp.'

I realise that none of this is helping my cause. 'I'm not here to discuss this. I need your help.'

'For your information, I never took a cent from any cricketer I promoted.'

I say nothing. He looks at me a long time, all the while stroking the book. 'Lend me this. I will return it.'

'I'm not a library, Newton. I need cash.'

He looks at me a long time. His words appear carefully chosen. 'If you promise to keep shut, I will tell you how I bought this Mercedes.'

'I'm too old to coach the national blind team…'

He bursts out laughing. 'You think SLBCC gives the women's coach enough to get a Benz?'

He looks around and then leans forward. 'I will help you, not for this book, but because I am the bigger man.'

I look at the tyre of fat around his belt and nod.

'Cricket betting is run by two families. The Punchipalas and the Sumathi-Silvas. But there is a third. Newly opened. Attached to a casino. Run by Filipinos who don't know a ball about cricket. If you promise not to repeat this to that thug friend of yours, I can give you a tip.'

'Definitely.'

He then asks if he can borrow my book. I smile and mentally say goodbye to it.

Turf Accountants

'No, Wije. That is madness.'

'Let's just go in. Then we shall take a call. What is there to lose?'

Ari shakes his head.

The Neptune Casino sits on a seaside lane in Colpetty. There is a gold-plated sign saying 'Foreigners Only' on its white entrance and a single file of taxis that transport oriental women and Arab men to and from hotels. Next to it is a narrow lane of crumbling brick and the whiff of urine. Brick gives way to white plaster which widens into a courtyard of fluorescent shadows. To the left is a door with two burly men in white shirts sitting at the entrance. To the right, a large roti shop with a sign saying 'Turf Accountants'.

This is the back door of the Neptune that Newton spoke of. The well-dressed brutes direct us towards the curry house. It smells of onions, fried chicken and deep coriander. The floor is a mess of newspapers and coloured rice, but I see no flies.

We are not the first drunk old men to darken these doorways. The room is large, but clumsily placed pillars and tables make it look small. The lack of lighting doesn't help. The dress code here is messy casual. There are men in trousers and men in sarongs.

A shuffling man with a thick moustache points us to a table and places two printed sheets and two Reynolds pens on the dust-ridden formica.

I have been in places like this many times. A lifelong commitment to drink is not for the squeamish.

The dark corners of the room conceal dark strangers. Chattering, sipping from greasy cups, stuffing themselves with vade. Everyone staring at the paper in front of them. I put on my glasses, Ari removes his. Even our eyes take opposing views.

Cardinal's Steelers 19/3
Average Outburst 2/12
Upekkha 11/4
Apple Rain 21/3
Genuine Risk 11/5

'This looks more complicated than your diagrams, Byrd.'

Ari scratches his bald spot. 'You brought me here to bet on horses?'

I flag the moustachio. 'You have Old?'

'We don't serve liquor.'

'All these fellows are drinking, no?' says Ari with a wave of his arms.

'Drinking only for members,' he says and walks away.

'We are friends of Mr Newton. Did he call you?' I say.

We are asked to fork out Rs 1,000. Ari refuses. I have to pay from my own pocket. We are each given a cyclostyled red sheet with black lettering. We are not offered drinks.

It is just like Newton said. The cricket betting.

Ari looks up. 'These odds are odd.' He chuckles.

'Very funny,' I say while scanning the page. Indeed. The odds were cockeyed.

'So if we put 50 on South Africa beating the UAE, we get 80? That can't be right.'

'Not just the win. You have to specify top scorer, top wicket taker and winning margin.'

'So that's hard, no?'

'You're the mathematician.'

'I'm not a fortune-teller. At these odds they would be bankrupt.'

'Apparently, all our buggers bet on Sri Lanka. No matter what the odds. That's how this place makes money.'

I look down the list of World Cup fixtures. Pakistan vs Holland. Australia vs Kenya. Even to my Grade 7 maths brain, it seems incredible. The trick now is to convince the man with the cheque. The puritanical Ariyaratne Cletus Byrd.

He looks up solemnly.

'Ari, do not think of it as gambling. It's like the silly bets we have at Jonny's.'

'What if we lose?'

'How can we lose?'

'If there is an upset.'

'South Africa are unlucky, but they are not going to lose to the Arabs.'

Jonny has a theory that South Africa are doomed to choke in every major tournament for the next fifty years as payback for apartheid. He also believes that England will spend centuries working off their colonial sins by performing miserably at sport. I then ask him why

Australia, who wiped out generations of Aborigines, win everything in every sport, and he shuts up.

There are gamblers in the corner praying at a TV. I do not mean this metaphorically; one of them is actually on his knees. If both teams pray for victory whose prayer does God answer? Does he decide who is more worthy, does he throw dice, or does he ignore everyone? What about during a war?

'You want to put all of it?'

'Let's put and see.'

'I don't like it.'

'You want to sit waiting for Graham Snow?'

Ari scratches his bald spot and shrugs. 'If we lose, you better explain to everyone.'

I wish everyone were this easy to convince.

On the way home, we argue over whether to place the full amount. I tell him there will be no point otherwise. He says nothing, but when we meet the next day he has an ola leaf with strange markings on it.

'If we are betting everything, we need outside help.'

'You know a match-fixer?'

'No. A fortune-teller.'

He does not reveal his source, but tells me we should place the remaining 50,000 on South Africa beating the UAE by 150 runs, with Kirsten scoring and Donald taking wickets. We both agree to be discreet, knowing very well that if Brian, Manouri and Sheila got to know there would be death. One of us would do the deed. Like any casino, management got suspicious of the same faces taking home winnings.

Ari has bought a hat and a long coat. I talk him out of wearing them. He sulks.

I walk down the long alley by the casino and wait ten minutes inside the curry house. I nurse a plain tea and some cutlets, while Ari walks in. He has discarded the hat, but kept the raincoat and added a cigar. He has forgotten to look up the word discreet in the dictionary.

When the waiter arrives with the betting sheet, Ari announces he is placing a large bet and would like to be allowed into the sports bar. The cashier explains that the sports bar is members only, and that all bets are placed from here.

Ari catches me glaring and places his bet, muttering insults at the cashier. Once the money is accepted, the bouncer has a quiet word with him.

'How dare you? I am a paying customer.'

'For you, betting closed,' says the bouncer, pulling him by the arm. For a moment I am petrified that Ari will throw a punch, but even he is not such a fool.

Later Ari laughs. 'They must've thought I was a cop.'

'Did you at least place the bet correctly?' I ask.

Fourteen hours later, the Africans trounce the Arabs by 169 runs, despite the best efforts of Lankan-born UAE all-rounder Johann Samarasekera, who Ari reminds me was a Thomian. His brother Athula was a swashbuckling batsman who retired prematurely before the World Cup.

Kirsten scores 188, Donald gets 3 wickets. Our side bets net us Rs 90,000. Ari's ola leaf predictions were spot on, a fact he reminds me of at ten-minute intervals.

In the interim, Danila calls to find out how the project is going. I reply, perhaps a bit too curtly, that we are batting on, despite getting no support from the Cricket Board or Graham Snow.

'I have good news, Mr Karuna. I convinced MD to grant a bit more budget.'

My hard-nosed businessman routine evaporates.

'From Graham Snow?'

'He's busy with the World Cup. We can forward this to you as a loan, provided you don't feature Mathew.'

'How much?'

'Two lakhs.'

'What can we do with that?'

'It's a start, no, Mr Karuna? But no Mathew, ah?'

'For two lakhs, how to promise that?'

'Have you located him?'

'Not yet. You knew him?'

'Not really.'

I decide to change the topic. 'Can we pick up the cheque tomorrow?'

'Only if no Mathew.'

Mathew would be the first documentary we shoot, but best not to argue with a lady bearing a cheque. Instead I decide to be nosy.

'Bit of a question, Danila?'

'Ask away, my dear.' Was she flirting? Dream on, old fart.

'I heard Graham was in love with a girl from the Cricket Board. Was it you?'

There is laughter at the end of the line. 'Aiyo, no. Give me some credit. He had an affair with Saleshini.'

'Who?'

'You know her. Came to our meetings.'

'The mouse?'

Danila giggles. Unlike her voice, her laugh is lyrical. 'Yes. The mouse. Don't you know, Uncle? Sometimes mice can attract rats…'

Uncle? Ouch.

Shrewd Investors

On my way to collect the money, I think about Ari's ola leaf and wonder where he got it. Some fake guru in Maradana or the charm shop in Bamba probably. Ari had now gone to procure a prediction for the Pakistan–Holland match.

The mousey girl meets me at reception, announces that Danila is at a meeting, and hands over a cheque. For some reason, she does not ask me to sign anything. My bus home passes the Neptune Casino and I decide to ring the bell.

I do not wait for Ari's sorcery; I will follow my W.G. instinct and place it on Sri Lanka against Zimbabwe. The waiter smiles at me and asks me to stay for a drink. My bet for 293,000 gets me entrance to the back room, where the lights are dimmer and the seats comfier. There are TVs broadcasting karaoke and cricket matches. Local women in tight clothing serve drinks. I enjoy half a bottle, and place side bets on Aravinda top-scoring and Streak getting wickets.

I make the mistake of telling Ari.

'You bloody fool! We agreed we would put it on the Holland game. I even got the prediction. How can you be sure we can beat Zimba?'

'I'm sure, I'm sure,' I slur.

'What margin?'

'100 runs or 6 wickets.'

He does not speak to me for two days.

On the third day, the Guru and Aravinda take us to the target in style with 13 overs to spare. I get a call. It is the only time I have heard someone whisper and shriek at the same time.

'Wije. Wije. We have almost eight lakhs. I calculated. I calculated. Streak got 3, Ara got 91. Let's tell Brian. 6 wickets exactly. You are a genius. I told Manouri!'

Heaven help us.

We get a stern talking-to from the wives, but Brian's presence soothes their fury.

'Aunties. I know. I know. But it was a calculated risk. Your husbands are shrewd investors.'

'They are fools,' says Sheila. 'Gamini, if you use any of our money, I will skin you.'

'The Bible says gambling is a sin,' says Manouri.

Brian laughs his laugh and gets down to business. 'Uncles. This is your money. To tell the truth, I had actually given up on this. Here's my suggestion. We increase the budget to six lakhs. That way we can do the script we want, the way we want.'

It sounds fair enough and we are nodding, all except the wives. Sheila enters the negotiation. 'What about Garfield? Sorry, Brian. I need money for my son's education. I am sorry.'

'It is our husbands' money. They owe to their families. Brian, we will refund your 50,' pacifies Manouri.

'How can you say it is your money?' says Brian, his voice quivering.

Ari and I look on like eunuchs. I decide to intervene. 'There is the Pakistan–Holland game. We keep 50 for security. Take a small share for Garfield and Manouri. And place the rest on Anwar, Waqar, 130 runs or 7 wickets. We have been picking the group games well. If we win, which we will, Garfield can go to Harvard, we can go to Hollywood and Manouri can build a church.'

Then Ari opens his mouth. 'I even have an inside source.'

'That's from Uncle Neiris's woman?' asks Brian.

'Who's Uncle Neiris?' ask Manouri and I at once.

'He's an ace con artist. Looks after the Tyronne Cooray cricket ground.'

'The midget?' I ask.

'I think he's a dwarf,' says Brian.

'Not him, men,' says Ari. 'His wife or sister is a super fortune-teller. She sells predictions for 100 bucks.'

'You're getting betting tips from a saasthara lady?' I mock.

'Ari,' says Manouri, 'I am not happy.'

An argument erupts between Brian and Sheila and I am unable to get a further word in.

Garfield

Waqar held down the Dutch while Anwar and Ijaz punched the daylights out of them. The Netherlands team featured another Lankan, former pre-test player Flavian Aponso. Now it's my turn to be livid. I drag Sheila over to Ari and Manouri's.

'17 for 1!' I yell across the pantry. 'Forget saasthara. I got everything right. If we had put half the amount, we would've all been millionaires.'

'Who has the money?' asks Manouri, ignoring my outburst.

We all look at Ari, who looks at me. 'I can't go in there. They think I'm a cop.'

'You mean you fools haven't collected it?' says Sheila. 'Go now, before the place goes bankrupt.'

They forbid Ari from buying any more tips and send Garfield with me to make sure I don't do what I want to do. He sits in the trishaw listening to noise on his earphones and looking the other way.

'Why are your jeans torn?'

I repeat myself thrice and get no reply.

The portly trishaw driver's eyes twinkle at me through the rear-view. 'Just like my daughters. Always sticking the plugs in the ears. But if my ones wore torn clothes, I would flog them...'

The day I take parenting advice from a trishaw driver is the day Israeli cricket gets test status. I nod politely and gaze at the Slave Island morning. Checkpoints and road closures force us to take the less-than-scenic route.

Your children's faults are always magnified in the same way that yours are invisible. Truth be told, Garfield was better than me. He was gentler, politer and kinder. But those qualities don't get you anywhere. He was a typical twenty-year-old, a fool who did not know he was one.

We get out near the bus station, walk down the alleyway and stop off at the curry house. An urchin wearing a Titanic T-shirt serves up two steaming cups, a masala stain covering Kate Winslet's face like a veil. The place was more crowded than before. Maybe word of its odd odds was spreading.

'Garfield, you realise, all this money is not for you.'

'Thaathi, no one calls me Garfield. My name is S…'

'No need to tell me. I gave you both your names.'

'I know.'

'Listen, son. There is only about eight lakhs there. Once Aunty Manouri takes her share and Brian gets some for the documentary, you'll only be left with one or two lakhs.'

'I thought you were asking Mahappa.'

'Your uncle will not give.'

'He said that?'

I say nothing. But give the impression I'm saying yes.

'Son. Tomorrow West Indies play Kenya. We can play it safe or play it smart.'

He grabs the betting sheet I've placed before him. 'West Indies are not as good as they were.'

The boy was not a complete fool.

'True. True enough. But Kenya? Can you imagine losing to them? Lara always top-scores and Ambrose always gets wickets. They will win by 80 runs or 5 wickets.'

'It's risky.'

Ragged men in sarongs jostle through the narrow shop and request roti and some curry to dip it in. Gamblers pour from one room to the next. Hungry men who will never be full. Their eyes look exhausted and enthralled at the same time.

'What risk? If we had put on Pakistan like I said, we wouldn't be here.'

'Did Mahappa really say he couldn't give?'

'Will you place the bet for us?'

He says nothing. But gives the impression he is saying yes.

Steve Tikolo

I tell him thrice how to fill the betting slip. He keeps saying, I heard you the first time, and then completely screws it up. He gets the winning margin (80 runs/5 wickets) and the best bowler (Walsh) right. But he comes back having put Rs 753,000 on Kenya! And instead of putting on Lara, he has put money on the Kenyan number 4, some guy called Tikolo.

I call him a buffoon and send him back to change the bet. He comes back saying they would charge a 6 percent transfer fee. I call him an imbecile and send him back in. He returns with the correct bet, on the favoured team. West Indies, Lara, Walsh at safe odds. After all, we are neither gamblers nor fools. We ride back in silence and tell the others that the payout is on Friday. The reaction is not good.

'Are you sure they will pay?'

'Yes. Yes,' I insist. 'Ask Garfield.'

Ari whispers to me as they grill Garfield. 'Tell me you didn't do it, Wije.'

I smile at him and put my fingers to my lips. He frowns back.

None of us are to know that chasing a paltry 166 against a non-test playing bowling attack, the Windies would collapse to 93 all out, causing one of the great upsets of the modern game. That Steve Tikolo's 29 would be the highest score of the game.

Ari does the calculations much, much later. If Garfield's initial mistake had stood, we would have made 6.7 million. Instead, we end up losing 7.5 lakhs.

Halal Meat

On Saturday, Garfield disappears. In the confusion, no one notices we haven't claimed the bet money. A note is left:

> Ammi. Thaathi.
> Leaving for Dubai. I have no choice. Will be in touch.
> Don't worry.
> G

For a while, hysteria reigns. Then Ari's daughter Melissa spills the beans.

'He ran off with that girl down the road. Sara.'

'That's Marzooq's daughter...'

There is a crash of metallic rust outside. As if mammoths are battling robots. We look through the window. My gate is still shuddering. There are three bearded men with mosque hats. The oldest one is the biggest; he is wielding a stick and being restrained by the younger two.

'Bring her now or I will smash this house!'

Ari shouts from the balcony. 'Mr Marzooq. What is the meaning of this?'

'Where is my Sara?'

Faces are peeping from behind curtains and trishaw drivers are exiting their vehicles and approaching Ari's house.

'We are also missing our boy,' I say.

'I will break your boy's face.'

I run down the stairs. I have been drinking all morning and my run is more a tortoise-like shuffle. 'Gamini, wait!' shouts Sheila. Ari comes after me, the snail in hot pursuit of the tortoise. In the three minutes that it takes for us to reach the gate, a crowd has gathered.

'Come back, Wije! They will turn you into halal meat!' says Ari.

The Marzooq brothers are attempting to prise the stick from their father. The stick flies off in the scuffle, bounces on the tarred road and lands at my feet. I pick it up and begin swinging. The crowd coos with delight and takes a step back. The Marzooqs advance. 'Uncle. Don't try anything.'

'Where is that bloody son of mine?' I scream. 'I will make hal... mincemeat out of him.'

In the distance I hear Sheila wailing. The Muslims stop in their tracks.

'Come, Marzooq. We'll find this fool and we'll thrash him.'

I begin walking to their car. The crowd parts like the Red Sea.

Even though I feel like a lie-down, I keep up my bravado. I lift my baton to hammer the de Saram Road signboard. 'Let's go! I will break his head!'

And suddenly there are people restraining me. They drag me into my home and lock the door. I am force-fed cups of tea and asked to sit still.

An hour later Mr Marzooq enters with his sons. We share more tea. Melissa Byrd tells us the rest of the story. My son and Sara Marzooq have been seeing each other for over two years.

'You knew this?' bellows her father.

'No, did you?' I snarl back.

'They did.' Melissa points to the two boys. She had evidently inherited her father's talent for subtlety.

The eldest boy receives a slap. There is a flood of Tamil exchanged between father and sons. That is when Sheila hands me a letter that has just arrived. She gives me a look that could curdle beer.

> Dear Ammi/Thaathi
> I'm sorry for causing drama. I am in Dubai and have a contract to play bass with Capricorn. I can save money for studies.
> I am with my wife, Sara. This is the only way for us to be together.
> Please do not be upset. I will stay in touch and send money.
> Your son,
> Garfield
>
> PS: Do not show to Sara's family.
> PPS: Don't blame Thaathi about the money. I am the one who placed the bet.

The elder Marzooq boy grabs the letter. 'Come, Vaappa. We will bring her home.'

Sheila runs after them. 'Mr Marzooq. Don't you dare hurt my son...'

I rise to go before realising that the entire Byrd family is staring at me.

'Tell me you didn't put all of it, Wije?'

'How much did you put, Gamini?' asks his wife.

'What did Uncle Wije do?' asks nosy Melissa.

I tell them very quickly. In the second that it takes for the truth to sink in, I make a hasty exit, chased to the door by raised voices and fists.

Check-up

Last week I woke up shivering. This week I wake up sweating. Sheila spies a note from Nawasiri in the post. It is the hospital calling me in for my annual check-up. My body notifies me that the prognosis will not be good.

'Didn't you just go for a check-up?'

'No. That was to make an appointment.'

'When is your appointment?'

'Sheila, I have writing to do.'

I lock myself in my room and decide to leave it till after next month's World Cup.

Persona Non Grata

Just as the Marzooqs begin assembling a SWAT team, young Sara comes home by herself. The sixteen-year-old realises that being a little princess is far more pleasant than being a musician's wife. The Marzooqs have the marriage annulled. My son calls and I refuse to talk to him.

The Byrds take turns in coming over and blasting me. Brian Gomez rings up and calls me every name under the sun. Everyone insists I pay back the Cricket Board from my personal money, of which I have none. Garfield stays in Dubai and sends a cheque for 5,000 dirhams. I tear it into pieces and post it back to him. A week later, following a blistering arrack-fuelled row, Sheila asks me to leave the house.

I find myself in the same position as the internationals who dared tour apartheid South Africa in the 1980s. I am universally shunned. It would be a few years later that men more famous than me would be banished for committing the very crime that I had. Betting more than they could afford on a game of cricket.

Nineteen Ninety-six

Where were you in 1996? Who did you hug when Ranatunga hammered that 6 off Warne? I hugged a sweaty trishaw driver with a scar running down his cheek. As far as hugs go, it wasn't bad. Though I, who grew up in a no-hugs-please-we're-Sinhalese atmosphere, am hardly an expert.

I was at the Kaanuwa in Moratumulla. A place where I was sure no one I cared about or didn't care for would see me. A place where men in sarongs drink to forget why they drink, smoke cigarettes past the filter and start long-running arguments.

Jonny Gilhooley had invited me to his bungalow in Bolgoda to watch the final. But recent events had put a dampener on my mood. A mood that I only wished to share with strangers.

It is the first time I've seen chairs and tables in the Kaanuwa. Till today, it was a transit bar near Moratuwa's central bus stand that served every type of arrack – Pol, Gal, Blue, White, Old, Old Reserve, Double Distilled, Extra Special – to every type of customer, regardless of how ragged they looked. After today, the furniture and the TV would be a permanent fixture. And it is the first weekend in the Kaanuwa's thirty-year history that no fights break out and no one is evicted.

The bar is already full when I walk in, and everyone is wearing free Regnis hats. The floor is sodden, with leaflets advertising washing machines and fridges soaked in spilled arrack and fallen stout.

The table next to me is taken by trishaw drivers. The one who sits alongside me is well built, with copper-tinted hair, a mosque hat and a scar on his cheek. He is the only one of them who doesn't unnerve me. He gives me the first of a million grins as he sits, creating a buffer between me and the barroom beasts.

I recognise a few of them. Comrade Bandara sits under the fan with a bottle of strong beer. He once lamented that countries who play cricket never become communist. Bandara lives in Mount Lavinia, close to my place. His nephew was murdered in the 1989 Janatha Vimukthi Peramuna purge – the government-sponsored mass execution of thousands of suspected university Marxists. 'I hope this team doesn't win anything for the next hundred years,' he once said. Today he is wearing a Sri Lanka T-shirt and hooting.

It had been an eventful two weeks. I had lost seven lakhs, a son and a home. I was staying with my born-again sister and her holy husband in the suburbs of Battaramulla, and my face ached from all the smiling I had to do. The youngest of Akka's three children had just left for studies and I was taking full advantage of her surplus mothering instincts. While the food was good and the sheets were clean, I was unable to drink and I had to join them for evening prayers.

I need not waste too much ink on the 1996 World Cup final. You all know what happened. Taylor and Ponting posted 137 for 1. Sri Lanka's spin quartet of Murali, Dharmasena, Jayasuriya and de Silva applied the skids. Our spin quartet were no Chandra–Bedi–Venkat–Prasanna. We had only one genuine spinner of the ball and two part-timers. But coupled with our agile fielding and aggressive spirit, it was enough. 170 for 5. 245 for 7.

245 wasn't impossible, but it was difficult batting second in a Cup final against the likes of Warne, McGrath, Fleming, Reiffel and the Waugh twins.

By the time the scoreboard read 20, both our openers were in the pavilion, removing their pads and shaking their heads. Amid the perfume of sweat, smoke and distilled spirits, we begin shaking our fists and cursing. Unfit drunks swearing at professional athletes.

Plates of steaming fried rice and devilled beef fly past my face. The bar is filled with sellers of kasippu or illegal liquor from Soysapura, fisherfolk from Lunawa, shopkeepers from Rawatawatte and the sum total of zero women. These are men escaping their obligations. Men who have nowhere to be. Men who lean against the filthy walls, oblivious to the cockroaches crawling across the ceiling wires.

Then Aravinda and Guru steady the ship and, united by a hatred of Glenn McGrath, a brotherhood begins to bind us. Outside on the streets nothing moves. As if even the cats and the crows and the beggars have found TVs to crowd around.

My companion gets chatty. 'Ade. I can't believe. We are winning. We are winning.'

I spy a ponytail under his mosque hat, a tattoo under his shirt sleeve and shiny chains on his throat.

'Shut up, fool,' growls Kalu Daniel, notorious kasippu distiller and gambler, seated below the TV with his entourage. 'If we lose I will smash you.'

Mosque Hat lets out a nervous giggle, lights a Gold Leaf and extends his hand. 'Uncle, fit, no? Fit.' He is pouring with sweat and 147 minutes away from hugging me.

The Aussies crumble as Aravinda and Arjuna take us home. Intoxicated by hours of drinking and the possibility of the improbable, we begin hitting the tables and chanting. Outside firecrackers pop, first like machine gun pellets, then like dynamite.

'Uncle! We are the champions!' shouts my sweat-drenched companion, mid-hug. Colombo explodes into fireworks and men embrace strangers. The party goes on all night and continues for the next three years. Sri Lankans across the world stand taller, believing that now anything is possible. The war would end, the nation would prosper and pigs would take to the air.

We watch the victory lap. Gurusinha is caught wrestling a souvenir stump away from a spectator. Glaring at the man as if to say, 'Sorry, mister, but I have taken too much crap from too many people for far too long to get to this point. This stump is mine. Go get your own.'

We watch Arjuna, next to Pakistan Premier Benazir Bhutto, thanking Wasim and Azhar for supporting us after Australia and the West Indies refused to play in Sri Lanka, following a bomb blast. My friend, his tongue fully lubricated, lets out a giggle.

'Ado. Uncle. London, there are more bombs, no? No one boycotts Lord's. What do you say?'

I nod and smile. 'Johannesburg, full of AIDS and guns. No problem. Bloody bullshit. They are scared to play us.'

We watch Arjuna hoist the Cup. And we watch rerun after rerun after rerun. Credit and kudos are multiplied and then divided. And our cricketers transform from international punching bags to national gods.

My companion's name is Jabir and even though he looks and acts like a juvenile, he claims to be a father of four, an electrician and to have driven a trishaw to the SSC over twenty years ago. He tells me how Arjuna Ranatunga used to come by bus in tattered shorts to practices. How two players of yesteryear courted the same woman for over a decade. How Sanath once had a full head of hair.

His scar begins from his ear and reaches his chin. He tells me he got it in a gang fight at a Marians Concert in Panadura. The Moratu Boys vs The Chilaw Gang. 'We had fists, they had knives, we still won. Marians had to go home.'

I tell him about my friendship with Graham Snow and try not to appear boastful. I ask him about Pradeep Mathew and he says he has never heard of him. I ask him if he can take me to Colpetty; he says he will, but only after one more stout.

* * *

Two days before the final, I'd got a call at my sister's house.

'It's some girl,' said my brother-in-law more loudly than necessary. He and his wife both watched me as I picked up.

'Mr Wije. How you doing?' The vatti amma voice and the sing-song delivery.

'Been a bit unwell, Danila.'

'Take a break from your scriptwriting, Uncle. We are about to win the World Cup.'

I laughed. 'How sure are you, my dear?'

My sister and her husband registered looks of shock. I ignored them.

'How can you ask that, Uncle? Kangaroo meat for dinner.'

'Yum.'

'I called to say it's your lucky month. Your friend Mr Snow sent a present for you.'

'Really?' Probably a World Cup tie. Useful to strangle my sister's husband, who was now pretending to read the paper.

'He's upset about the mix-up. He wants to donate three and half lakhs to the cause.'

'Mr Wije. Are you there?'

'Of his personal money?'

'Yes. I have the cheque in front of me. Would you like to pick it up after the World Cup?'

'No,' I said, and watched my sister pretend to sew.

* * *

Firecrackers and music at every corner. Dancing urchins come up and shake our hands as if we are personally responsible. All the shops are open. Except the twenty-four-hour communication ones. It takes us an hour to locate a telephone, by which time the fumes from my liver are baking the insides of my head.

First I call Jonny. He doesn't pick up. Then I call my sister and tell her I'll be taking them all out to lunch tomorrow. Then I call Ari.

'Wije! Wije! Where are you?'

'I can pay you back the money.'

'How can you talk money, men? We did it, you bugger! We hammered the bastards!'

'I told you Aravinda would do it.'

'Excuse me. I only told you!'

'Not going to sleep?'

'I am giving up drinking after today. Let's put a final shot.'

'Don't be a fool. I'll come. I'll bring your money.'

I cannot bring myself to call Sheila. I slump back in the red trishaw, feeling faintish. A long-haired lout in a tophat points a guitar at me from the sticker behind Jabir's seat. The caption reads 'The Guns and the Roses'.

Jabir has also let his hair out; his also has the texture of an old broom.

'Jabir. It has been a pleasure to have shared this day with you. I now want you to take me to my wife.'

'No problem, Uncle,' he says in harmony with his tooting horn.

'But first, one more stop.'

* * *

The odds weren't as good as the Holland or UAE games. Probably because the result was harder to pick and the bookies more emotionally vested in the result. Not surprisingly, the curry house behind the Neptune was more crowded than usual. I spotted a misprint on the red cyclostyled paper. The odds of Aravinda being top scorer were inverted, paying out far more than they should. I took it as a good omen.

I had watched the semi-final in India keenly and had observed Aravinda bowling. He was in good form and the Lahore pitch might suit his gentle off breaks. I had no time for Ari's ola leaf predictions, I jumped in with both feet. Put down Aravinda for best batsman and bowler and bet on a convincing Lankan victory (90 runs/7 wickets). Three and a half lakhs would yield returns, provided all my horses came first.

So an hour before the toss, for neither the first nor the last time, W.G. Karunasena bet with his heart and not with his head. People stared at me as I handed over the bundles of cash. 'Aravinda best bowler? 7-wicket win? Fool,' said the drunkard next to me. I smiled. All or nothing. I would have enough spoils to share if Sri Lanka pulled it off.

On the big day, Aravinda took 3 wickets and scored 107 not out and we got there with 7 wickets to spare. God bless Lady Luck. God bless Graham Snow. God bless the Guns and the Roses. God bless Sri Lanka.

* * *

Jabir cranks his radio up. His trishaw is cobwebbed and falling apart, but he has a gleaming stereo and a box speaker behind my head. I am not a fan of rocker music. I prefer Jim Reeves. From modern music I like ABBA and Shakin' Stevens. Jonny once bought me a cassette by a singer called Meat Loaf; he said it was modern opera. It only had one good song.

On the side streets, cricket games have sprung up along the gutters. Children in baseball caps and mosque hats re-enact the glory of Lahore, watched by smiling soldiers with guns. Dancing fools, papare bands and giant TVs greet the awakening sun.

I feel euphoria. My bag is filled with more money than I can spend. I will tell everyone that it is my gratuity and not care if they believe me. Either it is a random universe and the lottery has delivered me my numbers. Or it is presided over by a deity who does not despise me as much as I thought. Either way it is good.

I will now finish my documentary. Sheila will take me back. Garfield will come home. As Meat Loaf would say, 'Two out of three is not bad.'

Before leaving, Jabir shakes my hand. 'I only tell this to my good friends. After today, I think you will be one of those. This scar wasn't in a gang fight. I fell off the mat slide in Sathutu Uyana when I was small. Don't tell anyone.' He lets out his hyena giggle and pockets my generous tip.

So now you know how I can afford to place an ad in the Sunday papers every day for the next six months. And how I can afford, at least financially, to drink to my liver's discontent. It is now time for us to explore the rest of the iceberg.

Charith Silva

I fall sick straight after the victory. Delighted by the money I bring home, Sheila nurses me with love. Manouri, now my best friend, brings in roti, lunumiris and her blessings. Ari sets up the TV in my bedroom and we enjoy the afterglow of highlights and interviews. It is evident that the world shares our joy. A world that warms to underdogs and cheers those who humble Australia.

The World Champions return the next day to be greeted by Buddhist priests chanting blessings and cash rewards from Kandy's sacred Temple of the Tooth.

'That's ludicrous, Wije,' says Ari the spoilsport. 'What if a Sri Lankan becomes world boxing champ? Will the Buddhist clergy pay him a lakh for beating a man to a pulp?'

Buddhism is a non-violent, non-materialistic philosophy everywhere, that is, except for this fair island of ours.

On the same day eighteen soldiers are killed and ten are injured in a landmine in Mallakam in the war zone up north. Almost the same number as the squad that returned from Lahore. Does the nation decide to celebrate victory or mourn the dead? What is more important, Sport or Life? Stupid question.

The same benefactors that cursed my foolishness now praise my good fortune. 'Who knew you had so much gratuity?' says Sheila, rubbing Tiger Balm on my brow. Brian arrives with a camera crew and a bottle of whisky that is confiscated at the door by my sweet wife. His face is everywhere, pointing microphones at anyone associated with bats or balls.

I refuse to be filmed on my sickbed. Ari attempts to give learned answers to Brian's dumb questions. All it takes to transform Brian from a likeable chap to a rambling fool is the turning on of a camera.

'So Mr Byrd, would you say, that, as a distinguished follower of Sri Lankan cricket, that Sri Lanka, who, as you know, are world champions, having comprehensively beaten Australia, will Sri Lanka, who are in peak form, Mr Byrd, will they do well, in the upcoming Sharjah tournament?'

'I predict we will win every one-day tournament for the next year.'

Brian nods and smiles.

'And then the bubble will burst. And we will fail to build on this glorious moment.'

'CUT!' yells Brian to his crew. 'Uncle, you can't say negative things.'

'Then our friend will have to be silent,' I croak.

'Wije has found money to do the documentary,' says Ari. 'Almost nine lakhs.'

'Ah. Superb.' A month ago, Brian would have leapt in the air. 'Let's do something,' he says, with the vagueness of a man who has much on his plate. 'Definitely.'

Ari looks at me. 'Wije. Let's wait. Now too much cricket on TV. See. See.'

On Ari's TV, Sanath Jayasuriya is diving to catch a tin of powdered milk.

I disagree. I tell him that if ever, the time is now. Brian and the camera crew pack up and leave us. 'Get well soon, Wije,' says Brian. 'Definitely, we shall do something.'

Highlights are interspersed with more commercials. Murali selling life insurance. Mediocre spinner Pramodya Dharmasena holding a pot of jam and grinning. Garlanded coach Tom Whatmore selling refrigerators. World Cup reserve Charith Silva drinking a colonial brand of Ceylon tea.

'Sha. Our Silva is also cashing in,' I exclaim.

'Wije, you and I played more cricket during the Cup than he did! What do you say?'

We have a laugh as the portly paceman sips tea and wobbles his head from side to side. We then watch Ravi de Mel, retired and greying, discussing the biomechanics of Murali's action. On the other channel we see former MD Jayantha Punchipala accept a nomination for president of the SLBCC. Danila is absent from the press conference. As is the former president, who was ousted a week after delivering World Cup glory.

Sheila demands that she accompany me to my check-up. While the return of the money won me my civic rights, the upper hand in our marriage still eludes me. I relent and agree to go with her on Friday. I then make an appointment for Thursday and visit Nawasiri Hospital alone. I rue my mistake. This privatised hospital runs like a government department. I have to present my letter to reception, get it stamped by accounts and then obtain three separate results from three different departments. The results are as lucid as Ari's hieroglyphic notebooks.

Perhaps the hospital's aim was to source business by rendering everyone who came there ill by shunting them up and down poorly ventilated corridors. It was working.

I have to channel a doctor who is seeing his thirty-fifth patient for the day. I take number 74 and hope that Nawasiri's chronology is as garbled as its service. I sit back and sigh. A drink would be nice. A fan would be nice. And then I notice everyone staring at me.

The nurses are giggling, the children are whispering, the sick and their minders gape in my direction. I check my zipper. It is up. I check my shirt. It is clean. I check behind me.

'You are Mr Karuna, no?'

It is Charith Silva, career reserve and public tea drinker.

'Ah, Charith.' I always assume first name with young cricketers. Makes me appear closer to the pulse than I am.

'You are with *Silumina*, no?'

'I write for *Sportstar*.'

'Wow,' he says, not caring. 'Uncle, please, can I sit next to you?'

I look around. The whole hospital has stopped to stare.

His gold chains jingle. He sits down and mutters.

'Please talk to me, Uncle. Don't look.'

It is then that I realise that only I stand between this B-grade cricketer and an autograph stampede.

I comment on the heat and ask if he's waiting for the doctor. He says his wife is expecting and gradually the hospital returns to normal. Aside from a few children who approach for autographs, we are not bothered.

'Uncle, I also can't believe. Two TV ads and I can build my house. Everyone is giving bonuses. I didn't even do anything.'

I am sure that up till now the only signature Charith had to part with was when he signed his contract with the SLBCC three years ago. In that time the career reserve had gone on four tours and played two games.

'Charith Silva. Ella. Ella.' Two young men in slacks offer their hands. 'Well done, machang. Well played.'

'So what are you writing for *Sportstar*?'

'I wrote the Best of Sri Lanka series.'

'Ah. Yes. I remember. Very good articles.' Charith smiles.

'Which one did you like?'

'I didn't read them, but they were superb.'

There is too much oil in his hair, too much paunch in his belly. He has remained a simple boy from Galle, which is probably why he has remained a reserve for most of his career.

I decide to ask the question. His face lights up.

'Why not? Why not? Pradeep was very good friend of mine.'

'Where is he?'

'No one knows. I heard he went to get surgery in Australia.'

'For what?'

'Fellow had wrist problems. Naturally, no? You know the way he used to spin, no?'

'I met his sister. Apparently he has passed away.'

'What?' Silva drops his phone. Attention is redirected at us. 'How?'

'Car accident.'

'Where?'

'In Melbourne, I think.' I really should stop spreading unconfirmed rumours. 'This is just what I heard.'

'I didn't know he had a sister,' says Charith, with eyes wide and hand over mouth.

He is silent for a long time. When he speaks, his gaze is on the floor and his voice is low. He tells me that Mathew joined the national side to impress a girl named Shirali Fernando. He tells me that Mathew was one of the most feared bowlers on the domestic circuit. That he was one of the few youngsters to snub the SSC. And that most of the senior players found him arrogant.

'But I remember, every season, when he came for practice with the cricket pool, he had some new deliveries. He had over twenty different balls.'

I nod. I know. Actually, according to Ari's count, the figure was fourteen. Still impressive. 'Did he get into trouble with management?'

'You know the scene, no, Uncle? You have to be good with the seniors.'

'And he wasn't?'

'He was a mad fellow. If I had his talent, I would be a top-class bowler. Didn't even listen to the coach. Said he had his own coach.'

'Who was that?'

Charith pinches between his eyes and wracks his modestly sized brain. 'You must be knowing. That fellow with six fingers, men. Coached around Moratuwa.'

'Gokulanath?'

'No, some other name. He had six fingers.'

The door opens and a round-faced girl with an oval belly exits. Charith gets to his feet.

'Here, Uncle, take my card. Let's later put a chat.'

'Can I call you?'

'Definitely.'

I shake the boy's hand as he takes his wife's hand and steps into the doctor's office, leaving me to my morose thoughts. Mathew was probably dead and I am possibly soon to be. Arrack-swilling, meal-missing I. I who now had an inside source and thirteen lakhs in the bank.

Or maybe not. Maybe the doctor would give me the all-clear. I would run out of here and find the coach with six fingers and the spin bowler with fourteen different balls.

Charith interrupts my reveries. 'This is my wife Dinusha.'

A former southern belle, now sporting a bell-shaped body. I smile and shake hands. Charith whispers in my ear.

'Your doctor is my good friend. I had a chat. You can go in next.'

I enter the doctor's office wishing there were more cricketers like

Charith Silva The doctor gives me a year or two. Maybe more. I leave resolving to make a halfway decent documentary on Sri Lankan cricket. There is nothing more inspiring than a solid deadline.

Hoop Dresses

Bowlers have always had the wrong end of the stump. The job that no one wanted. All innovations over the last century from the helmet to the bouncer rule have conspired to favour the batsman. In fifty-fifty decisions, the batsman enjoys the benefit of the doubt. What's harder? To hit a ball? Or to make someone else miss one?

When the game was introduced in the colonies two centuries ago, the fat masters batted all day, while the emaciated slaves bowled. At charity amusements, the lady folk were relegated to bowling, their impractical hoop dresses leading to the invention of the over-arm action. Centuries later, bowling still remains a thankless job. But thanks to a few it may also have become something of an art.

Red Trishaw

By the beginning of '97, we have all forgotten about documentaries. We are too busy watching cricket. For the past year Sri Lanka has been thrashing everyone in sight. Pakistan, Australia, India and South Africa. Ari remains unimpressed, claiming that only one of these victories took place outside of Asia.

I am thinking of turning Pradeep Mathew into a book when Brian comes calling. 'Uncles. Shall we do the doco now?'

Brian is now wearing sunglasses that cost more than my entire wardrobe. The past year has been a good one for him. He has been getting a regular gig with Maharani TV.

'Now that I have contacts, I can get interviews.'

'Only if we do one on Mathew,' I say.

'I don't think SLBCC will approve a show on Mathew.'

'So? Tell them to hang. I have five lakhs left from betting money.'

'No need for the money. I will get funding. You get me the scripts done.'

'Only if we do one on Mathew.'

'Forget Mathew,' says Brian. 'We will call it "Lanka's Top 5 Super Best"...'

'We will call it "Chinaman: Sri Lanka's Greatest Unsung Hero",' I suggest.

'That's a stupid name, Uncle,' says Brian.

'Yes, Wije,' says Ari. 'No one will want to see that.'

* * *

> 'I was involved with coaching Sri Lanka cricket at various times in the 1980s. I have never heard of this boy Mathew.'
>
> Sir Garfield Sobers, world's greatest all-rounder
> Interviewed by Brian Gomez at Colombo Cricket Club,
> December 1996

* * *

Now whenever Ari comes over to help with the scripts, he brings over a coloured concoction in an Elephant House bottle. This one looks like blood, even though he tells me it is watermelon mixed with lime.

The fool had made a vow to Manouri and his five daughters that if Lanka won the Cup, he would give up booze and cigarettes. Instead of doing what any red-blooded, lily-livered man would do, that is, find a loophole to wiggle out of, Ari kept his word. 'A Thomian's word is his honour.'

He replaces gin with thambili, whisky with kola kenda, and Gold Leaf with fruit. And refrains from grumbling. I ask him how he's coping.

'Fair exchange, Wije. To see Ranatunga hammer Warne over the ropes with 44 balls to spare is worth all the arrack in arrackland.'

Who can argue?

'Do you know what I found in my filing cabinet?'

'Termites?'

'All those tapes that Mrs Kolombage got for us. You had forgotten about them, no?'

The next two months are bliss.

We sit at Jonny's and pore over the televised history of Sri Lankan cricket since 1978, the year of televisation. We spend a week there. No wives. Jonny and I boozing. Ari juicing. The lake reflecting orange into Jonny's veranda. Ten hours of cricket watching behind you. And hundreds more before you. I cannot think of a better description of heaven.

* * *

> 'Fellow had talent. I won't say no. But bugger was lazy. And to tell you frankly, quite arrogant. Actually I don't know why y'all are doing a show on him?'
>
> Ravi de Mel, Sri Lankan opening bowler (1984–93)
> Interviewed by Brian Gomez at ITL Studios, January 1997

* * *

The three twenty-minute pieces on the World Cup heroes are effortless. Everyone Brian interviews has plenty to say about Captain Cool, Mad Max and the Master Blaster.

We then set to work researching Satha and Mathew. There is some useable footage of Mathew's thirty-four-match career, but obviously none of Satha's which ended in 1951.

Mahadevan Sathasivam was jailed for the murder of his wife in the early 1950s. It is universally accepted that he was innocent; that his wife, cognisant of his numerous affairs, was granting him a divorce; that the real murderer was William, the domestic aid. That's right, apparently the butler did it.

Those cuckolded by Satha's amorous activities or slighted on the field by his delicate blade were glad to see the playboy batting hero get his comeuppance. Having controversially captained Sri Lanka vs Bradman's Invincibles, Satha went on to captain Singapore and Malaysia, perhaps the only man to captain three countries at the sport.

Opinion on his character was divided. Praise of his deft strokes and fleet footwork was unanimous. Sir Frank Worrell described him as the best batsman he had ever seen.

Pradeep Mathew elicited no such outpouring of anecdote. Those who remembered him, remembered him vaguely. Everyone seemed surprised by his death, but none too concerned.

* * *

> 'Mathew, Mathew, like a statue,
> When in form, none can match you.'
>
> Reggie Ranwala, Sri Lankan cheerleader
> Interviewed by Brian Gomez at SL vs Pak, Kettarama Stadium, April 1997

* * *

Brian is too busy interviewing players and pundits and ex-players and ex-pundits to find a sponsor. Jonny says he knows the media director at SwarnaVision, a state-of-the-art channel not belonging to the state. He says they have huge budgets, international sponsors, studios and directors from India.

The meeting is set up and we take our five scripts, our three films and our waning enthusiasm to plush offices in Pannipitiya. I don't bother to iron my shirt or shine my shoes. We are kept waiting for half an hour and then greeted by a blood-curdling polkatu accent.

'To what, pray tell, do we owe this pleasure?' says Rakwana Somawardena, newly appointed director of SwarnaVision.

'A pleasant surprise,' says Cassim.

'Surprise, surprise,' says Mrs Kolombage.

* * *

> 'Statistically Pradeep was Sri Lanka's best ever spinner. Statistically I am the best left-handed batsman in test cricket next to Gower and Sobers. That is, if you only take my average when I batted at number 3 and 4.'
>
> Uvais Amalean, SL wicketkeeper (1987–93)
> Interviewed by Brian Gomez at Port of Spain, June 1997

* * *

I stayed away from the production. Sponsors had been obtained and while the scripts survived unscathed, additions were made to the production which I didn't understand. They were employing a computer graphics division and had commissioned composer Dilup Makalande and his guitar-shaped keyboard.

Ari seemed excited and I left him to it. He got his daughters, Stephanie and Melissa, both drama teachers, involved in set design and wardrobe. Sheila tells me that Stephanie, the tall one, is divorced and carrying on with a married man. Melissa, the round-faced one, is a local nightclub queen. Ari, as usual, is oblivious to all this.

* * *

> 'One could say that Prasad Mathews was a mediocre spinner who lacked discipline. One must have discipline if one is to succeed at international level.'
>
> Famous Lankan Commentator
> Interviewed by Brian Gomez at SLBCC Ball, August 1997

* * *

I dream of trishaws. I am in the back of what appears to be Jabir's red one. I am reaching for a bottle at my feet which keeps rolling from my grasp. I ask the driver to slow down. He speeds up. I scold. He turns around and holds up his hand. 'How many fingers am I holding? How many fingers?' I recognise his shaggy hair. He is Pradeep Mathew. 'I thought you were dead,' I say. 'We will all be soon,' he says, and drives into Beira Lake.

* * *

After all that drama with the World Cup betting, we don't even use any of the spoils. SwarnaVision agrees to finance. They say they will pay for the scripts and for Brian's interview footage. Brian agrees on the condition that he is retained as presenter. I agree on the condition that a Mathew episode is shot.

We sign documents, hand over our footage and wait.

The cracks in Ms 2ndGeneration's political regime, which we voted in three years earlier to deliver us from civil war and economic ruin, are starting to show. There are rumours of impending power cuts as droughts cripple our hydro power catchment areas and war rages in the north and east.

We are finally allowed to see a rough cut in October. It is unveiled for the board of directors of SwarnaVision in the boardroom on the seventh floor.

We take our seats and make nervous jokes. The film opens with Sir Garfield Sobers talking about Sri Lanka's talent. Music that is glorious, but somehow inappropriate, swells to a crescendo as Brian reads out my intro line: 'For Sri Lankans, cricket is not a game of gentlemen. It is a game of geniuses…'

The action cuts back to Sir Garfield, who is now talking about Aravinda de Silva. The shot reverses to show the interviewer nodding ponderously with furrowed brow.

Cassim and Mrs Kolombage giggle with surprise. I look at Ari in horror. The interviewer is not Brian. The man with the microphone is not tall, dark and funny looking. He is short, fair and speaks with an accent.

Brian gets up from his seat and, before the SwarnaVision board of directors, in raised voice, with raised finger, begins describing the genitalia of Rakwana's mother.

* * *

> 'Aside from my good friends, Sri Lankan cricket gurus Dublew Gee Karoona-sayna and Aree-ya-rat-ney Byrd, no one really remembers Pradeep Mathew. And that my friends, is one of cricket's greatest tragedies.'
>
> Graham Snow, England cricketer (1968–82)
> Interviewed by Rakwana Somawardena, SSC,
> October 1997

Shirali Fernando

'He only took cricket seriously because of a girl,' says Kamal Kiriella.

Kiriella works in finance, sweats a lot, and gives the impression that he sleeps in his tie. He is a busy man so I have to go to his office, where I am served biscuits and given fifteen minutes.

'You are a relative or what?'

Kamal and Pradeep met at an Old Royalists Law vs Medicine match.

'Our buggers, any excuse for a match. Half the buggers weren't doctors or lawyers. I don't remember Pradeep ever being at Royal.'

They then tried out for the Hampshire University XI in '84. Neither made the grade, but both made the squad.

Kamal has few illusions about his abilities. 'We were fresh off the boat. Pradeep bowled googly. I hammered pol adi. We were unfit, lazy buggers. They just kept us in the squad because we were brown.'

Pradeep had been sent to his mother's sister in Southampton. He enrolled to study accounting. Which he changed to computing. Which he then changed to physics.

'Moody bugger. Didn't get on with the aunt. Didn't mix much with the suddhas. He had one friend, this tall physics nerd, that was it.'

In what was neither the first nor last example of serendipity in Mathew's life, the University 2nd XI happened to be practising at the county ground alongside the visiting Lankan team. The students were asked to bowl at Mendis, Dias, Wettimuny, Madugalle et. al, who, though international test cricketers, were unknown outside of the Sinhalese Sports Club.

'Matty had real talent. Real talent. Fellow played the fool. Can you imagine? He bowled to the national side in the style of Ian Botham. He imitated each of the English bowlers. Agnew, Allot, Ellison, Pocock. The whole Lankan team were stunned.'

Pradeep and Kamal were invited to the Lankan High Commissioner's house for a rice and curry dinner. The Minister was present, as was the manager Abu Chanmugam, who asked Pradeep if he would like to try out for the national team. Pradeep smiled and declined.

'No one asked me. I suppose Lanka had enough and more pol adi batsmen,' reasons Kamal.

Throughout this monologue, several boys in ties bring Kamal papers to sign. He does so without breaking eye contact or breaking narrative.

Outside I hear someone shouting at a peon. You can tell a lot about an organisation by how they treat their peons.

Several cricketers came up to them and asked Pradeep about his effortless action mimicry and his promising chinaman bowling. But Pradeep, ill at ease in mixed company, said little.

Batsman Wettimuny, on the eve of a career-defining century, thanked the boys for bowling at them. 'I feel I have already faced the English attack. You should improve your talent.'

The skipper got drunk and started a baila. Those days Sri Lankan cricketers weren't afraid of making fools of themselves in public. This they did on the field on a regular basis.

Kamal Kiriella describes the party as 'full arthal' and 'maara jolly'. Aside from the cricketers there were Sri Lankan families and their sons and daughters. Mathew followed a group of them upstairs, drunken baila clearly not his thing. Kamal tagged along.

'These British Lankan chicks you should see, ah? Full sexy, but also hi-fi.'

It was in the High Commissioner's office that Mathew saw the girl of his dreams. Away from the festivities, the expat kids were watching a show called *Top of the Pops*.

'These two sexy girls were dancing like…what's that woman with the hair…'

'Boney M?'

'No, men. Cyndi Lauper! That's the one.'

I nod as if the name had been on my tongue's tip.

'The hot one sat down; the chubby one, Shirali, the High Commissioner's daughter, was begging people to dance. No one would.'

According to Kamal, Shirali was a 'tease' and everyone was taking her for a 'bite'. It was supposed to be her farewell, as her father was about to be transferred back to Sri Lanka.

'Then suddenly our man jumps in, pulls her, and starts break-dancing. He couldn't dance for toffee, but everyone thought he was being a clown. After that, he starts chatting to Shirali. Didn't even know the bugger could chat up.'

When it was time to go, Shirali kissed him on the cheek to roars from the expat kids. 'He's the only cute guy at this party,' said Shirali. Mathew turned 'pink like a jambu'. They shared a ride home with batsman Roy Dias who invited Pradeep to another team practice. Pradeep said he would think about it and showed Kamal a piece of paper with a number written on it.

'I told him, it's only 'cos she thinks you're a cricketer. Once she finds out you're flatting with seven illegal Tamils in Southampton, see if she thinks you're cute.'

The next day, Pradeep announced that he was planning on trying out for the national team and may even drop out of uni. He spent his tuition on the airfare back to Sri Lanka and joined the team as a net bowler for the Sharjah tour.

'At the time I thought the bugger was mad. But in the end he managed to get into the team. At least for a few games.'

'What happened with the girl?'

'High Commissioner got transferred back to Colombo. Pradeep followed her. I saw her a few years later, she had put on a bit. Said she was studying in Australia.'

'Did he have an affair with the girl?'

'Are you mad? She told me the loser sent her love poems and screwed things up.'

'What happened?'

'Who knows? She was too hi-fi for him. Never heard from Pradeep after that. Actually, do you have his email?'

Coconut Tree

I am once again in the red trishaw, but this time I am the driver. In the back seat is Pradeep Mathew, circa 1987, with shaggy hair and headband and a girl. He is writing on one of Ari's pink notebooks. Now and again he attempts to touch her breast and she slaps his hand. I am spying in the rear-view mirror. Mathew catches me and glares. 'Uncle. How many fingers do I have? How many sixers will I hit?' We crash into a coconut tree. Each coconut that falls has the number 6 on it.

I wake up fumbling for a pen. Sheila curses me with an f-word. 'What the f…fruit are you doing, Gamini?'

I find a pen that doesn't work. I end up carving three words on Sabi Amirthalingam's envelope before succumbing to a coughing fit.

Sheila sits up in bed. 'No excuses. Tomorrow we are taking you to a blooming doctor.'

The Six-fingered Coach

Ari retires from teaching and wastes his pension on his 1979 Ford Capri. He puts in leather seats, fixes the radio and the air conditioning, but is still unable to make it move.

'No, Wije. I need to work on this more. We'll have to go with Jabir.'

It is then that I tell him about my red trishaw dreams.

He looks at me with suspicion. 'Is that why we are going on this goose chase?'

'It makes sense. He wasn't close to his family. No real friends. Someone must have helped him in those early days with the Sri Lankan team. Charith told me at Nawasiri…'

'Nawasiri Hospital? What were you doing there?'

'Charith told me Mathew never listened to the Skipper or the coach. That he had his own personal coach…'

'Are you sure he said six fingers? Or did you dream that also?'

'No. No. Charith said.'

'If I dreamed of coconuts with the number of the beast on them, I would go straight to confession.'

'You think it's OK to go in Jabir's three-wheeler? We won't crash like in the dream?'

'It is always the opposite of dreams that comes true.'

Ari begins as he begins everything in his life. With a list. He types at a snail's pace, making no mistakes.

SIX-FINGERED COACH – SUSPECTS

- Lucky Nanayakkara, U-17 Thurstan coach
- Sir Nihal, Royal 1st XI fitness coach. Instigator of so-called Closed Pavilion Policy
- Gentleman Cricketer of Yesteryear, national coach for three seasons. Got on well with Mathew

'Exciting,' he says. 'Like searching for the one-armed bandit. More Hadley Chase than Conan Doyle.'

I add two more to the list:

- One of the Bloomfield coaches?
- Gokulanath, Royal fielding coach

Ari pulls out a magnifying glass. I give him a look.

'I broke three specs this year. Manouri won't let me buy another pair.'

Ari scrutinises my scribbling through the glass, like Sherlock in a sarong, one eye thrice the size of the other. He frowns. 'That fool Gokulanath?'

'Worth a shot, no? Do you remember how many fingers he had?'

'I remember how many brains he didn't,' says Ari.

Sir Nihal

First stop is Rosmead Place, where we are met by two Great Danes and a suspicious servant.

'Heel, boys,' grunts a giant of a man with a walking stick and a grey twirled-up moustache. 'These are my guests.'

We enter through a lush indoor garden. The walls are lined with pictures of Sir Nihal's family. And pictures of Sir Nihal posing with cricketers in various countries. He then brings out his books and brings our attention to his feats playing for Royal in the 1960s. And representing Ceylon in athletics. He then talks about his distinguished career at Lanka Insurance.

Ari cannot take any more. 'Mr Nihal, we are not writing about you.'

'Oh. Really?'

'No, Nihal Sir,' I say. 'We are writing about a boy you coached. Pradeep Mathew.'

The fossil smoothes down his moustache. 'Never heard of the fellow.'

'He trained with the Royal squad in 1983. When you were coaching.'

'Never heard of the chap,' he says, rising. 'You were the fellows calling around last year about the 1983 Royal–Thomian?'

Ari swallows hard. 'No, Mr Nihal. What happened in '83? Did you get bowled out for 9 runs again?'

'I'm sorry I don't know this Mathew and I am very busy.' Sir Nihal rises and gives us a look that says that in two minutes he will release the hounds.

Lucky

When we get to Thurstan, we notice immediately. Lucky Nanayakkara uses all five fingers on his left hand to hold the saucer and all five fingers on his right to hold the cup.

'I don't mean to boast, but I taught him to bowl the flipper.' Today, Lucky Sir's voice is ebony with an extra coat of varnish on it. He is not puffing his pipe.

'Really?' I ask.

'His fingers were supple. I taught him Clarrie Grimmet's technique.'

Grimmet, who made his debut at thirty-three, was perhaps the greatest right-arm leg-spinner of all time. Ari is rummaging through his school satchel.

'I only advised him to play for Royal.'

'You didn't tell me that when we last spoke.'

'You didn't ask,' says the gentle lover of cricket.

We are at the same pavilion, overlooking the same ground. The same band of cub scouts go marching in the distance, singing an African song in a Swedish accent.

'Were you in touch with him when he played for Lanka?' asks Ari.

'Many coaches tried to ruin him. ICC sent guys like Terry Mallet, so-called spin coaches. How many of our local actions did they ruin? Pradeep would visit me and ask "Lucky Uncle, why am I not being selected?" I only designed his action and helped him develop new variations.'

'Which variations?'

'The flipper. The googly. The double bounce.'

'The double bounce?' I ask.

'The greatest ball ever invented. I only taught the fellow.'

Ari stops rummaging and leans forward. 'What about the leaper, the floater, the darter and the lissa?'

Lucky folds his arms. 'Of course. I only taught him.'

Ari puts his hand back in the satchel and fishes out a junior cricket ball. 'Show us.'

He lobs the ball to Lucky Sir. Lucky Sir catches it in his left hand and spills his tea with his right.

The GenCY

'Bloody ace conner,' says Ari. 'I knew he was a bullshitter soon as I saw. Wije, you are too gullible.'

Lucius's spinning grips were out of a coaching manual long out of print. They were nothing like how Mathew bowled.

'OK. OK. You only put him on the list, no?'

'Based on what you said.'

'Uncles are doing what?' asks Jabir as he lets rip on Parliament Road. We drive past the parliament grounds, where cricket games overlap like stories.

'A cricket book,' I say.

'One fellow I know who might help you.'

'Who? Who?'

'At Tyronne Cooray. Uncle Neiris.'

'Mad Neiris?' says Ari. 'That dwarf? No thank you.'

'You know him?' asks Jabir.

'I get betting tips from his woman. He's fully mad,' says Ari. 'What, Jabir? No wonder you are sending your children to Royal.'

Jabir laughs hard as we are pulled over at a checkpoint. I am still not sure if he laughs because he is good-natured or because he is slow. A kid with a T-56 six sizes too big for him asks us where we are going.

'Pelawatte,' we say in unison.

The GenCY also sits in a room of photographs. But none of them feature him.

'Your family?' asks Ari.

'Ah?' says the frail man, settling back into a haansi putuwa.

'Your family?'

'Whose...family?'

'The photographs.'

'I don't...take photographs.'

Then he stares into space.

'You coached Pradeep Mathew?'

'Who?'

'Pradeep Mathew?'

'I think...I don't.'

A woman whom we recognise from the pictures, now with a big bum and her hair in a bun, enters the sitting room.

'Sorry for keeping you waiting. Thaathi is not very well. I don't know how much help he will be.'

I consult my notebook and sit up straight like the professional that I am. 'He coached the national side in '87 and then again in '93?'

'That's right.' She lowers her voice. 'He was diagnosed last year.'

I look at Ari. He holds up five fingers and shakes his head.

The daughter turns to the GenCY. 'Thaathi, did you know of a Mathew Pradeep?'

'Pradeep Mathew.'

'There was a fellow...called Iverson...in my team...'

Ari gathers his notebooks. 'Thank you, miss. We won't trouble your father…'

I remain seated. I saw this skeleton, now covered in wisps of white, score as flawless a 50 as I've seen against Bradman's Invincibles. He was invited to play a game for the MCC, but turned them down for unfathomable reasons.

'Iverson didn't listen to me... He had his own coach.'

'Come, Wije.' Both Ari and the daughter are standing.

'Who was Iverson's coach?' I ask.

'That chap…'

'Did he have six fingers?'

'Wije. Come. Come.' Ari gives the daughter number 37 in his collection of fake smiles.

'Six fingers… Yes. He did. Bloomfield chap, I think. Was a scoundrel …'

'Who?'

The old man looks at me as his daughter wipes a bit of spittle collecting at the corner of his mouth.

'Who?' asks the old man.

'Iverson's coach.'

'Who is Iverson?'

'Pradeep…'

'Pushpa…who is Pradeep?'

Police Report

I am shocked to read in the *Sunday Leader* that the body of an S. Gokulanath was found in Soysapura Flats. Baulking at the prospect of being shunted around the Moratuwa Police, we give Jabir a few thousand-rupee notes and send him on his way.

'I think this six-finger thing is bullshit,' says Ari.

'We have two people…'

'You just have Charith. You can't put words into the mouth of a senile man.'

'OK. Fine. Shall we visit Bloomfield? We can chat to teammates, coaches also.'

'Why are we doing this, Wije?' asks Ari, cleaning his magnifying glass.

'Doing what?'

'The documentary is over. We have given our inputs. Why are we spending money?'

I have thought this over. 'I want to do a book.'

Ari extends his hand and grins. 'Praise the Lord. Finally. If you are going to do that, I will support. What about?'

I shake his hand, but stay at arm's length. Ari has no qualms about hugging other men. Bless the old fool.

'What else? Pradeep Mathew.'

'As long as you don't call it Chinaman. That is a racist term. Would you call a book Nigger?'

'Joseph Conrad did,' I say, showing off. 'So did Agatha Christie.'

Jabir comes in sweating with a copy of the police report. 'Found your fellow. Need more cash. Had to bribe four fellows.'

The report was eleven pages long; the main points were as follows: Gokulanath had been stabbed. He was unemployed and owed money around the neighbourhood. He lost his job at Royal for misconduct and was separated from his family. His death had been the seventh homicide in that apartment complex for the year.

'Wije. Do you think we are uncovering something dangerous?'

'Don't be a girl, Ari. Soysapura is like that. Jabir, you asked?'

'Ah. Forgot, no.' We glare and Jabir can hold a straight face only for a few seconds. 'Joking, Uncle. Yes, yes, I asked. Both hands had five fingers.'

Bloomfield

I have to restrain Ari when we enter Bloomfield.

'No. No, we can't. He only is the one who gave us the betting tips.'

'So who cares?'

'No. No. It's not nice.'

The Sri Lanka women's team is practising at the Bloomfield ground and Ari's nemesis Newton, with his glove and bat, is teaching them to catch.

'Can I at least throw buriyani at him?'

Newton misses a ball and Ari applauds. We get 1,000 yard glares from the women and their coach.

'Maybe he has six fingers.'

'He doesn't even have two balls,' says Ari as we enter the main office of the Bloomfield Cricket Club.

The club secretary is a shuffling young man with the fluffy facial hair of a teenager. He shows us their coaching list. Bloomfield currently have seventeen coaches on their books from U-11 to indoor to women's teams. The secretary asks if we know that Pradeep Sivanathan Mathew is no longer part of the club.

Ari nods. 'Yes. Yes. According to my records he played for Bloomfield Cricket Club from '86 to '94. 590 first-class wickets. 27 Man-of-the-Match awards. Member of the P. Sara winning team of 1994/95. Best bowling 9 for 17 vs Saracens.'

All this would have been impressive if his notebook were not pink, and if he wasn't wearing a golf hat and holding a magnifying glass.

'You know more than us,' smiles the secretary. 'How can we help?'

'Could you get us a list of coaches who Mathew played under? And a few teammates who may remember him?'

I notice a slight grimace on the young man's face. To him, what we were asking for must have sounded like work. 'Y'all are writing about Bloomfield?'

Ari tramples my foot under the table. 'Yes. Yes. Great Bloomfield cricketers.'

'Like Mahanama, D.S., Kuruppu, Warnapura, Dharmasena,' I say, prying my foot loose.

'Why, Sanath?'

'Of course Sanath. But here, Mr…'

'Rideegamanagedara.'

'Of course. We have info on the others. We are looking only for info on Pradeep Mathew.'

'I will find out and let you know,' says the man with the long name.

I let my gaze wander. Three separate practices are overlapping on this modest ground. Newton is keeping wickets to a young girl bowling surprisingly competent medium pace. The Bloomfield 1st team is having a net session. I recognise the captain, Villavarayen.

The clubhouse is not as regal as the SSC. It has neither the heritage nor the ostentation nor the visible trophy cabinet. I have a cutting of my *Observer* classified ad.

'Do you mind if I paste this on your notice board?'

'Have to actually get permission, but go ahead. Shouldn't be a problem.'

I take one last glance at the coaching list. One name leaps out.

'Does Asiri Ranasinghe still work for the club?'

The secretary closes the book and shakes his head. 'That fellow we gave enough and more chances. Always bloody drunk. He got sacked last month.'

I see Newton Rodrigo leading the women off the field and decide it's a good time to lead Ari home.

Long Names

Sri Lanka is considered the land of long names, long waits and long promises. But, contrary to popular belief, most pages of Colombo's phone book are taken up by shorter Portuguese derivatives like de Silva, Perera and Fernando.

That said, Sri Lanka has also produced leg spinner Ellewellekankanage Asoka de Silva and Kurunegala first-class player A.R.R.A.P.W.R.R.K.B. Amunugama. I was going to type out his entire name, but life is too short, mine especially.

When a New Zealand journo, with a nose resembling the beak of his national bird, asked me why Lankans have long names, I told him I would rather have a long name than a long nose. He replied he'd rather have a long you-know-what. Such is the insightful cricketing analysis that goes on in the press box.

As Kiwi journo whinges on, I point out that John Wright could be pronounced Jo-Ha-Na Wa-Ri-Ga-Ha-Ta, but that our Sri Lankan names regardless of length are pronounced as they are spelled.

Most Sinhalese and some Tamil names follow the adjective–noun formation:

Jaya-suriya: Victory-Hero
Guru-singhe: Learned-Lion
Rat-nayake: Golden-Captain
Siva-nathan: Shiva's-General
Karuna-sena: Benevolent-Army

The only nation that can rival us for name length is Thailand. In contrast to our adjective–noun formulae, names like Thaksinatrakulyingyong appear to be harbouring full-blown sentences.

So why did a boy born Mathew Pradeepan Sivanathan decide to shed his surname when joining Sri Lankan cricket? I could be wrong, but I suspect it had little to do with length.

Asiri Ranasinghe

'Wije. Sometimes you're not as stupid as you look.'

It is a week later and Ari has managed to make his Ford Capri mobile.

We are travelling with a mini-fan and a radio crackling commentary from Sri Lanka's game in Sharjah.

'Asiri Ranasinghe's grip was very similar to...'

'It was identical.'

The fight for the eleventh place in the side to face England in Sri Lanka's inaugural test match in 1982 was between two players with identical initials. Asiri Ranasinghe was the hard-hitting batsman and orthodox left-arm spinner who was the Schoolboy Cricketer of 1976. An aggressive cricketer. He was known for his raw talent and his lax discipline.

Of course the eleventh place went to another schoolboy cricketer, a wristy left-hander who had caught Sobers' eye. Arjuna Ranatunga scored a half-century in the test and went on to captain Sri Lanka and lead us to '96. Asiri Ranasinghe played three games, was dropped from the side and joined the 1982 rebel tour to South Africa. Rich and banned from the game for twenty-five years, he built a house in Malabe. The one we are about to visit.

The Arosa Sri Lankans were the first non-white national team to tour South Africa during the apartheid era. The South African Cricket Board offered the rebels five years' salary to play one series. Ironically, the key instigators Mendis and Dias were bought out by the SLBCC at the last minute and appointed captain and vice captain. A second-rate B-team of a weak side lost all their matches and were thrashed like Bantu agitators in an Afrikaner cell.

The Lankan rebels were banned from playing any form of cricket for life. Many migrated. Asiri Ranasinghe, who was only twenty-four at the time, went from job to job, leaving a trail of enemies and empty bottles.

The house he built in Malabe still stands. And as we enter the gates, we see that we are not the only visitors that day. A crowd is gathered and the garden is filled with vehicles. We are informed by a distraught servant that the master was found dead in his bedroom the night before. The death was not unexpected.

On the way home, listening to Sri Lanka collapse to 21 for 4, Ari asks me if we should not abandon this wild-goose chase for this possibly non-existent coach. I am silent. If I was a talented cricketer and paid more money than I could imagine not to play, what would I do? As we crawl through Kotte traffic, and Sri Lanka loses its sixth wicket for 47, I realise I would do exactly what Asiri Ranasinghe did. I would build a mansion and drink myself to death in it.

Big Gloves

This time Mathew is not in the trishaw. He is on the side of the road, carrying his cricket bag and wearing gloves. He hails the three-wheeler. Jabir who is driving says, 'Sorry, have hire.' Mathew ignores him and addresses me in the back seat. 'You know what they say about men with big hands?' he asks. 'They wear big gloves,' I reply. Mathew bursts out laughing. I join him.

I wake up with a smile on my face and Sheila in her nightdress eyeing me suspiciously. It takes me all morning to convince her that the word I said in my sleep was glove and not love.

The Bloomfield club secretary does not return our calls. Walking through the entrance we are stopped by the security guard. He checks our IDs and enquires about our business. We mention the club secretary and he mentions he has not been informed. We drop as many names as we can remember. Kaluperuma, Dharmasena, Jayasuriya. Ari tries to slip him 200 bucks and we are asked to leave. It is then that I mention Newton.

'You are here to see Rodrigo Sir?'

We nod.

'Let's ask him.'

Newton comes carrying a cricket bag. He gestures to the security guard and takes us aside. 'Wije. Go. You are not wanted here.'

'We have an appointment,' says Ari.

'Did I speak to you?' says Newton, not looking at him. 'Wije. Did you put that notice about Pradeep Mathew on the board?'

I nod.

'Club management issued a memo that anyone speaking to journalists about Pradeep Mathew will be fined. You will get nothing here.'

'Wije, look,' says Ari.

This time Newton turns to him. 'I told you once not to talk to me. Kindly get out from here.'

I look where Ari is pointing. And then I see what he sees.

'Show me your hand, Newton,' I ask.

'If you don't leave this minute, I will show you both my hands.'

And then the security guard comes to escort us from the premises.

Let's be Friends

She asks me how much I would pay if she gave me a letter written by Pradeep Mathew. I tell her three thousand rupees and she agrees to come over.

'This could tell us where he is,' says Ari.

Power cuts are scheduled for June. The airing of our documentary is scheduled for March. Ari and I pretend not to care. Garfield joins a band in Geneva. He sends us a money order for five hundred Swiss francs. Sheila does not let me touch it. There is no more talk of sound engineering or further education. There is no more hope that my son will turn out better than me.

He will drift around the world and return home penniless and hopefully I will not be around.

Newton refuses to talk to us. My calls are unanswered. My book is not returned.

I have ignored doctor's orders and suffered no consequences. I decide that it is work that is keeping me young. I drink to more work and staying busy. Ari keeps his World Cup resolution.

She is in her early thirties and wielding three children, two girls and a boy, all under five. She has thick glasses and frizzy hair.

'Harini Diyabalanage.' She extends her hand. 'I have to be at Montessori in half an hour. Here is the letter, have a look.'

The boy is sitting on Ari's carpet patting the ground. The two girls are chasing each other around Ari's desk. 'Here. Here children. Come, I'll show you some magic.'

'Heshika. Nerissa. Behave,' barks the mother.

'This is not written by Pradeep Mathew,' I say.

'The poem is,' says Mrs Diyabalanage.

I hand the poem to Ari, who has got the girls drawing on file covers.

Skin is silky
Hair is honey
I will serve you
Reach your star
At your smile
Lovely lady
I am yours

'It spells…'

Ari nods. 'I can see.'

Harini Diyabalanage went to Visakha College with Shirali Fernando. The two were pen pals till Harini got married a few years ago. The letter was written in 1986. Shirali had just migrated to Australia and was bombarded with love letters from a cricketer called Pradeep Mathew.

'We were popular girls,' says Harini.

'Where is this Shirali?' asks Ari.

'I heard she got married and moved to New Zealand. But then I heard she was working at the Cricket Board. I also lost touch. Can I collect the money?'

The letter is handwritten on ruled paper written in light green and sprinkled with glitter.

'Miss. This is not the letter we were expecting. Do you have anything written by Pradeep Mathew?'

'How should I have? I didn't know him. I was friends with Shirali. That poem is written by him. We agreed on the payment.'

'Fine, fine. We will pay,' says Ari as a puddle appears on his carpet, right where the boy is sitting.

'If I find out more, I will call,' says our visitor as she pushes her bundles of terror out of the room.

* * *

> 'Pradeep is soo sweet. He sends me presents and writes me poems. I've attached one, its soo cheeesy. Please don't show it to anyone. I hope I'm not leading him on. I told him I want to just be friends, but you know how Lankan guys are. Oh my God. I forgot to tell you. I met this guy called Larry. What is it with me and cricketers...'
>
> Excerpt from a letter from Shirali Fernando to
Harini Diyabalanage
Postmark Melbourne
11/12/86

The First Note

This Sunday's *Leader* has the headline, **The Norwegians are coming, the Norwegians are coming**. Men with briefcases from Scandinavia are attempting to succeed where bombs and guns have failed.

'Newton can't be who we think he is,' says Ari. 'He hates Mathew. Thinks he's crap.'

'So what?' I say. 'Elizabeth Taylor said she hated Richard Burton. That is after she had married him twice. It is easy to hate the thing we love.'

'Ammataudu. When did you become Mr Philosophy?'

I have been reading a Ladybird book about the Golden Age

of Hollywood, permanently borrowed from the now defunct Rawatawatte Lending Library.

'Here. You remember telling me about Montgomery Clift?' I ask.

'Of course. He was the Pradeep Mathew of the silver screen.'

'Can you name the films he turned down?'

'*Sunset Boulevard*, *On the Waterfront*, *Rebel Without a Cause*, *The Hustler*.'

'If he had taken those roles, he would've been the greatest star of all time. And no one would've heard of Holden, Brando, Dean or Newman.'

'What have you been reading?' asks Ari. 'Books?'

The nuisance calls precede the notes. A throaty voice in Sinhala, 'Hello, who is speaking?' When my son was in the house nuisance calls were a common occurrence and there are many ways of dealing with them.

Indignation: 'You called me. Who the hell are you?'

But this will only result in a 'Who the hell are you?' competition.

Filth: 'I am the <expletive> who <expletive>ed your <expletive>ing mother.'

But, for a mind that thrills in nuisance calls, these exchanges delight more than they offend.

I usually answer with the surreal. Unrelated nonsense delivered deadpan.

Gruff Voice: Who is this?

Me: Burton.

GV: Who?

Me: I was born Burton Richard. But I changed my name to Clift Montgomery.

GV: Where are you speaking from?

Me: Norway.

GV: Ah?

Me: You can get a ferry through Helsinki.

By this stage bewildered callers usually hang up. Not this one.

GV: Helsinki is in Finland.

I decide to switch gears. I talk in rapid Sinhala.

Me: Gokul dead. AR dead. GenCY dying. Nihal liar. Lucky liar. Is it Newton?

GV: Are you mad or senile?

Clearly not working. I seek refuge in technique number 4. Radio static. Sudden bursts at high volumes. My pocket Samyo transistor can pick up the BBC commentary perfectly, but every other frequency crackles like an oven of bees. I hammer it at full blast for thirty seconds. The caller hangs up.

The same caller, two days later.

Gruff Voice: Mr W.G., please.

Me: Who's speaking?

GV: Pradeep.

Me: I thought you were dead.

GV: Why are you putting ads about me in the papers?

Me: So that you would call me…

GV: Who are you?

Me: Can we interview you?

GV: No. I will interview you.

Click.

The next day a note arrives. It is a computer printout with a few typed sentences:

> Why are you interested in Pradeep Mathew?
> Who is your employer?
> Write answers below and return in very same envelope to your own letter box.

In detective novels, you can trace the make of the typewriter and track down the phantom note writer. I can imagine going to the Mount Lavinia Police Station with such a request.

Me: Ralahamy, can you analyse the writing on this?

P.C.: Certainly sir, I'll get ballistics onto it right away.

That is, sadly, a load of – pardon the French – bollistics. The response will be, Uncle, where you from, full name, date of birth, religion, race, caste, time of day, alignment of planets, blah, blah till the khaki-clad penpusher fills up one foolscap page with squiggly, indecipherable handwriting.

Then he will ask you to come back next Wednesday when he has typed it up and shown it to the SSP and the ASP.

But I could not deny that this was exciting.

I call Ari and tell him the news. He is over in minutes. He enters with a bottle of greenish juice. I decide not to ask.

'Ari, why are you wearing a raincoat and a hat?'

He pulls out a cigar and begins pacing and talking like he has a mouth full of bulto sweets. 'What we have here is a sap who is trying to play games. Let me see the note, Jimmy.'

'Who's Jimmy?'

'Just as I thought. Guy's an amateur.'

'How the hell do you know he's an amateur?'

Ari waves the cigar. 'You gotta lot to learn, son. A pro would misspell words to throw us off the scent.'

'What scent? The only scent here is coming from that green stuff in your bottle.'

'It's important how we respond to this.'

'I already have,' I say, handing him a typewritten paper.

Who are you working for?

I, W.G. Karunasena, Ceylon Sportswriter of the Year, 1969 and 1976, have worked for the *Observer*, *Daily News*, *Island*, *Kreeda*, *Ravaya*. My work has appeared in *Sportstar*, on the Sri Lanka Broadcasting Corporation, SLBC, sports round-up and will appear in a SwarnaVision TV documentary. Now retired, I, with my colleague, Ari Byrd, am writing about the life of Pradeep Mathew.

Why are you interested in Pradeep Mathew?

Put simply, I believe him to be the greatest Sri Lankan cricketer of them all. I remember his performances in the '85 World Series, the '88 Asia Cup, the '87 Test series vs New Zealand. At his best he was better than anyone I have seen. Are you really him?

Ari frowns. 'As usual, you have written an essay. And why mention my name?'

'Why? Scared?'

He adopts that silly bulto voice. 'Kid. I'm an undercover cat. I don't need the publicity.'

I fold the paper. 'We put this in the envelope and we keep the original.'

'Let me get a siri-siri bag. We must preserve the fibres on the note.'

Ari comes back with a supermarket bag and a permanent marker. He gingerly places the note in the bag. He crosses off the word Cargills and writes 'Exhibit A'.

Sheila walks in with the tray of tea; she smirks at Ari in his raincoat and sarong. 'Who's this? Kalisama nathi Bogart?'

Ari allows a grin. 'Who's this broad? Of all the tea joints, she had to walk into mine.'

Sheila looks at our evidence bag and walks out, saying, 'Y'all are mad.'

Ari suggests we spend the night on his balcony, where we take turns doing surveillance on my letter box. The plan is hatched and the bottles are opened. We put the note in the envelope. We drink and stay up till dawn. Ari, his juice; me, my arrack. We discuss who the letter writer might be. Bloomfield? Newton? Ari suggests it's someone playing a prank.

'How many know about what we are doing?' asks Ari.

'No one cares. You, me, Brian, Sheila, Manouri.'

'I bet Sheila is up to something.'

'Maybe Brian or Jonny.'

'Ah. What are you saying? Of course it is Jonny. Who else?'

'Have you heard from Mr Jonny?'

'No, fellow has been a bit strange lately.'

'How?'

'I don't know, something is going on with him.'

We fall asleep at sunrise and Manouri shakes us both awake at nine. 'Like children y'all are.'

Ari gasps. 'Postman, postman.'

A bald man on a bicycle in a dung-green uniform is inserting letters into the box of 20 1/1 de Saram Road.

Ari croaks, 'Oi, don't remove the letter already there.'

The postman looks up. 'What letter? No letter, sir.' And rides off.

By the time we rub the sleep from our eyes and will our bodies to brave the stairs to the letter box, both he and our letter are nowhere in sight. Just junk mail from Regnis offering easy payment on sewing machines. In the evening comes the call.

Gruff Voice: Mr W.G.?

Me: Yes.

G.V.: I told you to write on that very page.

Me: Didn't have room.

G.V.: I suggest in the future you do exactly what I say.

Click.

And for a while at least, that, as they say, is that.

Cricket Café

One week to go. 'Which will they air first?' I call Rakwana. I am the only one still speaking to him.

'Not entirely sure. We're still putting the finishing touches. The edit is complex and nefarious.'

'I thought Aravinda, Pradeep, then Sanath, Satha, Arjuna would be a good sequence.'

'No sirree. There are other factors to consider, Mr Karoona.'

'Have you been to Texas recently?'

'No. Why?'

'No. Just.'

'Power cuts may happen later. In the second month. We'll save Mathew and Satha for then. Put the important ones first.'

I bite my tongue. 'Can I get a preview?'

'Even I may not get a preview. But I'll try my best, pardner. Definitely.'

Danila Guneratne asks to meet for coffee. Sheila sees me polishing my shoes and combing my hair. 'Wedding or something?'

'Business meeting.'

'Me and Manouri will watch your show from here. Can't come all the way to Bolgoda.'

'Aiyo. In vain. Would've been fun,' I say, hiding my delight. Jonny's place is no place for maidens.

Danila is to meet me at the Cricket Café in Colpetty. Is this what the youngsters would describe as a date? The room turns its head as she enters and even though she walks bow-legged and wears glasses, her allure is undeniable. Miniskirt, red blouse, straightened hair.

'Ah. Uncle.' She kisses me on the cheek; her perfume sweetens the air.

We sit in a corner next to a framed photo of Curtly Ambrose in delivery stride. The café walls are adorned with cricketing memorabilia. Autographed bats, framed newspaper cuttings, photos, caps. The furniture is varnished wood and the menu is laden with pub food named after cricketers.

Sometimes the links are obvious (Allan Lamb's Lamb Chops), sometimes tenuous (Augustus Logie's Caesar Salad), sometimes unappetising (Merv Hughes' Meat Balls). The prices appear designed to keep locals away.

'I heard your documentary with SwarnaVision is going to air.'

I nod as Danila stirs her coffee. I watch the men with women at other tables trying not to get caught copping a look. She fiddles with my cufflinks and plays with her hair. I remain calm.

'Uncle. I'm telling you in confidence. I don't think the documentary will run. ITL are planning on suing. The SLBCC is also very powerful these days.'

She ties up her hair and plays with her teaspoon. 'Not that. I had something else to ask.'

Steady old boy. Play it cool.

'What can I do to you?'

Idiot.

'I'm sorry…for you.'

She giggles. 'Shall we ask for the bill?'

The waiter arrives and she places a gold card on the table. I don't even pretend to reach for my wallet.

'You're the one putting classified ads about Pradeep Mathew.'

'Unless there's another W.G. Karunasena.'

'A lot of people are upset at the Cricket Board.'

'Why?'

'Mathew wasn't very popular. He let a lot of people down when he left.'

'Like whom?'

'He owed money. He fought with everyone. Be careful, Uncle.'

'The G in my name stands for Gutsy.'

'Why you're so obsessed with Mathew?'

'He is the greatest cricketer this country has ever produced. If you knew…'

'Do you know where he is?'

'It seems he may be dead.'

Her face flattens and her eyes cave in. Her voice becomes a squeak. 'How?'

I tell her about the sister and the notification of death.

'Personally I don't believe…'

She is not listening to me. Her gaze is directed at the table between us. Her eyes turn glassy. The glass turns to liquid. A drop spills from the corner of her eye, leaving a trail of mascara down her cheek.

'Danila?'

'Sorry, Uncle. I have to go.'

She grabs her bag and leaves me to sort out the tip.

The Premiere

I don't tell Ari about Danila, knowing he would disapprove of my unchaperoned visit. It has been raining in Bolgoda; the lake and the air around it are murky. It is just us men and our bottles and our widescreen TV. About to witness the fruit of two and a half years of labour. This time I bring the Chivas Regal. Ari brings the cutlets and the litre of apple juice.

'Ah, bless the rain,' says Jonny. 'Reminds me of Newcastle.'

'That Shearer fellow is a bit of a flop, no?' I say.

'He'll keep,' says Jonny.

Ari pours drinks and eyes the sky. 'At least these rains will keep the power cuts away.'

The sound of an over-revved engine cuts through the sound of water hitting rooftop. In tumbles Brian, carrying a crate of beer and grinning. Brian appears to have a suntan which has turned his black skin purple.

'Thought you weren't coming,' says Jonny.

'Otherwise? Jonny my bonnie. Would I miss this?'

By 8 o'clock we are seated and restless.

'Don't know if they'll even put our names,' says Ari.

'Uncle Wije's name will be there,' says Brian. 'Him and Rakwana are thick pals.'

'Dr Rakwana…' reminds Ari.

'Yeah, right,' says Brian. 'And I'm a chinaman with a ponytail.'

Then the plink-plinks of Dilup Makalande's piano and soft dissolves of Aravinda, Sanath and Satha fill the screen. We all cheer. The title appears: 'Sri Lanka's Finest.'

'Your title, Wije?' asks Brian. I nod my head.

The next title appears: 'Pradeep Mathew. The Mystery.'

We all gasp. Everyone looks at me. I shrug.

And over cricket footage, carefully selected in this very room, the following credits appear. Most are greeted with catcalls and shrieks of disbelief; some with applause, some with cheers.

SwarnaVision presents
A Dr Rakwana Somawardena Production
Assistant Producers M. Cassim, B. Kolombage, B. Gomez
Set Design Stephanie Byrd, Melissa Byrd
Graphics SwarnaCyber Ltd
Music Dilup Makalande

Voice-overs Dr Rakwana Somawardena, B. Gomez
Script W.G. Karunasena, A. Byrd
Produced and Directed by Dr Rakwana Somawardena

Brian is yelling filth at the TV. 'Calm down. Calm down,' yells Jonny. 'Let's watch the damn thing.'

They had remained faithful to my script. Almost to the word.

Video: Mathew's googly to dismiss Vengsarkar in '85.
Audio: VO (Brian): Incredible talent. Brilliant variations. A mystery on the pitch. And off it.
Video: Montage of Mathew's 5 wickets in the World Series.
Audio: VO (Brian): When Pradeep Mathew bamboozled the Australians at Adelaide, taking the wickets of Border, Jones and Boon, it seemed to be the emergence of a new talent.
Video: Graham Snow speaking to Brian. Brian not visible.
Audio: Graham: Pradeep Mathew was the cricketer who never was. He was tried young. Discarded. Tried again. Dropped. No one said, hang on. We have a real talent here. We have to nurture this.

Ari looks at me. 'How many times has he come to Sri Lanka? Not even one call.'

'Aiyo, Ari. Don't start.'

'Shh!' says Jonny.

'&@#%$,' says Brian.

Video: (New shot) Rakwana Somawardena clad in MCC whites, wearing a V-necked woollen jumper and stroking a ruby-red cricket ball, walking into the Kettarama pavilion.

We all erupt in laughter. 'Very good for the bastard,' says Brian. 'Look at him, sweating like a pig.'

Audio: Rakwana (Speaking to camera. Accent: deepest, darkest Oxford): Why did Pradeep Mathew only play four tests? Why did he never blossom into greatness? The answer can be summed up in one word: …

Right then, the lights go out. The image on the TV collapses like a dead star. We sit in darkness, pupils dilating, listening to the rain hitting the lake, waiting, hoping for it to only be a short powercut, but knowing it won't be.

Powercut

Brian and Ari jabber on their cellulite phones. Jonny and I light candles and open the French windows. The rain has stopped and the night is cool.

'Brian! Language!' calls out Jonny. 'WeeGee, mate. I'd like to talk to you after this fool goes home.'

'Something serious?'

'Hope not.'

'I'm going home,' announces Brian. 'All-island powercut. Will continue till midnight.'

'Isn't there a place with a generator where we can watch?' I ask.

'By the time we drive into town, show will be over.'

After he leaves, we sit by the lake.

'How can there be powercuts with all this rain?' asks Jonny.

We speculate that there is a drought in the hydro catchment areas. Or that Ms 2ndGeneration's regime is helping itself to more than the usual quota.

'Why are we still relying on hydropower?' asks Ari.

'Imagine if we had nuclear,' I say.

We all shudder at the thought of Lankan bureaucrats splitting atoms.

Jonny tells us how much he loves this country. 'But your idiots are fucking it up. You're killing the wildlife, robbing the holy cities and sticking DVD shops in the Galle Fort. The only people who care about preserving this island are suddhas like me.'

A mild breeze ripples the lake. Jonny is wearing a batik sarong and no shirt; his skin is hairless and freckled pink. He has seen more of this country than Ari and me combined. He once tried to build an eco-resort in Dambulla, but was blocked by the local authorities.

'Most of the local council are hunters. Found this beautiful place in Digana. Government wouldn't let me buy it.'

The word Jonny should have used was poachers. Hunting is what his ancestors did in those very same forests hundred years ago. I keep my thoughts to myself.

'Lads. I want you to hear this from me.'

Bats skim the night sky in silence. Ari and I exchange glances.

'There's some trouble around the village near Lunawa. To do with some of the locals. It's all bullshit. Most rumours are.'

'What kind of trouble?'

'They're making out that I'm a…you know…like Arthur C. Clarke.'

'That you're a scientific visionary?'

'No. That I'm friends with young boys.'

Ari bleats like a lamb. 'Who? Who? Who is saying? I have played table tennis with Sir Arthur. He is a gentleman and so are you. That is defamation. I know some lawyers.'

Jonny sips from a can. 'I already have lawyers. It's gone to the cops. Don't think they have a case. Just thought you should know.'

The lights come on at midnight as promised. The newspapers announce powercuts from 7 to 9 every night for the next two weeks. These powercuts are less than punctual. Some arrive at 6, some well after 8. Some last for forty-five minutes, some for three hours.

As a result, we manage to catch seventeen minutes of the Sanath show, six minutes of the Sathasivam show and twenty-five minutes of the Arjuna show. Aravinda is not seen, Mathew is not repeated. Ari reckons the timing of the powercuts is political; that it is no coincidence which shows ran for the longest. I remind him that Arjuna is our only international cricketer not to appear in commercials and that he probably deserves some airtime. Ari scratches his bald spot and tries to think of a response.

'Don't worry, Gamini,' says Sheila. 'They will repeat the shows after these powercuts are over.'

I do not worry, even though I know they will not.

During the powercut months, families get closer, sales of battery-powered inverters increase. Ari makes a few from car batteries in his garage and makes a buck. People go for walks on Galle Face and parliament grounds. Isso vade salesmen do good business. Tales of gross mismanagement flourish. The government spends half the rescue budget on generators from Singapore that don't work. Advertising revenues plummet. ITL goes out of business. And I, W.G. Karunasena, sit in the darkness and drink.

Murali

The first test meanders across the screen, punctuated by so many ads that we sometimes miss the first ball of the next over. Even though the action takes place in Cape Town, RupaVision have found a way to pollute what we see with their logos, their sponsors' logos and an unending stream of selling messages at the foot of the screen.

Welcome to Sri Lankan cricket in the dot-co-dot-lk era. Ari is about to invest in a computerised internet thing. I gaze at my browning papers and the scrappy books crowding my Jinadasa typewriter and realise that I am too old for new tricks.

I pour another shot. On African pitches, Sri Lanka's bowling attack looks particularly pedestrian. Cullinan, Cronje and Kallis help themselves to runs. 'This is buffet bowling. Help yourself,' says the Yorkshireman in the commentary box, reading my thoughts.

The creditors representing ITL sue SwarnaVision for violation of copyright. SLBCC sue SwarnaVision for unauthorised use of images. All live shows are confiscated by the court. All revenues are frozen.

On TV, Muralitharan is the only bowler who is testing the batsmen. What a bowler he has blossomed into. His wrist flapping in the wind, unleashing curling deliveries that drop just out of the batsman's reach and turn at impossible angles.

I have spent the morning checking my books. As far as I can ascertain he is the only wrist-spinning off-spinner in the history of the game. While he may not quite have the genius of Mathew, he appears to have a discipline over his art that eluded Mathew. Even though his career had some overlap with Pradeep's, sadly, we are unable to interview him for our articles.

'What a bloody pigsty.' Sheila enters and grabs the glass from me. 'Gamini. It's 9.30 in the morning.'

She is right. It is too early in the morning for a domestic row.

'Very nice. Now your documentary is over, you're just going to sit around drinking. Is that your plan?'

'Sheila, leave me alone, I'm tired.'

'Today the powercut will be six hours. Enough time for you to drink. Come, let's tidy up this mess.'

'I don't know what y'all are writing.' Sheila is filing Ari's diagrams and dusting the shelves. I am collecting empty crockery. Glasses outnumber plates by 4 to 1.

'What happened to your book?'

'It's been shelved,' I murmur.

In forty-five minutes the room looks liveable again. I give Sheila a hug, she pushes me away.

'Aney, brush your teeth, men. Smell like a tavern.'

We do not mention last night's argument, which had me sleeping in the office room. Garfield had sent a letter. His contract in Switzerland was being extended. He was getting married to a Swiss girl named Adriana.

The boy would end up a performing monkey with zebra-coloured children. Another failure to add to my trophy cupboard. With the money from the World Cup all but over, I discontinue running the classified ad.

I spend the next few days slumped in my chair, watching the so-called World Champions being outplayed by Hansie Cronje's men. There have been rumours of corruption and match-fixing in South Africa, though it is hard to believe, judging from this polished South African performance.

Images flash across my face. My eyes droop. I do a cost–benefit analysis of walking to the wine store vs lying here thirsty. And then Ari bursts in and tells me that Jonny has been arrested.

Inside a Rambutan

Jabir's trishaw arrives from Dehiwela and takes us south on Galle Road.

'How much are you drinking, Wije? Sheila is very worried. Me and Manouri as well.'

I have agreed to associate with Ari since he gave up booze on the condition that he doesn't try to convert me. He is about to give me an I-have-seen-the-light speech.

'Wije. I have seen the light…'

'You will see stars soon, if you don't shut it.'

Neither of us discuss Jonny, the charges, or the possibility of his guilt. We have known him for almost twenty years. That is all we need to know.

At the Moratuwa cop shed, Jabir tries the back door, Ari tries the front.

But no favours are being offered. Jabir reports that the suddha was arrested last night.

Ari calls DIG Raban, an old Thomian. I watch Ari's tone simmer and his body language atrophy. The news appears bad. Ari hangs up and shakes his head. 'Three different boys around Moratuwa have brought complaints. All are under sixteen. The bail hearing is tomorrow.'

We and the lawyer are the only ones in the court on Jonny's side. Though at times I am not even sure about the lawyer. No one from the

High Commission shows. Bail is set at Rs 50,000, which the lawyer has managed to raise. Ari and I sign for the defendant.

Jabir helps us jostle the crowd. A crowd who are hooting and jeering. A rotten guava hits Jonny on the side of the head and the police jump in with their batons.

'Good arm, whoever threw that,' smirks Jonny.

'Must've been Jonty Rhodes,' I say.

The first words he says when we climb into the lawyer's car are 'Ari, WeeGee, I didn't do what they say I did.'

'Of course. Of course,' says the lawyer. 'Even if you did do it, they can't just arrest you like that.'

Ari and I sit in silence as the lawyer advises how to set about the trial.

'Does it have to go to trial?' asks Ari.

'Of course, Uncle. Child abuse is not a joke. Especially by a foreigner.'

Jonny gazes out of the window. Arms on his drooping belly.

'The foreign service fired me. Do I have a case for wrongful dismissal?'

'Otherwise? Of course you do, Mr Gilhooley.'

'Why don't you leave the country for a little?' I ask.

'Court has his passport,' says the lawyer.

We drop Jonny in Bolgoda. We offer to stay with him, but he says he prefers to be alone. Ari hugs him, the lawyer hugs him. I shake his hand. Dark thoughts accompany me home. All the good in the world you can fit inside a rambutan. And still have enough room for you and me.

Joy

The match is on and there is no powercut. Ari sips tea as I find the bottle I had hidden behind my *Wisden Almanacks*.

'You think he did it, no?' asks Ari.

'Has he ever talked about women since we've known him?'

I begin clearing the floor of notes from the previous months.

'Jonny doesn't talk about anything except cricket and Newcastle United. That doesn't mean he's a homo.'

'I will support him.'

'So will I.'

Ari joins in the clearing. Some paper napkins fall from a folder that Ari is shelving. They are in Ari's handwriting and we both recognise them.

'I say. You kept those napkins from when I hammered Newton?'

I nod with a grin. I have bus tickets from 1963, when I was courting Sheila. I have notes passed in class at Maliyadeva in the 1950s. Throwing away is something I do reluctantly.

'Gamini. Phone call.' She is looking sternly at me. 'Now speak nicely.'

I take the receiver.

'Hello, Thaathi.'

'Hello. So how are things?'

'Going well. Working…'

'Do you need money? Is that why you're calling?'

Pause.

'No. Do you?'

'Ammi says you're getting married?'

'I got married this morning.'

'Is she pregnant?'

He laughs. The way I do when I'm upset.

'No. But she will be soon.'

'And you can support your family playing your music?'

'Musicians make a lot more than journalists.'

I hand the receiver to Sheila and walk off.

'What did you say?' she squeals into the line.

In the room, Ari is smiling, scribbling and looking through the napkins. Sri Lanka is 290 for 8, chasing 377. Donald and Ntini are machine-gunning the tail-enders. The match is all but gone.

Ari hands me the napkin. I recognise the list that caused a punch-up at a wedding. Hobbs, Gavaskar, Tendulkar, Richards, Bradman, Sobers, Akram, Lindsay, Barnes, Lillee, Mathew. I realise that it was almost five years ago. Ari hands me a piece of paper, one he has just written on. It is an all-time Sri Lankan team and to me it borders on the surreal.

Openers

- Madugalle (80s)
- Jayasuriya (90s)

Middle Order

- Aravinda (90s)
- Sathasivam (40s)
- Mendis (80s)

All-rounder

- Goonesena (50s)

Wicketkeeper

- Navaratne (40s)

Bowlers

- Kehelgamuwa (60s)
- Mathew (80s)
- Vaas (90s)
- Jayasundera (40s)

I drain my glass and snort. 'Kehel Yaka? Madugalle?'

'Even though Madu was a Royalist, he was class. You know he started as an off-spinner and when he was fifteen he took 8 wickets against…'

'Pakistan, yes. Why no Ranatunga?'

'There are better batsmen, no?'

'No Murali?'

Ari looks at his shoes. He rises and looks at his watch. I eyeball him.

'Why no Murali in your team?'

There is a pause. I begin smiling. 'Did you forget? Useless fellow.'

Ari looks me in the eye and speaks, but his voice sounds different. 'No, Wije, I didn't forget.'

'So? Shall we put him instead of Jayasundera?'

'No, Wije.'

'What do you mean, no?'

There is a longer pause than before and I know what Ari is going to say before he says it. 'I'm sorry, Wije, but I think he chucks…'

Sheila enters about to castigate me for not speaking to my son. She sees the look on my face and backs out of the room, closing the door. I lower my voice. 'The ICC have cleared him.'

'If he was white, you would've asked for his head.'

'What colour is the ICC? Purple?'

'Today the ICC is the same colour as you and me.'

'It is a bloody optical illusion, Ari. You of all people should know that. The wrist…'

'I do not want to talk about this, Wije.'

And so begins the ugliest argument I've ever had. More foul-mouthed than when Ceylon Electricity overcharged me Rs 10,000. Angrier than when my wife found out I had been fired from my third successive job. Louder than when my son told me he was quitting the cricket team.

I remember every word, but I do not wish to repeat them. I also remember how it ended. With me holding my abdomen and falling to the floor. Feeling paralysis go through my right shoulder and sharp pains stab my stomach.

As I lie on the floor of my study I can hear Ari shouting for Sheila. I hear footsteps and raised voices. In the distance I hear the last wicket fall and the test being lost. Sri Lanka all out for 306. The last man, run out by Jacques Kirsten, is none other than Muttiah Muralitharan. I can no longer feel below my neck and warm liquid is escaping my lips.

In my mind, I go through lists of my own. My proudest moments on earth in no particular order. Marrying Sheila at Galle Face Hotel. The birth of Garfield. Watching him hit three sixers against his cousins eight years later. Being awarded Ceylon Sportswriter of the Year in 1969. Winning it again in 1976. Watching Wettimuny at Lord's in 1984, the first time I realised that a Sri Lankan could be as good as anyone else.

Someone is shaking me, but I do not feel like waking. I am at Bolgoda. With Ari and Jonny. The lake outside is orange and there is footage of Mathew on the giant screen and scotch in our veins. In a time before powercuts and court cases. I close my eyes. I feel no pain. Only joy.

Second Innings

'I've missed more than 9,000 shots in my career. I've lost almost 300 games. 26 times, I've been trusted to take the game winning shot and missed. I've failed over and over and over again. And that is why I succeed.'

Michael Jordan, Nike ad

Chopped Liver

It is nothing like the films or the books. There is no floating, no white light, no wings or hooves. I'm at my desk, back to the window, face to the typewriter, scene before me. I attempt to hit a key, but the key does not notice. I watch my body shuddering on the floor and witness the hoo-ha it inspires.

I look smaller and scruffier than I always imagined. My glasses are halfway down my nose, there is vomit forming a bib over my shirt. Ari is directing ambulance men in white smocks and Sheila is wiping my face and blubbering.

I try to type these words, but these words remain un-typed. My fingers touch objects, but objects fail to respond. The ambulance is only fifteen minutes late, which is not bad. They say ambulances in Sri Lanka barely make it to the funeral.

My room, my books and my clutter are all blurry edged. The men in white smocks are manhandling my twitching torso. There is no sound. There may be music, but I do not notice. Ah, here comes the white light. You're late, you bugger. Does even divine light work on Sri Lankan time? And here comes the music. *I'm born again, I feel free.* Is that my Samyo radio? *No longer alone.* White light is usually blinding, this makes you want to open your eyes more.

'Centuries of music, WeeGee. Mozart. Sinatra. The Beatles. You have to choose Boney bloody M?'

And now I am in the SSC pavilion with Jonny Gilhooley. The grass is green, everything else is white. The pavilion, the scoreboard and Pradeep Mathew bowling to a young Ian Chappell. Chappell has his collars up and his shirt open. His chest is hairless and pink, not unlike Jonny's. Mathew bowls a full toss and is hammered for 4.

'You also died?'

'No, WeeGee. Neither did you. Bite?'

He hands me a plate of devilled liver. It has the texture of rubber and when I bite I hear screams and feel movement against my teeth. I spit out onto the plate and see that the plate is alive. A mixture of liver, onion and capsicum writhing like maggots.

'Uncle, don't eat that.' The words are not called out by Jonny. But by the man about to bowl. None other than…you guessed it. His voice is thin and filled with treble, but it manages to reach us.

Chappell leg-glances and Mathew sprints after it. The other fielders sit back and let the bowler give chase. At the beginning of his career, Mathew would slouch like an orang-utan as he trundled after the ball. By the early 1990s, however, Mathew's posture had straightened and he looked less awkward in the field. Today he gallops after the ball and saves it from the boundary with a well-timed dive. The throw is flat and hits keeper Silva's gloves. Walking back to the boundary, Mathew shouts out, 'Go home, Uncle. I will visit you.'

'So will I,' says Jonny, as I hand him back the plate of liver. I walk back through the gates of the SSC.

Things You Will Never Know

I am lying on a bed in Nawasiri Hospital. There are tubes attempting to pump death from my body. I open my eyes and know I am to live at least for a while and I am happy. Even though that may seem an obvious emotion, for me it is unusual.

The nurse adjusts my bedpan while Sheila smothers me in kisses. It is the closest I have come to a *ménage à trois* in my wretched, uneventful life. Ari is seated in a clean shirt against a dirty wall. No matter what the circumstances, Ari is well turned out. Perhaps the Thomian education has its merits.

'You should have told us you had liver problems,' he says.

'You should've told me you thought Murali was a chucker,' I retort.

All of us, including the nurse, burst out laughing, and for a moment the fear of death is expelled from the room. Sheila is opening a flask of something likely to be unpalatable. She begins her nagging. 'What is wrong with you, Gamini? Why are you drinking like this? At least think about me.'

She starts welling up and I swallow my rebuttal. Tears should be made illegal in domestic squabbles. From where I am lying I can count the greying strands of hair that cover Ari's scalp. I fix my gaze upon them.

'So tell me, my friend, about Muttiah.'

'Doctor says you shouldn't get excited.'

'Doctors only say that in your Bogart movies. How long have you felt this way?'

'How long have you been sick?' asks my wife.

I pause and sigh. 'Sheila darling, I will stop drinking when I finish my manuscript. I promise.'

Sheila gets up and walks out of the room. 'You are such a b…bloody b…baby. Ari, I can't when he's like this.'

She hands the baton to my drinking buddy, who mumbles something about me and my disease and my responsibility, and my head begins to hurt as much as the rest of me. I decide to change the subject to something harmless. But I can't think of anything.

'So. You think Murali is a cheat, do you?'

I catch Ari in mid-lecture and he is shaken by the shift in gears. He takes a breath, cups his hands as if he were explaining friction to his O-level class. 'Wije. Imagine Muttiah being some random bowler from Transvaal or Bristol. Then what would you say? I know what you would say. You would say his arm bends.'

'But his arm doesn't bend.'

'Just because he's from Kandy?'

'Hallo. He has been tested by the ICC…'

'That is everyone's argument. The ICC are petrified of the subcontinent.'

'How can you argue with science?'

'Putha. What happens in a lab and what happens on the turf are two very different things. I know, no? I have seen him bowl with a straight elbow and I have seen his elbow bend in four. Sometimes to get more spin, he throws...'

'You fool. It is the wrist that turns. Not the bloody elbow. It is an optical illusion.'

'Many people outside Asia think he chucks and his wickets are illegal.'

'Typical. Always giving the arse to people outside Asia.'

We go on for a few rallies. In the end, as always, Ari backs down.

He takes another breath and smooths a crease on his sleeve. 'I admire Murali. I'm glad he's a Sri Lankan. Even if I bent my neck, I couldn't do what he does. I may be wrong. But it is my opinion, no?'

He is right, even though he is wrong. I ask him to go and check on Sheila and I am left with my white sheets and my tubes and my imminent death.

Ari is a maths professor in everything but name. Maybe he will help calculate the mathematics of my situation. Alcohol Consumption to Proximity of Death ratio. A bottle a day = Two months. Half a bottle = Six. A few shots = A year. Never = Forever?

Doctors can't give you this information. Some things are not knowable. If Pradeep Mathew had played for India or England, would he have gone on to be the greatest spinner of all time? Not knowable. How many poor bastards have perished in this bed before me? Not knowable.

Ari returns, Sheila does not.

'Ari, do you have a name for numbers that can't be found?'

'Ah?'

'For instance, how many bullets have been fired in Sri Lanka's civil war so far?'

'Nurse put whisky in your saline?'

If only.

'A figure exists. We will never know it,' I mumble.

'That's interesting,' yawns Ari.

'How many bullets were fired in anger? How many in fear?'

'Sheila will fire bullets into me if I don't talk sense into you. What are you going to do, Wije?'

'Forget war. Think cricket. Which bowler has got the most wickets off bad balls?'

'That's easy. Charith Silva.'

'How many geniuses have played test cricket?'

'Genius is a tough thing to quantify, Wije.'

'It is finite and measurable. If you knew which things to measure.'

Then Sheila enters and there is a discussion in low tones about my health. We do what every pointless committee in this country does and decide to postpone talks till we have more information. We all know that once the chase is cut to, it'll boil down to me giving up drinking or refusing to do so. Silently knives are sharpened.

That night I think of other unknowables. How much love does one need in a lifetime? Is there a quantity of brain space that is allocated to love? And for those of us who have loved less, does this space become occupied by something else? Like cricket, or religion, perhaps.

How many minutes of an average life are spent happy? How many are not? Does the sum of one outweigh the other? By how much?

Has alcohol brought misery to humanity or kept it at bay?

I was teetotal in my twenties and wrote clichés. In my thirties, my most prolific period, I began sipping in the afternoons. In my forties, when I wrote wonderful pieces for the *Daily News* and the *Island*, I was drunk by the 10 o'clock tea break. Did the drinking make me a thinker or did the thinking make me drink?

I attempted giving up in the early '80s. Once for as long as five months. But it is pointless. Once the amber tint leaves your glasses, you are left with unused energy and rage. People's failings grate on you. Hatchets get harder to bury. You spend your time barking at your son, evaluating your bad luck and worrying about other people's thoughts. And no matter how much clearer your skin, fresher your breath, or springier your step, you see that you have become a bitter bastard and you reach for the sweetener.

Alcohol strips my mind of noise and helps turn my thoughts to words. It keeps me smiling and guarantees me a dreamless sleep. It stops me from thinking of things that thought cannot cure.

The next morning, in the presence of Ari, Manouri and Sheila, the doctor announces that my liver has suffered damage, but it is not irreversible. And that unless drinking stops I will be dead in months. This time he does not smile. Sheila squeezes Manouri's hand and sobs quietly. Ari stares at me, knowing that I would reconsider our friendship if he cried.

I ask for specifics, ratios, probabilities. I explain the importance of my project and why without alcohol I would find it impossible to complete. Then there is shouting. And then there is silence.

There are things that Sheila will never know. She will never know how much I regret. She will never know that I disappoint myself more than I disappoint her. She will never know that even though I love her more than anything, I will always hate myself a tiny bit more.

Newton Rodrigo

Newton Rodrigo is my seventh visitor in my week at Nawasiri. Seven people who aren't married to me or Ari come to see this old dog in hospital. Considering the mountain of contempt I have accumulated over the years, I am flattered.

Newton sits by my bedside and says nothing. He has put on weight and wrinkles, but his hair and moustache are unnaturally jet black. He clutches a white envelope and examines every square inch of the hospital room. My saline, my reports, my bottles of juice, my hamper of inedible food, my view of the harbour. He looks into everything except my eyes.

'How many people did you tell about the Neptune betting scene?' he asks.

'No one,' I lie.

'The place went bankrupt after the World Cup. There was a misprint in the odds. Kalu Daniel, the manager, is in hiding. How much did you bet?'

I tell the truth. 'Everything I owe.'

On his lap is not my copy of Bradman's *The Art of Cricket*. It is the white envelope he has been holding.

'I forgot your book. I will drop it off tomorrow. But here's a little present.'

He hands me what looks like a giant get-well card, but instead has 'Thank you' embossed in a gold flowing hand on its white cover. It isn't for me.

Inside is a trite verse also embossed in gold. Below it is handwriting. Spidery and left slanting.

> Dear Newton Sir,
> No matter what misunderstandings there may be, I will always be thankful for your advice and guidance.
> Yours truly, Pradeep.

Trust Newton to cover a boast in wrapping paper and call it a present.

Kakka Gangsters

Jonny Gilhooley is my first visitor. He has a hunch, a droop in his gait, charcoal under his eyes.

He brings me a CD player and a bag of CDs that I do not listen to. Correction. I listen to one of them because it has the word BAT in the title.

'You look worse than me, Jonny boy.'

'Spoken like a man who has not seen a mirror in a while,' says Jonny with a smirk.

'How? How? We're thrashing Zimba, no?'

'Haven't been watching much cricket,' says Jonny, looking out of my window at the view of the harbour.

'How's the case…'

'I sold Bolgoda.'

'What?'

'Villagers came and shat in my pool.'

I am silent and then burst into giggles despite how much it hurts my stomach. Thankfully, Jonny joins in.

'Be careful, Jonny. They may hire a gangster to throw kakka on you. Only 750 bucks.'

'500 if you provide your own turd.'

The urban myth is that for Rs 750 a man on a motorcycle carrying a lump of excrement in a siri-siri bag would fling it at whoever you took the contract out on. Just because no one had seen it didn't stop us from believing it.

We laugh. Even though it tears my stomach. I do not tell him of my dreams. He does not tell me how scared he is.

When I Curse

Newton coached softball cricket at the Soysapura Cricket Grounds during the mid-1980s. That is where he is said to have discovered his protégés.

Softball matches attracted most of Moratuwa's cricket urchins. Sons of fishermen, carpenters and prostitutes. Newton was one of several Fagins who received a salary from the Sports and Youth Affairs Ministry to run this tournament.

'My, you should see the talent those days. There was Val Adi Sarath from Maradana. Faster than even Ravi de Mel. Got sponsored to play for Chilaw Marians.'

Newton, *Lankadeepa* stalwart since the late 1960s, was not a sportswriter who thought he could coach. He was a much rarer creature. A cricket coach who thought he could write.

On the advice of Aussie cricket consultant Pat Philpott, the Sports Ministry halted the funding of Colombo softball tournaments, seeing it as a breeding ground for unorthodox bowling actions and bad batting technique.

'What rot! Even Paulpillai, the most technically perfect schoolboy batsman since Satha, played softball. He scored seventeen 5-over 50s. Later got into NCC side.'

Newton was a political sportswriter. He took payment to write propaganda. He proudly claims to have helped get rid of two Sri Lankan cricket captains and four selectors with his poison pen.

'When I curse someone, they stay cursed.'

He also claims credit for helping reinstate the Captain in 1993 after he was dropped for failing a fitness test.

Having spent years writing dense, unreadable articles about the oldboy network quashing cricket at grassroots, Newton decided to join those he couldn't beat. He began scouting for talent and charging clubs sizeable finder's fees.

'People say all my players could never last more than a season. But what about Galappatti, Villavarayan, Waragoda? All played club for over ten years.'

'Didn't one of your cricketers get to play for Sri Lanka?'

'Why not? Granville. Karnain. Von Hagt.'

I note that none of these players lasted over a season, but I keep schtum.

'Not Mathew?'

Finally Newton looks me in the face. 'Pradeepan, I met at Soysapura. But I never promoted him.'

'Then?'

'I taught him everything he knew.'

'When he played softball?'

'No. When he played for Thurstan.'

The Ratio

My sister brings food and gossip. Loku's youngest daughter has an Australian boyfriend. Bala has been planting teak trees on Maddhu's land. Her son is joining IBM in Chicago.

I ask for pastries, but I am allowed only fruit and crackers. After an appetite-less life, I crave food now that I am denied it. I yearn for a karola badun floating in crisp onion, a roast leg of lamb wrapped in crunchy crackling, or a burgundy katta sambal on kiribath mixed with umbalakada.

But none as much as I crave a shot.

I let my sister say a prayer over me. It is so lengthy that I doze off, waking to her kissing my forehead and stroking my head. 'God bless you, Sudu.'

Brian and Renga drop in that same day. They inform me that the SwarnaVision lawsuit over the documentary that no one saw is finally over. ITL, which had been closed due to bankruptcy, won unprecedented damages and soon returned to air.

'That Rakwana is countersuing. The dumb buffalo,' says Brian with relish.

They bring good news. Mr Sulaiman from ITL agreed to pay my script fees when he heard of my health problems. It is a blessing. The saline does not pay for itself.

'You saw Ranatunga's innings vs Zimbabwe?' booms Renga, swaying on his chair. 'Best innings by a Sri Lankan in Africa.'

Brian complains about the TIC and FLC, who appear to be monopolising the cricket commentary scene. 'Bunch of clowns. They throw parties for all the Chappells and the Bothams and the Greigs and get the job.'

I thank Brian for the ITL money with the lie that he is a better commentator than both of them and he will one day make the cut.

The doctor says I should be able to go home by the end of the week.

I ask him about the mathematics of my last days. He gives them to me straight.

1 sip = Death.

History

'I thought Lucky Nanayakkara was the Thurstan coach.'

'Ah. You met that fool,' says Newton, scratching his moustache. 'Fellow was only master-in-charge. Didn't know balls about coaching. All he does is smoke his pipe. I only coached U-15 from '76 onwards.'

'How did you get a school coaching job without any experience?'

'How did you get Ceylon Sportswriter of the Year without any talent?'

'Twice, remember? Imagine the talent that takes.'

Newton smiles. It was his inability to rile me that always riled him. 'I was an old boy of Thurstan. I had a knack for coaching. And a knack for finding talent.'

He claims to have coached Mathew from the time he was eleven. Even then the boy would squander his abilities.

'First few matches fellow would bowl his heart out. By the end of season he would be in the reserves. Hardly came for practice.'

'When did he become a left-arm spinner?'

'I only advised him. After the Royal–Thomian match.'

'I heard some things about that match.'

'Do not ask me, because I will not tell you.'

When I tell him I have spoken to Gokulanath and Sir Nihal Pieris, he is taken aback. I ask him if he knows anything about the former's death.

'Never heard of him.'

'He coached at Soysapura as well.'

'That was that fielding coach, no? I heard he got sacked for stealing from the Royal Sports Fund. Must have drunk himself to death.'

I tell him he was stabbed.

'That area is full of thugs. He must've owed money. Typical Jaffna crook. Too many pretend coaches in this country.'

Newton tells me that he advised Pradeep not to play the Royal–Thomian and that it was not the first or last time Mathew refused to heed his advice.

'He could copy every action reasonably well. But when he mimicked Malik Malalasekera, the left-arm spinner, there was magic.'

Newton did not encounter Mathew till two years later, at the Soysapura Softball Tournament. When Newton asked him to bowl for the Cooray Park 6-a-side, the gangly, shaggy-haired youngster not only asked 'Fast or spin?', but also 'Left or right?'

'The fellow dropped out of university in the UK to try out for the Sri Lanka team. Must've been around '84. I told him he was a fool and advised him to bowl left-arm chinaman.'

Newton also organised that Mathew board with a family in Dehiwela when the Sivanathan family fights reached unbearability. And asked him to cut his hair and stop slouching.

'What a bowler he was. Bowled out Val Adi Sarath. Dismissed Paulpillai. Had both Japamany twins stumped. Cooray Park won the tournament.'

Newton then introduced the boy to the Bloomfield Cricket Club. And in 1985, the bowler formerly known as Sivanathan was taken to Australia for the World Series and then selected to play the first test vs India at the SSC.

The rest, as they say, is history. Or should have been.

Purple Green

On my fifth day in Nawasiri, Garfield calls. He tells me he does not want to fight. That he and his wife are settling in Zurich. That he has regular work with a band called Purple Green.

'Is it green or is it purple?'

'Both. Kind of.'

'Why are you speaking in that accent, men?'

'I have to learn German to apply for citizenship.'

First Japanese. Now German. Is he training to be a World War II spy? This is what I think. What I say is, 'How is your wife?'

'Adriana is good. You'd like her. Big football fan. How are you, Thaathi?'

'Have to give up booze. Otherwise, fine.'

'I'll try and come there for Sinhala New Year.'

Since when did Garfield Karunasena care about Sinhala New Year, I think. As if your Swiss German wife will eat kavum and ride onchilla, I think.

What I say is, 'OK. Take care.'

Sheila is very proud of me.

Cricket Uncles

Who sends a driver with a cellulite phone to visit a sick man? An idiot cricketer who has just got rich on tea and margarine commercials, that's who. The man is dressed in ministerly white and hands me the phone, as if it were a message from God. It is a much sleeker model than Ari's brick. The man on the other end is pretending to pant.

'Hello, Uncle. Sorry…have training, otherwise I would've come.'

'No problem, Charith. Thanks for calling.'

'Uncle is OK?'

'Liver problems, but if I stop…'

'Super. Super. When will Uncle be back at home?'

'Tomorrow…'

'Superb. I will call. I have a small job.'

I wince, but say nothing. I know what the job will be. That morning's *Daily News* had the squad for the 1998 tour to South Africa. Charith wasn't on it. He would need a PR article saying how fit and talented he was. There was a time I would have whored myself for this kind of project.

Like when I wrote a scathing piece for a government rag about the 'cricket uncles' who exploit the outstation pool of cricketing talent and hold clubs and the Cricket Board to ransom. I was called by the Sports Ministry and told what to write and they paid me. But that is not why Newton Rodrigo did not talk to me for fifteen years.

The Apple

'What happened to you, Wije?'

Newton is getting ready to leave.

'I'm sorry I wrote that piece about "cricket uncles". I needed the money. And you had…'

His head falls back, his nose elevates a fraction. 'Forget it. Look at you. Ceylon Sportswriter of the Year turned Cricket Board stooge. You had the talent, not me. What happened?'

He asks these unanswerables while stroking the keys of his Benz.

'Some of us don't judge our lives by the money we can steal.'

'For your information, I never took money from Mathew.'

At that moment Ari walks in with his camera. Newton rises in disgust.

After a few minutes of name-calling I manage to calm proceedings. My gaze falls on a red apple my sister brought. The type that Eve ate, the type that killed Snow White, the type that I cannot stomach. I recognise the huge scar on Newton's left hand. The one Ari had spotted at Bloomfield. It does not look like he got it from the mat slides in Sathutu Uyana.

'I don't remember you having six fingers.'

'That's because you were drunk all the time. And I used to hide it. I was embarrassed.'

'But he doesn't have six fingers,' says Ari.

'I got it removed when I could afford to,' says Newton, looking at me. 'It only helped me when I coached left-arm spinners. And I stopped doing that years ago.'

I pick up the apple. 'Show us.' I extend my hand awkwardly, like a granny using a remote control.

Ari gazes with contempt at the scar between thumb and index finger.

Newton scowls. 'What?'

'Show us.'

'But I don't have the finger any more.'

'Why don't you use both your hands?'

'How?'

I place my right index in the webbing between my left hand index and thumb.

'Mine wasn't that long,' smirks Newton. 'More like this.'

Newton inserts his pinkie on the webbing at a strange angle. He cradles the apple on it and rolls it around his four free fingers, his gaze shifting from Ari to me.

'Something like this.'

And then, with a rosy red apple and two cupped hands, he shows us in minute detail every ball he claims to have helped invent from 1985 to 1994.

Sri Lankan English

Jabir is my sixth visitor. He brings nothing but his cheerful self and that is more than enough. I could have done without the gaudy green shirt, though.

He swoons over the batting of new boy Jayawardena vs Zimbabwe and says we have a good chance of keeping the World Cup if we win in South Africa. Ari and I hold our comments.

He tells us again that we should talk to Uncle Neiris at the SSC.

'I am the fixing his wiring. I know the electrical.'

This time Ari cannot be restrained.

'I am the person fixing his wiring. I am an electrician. That dwarf is mad. I told you before.'

'Don't correct Jabir's English. And he's a midget, not a dwarf.'

'If Jabir is going to speak English, he should speak properly.'

'I understood what he said. That was proper Sri Lankan English.'

'There is no such thing as Sri Lankan English. Even if there was, it wouldn't be proper.'

Jabir keeps smiling, but reverts to Sinhala.

'He has recordings of old matches. I have to rewire the full scoreboard. At least come and look.'

Ari says he is too busy. I say nothing, knowing that lying plugged into a drip-feed gives me more than enough excuses.

None of My Business

'You know Sobers had a sixth finger on both hands that were removed at birth?'

Newton rests the apple on his extra finger and lets the ball roll across his palm, each finger traversing its seam, blessing it with variation.

'Pradeepan had strong fingers. He could rotate his wrist to almost 360 degrees and deliver the ball with any of his fingers.'

The last finger to touch the ball determined the nature of the spin. The index and middle fingers made it a chinaman, the ring a top-spinner and the pinky, a googly. It was all in the fingertips.

In the 1986 Pakistan home series, the SLBCC had given players and umpires the directive that rules were to be bent. Against Newton's advice, Mathew refused to obey and subsequently lost his place.

Mathew spent the next few seasons honing his craft and made his mark for Bloomfield, with the help of his old Thurstan coach who he visited on occasion. Newton lays claim to the undercutter, my favourite Mathew delivery.

'That was my idea, a back-spinner that stays low,' says Newton, twirling the ball with both hands, mimicking the digit he lost. They fell out again for two years, just after the 1987 Asgiriya Test.

'Why did you have it removed?'

'I hated it all through my childhood.' As Newton raises his hand to display his scar, his gold watch slips under his sleeve. He pulls it out and tightens it back to visibility.

I ask Newton why they fell out and Newton asks if Ari knows why he and I did not speak for fifteen years. I shake my head. 'Because it's none of his business,' he says. 'And this is none of yours.'

I ask him if he thinks Mathew might be dead. He tells me it is possible. 'He moved with some shady characters. Didn't help his career.'

I tell him about Sabi Amirthalingam and the death notice. He tells me never to believe anything the Sivanathan family says. I ask him why; he tells me it is none of my business.

Discharge

On my final day, just before Newton's arrival, I get a call from Graham Snow.

'How are you, WeeJay? Heard you were feeling poorly.'

He apologises for being a stranger and I accept.

'Those documentaries turned out good. Who the hell is Rakwana…'

'Long story. Do you want to speak to Ari?'

'I will not speak to that time-serving crybaby,' yells Ari. It is loud enough for the next two rooms and for Graham Snow, half a world away. Ari exits the room, while Sheila packs up my things.

'Could you give me Ari's address, WeeJay?'

'You already have it.'

'Oh. That's right. Give it to me again.'

'Forgive him, Graham, he's a bit upset…'

'I know. It's my fault. What's the address?'

'17/5 de Saram…'

Newton does not approve of the unorthodox deliveries. 'That is our people's whole problem. Try to do everything. He might as well have bowled right-hand also.'

My suitcase is packed, my bladder is empty, my hair is combed, my liver is clean.

'When did you last see Mathew?' I ask.

'I met him with that Aussie girl of his.'

'Shirali Fernando?'

'No idea. That's when he gave me the thank-you card. Fellow was different. Short haircut. No longer slouching.'

'So you never saw him in the 1990s?'

'Oh yes. I took up coaching indoor cricket. He came to ask my advice.'

'On what?'

'On how to bowl the double bounce ball.'

Ari laughs like a jackal.

'Was that before or after you discovered the wheel?'

Mathew came to Newton in 1991, uncertain and jabbering. His girlfriend is described by Newton as 'tubby' and 'speaking with a hena accent'. Mathew had just returned to the side after being away for three years due to injury.

'Fellow, I think, had been drinking. Called me out of the blue and wanted to chat.'

They met at Newton's house and Mathew asked strange questions. Whether it was immoral to throw a game. Or to play with South Africa. Whether his carrom flick and his leaper were damaging his fingers.

'I told him he had too many variations. That throwing a game was a sin. I also told him not to take money from apartheid South Africa, unless there was a lot of it.'

We pile into Ari's Capri as Newton walks towards his Benz. I am convinced that there is a large chunk of something that he is keeping from us, something his pride will not allow.

'When did you last see him?'

'At that wedding of the great Sri Lankan opening batsman, Mr S…'

Ari puts his hand over his mouth and laughter fills his eyes. Sheila brings the last of my bags. Newton walks away. 'See you, Wije. Goodbye, Sheila.'

So that is why Mathew was staring at us at the wedding of the GLOB. We were stuffing buriyani down his old coach.

Newton rides off in his Benz and does not wave. Ari and Sheila help me into the Ford Capri.

'If you believe that liar, you're mad,' says Ari. 'Wish I had some roast chicken.' We burst into laughter and my stomach starts to hurt. Sheila does not smile.

Kola Kenda

Tonight is a powercut night and our battery-powered fan has run out of juice. We lie awake and listen to the background fuzz of Galle Road. We listen to the cats, the dogs and the man who beats his wife at midnight. I am unsure whose house the raised voices belong to.

'Gayathri Baranage. She should leave that drunk bully.'

I forgot that Sheila was treasurer of the Mount Lavinia Ladies' Charity Circle. For charity read chat.

'I thought it was the Marzooqs who beat their women.'

Sheila yawns and turns to her side.

'You say that because they came to hammer Garfield? Or because you're racist against Muslims?'

'That Marzooq can't handle his liquor.'

I turn and rub the side of her arm. It is soft and beautiful even if it is the size of my thigh. 'Unlike me.'

'No, Gamini,' she says and turns away.

'I'm just saying...'

She reaches for her bedside table and produces a half-full glass from the shadow. 'Here, darling. Drink this. Ari said the cravings stop after two weeks.'

She strokes my head and places the glass to my lips. The whiff paralyses me. It is even worse than Ari's fruity miracle cures. It is kola kenda, a green herbal tonic that makes your burps smell like farts. It looks like vomit served in slime. It is now my turn to turn away and say no.

Minus 750 ml

It begins with the alcohol counsellor two days after I am discharged. Before we go, Sheila gives me an article from the *Lanka Woman* on How to Overcome a Drinking Problem.

'I didn't know Lankan women had drinking problems,' I snort.

'They do. They're called husbands.'

Unlike me, Sheila doesn't laugh at her own jokes.

Sigh. The recent drama has made my sweet girl bitter and harder to outsmart. Sheila 1. W.G. minus 750 ml.

The alcohol counsellor is a Burgher girl in a white coat, even younger than my infant of a doctor. She addresses all her comments to my wife.

She tells Sheila that there is group counselling and individual counselling. She hands me leaflets. One speaks of Twelve Steps. The other of meditation and vegetarianism.

'I recommend you attend a few group sessions first.'

'What do they do at these sessions?' I ask, thumbing through a yoga leaflet, with a bald man touching his scalp with his foot. 'This kind of nonsense?'

The girl looks annoyed.

'No. No. You just listen to what others say. You talk if you feel like it.'

'I can't do handstands and eat carrots, ah?'

Sheila squeezes my arm. 'Let's just go and see.'

'Eat three meals and drink lots of water,' says the counsellor, not rising as we leave.

Counselling

'Last week I had sex with my wife.'

The old man and his old wife smile and nod. Everyone around the table applauds. I look at Sheila with terror. Then the young man in the tie starts crying.

'My daughter is afraid of me.'

The applause stops and everyone stares. I sit squeezing my walking stick, waiting for the final straw to break the camel's spine.

The meeting is at Dehiwela St Mary's. First bad sign. It is scheduled for 9.00 a.m. on a Sunday. Second bad sign. It starts at 10.20. 1.20 p.m. Sri Lankan Time. Three strikes.

It is chaired by a Dr Naomi Fonseka. Around the table are men chaperoned by women. Boys with mothers, husbands with wives, fathers with daughters. The walls are lined with crucifixes and filing cabinets.

Dr Naomi welcomes everyone. We begin with a young couple. The boy has spiky hair and the girl is dark and skinny.

'Last week, Rasitha, you said you didn't have a problem,' says Dr Naomi. 'Do you still feel like that?'

The boy leans back, folds his arms, and shrugs. 'No problem. I enjoy my drinking, I don't see what's the problem.'

'We are always fighting,' interjects the girl.

'Only when I'm sober,' says Spike. 'When I'm drinking there's no problem.'

I feel like applauding. But instead I stroke my chin and adopt the quasi-serious pseudo-concerned look of everyone around the table.

'You have a drinking problem, Rasitha,' says the doctor.

'I enjoy drinking. I'm earning well. What's the problem?'

The doctor's phone rings and she leaves to the side of the room. The tune is 'Yankee Doodle Dandy'. Inside me I feel a creature stirring. I do not know what the creature looks like, but I know he is in a bad mood.

Then the old man confesses he had sex. Then the young man in the tie starts crying.

'Every time I go near her. She'd cry. She thinks I hit her…'

The young man is comforted by the lady in a sari, the beneficiary of the old man's renewed sex drive. The old man looks less than pleased.

'Excuse me, son. I was talking. I'm sorry about your daughter, but kindly wait your turn.'

'Let him talk, Sepala. His wife has left him,' says the man next to me whose face I do not see. There is an argument and finally neither the old man nor the young man get to speak.

Dr Naomi returns to the table, oblivious to the drama, and calls out the next name on her list. In the next thirty minutes, three more grown men cry and the doctor's phone rings four times. I pinch Sheila. 'Can we please go?' She ignores me.

The doctor gets off the phone, looks around the room and stares at us.

'Y'all are new. Could you introduce yourselves?'

I know alcohol is killing me. I know I must stop. But surely.

'My name is Karuna.'

'Hello, Karuna.'

'I have an alcohol problem.'

'Tell us about it.'

Sheila clasps my hand and for the first time since arriving, looks at me in earnest. I hesitate.

'Tell us, brother,' says the old man who just had sex. 'We're all friends here.'

'I can't.'

Then Dr Naomi gets another call. The ringtone pierces my eardrums.

Yankee Doodle sits on the camel. That does it. The camel is now a quadriplegic.

'It is...my wife. She drinks like a fish. Every day. For the last twenty years.'

Sheila releases my hand and turns scarlet. Everyone around the table nods sympathetically.

The doctor hangs up the phone. She catches the drift of my monologue and gazes at Sheila. 'Could you tell us when you first started drinking?'

I throw my head back and laugh but no one else joins me.

High Catch

My punishment is that I am made to do chores. Little do they know that not drinking is punishment enough. I have to sweep the back of the house, do the dishes and hang out the washing. I offer Kusuma an extra five hundred bucks to do my sweeping for me early morning. She refuses.

Little do they know that not drinking is punishment enough.

The first day I smash three dishes. I fling them to the side of the pantry. I throw them in quick succession, knowing Sheila will come running. *Kling! Clang! Clatterbash!* Three darts of venom, released from my heart, my soul and my liver. The creature that has been sitting behind my throat since the meeting vanishes, and for a nanosecond I feel glorious. It is not much but it is sufficient.

When Sheila and Kusuma come in I am nonchalantly sweeping. 'They just fell,' I say, not looking at anyone.

The truth about withdrawal is that it disappears if you stop looking at it. But how to stop looking at it? The more you stare at the elephant in the room, the bigger it grows.

Like the young couple, Sheila and I argue more now that I am sober. I sit alone, sipping thambili in my office room, listening to the one compact disc. There is something about Meat Loaf's piano clatter that soothes my mood. I squint in the twilight and think.

The creature sips with me, both of us knowing it will not satisfy. I think of the pleasure I received from smashing those plates. I wonder if wife-beaters feel similar pleasure when breaking a spouse's arm.

The papers speak of Socialist MPs becoming Nationalist MPs as the balance of power in our permanently hung parliament swings from the chair to the elephant. Sri Lankan politicians change parties like European footballers change teams.

MP Dissanayake transfers to UNP for undisclosed sum

Cooray to strengthen SLFP's right wing

It is not ideological disagreements or divisions over economic policy that prompt these crossovers. It is petty squabbles, the other fellow getting a better ministry, a bigger Benz.

The youngest of Sri Lanka's Ruling Dynasty, the Minister who never became President, has changed parties seven times, always just before an election, always to the losing side. Here's a story about him that may or may not be true.

He once ordered the cordoning off of a Chinese restaurant in Mount Lavinia for him, his friends and his security, assuring management that he would spend more than the restaurant made in a week. Good to their word, they bust thousands on Chivas and lakhs on shark fin soup.

Then, in the early hours, paralytic from imported whisky, the Minister feels the call of nature, but is unable to get up. The guards try to help and receive an earful of raw filth as thanks. Then, the Youngest Sibling of the Ruling Dynasty has a bright idea. The bodyguards are told to form a semicircle in the middle of the restaurant. They stand to attention and stare straight-faced at the horrified manager and his staff, while the Honourable Minister, Youngest Sibling of the Ruling Dynasty, shits into four soup bowls. Ari swears this story is true.

In the 1970s, I was in transit at the Singapore airport on my way to cover the Asian Games. The Singaporeans then spoke of Ceylon as we now speak of New York. Their airport was little more than a leaf-thatched shack. Decades later, Singapore's Changi Airport is the toast of Asia. We dropped our high catch, while they took a spectacular, one-handed diving one.

I pick up the leaflet on the Twelve Steps. The garish printing and the overuse of exclamation marks sour the lukewarm water I am sipping. The leaflet contains tinpot philosophy in a corny typeface.

'You are not as worthless as you think you are.'

Neither am I as clever or as healthy or as lucky.

'What is more important? The car you drive or how often you make your children laugh?'

My son hates me and I travel by bus.

I crumple the leaflet and put down my empty glass, wishing it were full. It takes all the muscles in my soul not to hurl it against the wall.

Sports Fellowship Club

Ari and I, as members of the Moratuwa Sports Fellowship Club, are invited to a cricketers' dinner that week; a printed invitation has been posted to both of us. Speakers include Duleep Mendis, Arjuna Ranatunga and the FLC.

On the way to the Sports Fellowship dinner, Ari tells me he is proud of me. 'You have battled well. Shown true grit. Like a Thomian.' He even puts his hand on my shoulder.

'Ari. I went to Kurunegala Maliyadeva…'

'Yes. Yes. But you are strong. Once you have beaten these demons, we will find Mathew and you will write about him. That is what God wants you to…'

'Is this thing at the Masonic Hall?'

'Oh. Yes.'

We are both wearing ties. Manouri and Sheila wear saris.

'When did the fellowship get a dress code and start inviting wives?'

'After the fellows grew old. And became grandfathers,' teases Manouri.

'Of course. Of course,' says Ari, pulling onto Galle Road. Seven lanes of traffic pointing in different directions, each crawling at 20 mph. 'When is Garfield expecting?'

'In August,' says Sheila.

That was the weekend's celebration. Maybe the next Karunasena will play for Sri Lanka.

The traffic eases as we pass the cop who had been holding it up. Ari hums.

'Wije, you know what is the meaning of life?'

The creature is starting to scratch at my throat. I manage a grunt.

'Grandchildren. Your grandchild on your knee is the meaning of life.'

'Yes, Papa,' chimes in Manouri from the back.

'I hope the little brat torments Garfield.'

'Gamini…' says Sheila.

Ari grins as he brings the Ford Capri into the Masonic Hall car park.

The hall is filled and everyone is well dressed. The invitation mentioned dinner, but I see no tables. I recognise few faces. I see no

Mendis or Ranatunga. There is a large stage with a backdrop saying SFC and two microphones. The insignia has two swords crossed, a Christian cross minus the scantily clad gentleman nailed to it, and a phrase in Latin fluttering at the base. Not a bat or a ball in sight.

'How? Logo and all?' I smirk at Ari.

The Sports Fellowship Club had its heyday in the 1960s when it used to screen the previous year's test matches and collect donations for underprivileged sportsmen. It had been silent since the advent of TV. There had been a few events, but I had failed to go to any as, I suspect, had most of its members. Today was the first time they were offering dinner and guest speakers.

'Fellowship crowd has changed,' I murmur to Sheila. Then the FLC appears on stage and urges everyone to get to their seats. In the throng I am shoved into a corner next to Manouri. I am two seats removed from Ari, but it is too late to move.

After customary thank yous into a crackling mic, the FLC begins introducing the first speaker, who appears to have done everything and nothing. The FLC waxes pointless about the man's rugby career, stint in a band, job at the World Bank and finally his current role.

He talks of how Brother Sumith helped him when he gave up his cricketing career.

'Ladies and gentlemen, Brother Sumith is the reason I am a commentator!'

The packed hall applauds. Ari and I exchange glances and withhold comments.

'Woe to those who rise early in the morning to run after their drinks, who stay up late at night till they are inflamed with wine!'

Brother Sumith raises his arm as if conducting a choir. I look around for Duleep Mendis, then I see a face I recognise. An old man and an old woman who recently confessed to having sex. They smile at me.

'Woe to those who are heroes at drinking wine and champions at mixing drinks.'

Brother Sumith walks to the right of the stage and points a finger.

'Priests and prophets are befuddled with wine; they reel from beer, they stagger when seeing visions, they stumble when rendering decisions.'

He comes to our side of the stage and glares directly at me.

I turn to Ari and speak over the laps of our wives. 'You did it on your new computer internet gadget, no?' They all ignore me.

'Arrack. Whisky. Gin. Vodka. Kasippu. Satan! Satan! Satan!'

People start standing and raising their hands in the air.

I repeat, 'You printed the invitations with your fancy new internet gadget, no?'

Ari's eyes flicker in my direction, the women fold their arms and do not budge.

'If you allow the touch of Jesus on your brow, the demons that drive you, like swine to a trough, they shall be gone!' Brother Sumith is screaming.

'You actually forged an invitation to get me here? Maara impressive, ah? Maara impressive.'

Manouri, Sheila and Ari gaze at the stage where the action is and ignore me. There are cheers and more standing. I stand as well. I hold my stick aloft.

'Sheila, if you do not let me out, I will hammer these mad people with my stick.'

Sheila looks at Manouri. 'I told you…'

As I leave through the archways people are swaying and chanting. Brother Sumith's voice booms through the PA system. The creature is kicking at my chest and pounding my skull.

There is a stack of leaflets at the entrance. I grab one. I exit for a three-wheeler as Brother Sumith places his sweaty palms on the shuddering body of the old man who recently had sex.

Twelve Steps

'Yeah, Sheila,' says Jonny Gilhooley into his phone. 'I'll drop him home.'

His Attidiya home is not as flamboyant as Bolgoda. It is smaller, less open and less well furnished. He smiles.

'They took you to a prayer meeting?'

I hand him the leaflet.

> The SFC, Samaritans for Change, present Healing Sunday.
> 19 Sep 1998.
> Featuring Sumithra Warnakulatunge, Addiction Healer (alcohol, cigarettes, drugs).
> Presented by Distinguished Sri Lankan Commentator, R…

'They told me it was a Sports Fellowship Club dinner.'

'That's bloody funny,' says Jonny.

'No scotch?'

'How long?'

'Thirteen days and fifteen hours.'

'You're almost through the worst. You on the Twelve Steps?'

I hold up my hand as I blow on my tea. It is the colour of sunrise and smells of ginger. I have read up on the Twelve Steps and they are as follows:

1. Admit you're a screw-up.
2. Believe in God.
3. Make a list of reasons why you are a screw-up.
4. Ask God to take them away.
5. Make a list of those you have wronged.
6. Ask God for strength.
7. Lots of it.
8. Apologise to them.
9. And mean it.
10. Pray.
11. Don't drink.
12. Can't remember the last one.

'If you eliminate God from the Twelve Steps, it's just making a list and checking it twice.'

'Not a bad way to start, WeeGee.'

Then he tells me how he spent the 1960s stoned off his skull in Kathmandu, how he spent the 1970s in a rehab centre in California.

'Coke, Pills, Ludes, Booze, Weed, you name it, mate, I did it.'

'I am not a drug addict,' I say, meaning it.

'Yes, you are, bonnie lad.'

Ari and I had a game. We would try and speculate on Jonny's past. Ari's guess was that he was Charles Sobhraj, the gentleman serial killer of the hippie trail. Mine was that he was a UK mercenary, a James Bond type, looking after British interests in Kashmir, Afghanistan and here.

'You know, me and Ari had a game trying to guess your past. I thought you were a spy. He thought you were a killer.'

'I'm a homosexual.'

Jonny's Adam's apple bobs up his neck. I take a gulp of tea.

'He thought you were trained by the IRA. I said you were more Mossad-like.'

There is silence.

'This is damn fine tea. I don't go for tea, but superb.'

'It's Ceylon tea.'

'Don't tell lies.'

We sip. He looks at me, I return the gaze and nod.

'I didn't know he was fourteen. And I didn't force myself on anyone.'

'Jonny…'

'It's fine. I've lived in Asia for over thirty years. I've handled worse.'

'Don't tell Ari. Bugger's a Christian and all. They don't take kindly to…buggers.'

He laughs and so do I. He leans over and punches me, this bear of a man.

'I'll tell Ari when I'm ready.'

'I want a pavilion ticket when that happens.'

We keep laughing and I sip.

'Damn fine tea.'

'I'm giving you a crate. It'll help you give up.'

I stare at this fan of Newcastle United, Derek Underwood, The All Blacks…

'Statistically homosexuals are 1 in 10, yes?'

Jonny looks irritated. He scratches his head. His hair is not quite blond, not quite brown. His teeth are not quite white, not quite yellow.

'So statistically one All Black is a homo?'

'There's three in the current team,' says Jonny, pouring more tea.

'Who?'

'I'm not going to tell you. You'd publish it. Look what happened with Fashanu.'

Justin Fashanu, pariah of English football, played for the legendary 1981 Nottingham Forest side and admitted to being homosexual in 1990. Publicly disowned by his brother, footballer John, subject to crowd abuse and changing room jibes, Fashanu committed suicide just a few months ago.

'I love drinking,' I say. 'Without it I can't write, I can't talk…'

'Bollocks. The writing and talking comes from you. When you give up something, stop thinking of it as denial. You're gaining, not giving up...'

'Don't preach to me, Jonny. I've had enough.'

I do not tell him about the creature, even though he would probably understand. I try not to think of three All Blacks being homosexual. Or of my friend and a fourteen-year-old.

'When you feel like drinking, have tea. You don't have to believe in God, but you have to believe in a purpose.'

I believe in my powerlessness over alcohol and I believe in a higher power. Though I'm certain his name isn't God, Allah, Buddha or Shiva and I'm equally sure he isn't as unkind as those who claim to follow him.

'What purpose?'

'Ignore the cravings. Focus on the writing. If you fancy a drink, call me first. I'm the only one you drink with. OK?'

Jonny serves the only biscuits I consider palatable. Chocolate-coated things with marmalade in the middle called Jaffas. He gets crates shipped to the High Commission. Or used to.

'How's the case?'

He shrugs as I step into his car, clutching my tea like a lifejacket. The creature is silent.

'No one's shitting in my pool. Probably 'cos I no longer have one.'

As the driver puts the Jag into gear, Jonny leans into the window. 'If you feel better after a week, think about writing that list. It's the only step I recommend. And stop sulking.'

And that is how it happened. As slowly as the ending of the Cold War. As inevitably as the beginning of the oil war. After fifty years of distinguished liver abuse, I, W.G. Karunasena, gave up booze.

Midget in the Rain

The first time I saw him in the flesh was in '86 at the Tyronne Cooray Stadium. The stadium got its name from the Minister who presided over its upgrading and who, in the late 1970s, tried fighting, lobbying and cajoling the ICC into granting Sri Lanka test status. That failed. He then tried wining, dining and bribing. That worked.

These days, hardly any matches are played at the Tyronne Cooray. But back in '86, it hosted test matches.

I must warn you, the following story features midgets and racist language. While I myself may be something of a freak, I am certainly no racist. Sinhalese, Tamils, Muslims and Burghers all nauseate me in equal measure.

It begins under a bo tree, early morning, in a rainstorm. The bo tree is on the side road connecting the cricket ground with the town of Moratuwa. There I am, asleep under the bo tree, about to be woken up by rain. Two millennia ago a man, just like me, abandoned his wife, son and responsibilities to go sit under a bo tree. Unlike me, that man wasn't drunk after a cricket match. And so he ended up becoming the Buddha.

My bed of leaves receives spit from above, dollops of rain as thick as curd. I crawl to where the trunk curls inwards, to where the wood has wrinkled. I check my shirt and my slacks for unusual stains. There is a reason for this. I once woke up under a postbox to find the chest pockets of my borrowed suit filled with vomit – the previous evening's potato masala, if you must know.

It is the final day of the second test vs Pakistan. Sri Lanka are 45 behind with Arjuna and Guru new at the crease, negotiating grenades from Imran, Wasim and Qadir. Much to the glee of the crowd and the dismay of the touring team, the umpires halt play for bad light.

Rumour has it that the Minister and the SLBCC have instructed the umpires to deliver victory. I believe the bad umpiring is the result of incompetence and not partiality. No one at the clubhouse last night seemed to agree. I remember arguing this with Brian and Renga at one in the morning. I do not recall how I came to be lying here.

A prod in my ribs.

'Yann. Ah.'

'Uncle is asking you to go.' A female voice with a Tamil cadence. She is dark, with an apron over her sari, holding a bag filled with ticket stubs, plastic cups, cigarette butts and paper plates. Next to her, attached to the umbrella poking my ribs, is a midget in a white Sri Lanka cricket shirt. His head is shaped like a dented papaya and he is the height of his umbrella. Behind him is a cart filled with empty bottles. Both characters smell of garlic and sweat.

'Uncle says you can't sleep here.'

The midget continues his unintelligible grunts. His words are burped out at intervals and appear to have little connection with each other. The woman translates.

'Uncle has looked after this ground for forty years.'

I realise sleep is now an impossibility. The midget walks off. From a distance I observe the boils on his feet, the shuffle in his gait and the indecipherable tattoos on his arms. The woman gargles spit and squirts betel juice across the pavement.

'You both sell kadale in the stands, no?'

'We sell so many things. You want madana modakaya?'

A Double M is a mixture of cough syrup, ganja and foul-tasting herbs. Favoured by some drunks, it guarantees three hours of intoxication, a splitting headache and at least one erection.

'Too early, no? No thanks.'

'Uncle works in the scoreboard,' says the woman. 'He supervises the pitch. Because of Uncle, Sri Lanka has never lost here.'

I call out to the unlikely curator of the Tyronne Cooray. 'Uncle. You think we can draw this game?'

He snorts. 'Ani. Vaaren. Ekek. Out. Na.'

'Uncle says no Sri Lankan batsman will get out today.'

The sound of grasshoppers and frogs has given way to crows and distant cars. Light reflects off the metal chairs in the stands. The stadium is small and tacky. In three hours it will be full.

'Does Uncle think the umpires cheated?'

'Umpire hora.'

Uncle launches into a tirade. I only catch a few words. 'Para demala. Umpire Francis, Buultjens, Ponnadurai. Lansiya. Demala. Horu. Pradeep Mathews.'

'Uncle says the umpires are Tamil and Burgher and all crooks. Like Pradeep Mathews.'

'Aren't you Tamil?'

'Uncle is OK with me.'

'Tell Uncle he's a racist pig.'

Pradeep Mathew has done nothing so far in this, his second, test. He has stayed at the crease for two hours and scored no runs. He has not been asked to bowl.

'Uncle says you are a disgrace, but Mathew is a bigger disgrace.' She smiles to reveal dentistry that hasn't seen a dentist in a while and to distance herself from the messages she delivers. She wears a pottu and a sparkle of silver in her nose.

'Tell Uncle his ground is Asia's biggest disgrace. My grandmother could bat on it.'

The midget turns around. 'Mokek? Kiwwa?'

She tells him that I said Mathew was a crook.

Pradeep had walked for caught behind, even though the umpire had not given him out. He took a catch off Rameez Raja and then confessed to taking it on the bounce. Rameez went on to score 122.

The midget points the umbrella at me and bellows. The woman translates. 'Uncle says if Mathew had batted on, we would have scored 400. If he shut up, Rameez would have been out for 3.'

I get up. The scoreboard gleams in the morning sun. Arjuna 0 not out. Guru 4 not out. How long would they survive? I spy some of our players in cricket whites approaching the nearby nets.

The woman and the midget walk to the entrance, picking plastic bags out of puddles. The sun is now visible and it looks like there is no more rain to save us.

I pass the nets by the stadium entrance. The batsmen are Uvais Amalean and one of the Ratnayakes. Nervous tail-enders likely to be sent in early. The bowlers are medium pacer Kosala Kurupparachchi, hero of the last game, and Pradeep Mathew, zero of this one.

It takes me a while to realise something is amiss. Mathew, left-arm chinaman bowler, is bowling with his right arm, in the style of opposing spin wizard, Abdul Qadir. The mimicry is spot on. Amalean unsuccessfully tries to smother the ball with his pad.

I want to go closer, but I'm afraid they will mistake me for a beggar. In the distance the woman and the midget are removing leaves from the pitch. Mathew switches to left arm off a longer run-up. His shaggy hair is locked in a headband. He gallops in, a replica of Wasim Akram, turns his arm into a slingshot and bowls. Amalean succumbs to a yorker.

The batsmen change every fifteen minutes. Guy de Alwis, Duleep Mendis, Ravi de Mel, followed by the men of the hour, Ranatunga and Gurusinha. I stand behind the scoreboard, mesmerised as Pradeep Mathew, the honest cricketer who has not been asked to bowl in that game, imitates every Pakistani bowler including Imran and Zakir Khan. He even does the sideways delivery skip of Mudassar Nazar.

The Pakistan team arrives at the ground and the Sri Lankan skipper instructs Mathew to stop. While he walks away, I run up to him. He removes his headband and shuffles to the dressing room.

'Excuse me. Is your name Mathews?'

He turns his head, avoids my eye and keeps walking.

'Who taught you to bowl like that?'

His voice is deep and unsteady. 'Enakku English theriyadu.' I don't know English, he says in Tamil.

'Sinhala dannavada?' Do you know Sinhala? I ask in Sinhala.

But he has disappeared through a doorway that I cannot enter. The security guards are having their morning tea and eyeballing me. I begin the long walk to the press box. Below the scoreboard, the midget and the woman appear to be burying something in the outfield. I look their way and they stare daggers.

I fall asleep for the first session and wake up after lunch to the applause for Guru getting his 50. Some of the Sinhala journos take off to a nearby tavern, but I am unable to tear myself from the game. By the end of the day, Guru is unbeaten on 116 and Arjuna is 135 not out. The match is well and truly saved and the series remains drawn 1–1.

I arrive home shortly after nine, bringing Sheila her favourite, pittu and baabath curry. I had switched to beer after tea and am not fully drunk. Sheila sees none of these silver linings and locks me out to spend the night on the veranda's reclining chair.

The Spools

I am watching a teledrama with my wife and Kusuma, our servant girl. Every scene is interrupted by twelve commercials. Each scene consists of characters staring in opposite directions and crying. My medicine makes me drowsy and the evening's entertainment does not stay the drooping of my lids.

I am aware of visitors and of Sheila saying that I am asleep.

'Aney Sheila, is it OK if I move the spool player here?' says a familiar voice.

I open my eyes during the news break. Israel and Palestine are not getting on. What a surprise. Wonder how their cricket team is doing.

'Was that Ari?'

'Go to bed, Gamini. Instead of snoring here.'

'Not sleeping.'

She snorts and cleans her TV-watching glasses with the sleeve of her housecoat. I close my eyes and don't sleep as more teledramas roll by. The voice returns.

'Thank you, Sheila. Do you mind if I use the spool player. Just five minutes.'

'You stole ITL's spool player,' I murmur without opening my eyes.

Ari tugs at my arm. 'Come, come, Wije, you must hear this.'

The walking stick has become my permanent accessory. The swelling on my feet has all but vanished and I no longer need one. But I like how it looks on me. I now have the air of a colonial planter or a Victorian detective, or so I believe. Jabir is also there with a grin from eyebrow to eyebrow, cradling a cardboard box in his skinny arms. Ari helps him carry it into my office. In the distance, the same commercial is repeated thrice in the same ad break.

'Ari. Only half an hour, ah?' calls out Sheila. 'Gamini has to rest.'

'Hamu wants tea?' asks Kusuma.

'No need.' The creature is still asleep.

My room is neat and dust-free. 'You're not writing, are you?' says Ari, untangling wire.

'I will soon,' I say, trying to believe myself.

Jabir flicks the cobwebs from the casing he is holding.

'Eh!' shrieks Ari. 'Don't touch the spool!'

They exchange roles. Jabir plugs in the machine while Ari extracts the spool and I lie on my haansi putuwa.

'Ari sir, only for this weekend, OK ah? Uncle Abey is holiday. After Monday must give.'

'Jabir. If you can't speak English, stick to Sinhala.'

My gaze falls from the wall I no longer stare at, to the morning's papers on the desk. **Coup to oust SLBCC boss**. The recently appointed president, Jayantha Punchipala, is already unpopular with his employers. Punchipala's dirty betting links are getting another airing in the *Sunday Leader*. There is no mention of illegal cricket betting behind the Neptune Casino in Colombo 3. Meanwhile our cricketers are losing. We have suffered a series defeat to South Africa. The team of '96 is unchanged and unsteady.

The spool clicks into place. The room fills with static, bird sounds, cuts, blips, clips, taps, raised voices, long hisses, distant clapping.

> *We'll bat*... karkkark...crackle... *Isaywhat*... quiet... *Zulqi will play*... clipclipclip... *howzatt*... *Sidath*... *paduppadup*... whack... *Kaushik in*... crackle, silence, crackle... *Kosala out*... clap, clap...

And so on. And so on.

'You came all this way to give me a headache?'

Ari is consulting his notepad and tweaking knobs.

'Shouldn't you return this contraption to ITL?'

'End bit. End bit, I think,' says Jabir, evidently not to me.

'Thanks, Jabir,' says Ari. 'Very helpful.'

'Look, I'm tired,' I say, rising to leave.

'Wait, wait, here.'

The spool stops fast-forwarding. Ari flicks a switch and I stop and listen. Footsteps... clip...blip... woodhittingstone... footsteps... doorslam... silence.

And then two voices, barely audible but somewhat familiar:

> **You are a buffalo? You are deaf?**
> It's not his fault.
> **This fool's fault only. The series is gone.**
> We can't win, Aiya.

If we got 300, we have chance. Now no chance.
It's not easy. These Pakis bowl like bhoothayas.
[A third voice, shaky and quiet.] *I was out.*
Sha. It can speak, ah?
I was out.
The fucking ball didn't touch your fucking bat.
But it did.
Skipper asked you to occupy crease. Amalean and de Mel can't bat. Now we'll be out before tea.
Let him be, Aiya.

Poised between doorway and chair, I look at the cover of the spool. Pasted is a piece of paper, browned by time with shaky black writing: 'PaksTan Test, 86.'

Ari calls out, 'Kusuma, aney make us some of that wonderful tea.'

He sits on the stool before me. 'Wije boy. You better sit down.'

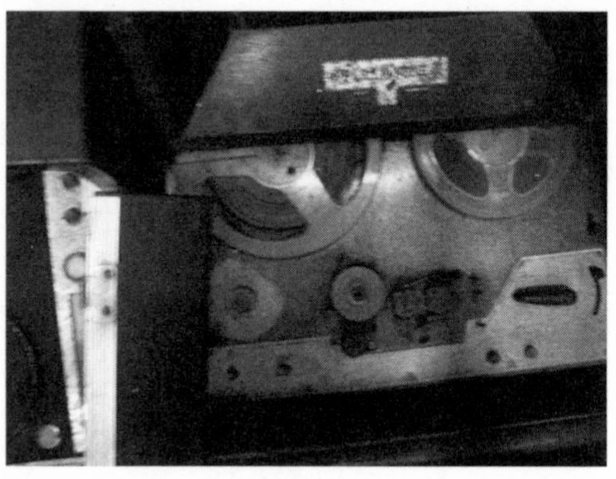

My Version

This is the story. It begins in the 1760s, when the Dutch dug tunnels and canals below Colombo to transport their plundered loot around the city and towards the harbour. It shifts to the 1830s, when the British closed the tunnels and shut the canals and began building roads and banks and cricket grounds.

It then shifts to 1941. After Nanking. Before Pearl Harbor. The Japanese had held ground against Russia, colonised Manchuria and believed they could take over Asia. The Allies had lost parts of Burma and the Philippines. If they lost Colombo and Trincomalee, the Japs would have access to India, the jewel in the melting crown.

So the Brits decommissioned one of Colombo's cricket grounds and turned it into a fully equipped aerodrome. It was a timely move. The Japs sent a fleet of bombers to disable Colombo harbour on 4 April 1942. The aerodrome at the cricket ground served its purpose. Her Majesty's Thirty Squadron shot down fourteen enemy planes and expelled the intruders.

The fight was not without casualties. Pilot Officer Don McDonald watched two of his comrades sink in trails of smoke over the Indian Ocean. When he exceeded his quota of hits to his tail, he aimed his plane at the sea swell. He missed the waves by 100 feet and crash-landed on the green grass of Galle Face.

He then climbed from the wreckage and staggered towards the Galle Face Hotel, wiping his brow with his gentleman's hanky, aviator cap blowing in the wind. He stumbled to the bar, watched his plane explode in the distance and turned to the bewildered barman. 'Mind pouring me a gin and tonic, chum?'

I repeat this story because I believe in the glory of Britannia. *The Stories for Boys* version. The empire that protected us from evil. The empire that no longer exists and probably never did. I repeat it because if you believe that story, you may believe the one that came out of Ari and Jabir's box.

The box contained half a dozen spools in various states of wear and tear. It also contained a logbook with neat scribblings in fountain pen. It was marked 'Property of the RAF'.

The aerodrome meant that the Royal–Thomian match, played at this ground in the 1930s, had to find itself a new venue. The world's longest running match, Eton vs Harrow, had already been cancelled as Britain exchanged bats for rifles. But in Sri Lanka, the match would go on even as the world crumbled, a fact duly noted by today's politicians.

The ground's scoreboard was demolished to make way for a landing strip. The pavilion was turned into a hangar, the dressing rooms into mess halls, and the Dutch tunnels under the cricket ground into bunkers. Two of these bunkers served as radio rooms, providing support for makeshift towers on makeshift runways.

Meanwhile more dogfights followed, but then came D-Day and then Nagasaki. Then Hitler committed suicide, Japan surrendered and the Royal–Thomian was shifted to the P. Sara Stadium. The British took away their equipment and their planes, the Canadians helped rebuild the scoreboard and the pitch. The tunnels were blockaded by rubble.

In 1948, Ari Byrd played for STC and forced a draw. On 4 February that year, a month before the game, the British took their bats, their balls and their viceroys back to Blighty, leaving behind the roads, the railways, the cricket grounds, the bureaucracies and, of course, the race divisions. In their haste they also left a bunker below a cricket ground fully equipped with radio equipment.

Harold de Kretser became curator in 1949 and supervised the restoration. The ground became the venue for school matches, the clubhouse was rebuilt, tennis courts followed. De Kretser hired Tamil labourers to clear rubble from the tunnels and stumbled across a hidden room. Not only was he surprised to find the equipment in working order, he also found transmitters rigged to the mess halls and the runways. The British had been spying on their own.

De Kretser knew more about electronics than he did about groundskeeping. Those duties he entrusted to Hewman Neiris Abeytunge, the midget servant boy who cleaned the mess hall during the aerodrome days and who stayed on to become gardener at the newly named…

'Wije. You promised.'

'People are going to guess anyway. We might as well tell.'

De Kretser first attempted taping the audio of live matches in 1956, with the arrival of the Indian national side. De Kretser's logbooks note that 'the mic positioning prevented clear transmission of onfield action'. He does, however, mention picking up 'a dressing room argument in Urdu between Nari Contractor and Polly Umrigar'.

The first spool is an inaudible mess of static. It is titled '1956–1967 Early Recordings, India, Pakistan, Gopalan Trophy, MCC XI, West Indies, Commonwealth'. The writing is neat, precise and identical to that of the journal.

Over the next decade, de Kretser, aided by his diminutive gardener, redirected the wires from the outfield and experimented with different mic positions. He tried under the turf, behind the umpire, before finally settling on the drinks hatch at silly mid-off for storing balls and beverages. The wires to the mess hall were easily redirected through the light fittings.

De Kretser's log, prodigious in its detailing of mic circuitry, offers precious little help in deciphering the shakily recorded dressing room mutterings.

He finally got it right in 1964, when Polonnowita and Lieverz bundled out a touring Pakistan side to give Sri Lanka a rare victory.

Each ball is clearly punctuated by the call of 'Well bowled, sir,' by gentleman keeper H.I.K. Fernando, in a time well before sledging.

The West Indian tour in 1966/67 is also well captured. Though it is difficult to distinguish between the calypso lilts of the Sobers, Kallicharrans and Lloyds. Snippets from these games and from unidentifiable domestic games feature on this spool.

The tone of entries is scientific and dry. It is unclear whether this logbook, covering almost twenty years, was kept out of boredom or Cold War paranoia.

The *Daily News* of October 1973 reported the death of Harold Bertram West de Kretser. An old boy of St Peter's, an engineer during the war, survived by a wife and two daughters. The logbook stops there.

Spool No 2 is titled '1970–1981. Taml NaDu, Gpalan Trophhy, Robet Senanyake, Tropphy, Inidia U-19, DH Robin IX'. The handwriting is less assured. The rest of the spools are marked in this hand.

Before I proceed I should tell you that the squadron guarding Colombo in 1942 were Canadians, not British. They claimed to have shot down fourteen planes, but only three metal carcasses were found. There was no 'jolly ole chap' business. Pilot McDonald was carried from the plane with minor burns and taken to a nursing home, where he asked for whisky and instead received iced tea.

Isn't my version a lot better?

The Bunker

Hewman Neiris kept no such journal, though he kept recording matches and then editing the highlights, just as old man de Kretser had taught him. His unmarked spool collection includes every match played at the unmentioned venue.

'Hewman? As in Human?'

'I think it's a cross between Herman and Hubert.'

'How do you know his name?'

'I met Neiris the midget during a 1986 Pakistan test match.'

'Are you making this up?'

'I was asleep under a bo tree.'

'You are making this up.'

Let us assume you accept this Hewman Neiris underground recording nonsense. Would you buy that a crazy midget, who had spent his life hiding and preserving secret recordings, would entrust a grinning trishaw driver and a balding maths teacher with his life's work?

'He's gone to Kataragama temple with his saasthara woman. Jabir let me borrow this for the weekend.'

'The saasthara woman who gives you betting tips?'

'That one only.'

'She gets her tips from the betting gods in Kataragama?'

Jabir is wearing a cap saying Ion Mayden. For once he is not grinning. 'Ari sir. Must return before Monday. Neiris Uncle will curse us.'

My head is twirling.

'How do you know the midget?' I ask Jabir.

'I fix his wires. I am electrical man.'

Ari frowns and Jabir reverts to Sinhala. He tells us that Neiris hired him to do the wiring in the scoreboards and in the pavilion.

'Wiring what?'

Jabir sits on my stool and eyes us both sternly.

'Uncle told me he would curse me if I ever told.'

'But he can't even speak properly.'

'I can understand.'

Aside from episodes under bo trees, I only knew the midget as one of the shabby people that populated local games. A grumpy 4 feet snack seller, who would scramble between seats with a tray of cadju hanging from his neck. Always annoyed if people didn't have the right change. He had barked at me in his mute yawp on several occasions.

'He's only half-dumb, Wije,' says Ari. 'When he wants he can say few words. But he's not deaf.'

'If he's eavesdropping on games, I suppose not.'

'Wije sir. You must promise not to tell anyone about this,' says Jabir. 'Neiris Uncle could get in trouble.'

'He's the groundsman. Can't he do what he likes?'

'He hasn't been the groundsman there for thirty years,' says Ari.

Shortly after de Kretser's death, a professional groundsman was employed, though Neiris was kept on the staff as a gardener and coolie. No one knew of his underground hobbies. People had bigger irrelevancies to care about.

Aside from his saasthara lady, only one other person knew how to enter Neiris's secret cavern. The man who had saved his life – a skinny, grinning, kind-hearted trishaw driver.

Ten years ago, Jabir found Neiris at a bus stop, surrounded by excitable bystanders, having a diabetic fit. He popped the midget into his three-wheeler, took him to Panadura Central Hospital, and kept an eye on him for the next few months.

'The fellow had no one. Wife died. Son killed by the army in '71.'

Neiris let Jabir visit him in the bunker, but had him sworn to secrecy, though how the mute communicated with the man who never shuts up is a mystery. Neiris Uncle found him electrical work around the neighbourhood and the two became friends.

Last month, Jabir visited the midget to find him livid. The saasthara woman told him the spool machine was broken. Neiris Uncle might not be able to record the upcoming domestic season. He asked Jabir if he could fix spool machines. Jabir mentioned the name of a maths teacher in Mount Lavinia who might be able to help.

'How did he know you stole ITL's spool machine?' I ask Ari, who is playing recordings and taking notes as I type. That's right. I am typing.

'How should I know?'

'Did you have conversations with the midget when you got your betting tips?'

'He's half-mute. How many times to tell you? He can make noises and mouth a few words.'

'Maybe he writes words on a chalkboard.'

'What?'

'Or maybe he collects words he needs from the spools, splices them together and plays the sentence back. Fix...my...spool...machine.'

'Now you're being silly, Wije.'

While I was in hospital, Jabir took Ari to the bunker. Neiris refused to let him in unless Ari agreed to be blindfolded. Ari was taken down a metal ladder to a darkened room, where a spotlight was shining on a broken spool machine.

'Over fifty years old. Can't believe it was still working. I told them I would have to return with my tools.'

On his way out, Ari secretly slipped a spool into his raincoat and brought it home. It was sound bites from the 1985 test vs India, our first test victory.

'Could hear all the Gavaskars and Madan Lals cursing our umpiring.'

Jabir is shocked. 'You stole from Neiris Uncle?'

'Relax, Jabba. I returned it afterwards.'

Ari used every trickle of Byrd charm and offered to transcribe the spools for posterity. Neiris grunted his disapproval. He threatened to rain curses down on whoever exposes his bunker. That, I suppose, would be me.

Jabir lets me in on the scoop with reluctance. I am only allowed to write about it if I can disguise the place well enough. I fear the last bit may need work.

A few days ago, while the midget was hospitalised for diabetes, Jabir let Ari into the bunker.

'Wije, I tell you, it was a dingy, cobwebbed, smelly place. But it was filled with treasure.'

'Sort of like your room.'

'Funny. More like a museum. Antique mics and headphones. I wanted to steal it all. Just joking, Jabba. That equipment won't last much longer. Neither will the dwarf.'

'Midget. Where do you enter from?'

'Ask Jabir.'

Jabir gets to his feet and shakes his head.

'Neiris Uncle says he will burn the bunker if I tell anyone.'

'Ari, can't you smuggle a camera down there and take some snaps?'

'And be cursed forever by the dwarf? Not me.'

The midget's spools contained 80 per cent garbage. Transcribing them was an exercise in tedium. Most of the dressing room chats were mundane and the onfield banter unintelligible. But hidden among this aural mess were three pieces of crucial Mathew-related information.

In the absence of a holy grail, the midget's spools represent the real prize of this story. I sometimes wonder if the recordings of Pradeep defending his sportsmanship were not forged by Jabir and Ari just for my benefit.

Who cares? It does not matter if the revelations are false. Perhaps an Indian player and a Sri Lankan did not fight over a woman during our first test victory. Maybe a junior player did not, in fact, refuse to cheat against Pakistan. Perhaps the ill-fated 1992 test was, contrary to popular belief, lost fairly and squarely. None of this matters.

What matters is that after one month of no alcohol, I am writing again.

The Chinaman

'Fancy being done by a bloody Chinaman,' said 1930s' English batsman Walter Robins in a jibe that today would have required a disciplinary hearing. It was Mathew's bread-and-butter delivery. Pitching outside the batsman's bat and cutting into him. Ellis Achong, a West Indian of Chinese descent, dismissed Robins with one such delivery, and sparked both the outburst and the term.

A ball turning in from a left-arm bowler is not considered as dangerous as one that turns away. The logic being that it is not difficult to combat something that moves towards you. Mathew bowled two variations of the chinaman. One with cocked wrist and one with rolling fingers. He would drift it to wide outside the off stump, giving it the appearance of a wayward delivery, and then rip it in at awkward angles.

The chinaman accounted for most of Mathew's early wickets and remained his stock delivery throughout his career. It can be difficult to combat something that moves towards you, if it arrives unexpectedly.

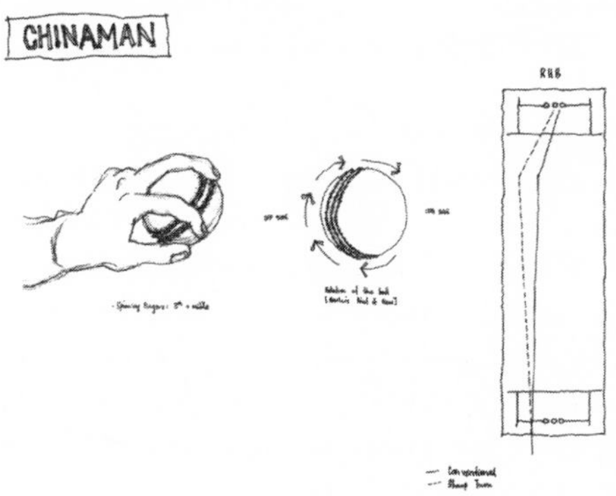

Reserve Captain

Charith Silva's call is predictably followed by him sending a Pajero with a driver. I arrive at Charith's Rajagiriya mansion alone and with a notepad. He leads me into the garden of his plush residence and sits me down on a cane chair.

'Have been made captain for the A-team tour to South Africa.'

'Congratulations…' I say, sipping a milky tea. Compared to Jonny's Seasonal Uva Broken Orange Pekoe this tastes like bathwater.

'What congrats?' He waves his hands. 'That means reserve captain. A-team captain means you never play for Sri Lanka. Look. Denham Fernando, Sajith Madena. Where are they now?'

Who? I put the tea down and brace myself.

'Uncle. I read your *Sportstar* articles. Your writing is not boru show. Easy to read. Can you write nice article saying I am taking wickets and bowling fast?'

'Are you taking wickets and bowling fast?'

'Definitely. Definitely. I am faster than that Pramodya. For sure.'

'But he is a spinner.'

'Uncle. I will pay two lakhs. If you can put in five newspapers.'

I then deliver a well-rehearsed speech. I would do it for free and I would have it published in the *Leader*. They have a novice sports editor, too young to be harbouring prejudices against the innocent W.G. Charith would pay the bribe. I would try *Sportstar*, the *Observer* and the *Island*, but no promises. In return Charith would tell me everything he knew about Pradeep Mathew.

Hands are shaken.

Love is the Magic

What follows was not revealed in one sitting. Neither was it revealed by one person. What follows is a stitching together of hearsay. I held the needle, so apologies if the seams show.

I have quoted only those who agreed to speak to me. I was refused interviews by many, including the Captain, the GLOB, Hashan Mahanama and even spinner Kalpage. Kalpage himself was later not selected for the World Cup, for refusing to carry the Captain's kit bag.

Charith Silva shared a room with Pradeep on the 1989 Australia tour. It was unusual for two juniors to be sharing a room. Juniors were either billeted with Sri Lankan families or packed in three to a room. The seniors got their own cabins. The tour stretched from Tasmania to Perth to Brisbane over ninety-three long days.

It was Pradeep's third test series. He had played tests against India and Pakistan and one against New Zealand, though the latter wasn't supposed to count. In addition to being a regular for Bloomfield, he had also featured in the '88 Asia Cup and the '85 World Series.

The spine was yet to enter Sri Lankan cricket. Our batting revolved around young men who would one day deliver a World Cup, but had yet to master the pressure of international sport. The pace bowling of Ravi de Mel, Labrooy and the Ratnayakes was pedestrian. The spinners Asoka de Silva, Madurasinghe, Kalpage and Mathew were used sparingly. Sri Lanka were crushed in most games, sometimes by amateur sides. Of the twenty-six games lost, Pradeep featured in three, Charith in two.

Charith knows about Pradeep's poems. He smiles when I hand him the letter from Shirali to Harini, recently valued at three thousand rupees.

'Fellow was going for English classes. He told me he had a manager. And a private coach. He studied all the books, but his English wasn't gooder than mine.'

Charith knows nothing of Pradeep's fortuitous practice with the national side in Hampshire. He remembers Pradeep bursting on the scene with a 5-wicket haul against the Colombo Cricket Club, CCC, in 1985. 'He was the best spinner I faced. Better than Murali, for sure.' The call-up to the national side a year later was as swift as the fallout the year after that. 'Unless you were good with seniors, was very hard to stay in Sri Lanka team.'

In 1988 Charith was selected for the A-team to play West Indies U-19. Pradeep Mathew, out of favour again after the '87 World Cup, was demoted to that team. Charith describes a carrom flick from Mathew that bowled a young batsman called Lara. 'I saw from first slip, the ball danced into the wicket.'

It was while seated in the pavilion, waiting for batting turns that never came, that the two tail-enders bonded.

'What are you writing?' asked Charith.

'Poem to my girl,' said the left-arm spinner.

'Where is she?'

'Australia.'

Solid performances in the '88 Asia Cup saw Mathew selected for the '89 tour to Australia. Along with him was the young medium pacer from Galle who had bowled economically against India.

'It's my luck that got me this. Labrooy was injured. The Ratnayakes were out of form. And de Mel was fighting with the Captain. So they took me just in case.'

I have watched Charith bowl for NCC on many occasions. While on a good day Charith could hold his line steady, his pace was unlikely to keep international batsmen awake at night. In fact, it was more likely to put them to sleep.

It was here that Charith learned the full extent of Mathew's obsession. Three phone calls a night to a number in Perth. 'Fellow was plucking flowers and feeding them down the phone.'

Charith and Pradeep spent their tour bowling to the seniors in the nets and sitting in their room talking about money they needed and women they did not have. 'I worked at Mercantile Credit, he was at Sampath National Bank. Some of the reserves had sponsors or club support. All we had was the money we made on tour and that was nothing.'

Charith describes Pradeep as having long fingers and being unusually supple. Some mornings, Mathew would be stretching, other times he would be reading his English books, some days he would be in the toilet vomiting.

'He told me his mother wanted him to give up cricket and look after his father. He was determined to become the first regular Tamil player in the national side. "Ado, Silva. As a Tamil I have to be ten times better than the Sinhala spinners. Now I am only eight times better." Sometimes fellow had swollen head.'

Mathew admitted to being in love with this girl for over five years and was a prodigious letter writer. Uvais Amalean, former Bloomfield wicketkeeper, remembers him scribbling on a foolscap notebook throughout the season. 'I can't remember. Stupid stuff. Some girl's name written like a poem.'

Amalean only speaks with me on one occasion, at the VIP lounge, during the Singer–Akai Nidahas Trophy. 'He was a solid servant for Bloomfield,' says Amalean. 'When he left, not even a farewell.'

Both Amalean and Charith remember the book of poems incident. It began as a dressing room prank, but spilled over to the post-match socials. No one knows how Ravi de Mel got hold of Shirali's scrapbook. Except me. I speak with Ravi a few chapters into the future and he gives me, among other things, photocopies of the cyclostyled sheets he pasted on Pradeep's locker. He even lets me take one.

No wonder we are getting thrashed!
Our spinners are writing poets.

Senshual and soft
Heating the senses
Incredible Feminine
Rosy with radiant
Anger not urs
Luvly beauty
I will pursue

Suppoze u not care 4 me
Have my heart
In my eyes u are womanhood
Rain wash over
Angwish and heartache
Love is the magic
Intentionz I have

From the pen of Pradeep Shakespeanathan

No doubt, in the quest for the hand of his intended, Pradeep had turned to the courtly wisdom of an *MD Gunasena Thesaurus*. Shirali had probably circulated these impassioned paeans as she had shared one of them with Harini Diyabalanage.

Mathew arrived in the dressing room to laughter and jeers. He threw a punch at the burly Ravi de Mel and was dispatched in a headlock. The GenCY broke up a very one-sided fight. 'You are gentlemen first, cricketers second.' Both Charith and Amalean agree that de Mel was a bastard. That the matter should have ended there.

But it didn't. As is confirmed by the bench warmer, the wicketkeeper in waiting and the bullyboy bowler, these poems were quoted extensively at the 1989 United Sri Lanka Association, USLA, Christmas celebrations in Perth.

Roshani Junkeer, member of the Perth Kandyan Dancing Troupe: 'Aiyo, Shiraligirl, look at the cheeks. Rosy with radiant. Hehe.'

Larry Donald, admirer of Shirali, friend of the West Australian Sri Lankan Community: 'Incredible feminine, you are womanhood, get us a drink, will ya.'

Both comments were within earshot of the reserves table where Pradeep was sitting. Mathew is reported to have glared. Shirali is reported to have looked 'full upset'.

Then Ravi de Mel, wielding a can of VB Bitter, put his arms around batsman Tillakaratne and Pradeep. 'Love is the magic, no? Intentionz I have.' Mathew freed himself from the paceman's elbow, walked up to Shirali and her drunken party, uttered the word thanks and left. A glass of wine was spilt. Opinion is split. 40 per cent of the interviewees claim it was thrown by Mathew at Shirali's face. 40 per cent claim it was thrown by Shirali down Mathew's shirt. Only Charith says that it was knocked over by accident as Mathew exited the Perth Town Hall.

Mathew and the Yorkshireman

Reggie Ranwala toured with the national cricket team as Percy the flag waver's sidekick. To call Reggie and Percy mascots would be unkind and insulting. To call them groupies would not be entirely inaccurate. The incident he relates about Pradeep Mathew took place in Melbourne, 26 December 1989.

It was the only Boxing Day of the last nineteen years in Melbourne that did not feature a test match. The Melbourne Cricket Ground, MCG, did not think the inexperienced Sri Lankan side of '89 was a big enough draw for a five-day fixture. It would be six years before

Melbourne cricket granted us the privilege of being sledged and accused of chucking for five whole days.

Mathew was not playing in the Boxing Day one-day game. But fate did a twist and Pradeep found himself on the field, substituting for an injured Ranatunga and on the receiving end of a cover drive from David Boon's blade.

Mathew, whose fielding has been described as 'roobish', 'lazy' and 'vedak nae' by various sources, reached out into the ether and was amazed to find that (a) the ball was lodged in his outstretched left hand, and (b) he was in midair, parallel to the turf of the MCG, and about to fall on his chin.

Man of the Match was Simon O'Donnell for his match-winning 4 wickets and his 57 not-out. Recipient of the CrocDundee2™ CatchoftheMatch was Pradeep S. Mathew. In the studio were team management and camera crew. Reggie had squeezed in to cheer on Mathew, but had been instructed to keep quiet.

The original *Crocodile Dundee* was funded by its cast and some private investors that included sports baron Kerry Packer, inventor of World Series Cricket and Aussie cricketers Lillee, Marsh and Chappell. It was Australia's biggest international film and spawned a sequel, which sponsored the award that Pradeep won.

The GenCY, anxious about the standard of English proficiency among squad members, had issued a memo before the tour, stating that in the unlikely event of anyone being selected Man of the Match, their speech should be confined to a selection of stock phrases:

'The boys played pretty well.'
'It was a team effort. I tried to do my best.'
'We have learned a lot on this tour so far.'
'They played better, but we gave a good fight.'
'We are getting used to conditions. We're looking forward to the next game.'

'Don't try and be pandithayas and talk big,' said the GenCY in his clipped accent. 'These Chappells think we are fools. Don't embarrass your country. Even seniors, ah? You may think you know your English, but unless you are sure, stick to the script.'

Many feared the West Indian pace attack less than the prospect of speaking to the cameras in English. And so it was that Pradeep found himself on camera with a famous Yorkshireman.

'Prah-deep Mathew. Winner of CrocDundee2CatchoftheMatch. Let's 'ave a look at it, shall we?'

Cue replay.

'Here we go. Ratnayake overpitching, Boon takes a swing and...out of nowhere, young Mathew diving to his right. I tell you, CrocDandy would've been proud of that.'

The crass sponsorship that has crept into the game and is now too large to be pushed back the way it came, frequently gets my goat. But I'm aware of its necessity. I can tolerate booze and cigarette companies putting on a show for us boozers and smokers, but to let a sequel to an Australian-Banda-goes-to-Hollywood film celebrate the art of fielding takes crassness to new lows.

Mathew, who according to Charith Silva and I.E. Kugarajah had seen *Crocodile Dundee 2* on Christmas Day in the company of three Melbourne females, stared at his shoes and muttered, 'It was a team effort. I'm tried to do my best.'

The Yorkshireman widened his grin. 'He's a hard hitter, is David Boon. That must have tickled?'

Mathew looked helplessly at the GenCY beyond the camera. 'They played better, but we gave a good fight. We have learned a lot on this tour.'

The Yorkshireman's grin stabilised, but his nose twitched the twitch of a man who wanted to roll his eyes but can't. 'If you ask me, you need to learn quickly. Sri Lanka are yet to win a game on tour so far.'

Off camera, the GenCY glared at the SevenSports studio producer. They had both briefed the interviewer to ask simple questions. The studio manager glared at the Yorkshireman and did the throat-cutting gesture with his index finger.

'We're looking forward to the next game,' said Mathew. 'Hopefully boys will play well.'

The Yorkshireman, a man who used the excuse of northern bluntness to be downright rude, was bored after a day's worth of ale. He was known for making enemies faster than he made runs.

'I saw you bowl in the game against Victoria County. You seem to be struggling with the local wickets.'

Mathew began shuffling and thought of Item 7 on the memo: When in doubt, smile and say, 'That's right.' He looked at the GenCY. Then at the Yorkshireman. He smiled. Shuffled and scratched his head. 'They played better, but we gave good fight. We are getting used to conditions. We're looking forward to next game.'

The Yorkshireman ran his tongue over his lips, squinted at the morsel before him and decided to take a bite. 'I saw you play in Colombo against New Zealand who, mind you, aren't the strongest, and you blokes struggled. Those were home conditions.'

Mathew dispensed with the smile, but kept scratching his head and shuffling. He dropped the unsure accent of a non-native English speaker and switched to his Lankan lilt. 'New Zealand took twenty years to win first test. Sri Lanka took only three years.'

The Yorkshireman smirks. 'That may be the case, but…'

Mathew's voice rose a key. 'England has played for hundred years...'

'But we're not talking history, are we, son?'

'… and they're still crap.'

The whole studio caught its breath.

'Is that right? You think you're better than England, do ya?'

'I'm better than you ever were.'

The Yorkshireman raised his eyebrows and gave his lopsided smile.

Behind the camera there was frantic signalling. The GenCY whispered, 'Reggie malli. This is not going live, no?'

Reggie shrugged.

'You think you'll play the next game, son? Or will you be carrying drinks again?'

There was silence. The GenCY hissed in the ear of the studio manager who grunted into his mic. Reggie watched Mathew look up at his bully.

'You think you'll ever do commentary? Or will you be doing CatchoftheMatch again?'

Obviously the English lessons had sharpened more than Pradeep's vocabulary.

'It was true,' gasps Reggie. 'That fellow only did CatchoftheMatch. They say because he was always drunk. But I think because no one could understand his accent.'

Mathew stormed out of frame, leaving behind a cheque and a stunned crew. He exited the room and then exited the ground. He had an argument with the GenCY on his way out. He was later seen by Reggie, returning to his hotel with Charith Silva at 2 a.m. the next morning. Not drunk, but with a bandaged hand and a smile on his face. The Yorkshireman was reprimanded and the interview never aired.

The Yorkshireman never got a stint in the commentary box on that tour, but a year later made a name for himself on radio as a straight-talking curmudgeon. Fortune was less generous with young Mathew. He had to wait three years before he could play for Sri Lanka again.

Almost Beating the Aussies

If we were to have a Big Match, an ongoing rivalry, who would it be with? India, Pakistan? No, we get on too well with our neighbours and they have each other to hate. The Kiwis are too nice and the Windies and South Africa are too far away. It'd have to be one of the Ashes teams.

'Would never happen,' says Jonny, when I present this theory. 'Problem is, Sri Lanka hates Australia. But Australia only slightly dislikes Sri Lanka.'

The reason we hate the Aussies is because of their umpires no-balling Murali, their bowlers calling our batsmen black monkeys, and their press calling us cheats. But most of all because they're tougher, better organised and impossible to beat.

Perhaps if we had won the '92 test, things might have been different. The '92 Australia test in Sri Lanka is remembered for magnificent centuries by Gurusinha, Ranatunga and Kaluwitharana, for 3 wickets in 13 balls by a young spinner named Shane, and as a shining example of Sri Lankan incompetence.

Having made Australia follow on, and chasing a target of 180 for an era-defying victory, Lanka slumped from 127–3 to fall short by 16 runs. It was a defeat of great immaturity. Many believe the match was fixed.

Aussie utility all-rounder Greg Mathews was awarded Man of the Match for his part in triggering the collapse. Another Mathew took a matchbag of 8–70, but received no mention by virtue of being on the losing side. It was the last game ever to be played at the Tyronne Cooray Stadium.

The Minister's Son

Ari trawls through hour upon hour of spool recordings, while Jabir stands by a broken-down Ford and looks at his watch. I am unable to be of much help as I cannot decipher anything aside from static and crackles.

'This was from one of the recordings titled "Canteen/Bar",' says Ari. 'Can you recognise the voices?'

De Kretser had mics in the scoreboard, the dressing rooms, the canteen bar and beneath the stumps. Last year, Jabir had assisted with rewiring them.

I am made to sit down in this air-conditioned garage and listen while Ari fiddles with screwdrivers. After hours of audio torture, we finally find something intelligible. Two voices. Both deep, both crude, one familiar, one not.

Why here of all places?
Because no one comes here. These fellows will be too drunk to remember anything.
They haven't played here since the Aussie test.
When was that? Two years ago?
Did you fix that game?
I don't fix obvious games, Mr MD.
Which ones do you fix?
Just the boring ones.
I'm not MD yet.
You will be. You have a good future. Drink?
I have to pick up my son. Price is OK?
Not enough. Luckily I found other sponsors. This time of year hard to organise.
You have to use suicide bomb? Can't use assassin?
For your budget? Suicide is the cheapest. They won't trace it back to you.
I don't want to kill civilians.
Nobody does.
When can you do it?
End of the month.
You should give me a discount.
Is that so?
You benefit from this more than me.
Really?
Don't pretend you don't.
The Jaffna library is ancient history. I don't hold grudges.
Who cares about libraries? He will close down all cricket betting. Maybe even nationalise the casinos.
That's just talk.
Is it?
The Minister is powerful, but he has no influence.
What about his son?
That fool. You want him done as well?
Can I get a buy-one-get-one-free?

I'm not selling soap.

He's gone mad. Last week he shot the mirror balls at the Blue Elephant. I don't want him to become a problem.

Ministers' sons are just like ministers. Easy to control if you have the right stick.

I can't believe you asked to meet me here. You're a strange fellow.

You want to hear something really strange…

Click…click…click…

Loose tape knocks the side of the machine. My ears feel like popping.

'Don't you recognise the voices?' asks Ari.

'Yes I do. They both belong to you.'

Ari has far too much time on his hands and a wonderful imagination. Bless the old fool.

Croc Dundee 2

It is important to reconstruct the events of Christmas and Boxing Day 1989, because they help answer two minor questions. Why the usually passive, shy Mathew lost his temper over the needlings of a Yorkshireman. And how he managed to end 1989 with the USLA New Year Queen as his new girlfriend.

In '89, Charith Silva shared the reserves bench with three lions or singhas, Hathurusinghe, Madurusinghe and Ranasinghe, and was yet to play his first test. Unlike other former Sri Lankan sportsmen I talk to, he does not give me excuses as to why he only played a handful of games for Sri Lanka.

'I didn't have the pace or the fire. And I wasn't very accurate. Don't put that in the article. Now I'm good. Pradeep told me not to bowl at the batsman, but to bowl at the mistake you want the batsman to make.'

The courtship of the USLA Queen took place over three nights: Christmas, Boxing and 31 December.

'That Shirali was going out with some Aussie dude. She was looking to be with a cricketer. Not a reserve.'

I.E. Kugarajah, who I will introduce you to soon enough, has a different view. 'I don't think she knew a ball about cricket. And she didn't need the money. I think she liked him because he was different. But I told him, forget looks, money, all are bullshit. To get women, you need to be strong. Finally he listened to me.'

Charith remembers his room-mate as messy and incurably lazy. 'On that tour he changed. I think all because of this girl. He stopped wearing batik shirts and rubber slippers. Was wearing Nike and Reebok. I don't know from where the money.'

When he wasn't bowling in the nets, Pradeep would be in his room watching cartoons or on the phone with a girl. But he would also disappear during certain evenings.

'That Shirali Fernando. Big fight after that poem business. I also didn't get to sleep.'

Charith cannot remember the details of this one-sided conversation, just that it began with Pradeep swearing and ended with them agreeing to just be friends.

Later Pradeep was seen sipping gin and lemonade and chatting to some of the prettier Bharathanatyam dancers at the East Melbourne Lions' Club Christmas party. 'I didn't even know that the bugger took liquor,' says Charith. 'These girls were drunk, easy to get. Even for us losers.'

The girls looked in their teens and called themselves the Sri Lankan United Tamil Sisters. 'We're the SLUTS and we're looking for a nice Tamil boy to corrupt,' slurred one of them.

Then Shirali arrived and Pradeep politely told the girls that they were meeting friends.

'Bloody fool,' says Charith. 'We could've had those sluts, but Pradeep obviously still had hopes.'

The crowd was a mixture of aunties, uncles and accents all in their Sunday best. The important and the beautiful flock around the big-name cricketers. Charith and Pradeep flock around Shirali and her group. To Charith, two things were clear. That Shirali had no interest in Pradeep other than as a little brother to bully. That Mathew could not handle his alcohol.

The Christmas Princess was crowned and it was Bronwyn Jones, friend of Shirali. A blonde Melbourne lass wearing a Kandyan sari. The protests from the crowd were good-natured and loud.

'Ado, why? Can't give one of our girls?'

'Why you're giving to a suddhi?'

'Machang, even at our own party, Aussies are thrashing us!'

According to Charith, while Bronwyn was undoubtedly sexy, the hottest BYT at the party was Shirali's other friend, Roshani Junkeer, a cleavage-flaunting vixen who sounded more Australian than the white girl.

'Who's the dark, handsome spunk, Shirls?'

Shirali introduced Pradeep to her friend and banter flowed. An hour later, after the GenCY delivered an after-dinner speech, Pradeep invited Charith to check out the Melbourne nightlife with Shirali, Bronwyn and Roshani. It was the first and probably last time that Charith left a party early with three women. He enjoyed the moment. 'All the seniors were looking at us. You should've seen Ravi de Mel's face. Like a pittu.'

The five of them scrambled into a taxi before team management could come to rain on proceedings by invoking the alcohol, drugs and sex ban (Item 3 on the Tour Rules). On the way, Shirali talked about how they were going to meet a guy called Larry who she thought was cute. Pradeep ignored Roshani, who was edging onto his lap with a stolen bottle of wine, while the Christmas Princess rubbed her bosom against Charith's arm.

'Uncle, I am not a fellow to cheat on my wife, no? Otherwise how many women I could've had?'

I look at Charith Silva's belly, man breasts and tennis ball haircut, and nod sympathetically.

They met this Larry character and decided to go and see the 10 o'clock showing of *Crocodile Dundee 2*. They were evicted twenty minutes into the movie when Roshani regurgitated her wine down the aisle. As they giggled their way out, the Samoan manager said, 'In this country, we don't go to cinemas drunk.'

By the time they got to the Bar Bodega and ordered tequila shots, Larry was holding Shirali's hand. Charith's descriptions of the gallons of alcohol they consumed and the chorus line of women who approached him for sex make me wonder if his words should also be taken with a pinch of salt and a squeeze of lime.

'Merv Hughes and Dean Jones also were there partying with us. One of the Aussies tried to camel Pradeep's BYT.'

I lose track of which one was Pradeep's BYT. 'The local one, Roshani. She goes off with Jones. Then Bronwyn, the beauty queen, sits on the bugger's lap. What a night!'

In the midst of proceedings, the Yorkshireman attempted to buy Bronwyn a drink. The blonde called him a 'paedophile' and slunk off with Pradeep. This may explain his belligerence at the next day's post-match presentation.

While waiting for a taxi at the end of the night, Charith, Pradeep, Larry and the three girls were accosted by two drunken skinheads.

Phrases like 'curry muncher', 'dairy owner', 'a thousand apologies', 'nargy bitch' and, inexplicably, 'nigger' were bandied about, not without malice. The night ended with the arrival of the taxi driver, but not before Charith was punched twice and Shirali spat at. Neither Larry nor Pradeep did anything.

The girls were dropped off at Shirali's place and the two reserves sneaked back into their hotel four hours after curfew. Mathew did not say a word all the way home. Team management did not find out.

Boxing Day

Pradeep was suspended and was due for a disciplinary hearing. While many players applauded him for telling off the Yorkshireman, senior members and management were less than impressed. No one knew of Christmas Day parties and brawls with skinheads the day before.

'Those days, we were the poor relations. No one would grant us games. Some years, we had to train 365 days to play one test,' laments Ravi de Mel. 'How to show the world that we are gentlemen, worthy of the gentleman's game, if fellows are talking like Maradana street thugs? Live on camera also. He was a typical Moratuwa thug. A tiger can't change its spots.'

They say bowling is the brainiest part of cricket. Ravi de Mel is not an example of that. He does not hide his contempt for Pradeep. 'I only recommended he be dropped. I don't believe in talent. Talent is nothing without effort. Give me a humble hard worker over a talented fool.'

Charith hadn't even heard of that day's Yorkshireman episode and was in bed when he received a phone call from an excited and drunk-sounding Mathew.

'Bugger was at the bar with girls. Madness, I told him. Management would massacre if we went out without leave on a match day.'

But leave without leave is what he did. He called the vice captain, saying he was unable to get through to the GenCY and the Skipper, and conveyed that both he and Pradeep were not feeling well and would be having an early dinner and resting.

At the Bar Bodega, Mathew looked like the Don. Not Bradman, but Juan. Roshani Junkeer on one arm, Bronwyn Jones on the other. There was a smattering of Sri Lankans at the bar, including Miss Sri Lanka and her date, who didn't look like a minister, but could have been the son of one.

Shirali Fernando was leaning on the lap of her new boyfriend, a tall curly-haired Australian called Larry. 'Charith Baba! Come drink, will you.'

The scene was good, but Charith was worried. The Bar Bodega was essentially a student bar, made to look like a working-class one. The faded pool tables, the battered jukebox, the peeling walls and the torn girly posters had been recently put in. Charith helped himself to a kiss and a squeeze from Bronwyn and Roshani and muttered to Pradeep, 'Machang, what if those skinheads come here?'

'Let them come,' smiled Pradeep.

And come they did. Four of them this time, at the nearby pool table. Dark jeans, big boots, black woollen jumpers, shaven heads. One had several strands of hair at the nape of his neck. He was the one who had thrown the punches the previous night. He was the one who noticed them while taking his shot.

'Strewth, it's the nargy club, back for some more, eh?'

Shirali's boyfriend got up from his stool. 'Steady on, mate…'

All four skinheads advanced with their cues. 'You fucking that curry bitch, mate?'

Larry pushed Shirali towards Charith and stood up to his full height. Charith drew the girls away and the other Sri Lankans at the bar looked on in horror, including Miss Sri Lanka and the boy who may have been the son of a minister.

The one with the pool cue pointed a finger in Larry's face, which went from pink to chalk. Pradeep stepped into the fray and stared up at the four men with little hair. The barman noticed and looked frantically for the bouncer. He spied him. Holding a pool cue with three of his mates, threatening a group of Asians.

I apologise for the language that follows. But this is the only bit of the story that Charith remembers word for word.

Pradeep employed his gruffest street urchin snarl. 'You guys are homos. You shave your heads because your dicks are too small, when you fuck each other.'

At first stunned silence, then a ripple of laughter wet the bar. What else? A skinny brown boy, standing behind a terrified white boy, questioning the sexuality of four stick-wielding, muscle-bound Nazis. If there was to be blood, and at that moment it looked a certainty that there would be, why not enjoy a moment of misplaced comedy?

'How did you end up like this? Your unemployed father raped you and dressed you up like a girl.' Mathew appeared to have practised his speech.

The leader took a while to process what was taking place. He shook his head. 'You smelly fucking curry…'

Mathew cut him off. 'You're the one who doesn't bathe, can't get a job, can't get a woman, can't…'

And then the smash and then the crash and the glass breaking over the head and the kicks and the punches and the shouted curses.

'I don't know where the bugger came from. I think he was with the Miss Sri Lanka crowd. He was dark and big and had a moustache. Looked like Prabhakaran himself.'

Just before the skinhead leader could break his cue over Mathew's head, the dark, stocky man smashed a glass jug into his face. As if it had been choreographed, Mathew began laying punches and kicks into the crouching leader. 'He looked like an ant hammering a horse,' laughs Charith. Two more jugs collided with skull as the dark, stocky man made quick work of the bouncer. The other two skinheads backed away. One of them tripped over a pool table on his way out.

Larry held back Pradeep, who was kicking the fallen skinhead. Both skinheads had stopped moving.

The dark, stocky man looked around. 'Everyone all right?' No one answered. He stared at Pradeep. 'Leave here now.' He then followed his own advice.

Larry drove Pradeep to the A&E, while the girls and Charith speculated as to who the dark man could have been. There were rumours that the West Australia Tamil Association harboured Tiger gunmen. Could this be one such sleeper? Could he be a neo-Nazi-hunting vigilante hired by the Mayor of Perth? Or was he just a drunk who landed a few lucky punches?

Pradeep had a hairline fracture in his index finger and a bruised rib. He removed his bandages as soon as he returned to the hotel. The next day his finger swelled up as he was called for the disciplinary hearing. He explained that his finger was injured taking the catch off David Boon. He blamed his conduct in the interview on being exhausted by the tour. Management decided to drop the matter, but a few players stored it away for future use.

Beauty Queen

On the day of the New Year's party, not only were the girls vying for the beauty crown, but also for the attentions of Mr Mathew. Roshani, Bronwyn and even the Miss Sri Lanka were seen speaking to him and playing with their hair.

'I remember, fellow was like a mouse,' exclaims Ravi de Mel. 'Suddenly, on this Australia tour, he is the ladies' man. Bugger didn't even play a single game. Even Aravinda, after scoring four centuries, wasn't as popular.'

'It was at the Perth New Year's party that I first noticed him,' says Serala de Alwis over the phone. 'He had a real I-don't-care-what-you-think-about-me look. He was awkward and clumsy, but there was something there.' Serala was a hotel exec and girlfriend of the vice captain.

The dancing round and the catwalk round had seen the exit of both Miss Sri Lanka and Miss Working Girl, much to the delight of a Sri Lankan expat crowd filled with drunk uncles and catty aunties. Everyone agreed that it was the question round that clinched it. 'If you were to win the prize, a trip to anywhere in the world, where would you go?'

Kahatuduwa Twin 1: 'Rio, for the carnival! Because I'm born to party!' (Applause.)

Serala de Alwis: 'Africa, 'cos it's wild and wonderful. Just like me!' (Cheers.)

Bronwyn Jones: 'That would have to be Bali. 'Cos I love lying on a golden beach with nothing on!' (Hoots. Shouts of 'Keeyada darling?')

Victoria the Bomb: 'Chile. 'Cos I'm hot!' (Applause and cheers.)

Natalie the Singer: 'Japan. Because that is where my boyfriend is.' (Boos. Shouts referring to Japanese manhood.)

Kahatuduwa Twin 2: 'I also like Rio. But since Nanga said that, I'll say somewhere different, like…Brazil.' (Laughter. Hoots.)

Penny who Ravi de Mel banged: 'Sri Lanka, mate. You guys are cool!' (Huge applause. 'Suddhi sucking up!')

Some skinny Lankan girl who spoke with a French accent: 'I would sell the ticket and give the money to the poor.' (Catcalls. 'Ado! This is not Miss World!')

The judges were a starlet from a TV soap called *Neighbours*, the Sri Lankan cricket captain and the FLC who, referring to an LBW decision in the Boxing Day test, said, 'One would say that there's no doubt that there's a lot of doubt about that.' And the president of the United Sri Lanka Association, Mr Upali Manu. The shout of 'Ado Manu, give Sri Lanka its first win!' echoed across the auditorium and was greeted with laughter.

The last contestant was indeed one of our girls. This girl had done reasonably well in the dance and catwalk rounds, by wearing a red

Spanish dress that pushed out her breasts and unveiled her legs. It was good, but probably not good enough to compete with the models and the foreign nudists. But her reply for the question round did more than bridge that gap.

'I wouldn't go too far at all. Melbourne, Australia.' (Boos. Hoots. Jeers.)

'Hold on, hold on. Let me finish. 1992. The MCG. World Cup final. Australia vs Sri Lanka. And Sri Lanka…kicks…Australia's...ASS!'

The applause and shrieks drowned out the DJ. It was slightly louder when Roshani Junkeer was given second runner-up and when Penny Something won first runner-up. And twice as loud when they announced the winner.

'May we all be at the MCG when Sri Lanka beats Australia,' said a slightly inebriated FLC. 'The USLA New Year Queen is Miss Shirali Fernando from Perth!'

Charith was in disbelief. 'Shirali was my friend. But she wasn't the sexiest there. But guess what happened then. I couldn't believe when I saw.'

'She was on Pradeep's lap with her crown and her sash,' says Uvais Amalean. 'A minute later they were smooching.'

'What happened to Larry?' Charith asked Roshani. Roshani shrugged and walked off in the direction of the Minister's son.

'Pradeep and I were both dropped after that tour,' says Charith.

Shirali used her winning ticket to return to Sri Lanka, to work as an investment consultant at Sampath National Bank and to be with her new boyfriend. 'I only helped that bugger get that bitch,' says Innocent Emmanuel Kugarajah, the man you are yet to meet. 'I am the one who put them together.'

Get together they did. And together they stayed. They were together three years later when, contrary to the 1989 USLA Queen's predictions, both Sri Lanka and Australia were knocked out in the first round of the '92 World Cup. There was no Melbourne Cricket Ground final between these countries. The kicking of the ass would have to wait four more years.

* * *

Seamer to the Fore

Charith Silva is Mr Reliable of Sri Lankan cricket. He has been a valued servant for the CCC over the 1998 season and was a supportive member of the 1996 world-conquering squad. Earlier this year he

> ripped through the SSC defence with medium-pace bowling described by a spectator as 'the best he'd ever seen'.
>
> Known for his dogged accuracy, Charith has added pace and swing to his armoury and physically is the fittest he has ever been. Still in his early thirties, this solid, capable…
> Excerpt © W.G. Karunasena
> Published in *Island* 20/9/98 and *Observer* 17/10/98

The Carrom Flick

Jack Iverson, the 1950s Aussie spinner, bent his middle finger as if he were flicking a leech off the ball. He held the ball with his elongated index and ring and flicked it at the batsman, the ball spinning in whichever direction his thumb pointed.

The GenCY, team manager during Sri Lanka's '87 World Cup campaign, shared a photograph of Iverson's unusual grip with Pradeep. Mathew also began to bowl with a carrom-flicking motion.

While Jack Iverson is remembered as a genuine mystery bowler by the likes of Benaud and Bradman, the GenCY failed to tell young Mathew that despite a few 6-wicket hauls in his first few outings, Iverson was soon worked out by batsmen. His fragile temperament kept him out of test cricket and led to his suicide in 1973.

Mathew tried the carrom flick vs England, Pakistan and the West Indies, and while the trajectory was torpedo-like, the bounce low and the turn sharp, Mathew's directional control was abysmal. Of the nine balls that made it to the pitch, all were adjudged wides.

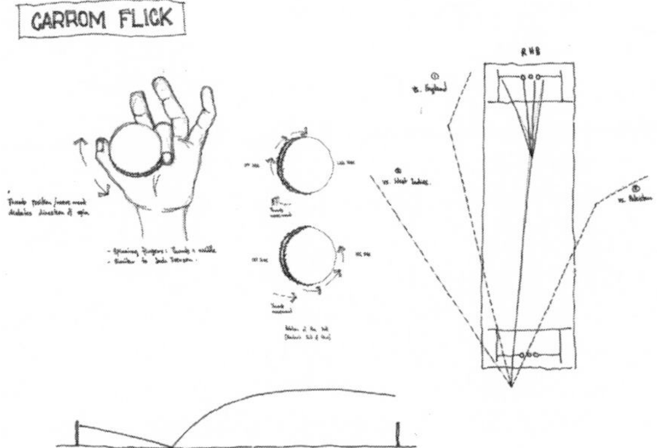

He was warned by the umpire of turning the game into a farce after the mid-wicket ball against Pakistan. And was taken out of the attack against England by the team captain for using that 'bloody carom bullshit'.

Different Rooms

Ari's office room and mine are roughly the same size. Mine is shaped like a D, his an imperfect square. Mine overlooks flowerpots and parapet walls, his looks over de Saram Road. Unlike his balcony, mine has no sea view. But every Sunday and poya holiday we get treated to a neighbourhood cricket match along our car-less street.

Sons of bloody bitches vs bastards from the seashore. I am sick of the taste of this thambili which I am supposed to sip. I cannot endure this saccharine spittle. Dear God. For the love of God. If you designed the liver, if you designed pain, I hate you. Are you the one who makes me shiver and sweat? This creature buried in my bowels. Is that you? I don't know why I'm talking to you. You don't even exist.

Breathe.

We watch through the grille as the youngest Marzooq boy bowls at pace to one of the boys from the beach. Our stretch of de Saram Road is wide and car-free; the Mount Lavinia Hotel traffic gets diverted at the S-bend.

'That boy chucks. Street cricket is ruining his technique.'

'What are you saying?' pounces Ari. 'Street cricket is our grassroots, it must be nurtured, treasured.' He shouts through the window. 'Well bowled, Tariq!'

He turns to me. 'I have a theory. A hunch.' Ari is not wearing the raincoat, but he is using the bulto voice.

'About?'

'Shirali Fernando, girlfriend of Mathew. She is either his wife or they have broken up. She is either here or abroad.'

'Superb theory. She is either alive or dead?'

On the street the beach boy thwacks the ball over the bowler's head. A catch is fumbled, a run-out attempted, a non-striker doubling as umpire shakes his head. There is shouting.

Ari continues stating the obvious. 'She will hold the key to where Mathew is. Why he disappeared.'

'This is your hunch?'

Ari has many theories and hunches about the way things are and how they should be. And 90 per cent of them are excrement.

Ari believes, for example, that if Mr BenevolentDictator had stayed alive, there would be no homeless people. I disagree.

'I was in Gampaha in '89,' I say, frowning at the memory of young corpses swinging from burning tyres. 'I don't think he was very benevolent.'

'But he achieved goals. People like winners, regardless of how evil they are. I bet even if a tyrant ended this damn war, we'd praise him as a hero.'

'Our people will never sort this out. Maybe the Americans can help us get rid of the LTTE. If only we had oil here.'

'Are you mad, Wije? Don't talk like an utter buffoon.'

'If the world has to have a class monitor, better America than Russia or China.'

'You don't know what crap you are talking. America are the worst devils. They have colonised our minds. Next they will colonise our stomachs. What if they colonise our sports?'

'Ah?'

'What if they take over everything and turn cricket into baseball, rugby into American football, replace hoppers with hamburgers?'

'I think you are the man talking the crap.'

My theories are less crass and less alarmist. But I believe them to be true. It takes three generations for a curse to be lifted and for the sins of a nation to be erased. If we are the generation that soiled this country, the mess should be cleaned up and sins forgiven by the time Garfield's children are voting age.

I believe the history of the world can be explained by climate. Year-round sunshine makes you want to sit under trees or dance in loincloths. Bitter winters make you want to invent heaters and guns and sail to warmer climes and scalp natives. The comfortable get docile, the uncomfortable get busy. Which is why, after centuries of European dominance, the pendulum has started to swing towards overpopulated Asia.

Ari strolls away from the window. His room is as dusty and overpopulated with junk as mine. But unlike mine, his is ordered into shelves, cabinets and stacks.

'So what's this hunch?'

'My hunch is based on observation and deduction.'

'Seduction? At your age?' Best to match idiocy with silliness.

Ari flips out a school monitor's textbook covered in brown paper. He flips the pages. 'I know who Shirali Fernando is.'

'Splendid. Shall we call her over for thambili?'

'What we know about Shirali is she was plump and pretty. When did Charith say they broke up?'

'Around '94.'

'Unmarried women tend to lose weight in their thirties. So let us drop the plump bit.'

He flips a few more pages. The Bogart accent has disappeared. 'Harini Diyabalanage, friend and one-time confidante, mentioned migration to Australia. Possible marriage. Or that she was, I quote, "working for the Cricket Board".'

'I don't remember her saying that.'

'You were too busy flirting with her.'

'You were letting her kids choo on your floor.'

Ari has the grace to smile. For a loudmouth, he has a grace that is enviable. His first wife Norma, mother of Rochelle, Michelle, Stephanie and Melissa, was killed by a wayward bus in 1978. He managed the family for three years, even missed the 1980 Royal–Thomian for the first time in five decades to take little Stephanie for an athletics meet in Kandana. The reason, Ari believes, why Thora didn't win that year.

In '81, he dealt with the fallout when he brought home holy Manouri, held the stable together amid fights and screaming matches, and became a father again at fifty-three. Great man, good friend, terrible detective.

'Worked at Cricket Board, pretty…' says Ari, now pinching his lip like Poirot.

'Or lives in Australia, plump,' says I.

'Remember our meetings with the SLBCC? Did you notice Danila's face every time Mathew was mentioned? Of course not, you were looking at her boobs. But I, my dear Wije, notice everything.'

I let him ramble and wonder whether I should mention a meeting at the Cricket Café and tears shed. I decide not to, because right then, Ari unveils his hunch.

'When we had that fight with Newton at that wedding, do you remember who Mathew was with?'

'Mohammad Azharuddin and some girl.'

'Do you remember what the girl looked like?'

'No.'

'I do. My dear Wije...Danila Guneratne…is…Shirali Fernando.'

Right then a ball is thwacked into Ari's window leaving a spider web of cracks. Then the nurturer of grassroots street cricket runs out into the street, screaming, and confiscates the ball.

Duckworth–Lewis

The Duckworth–Lewis method of resolving rain-affected games has divided the cricketing fraternity into those who do not understand it and those who pretend they do. Rumour has it that it involves calculus, astrology, quantum mechanics and the use of dice. Either way teams get screwed.

90 per cent Excrement

Ari believes:

1. That urinating on your feet can cure toe jam.
2. That Sri Lanka is a failed nation and will take more than three generations to heal.
3. That Sri Lanka's World Cup win of 1996 was merely a run of good form that lasted a few months.
4. That his daughters were all virgins on their wedding nights.
5. That Mr OldSchoolTie of the 1980s and Ms 2ndGeneration of the 1990s were worse leaders of Sri Lanka than Mr Benevolent Dictator.
6. That Sri Lanka cannot be considered a great cricketing nation till we consistently win test matches abroad.
7. That God is great and everything happens for a reason.
8. That the north should be given to the Tigers. But not the east.
9. That the Australians play good, hard cricket and it is unfair to demonise them.
10. That Pradeep Mathew was the greatest cricketer to ever walk the Earth.

To paraphrase Meat Loaf, 1 out of 10 is not bad.

Konde Bandapu Cheena

The term 'konde bandapu cheena' means a 'ponytailed Chinaman' and is a Sinhalese expression for someone gullible. 'Go tell that to the konde bandapu cheena.' The implication being that the said oriental will believe anything. 'You think I'm a Chinaman with a ponytail?'

To accuse the Chinese, who invented paper and gunpowder and built great walls and forbidden palaces, of being stupid is itself an exercise in stupidity. Like our technology, our racist stereotypes are decades, sometimes centuries, out of date. In the 1950s, prosperous post-war Ceylonese would refer to slums and shanties as Koreawas. Those days when we were a paradise, we looked down upon our impoverished, war-torn neighbours. I once caught Sheila using the expression some five years after Korea staged the Olympics.

Is this a story about a pony-tailed Chinaman bowler? Or a tale to go tell a pony-tailed Chinaman? That is for you to decide.

Checkpoint

Attidiya is beautiful at 8.30 on a Sunday morning. The sunlight is amber, the rooftops glisten and the road is not blocked by jostling metal snails. I sit in Jabir's red trishaw watching shops and palm trees disappear into narrow lanes. We bump along at 30 kph listening to the sound of horns not blaring. It is too early for the sea breeze to be stifled by the descending heat.

I feel better than I did when I awoke. The creature is asleep in my skull, curled like a banana-drunk monkey. He refuses to leave till I slake his thirst. His presence stifles all thought, allowing only fury to enter in bursts.

The last two months have been difficult and though it is getting better, it can hardly get worse. Garfield has abandoned his wife and child and is now in London as an illegal alien. So much for the Sinhala New Year.

Jonny's Flowery Broken Orange Pekoe is hardly a comfort. To expect it to douse my cravings is like trying to put a forest fire out by urinating on it. I'm not on my way to ask Jonny for more tea. I am going to get his permission to have just one shot. It will not be easy.

Sheila has borne the brunt of my petulance. It is she who glues together the broken pieces and feeds me on cracked plates. She tells me she has seen worse and reminds me of angrier times. Of my sacking from the *Daily News* and my falling out with my brothers. It is hard to defend yourself against crimes you cannot remember. Sadly for me, after my first bottle amnesia sets in. Sheila says I behaved like an animal; I take her word.

Ari arrives each morning with new revelations from the midget's spools. He tells me he has a recording of the SLBCC chief instructing the umpires during the Pakistan series. He plays it to me, but all I hear are indistinct croaks.

Today he tells me he has two English bowlers chatting about sharing bathtubs with Maldivian call girls. The creature hisses in my ear as Ari prepares to play the spools. It is a slow hiss that reaches unbearability in minutes. I tell Ari I have to see Jonny and refuse to let him come with me. Ari slips Jabir some money and instructs him not to take me to the tavern.

Jabir hoiks red spit onto the pavement and moves at the speed of a tractor. He keeps chewing the betel which will keep rotting his teeth.

'Jabba. Tell the truth. This Neiris Uncle thing is bullshit, no?'

'Then why is Wije Sir writing about it?'

'I'm not.'

Jabir looks at me in the mirror above his windscreen. I see his bloodshot eyes framed by a reflecting rectangle. The frame crops out his mosque cap and his betel-stained grin.

'I have known Neiris Uncle for so many years. He's not drunk, not mad, he just loves cricket.'

'Most people who love Sri Lankan cricket are drunk and mad. Look at me.' Jabir turns around and almost misses the policeman with his arm out.

'Oi! Stop. Stop.'

A decade ago, the Jerry Lewis of the Sri Lankan stage, Nihal Silva, creator of bald, bumbling Sergeant Nallathamby, a marginally racist creation, amusing if you like watalappan-in-the-face humour, was shot by soldiers after driving through a checkpoint. Some say he was too drunk to see the checkpoint and to know what hit him.

Colombo has become a city of camouflage and guns. When exactly it went from town by the sea to city under siege is unclear. Possibly, not too long after the LTTE's suicide attack in April 1987 that killed 113 and cut short a potentially enthralling New Zealand tour.

It crept up on all of us. Metal, sandbags and virgins with rifles took over Colombo's junctions while LTTE bombs took out the Central Bank and an Indian prime minister. They also took out civilians by the hundreds and destroyed a whole generation of Sri Lankan leaders, which included the Minister for Cricket.

'ID please. Can you get out of the vehicle?'

The cop's limbs are thinner than the rifle he holds. I do not recall ever seeing a checkpoint or a cop with a rifle on Attidiya Lake before.

'Where are y'all going?'

'Airport Road.'

'For what?'

'Meeting a friend.'

The cop is assisted by two men in white shirts and black slacks next to a parked Land Rover. The henchmen search the three-wheeler and ruffle through my satchel.

'These are CID men?' I ask the cop.

'What is it to you what they are?' barks the cop.

They let us carry on.

Jabir utters a filthy phrase that contains the words sperm and dog and translates poorly. 'Army are not rude like that. These buggers were looking for a bribe.'

We curse the government along the road to the Ratmalana Airport and Jabir tells me how Neiris Uncle's saasthara woman concocted a charm from Slave Island, which she buried under the pitch.

'So that's why we never lost on that ground?'

'Remember that record-breaking match? Neiris Uncle put charms on the bowler's run-up.'

'And I suppose during the last World Cup, he put them all over the pitch and scared away Australia and West Indies?'

'Must be.'

I slap the back of Jabir's mosque hat. 'No use going to mosque if you're lying like this.'

He grins, spits red, and rides off with two of my 100 rupee notes. It is only when I enter Jonny's house that I realise my satchel is missing.

Nineteen Eighty-two

Some people read tea leaves, some palms. I can tell a lot about a person from their taste in football games.

The 1982 FIFA World Cup was the first time Jonny, Ari and I drank together. Here are our favourite games:

Jonny: Hungary 10–El Salvador 1
Ari: Italy 3–Brazil 2
Me: West Germany 1–Austria 0

Jonny's game was the biggest thrashing in the history of the sport, a goal every nine minutes. It was light-hearted and fun, like the man himself.

Ari's game was a clash of greatness. Italy, led by Rossi, coming off a two-year match-fixing ban, knocked out Maradona's Argentina *and* Zico's Brazil to whack the cup. It was an intense game, savoured by purists, of which Ari is definitely one.

My game was the most disgraceful of the tournament. Group B

was well poised with three teams – Algeria, Germany and Austria – tied on points. Only two could qualify and the odds favoured Algeria. A draw or an Austrian win would have sent them and Austria to the next round. A 2-goal German win would have sent them and Germany to the quarters. In the last game of the group stage, both German-speaking nations mysteriously settled for a 1–0 win, the only result that would qualify them both and exclude the more deserving Algeria.

Both teams spent the second half kicking the ball around and refusing to attack. Flabbergasted, the crowd jeered, Algerians in the stadium began burning German flags and waving money at the players. It was a farce of a match, but it was also perversely compelling. The same fascination that makes me stare at road accidents and peek at my hanky after blowing my nose.

The other two think I am slightly mad for picking this game. They may be right.

Carrom Game

I am smoking a cigarette. It is the compromise. I can smoke a cigarette if I keep drinking the tea. Jonny doesn't argue or lecture or smile, he just gives it to me straight.

'You drink, you die. You don't drink, you feel like shit. The trick is to not drink and not feel like shit. This you do by keeping busy. Do your book, seduce your wife, go for walks, watch cricket.'

'It doesn't work.' I have tears in my eyes. Tears that neither my wife, nor my son, nor my best friend, nor Jesus Almighty has been able to extract from me. Before this giant homosexual in a Newcastle jersey I feel neither shame nor fear.

Jonny watches me powder his varnished carrom board. 'You need to change addictions.'

'I preferred your old place. This house is stuffy.'

'You must find another pleasure that helps you transcend. Meditation. Swimming. Marijuana.'

'Did you have to sell Bolgoda?'

'They put dead rats in my letter box. Threw rocks at my windows. How long before a drunk with a cup of acid broke in?'

'At least you've still got your TV.'

Acid is the weapon of choice of jilted men in this part of the world. It requires a cold-blooded sadism that is as horrific as the disfigurement it causes. I liked it better when we were discussing kakka gangsters.

'How about just one drink?'

'It's never just one drink.'

I wipe my eyes and miss an easy shot. 'I can control it this time. I don't want to exercise or smoke ganja.'

'How about cigarettes?'

After the fifth game and third cigarette, the compromise seems bearable. We discuss Sri Lanka's tour to England, my worthless son and Jonny's month in a Bangkok prison, though he does not tell me for what. It's not quite Bolgoda, but it's all right.

Pork Chops

Who would you rather be? Muhammad Ali or George Foreman?

In 1974, after the Rumble in the Jungle in Zaire, there was only one answer to that. Ali, back from wrongful suspension, dismissed as a spent force, destroyed Foreman, the malfunctioning cyborg, in a battle mythologised beyond redemption. 'It's a divine fight,' said Ali at the time. 'This Foreman represents Christianity, America, the Flag. I can't let him win. He represents Pork Chops.' There is prophecy in that last sentence.

Fast forward two decades to '94. Foreman regains the World Heavyweight title at forty-five, while Ali, crippled by Parkinson's, can barely give an interview, let alone step in a ring.

Foreman, made wise by his youth, hangs up his boxing gloves and picks up his oven mitts and markets the George Foreman Grill™, a phenomenon for the fat-free infomercial generation that bought its eponymous owner more wealth and fame than 76 wins and 68 knockouts.

Who would you rather be? The man who suffers first and laughs last? Or the man who suffers now, but will forever be known as The Greatest?

The Second Note

Jonny was right. It was the keeping busy that silenced the creature. I had replaced the classified ad in the *Sunday Observer*. I had classified all Mathew's balls from Ari's notebooks. I had written about Neiris, Shirali and the show that no one saw. The monkey on my back stayed quiet, the chip on my shoulder felt less heavy.

I notice a man standing outside Jonny's, smoking a cigarette. At first I think he is a spy for Jonny's prosecutors. I make up my mind to warn Jonny and ask him exactly how much trouble he is in. But I forget.

Then I see the man again on the bus, reading a copy of the *Sunday Observer*. I realise that (a) the man is familiar, and (b) it is Friday.

I return home ready to build a cathedral with words. Unafraid of the gargoyles that tell me it won't play, disobedient to the creature that haunts my thirst, drowning in tea, steaming in cigarette smoke. Sheila brings in a letter and sniffs at the air.

'I didn't drink. I'm not going to drink. So let me smoke.'

'I didn't say anything.' I hear her voice break and I want to hug her and say I'm sorry and that I'll try and be better, but of course I don't. I tear the envelope and recognise the computer font.

We enjoyed the documentary.
We would like to speak with you.
When can we pick you up?

It takes us a while to locate the first note in my mess of a room. Ari finds a siri-siri bag with the word Cargills crossed out and labelled 'Exhibit A' in black felt pen beneath my pile of *Cricketer* magazines. We compare. It is a match.

I call up Harini Diyabalanage and ask her what Shirali looked like. She describes straightened hair, short skirts and a shapely rear. I agree with Ari that it describes Danila Guneratne. And one-third of Colombo's female population.

The phone rings as soon as I replace it. Perhaps Harini can oblige with a strawberry-shaped birthmark. On an inner thigh perhaps. Now I am fantasising. How completely undignified.

'My boys will pick you up at Vihara Maha Devi Park tomorrow afternoon.'

The voice is gruff, hurried and familiar.

'Who are your boys?'

'You've met them. Come alone. Don't bring the schoolteacher or the homo.'

'Who are you?'

'Pradeep Sivanathan made me a lot of money in the 1992 test. You know the one I'm talking about.'

I cannot think of anything to say.

'2.30 tomorrow. Come alone.'

Click.

America's Favourite Pastime

Hard to believe, but in the mid-nineteenth century, cricket was America's favourite team sport. Cricket clubs flourished in over twenty-two states and the sport's first international game took place not between England and Australia in 1877, but between Canada and the US in 1844. True fact.

Around the 1880s, sporting goods maker A.G. Spalding spread the myth of baseball being invented by US civil war heroes. Baseball was positioned as an honest game for rugged Americans, regardless of the game's true origins, five centuries earlier, at the hands of medieval French monks. Cricket, by default, became the dull sport of English snobs and retreated from the American imagination. Meanwhile Spalding, a spin doctor long before the term was invented, sold a lot of baseball equipment.

Baseball, with its innings, its outs, its home runs and its pichers, is to cricket what Christianity is to Catholicism, or what Islam is to Judaism. Similar to the naked eye, and when put under a microscope, really not all that dissimilar. Despite violent cries, on both sides, to the contrary.

Innocent Emmanuel

Blindfolded, in the back seat of the white van, I ask for a cigarette. Not unlike a man facing a firing squad. There are mutterings in crude Tamil, the voice nearest to me places a hand on my shoulder. 'Come up front, Uncle. These windows don't work.'

My blindfold is an airline sleep mask and it sits over my eyebrows. I can dislodge it at any time, but I am urged not to. A lit cigarette is placed between my lips, I am nudged forward and pressed against the breeze. I hear no birds, no horns, no chatter, no traffic, just the rumble of our tyres navigating a bumpy road.

You are about to meet I.E. Kugarajah aka Emmanuel aka Kuga, the man you will not believe exists. Are you excited? Or are you, as I was, uncomfortable?

My feet hurt from hobbling across Vihara Maha Devi Park, my tongue is numb from sucking on an ice palam. I had spent the morning surveying the merry-go-rounds and the pony rides, trying to spot policemen wearing cloaks and carrying daggers. Named after one of Sri Lankan history's many matriarchs, the park has a golden Buddha statue at the entrance that turns its back on the scattered games of rubber ball cricket and the couples touching each other under flowering trees.

My glasses tint in the sun so I can observe the park without it observing me. I see balls being hit across pathways and breasts being fondled under umbrellas. Like our reefs and our forests, the sun is another blessing we take for granted in this ungrateful country. One day, it too may be gone. I expect men in uniform to point a gun at my kidneys and usher me into a jeep. Instead I get two sarong johnnies in cream shirts, both of whom are familiar. 'Come with us, Uncle.' As if they are prefects leading me to a sports meet.

I hesitate at the step of the Delica van. If threatened, I could hit them with my cane. The driver, dark and bearded, resembles the cop who stopped me yesterday. The passenger wears a T-shirt and gold chains.

The passenger speaks. 'Don't worry, Uncle. You can get in.'

I am helped into the last of three rows of weathered seating. All the back windows are tinted. I am handed an airline mask.

'Why must I wear this?'

'Everyone wears it,' says the passenger. 'Those are the rules. Uncle doesn't know me?'

'You stole my bag.'

'That's all? I have delivered letters to you. I have taken your bets. You have lit my cigarette at the Kaanuwa.'

Kalu Daniel looks different without his hair or his handlebar moustache.

'When did you take my bets?'

'When I ran the Neptune. You used to come there a lot. Please put on the mask.'

'Who are these boys?' I ask as I cover my vision with soft polyester.

'These are my boys. This is Sudu. That is Chooti.'

I peek through my blindfold. Chooti is a giant, Sudu is as black as a crow's rectum.

'Keep your mask on.'

'Sorry. Why does it smell of kerosene in here?'

There are sniggers.

'Don't misunderstand, Uncle. Have you had lunch?'

The tone is cordial, though I suppose I should feel threatened.

'Who did I talk to on the phone?'

'Boss called you personally.'

As I finish my cigarette, I can feel the road smoothing out, but still no background noise. My unreliable sense of time tells us we have been travelling for twenty minutes. Not enough time for us to exit Colombo on a Saturday afternoon.

The van takes some turns. The radio is switched on and I hear film music, though I cannot discern the language. With Sinhala and Tamil cinema aping Bollywood, everything sounds like a copy of a copy.

'Uncle is fully recovered?'

'From?'

'You were in hospital, no?'

'Ah. Yes. Much better. Thank you.'

'That is good.'

The van stops, the sliding door jerks open, I am led out crouching and my blindfold is lifted. They push me inside a doorway while my eyes get accustomed to the sun. The stairs are coated in red polish and the windows are grilled. The hall is all pot plants and paintings. I am shown into a room, a large room where light falls through an open balcony.

In the centre of the room, I see a padded swivel chair facing a wall and the top of a man's head. The room has a polished desk and a framed picture of Ms 2ndGeneration, present ruler of the land. A large plasma screen TV is playing my documentary on Pradeep Mathew.

Brian's voice: 'Mathew's best international bowling performance took place at Asgiriya in 1987...'

The chair swivels around and a chubby man in shorts with a moustache as dark as his skin, stares me down. On his lap is my satchel.

'Sit.'

I take the cane chair by the doorway and get a glimpse out of the window. The house opposite is a similar colonial-style cottage, all trellises and verandas and araliya trees.

'It's hard to believe this is Colombo, no?' says the man in the chair. 'Danny, ask Selva to make some lime juice. You stopped drinking, no, Uncle?'

I nod. Everything in the room is an antique, aside from the laptop on the desk and the screen showing Rakwana Somawardena talking to the camera.

'Hope you don't mind if I put a shot.'

'How did you get this documentary?'

'I taped it. I taped all of your films.'

'It was on a powercut night.'

Like Jonny, he throws his head back when he laughs.

'This street isn't affected by powercuts.'

I raise myself with my stick and look out onto the balcony. The road outside snakes into a series of dead ends like the arms of an octopus.

'This is Malabe?'

'Sit, Karunasena.' He points his remote at the plasma screen. 'Who paid for this?'

'We did.'

'You and Byrd?'

'And Graham Snow.'

'Not SwarnaVision?'

'Initially it was the SLBCC and ITL, then we funded, then SwarnaVision…'

'You spent your life savings on this?'

'We had some lucky investments.'

'I heard. The Neptune, no? That was a badly run place.'

'Was it?'

A man dressed like a waiter brings in drinks on a trolley. The man called Daniel pours me lime juice from a flask and fixes two Scotches.

'Danny. Have you recovered the losses?'

'Not yet, boss, shipment getting delayed…'

'Don't fuck around, ah? Minister is coming on Monday. You better have it sorted.'

I look at both of them. 'You work for the government?'

'Doesn't everyone?' says my host taking a sip. Daniel smiles.

'I have never seen a Johnny Walker Silver Label.'

'This is not Scotch, ah? Johnny Walker does an exclusive line of white arrack. Not available in Sri Lanka. Not available anywhere. In vain you gave up. Shall I add a bite to your lime?'

I shake my head and sip. The lime juice is filled with crushed ice and sugar syrup and is perhaps the finest non-alcoholic beverage I've ever tasted. Daniel scurries away to the balcony. The man in the chair watches me sip.

'Selva does the best lime juice in Asia. I picked him up in Chennai, then known as Madras.'

'Who are you?'

'My name is Innocent Emmanuel Kugarajah. I am quite positive you have never heard of me. That, Mr Karunasena,' he smiles, 'is the last question you will ask today.'

He closes my satchel. His voice has deepened.

'I repeat. Who commissioned and funded a documentary on Pradeep Sivanathan?'

'No one. I decided to do it. Ari and Brian agreed to help me.'

'Why?'

'Why did they help me?'

'Why did you do it?'

'Are you finished with my bag?'

Dilup Makalande's soundtrack to the show that no one saw invades the silence. The stocky man shakes awake.

'Of course, here.' He leans forward and places it on the low antique table between us. To call it a coffee table would be to describe a Stradivarius as a banjo.

'It was very interesting. I even understood some of those diagrams. You and your friend are cricket fanatics, no?'

I drain my glass.

'Do you work for the Cricket Board?'

'No,' he says. 'Do you?'

'What can I do for you?'

'I would like to know why you're putting ads, making documentary films and writing in notebooks about my friend who was apparently killed three years ago?'

'Because I saw him taking 10 wickets for 51 runs at Asgiriya in 1987.'

His beady eyes pop out of his chubby head. He leans forward.

'You saw that?'

I certainly did.

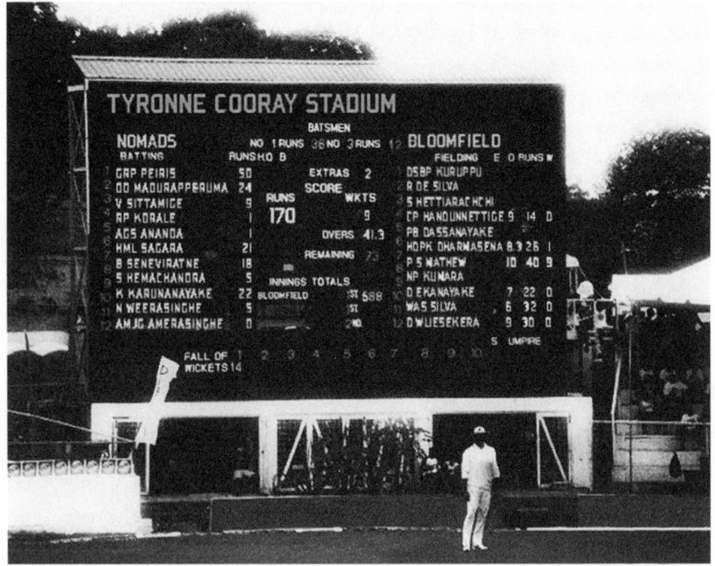

The Asgiriya Test

The first test of the 1987 New Zealand tour was known as the Kuruppu test, due to the aforementioned wicketkeeper-batsman spending every minute of it on the field. The match was as dreary as Kuruppu's unbeaten 201, the first double century by a Sri Lankan, quite possibly the dullest innings ever. Stretched over 778 soggy minutes, it remains the slowest double century in history.

Kuruppu was dropped on 31, 70, 165 and 181 and scooped most of his runs from pushing into the covers with his bottom hand. Then the Kiwis got in on the action with Hadlee and Jeff Crowe adding two equally yawn-worthy centuries as the match lurched to a non-climax. Days later, a car bomb at the Colombo central bus station killed 113 and wounded 300. The LTTE had struck at the heart of Colombo for neither the first nor the last time, as New Zealand cricket would find out again five years later.

In 1992, the exploding motorbike that disposed of Navy chief Clancy Kobbekaduwa in front of the touring team's hotel, landed body parts quite literally at the feet of the horrified Kiwis. Gavin Larsen, another medium pacer who could bat a bit, almost trod on a severed hand. That tragedy splintered the New Zealand team, with five players and manager Wally Lees returning home and Sri Lanka trouncing a weakened Kiwi outfit.

1987's bomb had no such compromise. As soon as the death count of Colombo's then biggest tragedy hit the headlines, the New Zealanders had their bags packed. It was the coaxing of the Minister that convinced them to play a second test in Asgiriya.

Three reasons: the Minister was instrumental in the construction of this stadium in the hills and guaranteed a closed event with tight security; the Minister was also instrumental in NZ dairy exporter Anchor's near monopoly of the local milk powder market; the Minister had a beguiling smile that was difficult to refuse.

The second test was closed to the public and only selected members of the press were invited. I then worked for the *Sun*, a short-lived tabloid that made up in free tickets what it lacked in print quality. I received an invitation to cover the match and I took Ari along as my photographer.

We were body-searched and stripped of our alcohol. Our stand was populated by the press and the players' guests. The pavilion was filled with politicians and VIPs, the stands around the players' dressing rooms were empty, and the rest of the stadium was bare.

These were the days before multiple cricket channels. Even school games and club matches attracted half-full stadiums. To see a test match in a cricket-starved nation played before an empty stadium was farcical. As was the notion that the Liberation Tigers of Tamil Eelam would want to assassinate curly-haired medium pacers from Waipukarau.

The Asgiriya pitch was not expecting call-up for international duties that year and had been hosting U-13 matting encounters between Trinity and St Anthony's. The surface had only three days' preparation, a fact kept from the already nervous New Zealanders.

The press box had a lone fax machine, a few typewriters and three dust-ridden overhead fans. There was a bar that served warm beer and a bird's eye view of the pitch. The commentary boxes upstairs sent rumbles across the ceiling. The usual suspects spread themselves across empty chairs and absorbed the action.

As members of the press, we were informed that this test was a goodwill game between the SLBCC and the NZCB and was yet to be officially recognised by the ICC. That due to the prevalent situation in the country, our match reports would have to be approved by the government censor.

'Cricket in Czechoslovakia must be like this,' said Ari as we took our assigned seats with a who's who of NZ sportswriting called this not for their fame or infamy, but because neither Ari nor I knew who was who.

New Zealand played an unchanged XI, while Sri Lanka replaced spinner Anurasiri and paceman Kurupparachchi with spinner Mathew and paceman Ramanayake. The first session proved a fascinating contest. Accurate bowling by the two Ratnayakes matched by cautious defence by Franklin and Jones. Pradeep Mathew came on just before lunch and made Jones jump in the way of a darter. He then dispensed of Horne with a googly.

The tourists went to lunch at 73–2 and we were informed that the ICC had officially bestowed test match status on this game. Invigorated by the buffet, the Kiwis came out guns blazing. Future rivals Crowe Jr and Turner, the wine and cheese man and the beer and pie man, hit our medium pacers out of the attack and within half an hour the score was 111 for 2. Captain Mendis tossed the ball to Pradeep Mathew, whose figures stood at 2–47.

What followed was the finest spell of spin bowling or any bowling, on this or any other planet, that I or anyone else could ever have seen.

Turner taunted the young chinaman bowler by imitating his ungainly action as he tossed the ball back to mid-on. Pradeep, unperturbed, returned to his mark with intent on his face. He adjusted his headband. He rolled up his sleeves as if to commit a long premeditated act of violence. He stumbled in to bowl three perfect googlies which Crowe read and avoided. On the fourth ball, Crowe attempted a cut, only to find the ball reversing onto his stumps.

With the new batsman, Mathew shifted to orthodox spin. The flight and drift were perfect, the ball curling just out of the batsman's reach. The trajectory was like a whip in mid-crack. By 1987, Mathew was not a stranger to Ari and me, though we were unaware he had weapons like the boru ball, responsible for Crowe Sr and Evan Gray's demises.

New Zealand 113 for 5. Turner knocked Gurusinha for a few boundaries at the other end, but made the fatal error of taking a single on the last ball. He faced Mathew who dished out an unplayable finger spinner, followed by the undercutter, the ball backspinning and staying low. Turner kicked the pitch in annoyance and said something unprintable to the bowler.

Mathew bowled him a chinaman and a googly, both of which he saw out.

Then out of nowhere a medium-paced leaper rose off the pitch and smashed into Turner's hook nose. The batsman advanced down the pitch and had to be restrained.

We watched in stunned silence as carrom flicks and darters were mixed in with stock deliveries. The variation was mesmerising, the control exquisite. Hadlee, Bracewell and Sneddon scatterd like hacked limbs as Mathew raced to his eighth wicket. Palitha Epasekera mentioned the words 'world record' and everyone in the press box became excited. Mathew's 8–50 was well ahead of the then Sri Lankan record, Ravi Ratnayake's 8–83 vs Pakistan.

'This is an upset,' said the Kiwi journalist with the beak.

'Just because you're upset doesn't make it an upset,' grinned Ari, snapping his flashing camera at ten-minute intervals.

The former Sri Lankan record holder himself stood at mid-on and shared a kind word with the bowler. The Sri Lankan field crowded the batsmen as Mathew sent down consecutive maidens. The shadows of the surrounding hills tickled the boundary line and the New Zealand team stood outside their dressing room in various degrees of agitation. Turner got a single. Smith fended off a looping chinaman. Then he bowled it.

It pitched wide off leg, like a misplaced carrom ball, cut onto the off stump, then darted back into the stumps. The double bounce ball, cricket's most magnificent creation. There was a loud boo from the New Zealand dressing room. Last man Chatfield swung at a top spinner, an edge flew by keeper Kuruppu, and they got a single.

Turner patted the wicket with the bat and shouted to the dressing room. 'This pitch is fucked!' Mathew then bowled another double bounce ball, this time turning from off to leg to take the middle stump. Turner stormed off in disgust.

New Zealand slumped from 111 for 2 to 117 all out. Mathew's figures sat plainly on the scoreboard. 10–51. Two better than Jim Laker. There was jubilation in the press box as the players went in for tea. This wasn't like Kuruppu's slow double hundred. This was a real world record.

But all joy is fleeting. The New Zealanders refused to take the field after tea, calling the pitch 'a shocker'. Intense discussions followed on the field between New Zealand tour management and the umpires. The Minister himself came down from the VIP stand to a standing ovation. The two captains were called and without pomp or ceremony the match was abandoned, as was the New Zealand tour.

The Minister gave an impromptu press conference minus anyone who was actually on the field. 'The pitch has been deemed unsuitable…'

The three sessions of play were declared null and void. We were told that any paper publishing a match report would have its licence revoked. We looked on forlornly as history was erased. Cricket in Czechoslovakia indeed. It was the match that would never exist.

Asgiriya would have to wait six more years to host another test match. Today there is no record of the record, even in *Wisden*. There is no record of a second test match taking place. But everyone who was there knows what they saw. And for once, Ari and I agree. Whatever the reason for New Zealand's collapse, it had very little to do with the pitch.

Wicketkeeper Conundrum

The fielder clad in armour who squats behind the batsman should be respected as a specialist and not treated as a dabbler. The wicketkeeper controls the mood around the pitch. His gloves hold most of the catches, his voice accompanies every appeal. He is the factory foreman, responsible for every ball.

In the early days, cricket valued its specialists. A wicketkeeper, like an opening bowler, was never expected to contribute with the bat. Times have changed.

Today, selectors face a wicketkeeper conundrum. Should we select purely on the basis of talent behind the stumps or should we consider batting? Do you pick a flawless keeper who averages 12.00 or a full-fledged batsman who may spill a sitter?

There is a young man from New South Wales who will soon replace Ian Healy as Australia's stumper. I have seen him bat and I predict that soon he will close the door on this debate.

Mr Average

My only meeting with former Bloomfield wicketkeeper and acquaintance of Mathew, Mr Uvais Amalean, is at the '98 Singer–Akai Nidahas Trophy final. The game is as good as gone. India are 230 without loss in the 40th over. India's nuclear warheads, Tendulkar and Ganguly, both on unbeaten centuries, are ready to begin meltdown.

Then, against the run of play, a wicket falls, followed by two more. Azhar, Sachin, Ganguly miraculously succumb to our assembly line of low-grade spinners and the stadium rocks to frenzy. 262–4.

The mantra of '96 had been: 'We can chase anything.' Our losses in South Africa had shaken this faith, but had not dented it.

Uvais Amalean had hung up his gloves years ago and was now a director at Singer, the name on the national team's jerseys. He stands on the steps of the Nidahas pavilion, sporting a shaven head, a walkie-talkie and an annoyed expression. For a keeper he is tall. He has the gangly build of a pace bowler, though retirement has added pounds to his face and midriff. Like most bald men he is probably unaware of the roll of fat by the nape of his neck.

I have just bought a copy of his autobiography *Mr Average* at the gate despite the mockery of my two associates. 'Pramodya Dharmasena's biography, *Not Fast, Not Spin*, out now, Wije! Hurry!'

Amalean, the last Thomian to play for Sri Lanka, managed to make the 1989 tour to Australia as understudy to Brendon Kuruppu, and played a few matches in the early 1990s. But the selectors played musical chairs with the keeper's berth and Amalean, reluctant to compete with younger men like Dunusinghe, Dasanayake and Lanka Silva, decided to bow out in '93.

Two more wickets fall, but Sri Lanka are unable to prevent the visitors from crossing 300. In the corner of the stand, a potbellied drunk in a straw hat falls off his chair, staggers to his feet and starts unzipping his trousers. The stand begins hooting and, encouraged, the drunk undoes his belt.

Uvais Amalean enters the scene, flanked by security. 'Kick all those buggers out,' he hisses into his walkie-talkie. I accost him as he is passing and ask him to autograph his book. He is visibly flattered.

Security descends on the situation like flies on dog poop. As the drunks are herded past the toilets, the papare band flares up an ode to Surangani and her fish and the rest of us cheer as India end their innings at 307.

Ari pretends he met Uvais during an STC Old Boys Stag Night and pours on the charm. I attempt flattery. 'In vain you retired, men. Look how many catches Kalu dropped.'

Jonny rolls his eyes, but Uvais nods. 'He almost messed up that stumping.' He then invites us to the sponsor's box, and that's when Jonny stops rolling his eyes.

The Premadasa Stadium, named after Ari's benevolent dictator, is easily our most modern. The ground is equipped with floodlights, an electronic scoreboard and freshly cropped turf. The VIP lounge puts Jonny's High Commission room to shame. The seats are padded, the bar is stocked, the air is conditioned and the view is sublime. We all grin at each other.

We receive seats up front and Ari and Jonny glare at me as I hesitate and then decline an offer of Bacardi and Pepsi, the unofficial sponsor. Uvais plonks himself in the seat in front of us and tells us that Sri Lanka will win.

'We are good at chasing.'

The sponsor's lounge is crowded with Singer logos, finger food and sycophants with smiles. Everyone who passes through the room comes over to our corner and shakes Uvais's hand. It is then I realise that Amalean is politicking.

'Petty politics has ruined this country and it will ruin our cricket if it is not stopped.'

Uvais is running for SLBCC president. His interaction with guests follows a very basic formula.

Long-lost brother greeting: 'Ammataudu, kohomada? After a long time.'

Small talk: 'Putting on, ah? How is so-and-so? You don't call us, no, now you're a big shot.'

Cricket talk: 'Otherwise? We will hammer them. We still have the classic batting line-up.'

Empty promise: 'Of course. Let's meet up. Definitely. I will call you.'

An Aravinda de Silva century, flanked by double-figure contributions by Messrs Jayasuriya, Atapattu, Kaluwitharana and Ranatunga, and the soundtrack of Uvais's election banter, punctuate a revealing evening under floodlights.

'They got rid of Ana Punchihewa, then Whatmore. What more?' Uvais has a high-pitched hyena laugh. The three of us laugh at the laugh and not at the joke.

'Selection should be on merit, not on favours. In my era, how many talented players were kept out?'

That was our cue. Jonny, Ari and I grab the mic at the same time.

'Did you play with Pradeep Mathew?'

There is more hyena giggling and then he tells us about the 1989 Aussie tour and Pradeep's courtship of Shirali Fernando.

The score reaches 200 for 4 just after the 30th. Sri Lanka looks on course. Amalean tells us how he kept wickets to Mathew for three seasons. 'Man was injured a lot. But in my last season, he was amazing.'

The wicketkeeper and the spinner had a secret code. Mathew painted the index and ring fingers of his right (non-bowling) hand brown with 'some Hindu powder from the kovil'. The painted fingers would indicate the direction of the spin, the unpainted ones the length. From there on, it got complicated.

'In the end it was too much to remember. How many variations? Pradeep liked bowling with me. The Silvas and the Alwises wouldn't put up with this hand signal nonsense.'

Uvais tells stories of Mathew spending the last three years of his career not talking with the captain or the vice captain.

'Hello, Uvais. My God, Karunasena and Byrd! How? How?'

The former MD, now president of the SLBCC, Jayantha Punchipala, is Uvais's opponent in the upcoming election. He has the blessings of the new minister and the establishment. His smile is as steely as his handshake. 'You've met Dhani.'

Danila is wearing a T-shirt and a cap and her smile looks dowdy.

'How? How? What happened with the documentary?'

'ITL won the case. They might recut it and re-screen it.'

She avoids my eye and speaks directly with Ari. 'I heard Rakwana is writing a novel.'

My blood freezes. 'About what?'

'About Rakwana. What else?'

There is awkwardness as two men who loathe each other smile for the public. Sri Lanka coast to 260 in the 40th with de Silva still at the crease. The journalists and cricket execs keep one eye on the match and one eye on the chatting titans beside us.

'I was telling them about your good friend Mr Pradeep Mathew.'

Right then de Silva is caught by Harbhajan off Agarkar and no one notices the look that Jayantha Punchipala gives Danila.

When they have left, Uvais whispers, 'That bitch has been with half the cricket team. Now she's being kept by the man who thinks he can be king.'

'Was she friendly with Mathew?' asks Ari.

'No one was friendly with Mathew…'

Then Upul Chandana falls to Kumble, then Dharmasena is foxed by Prasad. 20 runs from the finish line, the perahera of departing batsmen begins.

I have since read Uvais Amalean's *Mr Average*. It is the sourest bunch of grapes ever turned into print. Each chapter offers excuses as to why Amalean didn't play more than eleven tests. He uses formulae that baffle even Ari to show that if his best seven innings are considered, he would be the third greatest left-hander in the game.

It is halfway through the badly proofread text that I realise the title *Mr Average* is not a statement of modesty, but one of intent. He is not saying, as most of us believed, that he was an average player. He is saying that he is the Emperor of Averages.

He analyses each of Sri Lanka's wicketkeepers and gives them points for batting and keeping. Specialist keepers like Navaratne, Goonetilaka and de Alwis score poorly on batting. Kalu, Silva and Kuruppu score modestly on keeping. When all these averages are tabulated and put through an index, Sri Lanka's greatest wicketkeeper-batsman turns out to be, surprise, surprise, Uvais Ahmed Amalean.

That is only chapter three. The book is also highly critical of four tour managers, three selection committees and one captain. Why would he release this tirade while running for office? Perhaps he is running on misplaced idealism. Hoping that the establishment would favour the end of corruption. Not knowing that the end of corruption would be the end of the establishment.

Before the game goes to the wire, Uvais shares many interesting things. He tells us that seniors who earn hundreds of thousands of dollars cannot help but look down upon juniors who pocket rupee salaries.

He tells us that racism exists everywhere. Once he had tried to put his daughter into a prominent Colombo convent and was told that the Rs 15,000 entrance fee was only for Catholics. Buddhists had to pay 50,000, Muslims 100,000.

He tells us that he once accepted a lakh from a man in a bar to break the stumps seven times during a Sharjah game. 'I didn't think anything wrong. I didn't have to play badly. Just flick the bails.' Amalean gleefully broke the stumps every tenth over when receiving a throw and then, off the bowling of Wijesuriya and Jeganathan, he affected a couple of bogus stumpings. In the penultimate over, Fairbrother went for a suicidal run and was stranded by Tufnell. Amalean received the throw and hesitated.

'I had already done it seven times. But how not to run him out?'

On returning to the pavilion, instead of a cash reward, Amalean received a call blasting him in raw filth. 'Couldn't understand if it was Afrikaans or Urdu.'

That was the last time Uvais Amalean ever received a call from a bookie, though he says players were approached all the time.

'You're in a bar. A rich fan offers to buy you a drink. You can't be not polite. Next thing they send you a gold watch. Next thing they invite you to a party. Treat you like a friend. Then you get a call, asking to break the stumps seven times. How to say no?'

He tells us that Zimbabwean Anton Rose scored exactly 36 in 11 of his 21 innings. He once scored 40 against England and then followed it up with a 32.

'But I don't think Rose was fixed. I think the number 36 followed him around. Sometimes Allah controls the game.'

He scored 144 and 72 against Sri Lanka in 1994, putting Mathew, in particular, to the sword. Both numbers are multiples of 36. He followed those with six consecutive ducks, was dropped from the side and never played again. His average sits for all eternity at 36.00. Ari is more fascinated by this than me.

Uvais does not tell us why Mathew disappeared. Why he was never given a game on his final tour, despite scintillating domestic performances. Though he does tell us about Pradeep's role in the dressing room. Ignored by senior players, Mathew befriended the reserves and the juniors. As time went on, he became a senior outcast, a spokesman for the meek.

'The foreign coaches were correcting Sanath's technique. Backlift too high, too much wrist. Trying to mould him into a classical opener. Suddenly in a team meeting, Pradeep blasted all the coaches and the seniors.'

Mathew suggested that the young left-hander be allowed to play his natural game, to hit over the top. The seniors expelled Mathew from the meeting; the foreign coaches ignored him. But luckily, the batsman in question did not.

'Everyone claims to have invented the Sanath–Kalu combination,' says Uvais. 'Pradeep suggested it during the '94 New Zealand tour.' Uvais lowers his voice. 'This is for your ears only, I will deny it if you repeat it.'

He tells us of a young off-spinner from Kandy who was asked to change his action by management. 'We all thought he chucked. Only Pradeep, who was the most senior spinner by then, said the action was not illegal.'

Mahanama, our last recognised batsman, departs, and in waddles Charith Silva, recently recalled to the side and victim of India's nuclear eruption earlier in the game.

'Pradeep wrote a letter to the captain and the coach. 'If you let this boy bowl, he will be the greatest bowler of all time. If you change his action, he will be another forgotten Tamil bowler.'

Charith Silva is run out without facing a ball, Sri Lanka falls short by 6 runs and the crowd hoots. Unlike our subcontinental brothers, we do not throw bottles or light fires. We save our barbarism for the north and the east. We join the disappointed throng to the car park. I repeat Uvais's whispers to Ari and Jonny. Neither of them believes me.

Six months later, Jayantha Punchipala is elected SLBCC president in a landslide. Uvais Amalean scores less than a third of his batting average and receives 8 per cent of the vote. Two months later, the president, under investigation for corruption, is forced to resign and another interim committee is appointed on the eve of the 1999 World Cup. *Mr Average* sells out its first print run, but is never reprinted.

Wild Boar Curry

'I was in the VIP section,' says I.E. Kugarajah. The way he says it – as one would say 'I had eggs for breakfast' – it doesn't sound like a boast. 'I remember when the Minister ran down to save the match.'

We are on our second drink (non-alcoholic for me, of course) and I am still uncertain whether the person attached to the moustache before me is a friend or a foe. Kuga is delighted to hear I am writing a book.

'A book on Pradeepan? That is a pukka idea.'

'Is he really dead?'

'According to the family.'

'According to you?'

'I can't say.'

'I have a certificate from…'

'The fat sister? You also got that photocopy?'

'Why would the family lie?'

'Because they're afraid.'

For a thug there is something delicate about the way he caresses his glass, like a saxophone player looking for notes. The way his eyes linger on your face. The way he pauses after each sentence to consider what has been said.

'That letter was a forgery. I have people in Melbourne.'

'Meaning?'

'Friends. How much money do you need to finish the book?'

'It's a book, Mr Kugarajah. Not a documentary. It costs only time.'

Kuga presses the video machine and out pops what looks like a giant roti made from stainless steel.

'What is that?'

'Recordable Laser Disc. Soon this will replace cassettes and CDs.'

What about spools, I think. He inserts another silver disk and manhandles a remote control the size of Ari's phone. It is my Sathasivam documentary. One which, as far as I know, aired only once.

'My friend next door copied this for me. He also likes your programmes.'

'Who is he?'

'Rohana Vindana Kumara. Pirate king of Sri Lanka. You don't know him.'

'Why am I here, sir?'

While the Sathasivam documentary plays without sound, my host pours a third drink and lights a seventh Gold Leaf. My rumbling stomach tells me it is past lunchtime. The afternoon sun streams through closed windows and warms the room. Kuga turns up the air conditioner and doesn't answer my question.

'You will stay for lunch, I got some wild boar from Amparai. Selva is making…'

'I'm not supposed to have oily food.'

'Not oily. Juicy. Like those ones in *Asterix*.'

He laughs.

After the annulling of the Asgiriya test, I.E. Kugarajah invited Pradeep Mathew to dinner at the Citadel in Kandy. The tour had been abandoned, so the youngster was off duty.

'Why were you in the VIP stand?'

He jerks his head to the side, there is the crack of a bone. I wince, he smiles.

'Questions, questions. Bloody journalists. I was doing business with the Minister of Cricket. Will you let me tell?'

I put down my glass and pull out my notebook.

'Of course, this is for your book. You will not mention me.'

'Of course.'

At the post-game cocktails, no one was talking about the match or the pitch. The Minister had seen to it that no awkward questions were posed and as a result the evening was awkward. I remember the New Zealanders sharing beers with the Sri Lankans. I remember Rex Palipane arguing with Ari about the ethnic problem. I do not remember seeing the unofficial Man of the Match among the circles of chattering players. Kuga had found him sulking by the lobby TV.

'I told him "Great bowling, brother," but no answer,' says my host. 'Then I said the same in Sinhalese.'

It was only when Kuga spoke in Tamil that he received the flicker of an eyebrow. It was in this language that Kuga suggested they leave the party. Mathew easily received permission from the manager to be excused. It's hard to pretend a match doesn't exist when the record breaker himself is in plain view.

At the Citadel, the boy grew talkative. He said he had taught himself to bowl a lot of those deliveries, but that his school coach had also helped. He said he was not angry about the match being cancelled, but was disappointed that the tour was over. He said he hated playing for Sri Lanka.

Selva announces that lunch is ready. During this shuffling of feet, I look around and notice the bookcase behind me. It is adorned with curved carvings. At eye level are cheap thrillers by rich writers. Jack Higgins, Frederick Forsyth and Ed McBain's *87th Precinct*. There is a *Collected Works* of Shakespeare and Salman Rushdie's *Midnight's Children*. Standard issue in most Sri Lankan bourgeois homes and, more often than not, unread beyond page 7.

The rest of the shelves have books about Sri Lanka's racial problems and Tamil history.

'I told him it is hard enough being a Tamil in Sri Lanka, let alone in the cricket team,' says Kuga as we make our way to the balcony. 'I told him that our brothers Sridharan Jeganathan and Vinodhan John suffered the same prejudice.'

'What prejudice? They both had their chances.'

'Vinodhan John Jeyerajasingam couldn't make the side even after changing his name. Jeggie died in 1996. Just forty-four, the first Lankan test player to die.'

'As if Sri Lankan cricket killed him.'

'The president and the Minister kept him out of the side. He turned to drink. That is probably what killed him.'

The food is served on a marble table and unsurprisingly in this idyllic neighbourhood, there are no crows swooping down from the power poles. There are no power poles.

'You are working for the LTTE?' I ask as we sit down.

There is a stirring of menace as he reaches for the wild boar curry. 'You think just because I care about being Tamil, I am an LTTE-er.'

Selva decorates my plate with cloud-like clumps of basmati rice.

'What about Mahadevan Sathasivam?' I ask.

'What about?'

'He was even given to captain the side.'

'And what happened? Thrown in jail on trumped up…'

'Are you sure he didn't kill his wife?'

'What are you saying? Satha went around town with his Lankan wife and his English BYT. Wife knew everything. But the Sinhalayas were jealous. Satha could out-bat them and out-screw them!'

This man would have barely been an infant when Satha was out screwing.

I was a cub reporter on parliament duty. Those were the days of the Chelvanayagam debates. Do minorities get 50 per cent or do they get nothing? We Sinhalese knew the Tamils could out-bat, out-screw, out-think, out-everything us. So we gave them nothing. And made some of them hate all of us.

Pradeep Mathew's Tamil was better than expected. He told Kuga of how the Sinhalese mob had nearly turned his father's bakery to cinders in '83. How his family was pressuring him to give up cricket and enter the business. How his coach had advised him to drop Sivanathan from his name if he wanted to play for Sri Lanka.

'That's nonsense,' I say. 'Look at Chanmugam, Kasipillại, Schaffter, Pathmanathan, and of course, Muralitharan.'

'That is what you all say,' says Kuga, slapping an extra dollop of dhal on his curry-stained rice. 'Murali. Murali. You elevate a few Tamils for your pleasure and then you destroy them.'

We return to the living room and I gather my satchel and my notes. I ask to borrow the laser discs, but Kuga refuses.

'You will not mention this visit to anyone. Not Byrd. Not the suddha.'

Emmanuel Kugarajah offered to manage Pradeep's career that first night at the Citadel and the boy accepted. His first managerial act was to rid the twenty-two-year-old of his virginity.

'Fellow said he was waiting for a girl he loved. I said fuck that bullshit. Sorry, Uncle. Got him a Korean when we got back to Colombo.'

Kuga tells me he has an important visitor arriving and that we will make another appointment to meet. He begins putting the discs away and tidying the room.

'Sudu and Chooti will drive you back. I hope you will not mind the blindfold.'

'You are joking?'

Standing at full height, Kuga doesn't look as short as I thought. He is almost at my shoulder. On which he puts his dark paw and squeezes.

'Sorry, Uncle.'

'Why?'

'Because I know who you are.'

He increases the pressure on my shoulder.

'And because you know who I am.'

As he leads me down the stairs, I wonder if I should tell him that I do not have the foggiest.

The Armball

New Zealander Dipak Nathu had a beautiful armball that he employed a bit too extensively. So much so that unkind Aucklanders would hold banners saying, 'Beware of Dipak's mystery ball. It actually spins.'

ITL has this footage. It is from New Zealand's mythic 1992 World Cup where they beat everyone in the world, partly thanks to captain Crowe opening the bowling with his off-spinning armball practitioner. They then lose to a beleaguered Pakistan, who go on to whack the cup.

Nathu speaks to Brian Gomez, whose LankaTel T-shirt, cap and tie leave little doubt as to how ITL financed his trip to New Zealand.

'To be honest with you, mate, I picked up the ole armball in your country.' Dipak looks Punjabi and speaks fluent Kiwi.

'Your spinner took 10 wickets against us, eh? I was reserve. I watched that fella bowl in the nets. Beautiful armballs, eh? I can't remember his name…'

'Jayantha Amarasinghe?' prompts Brian, confirming beyond doubt that he is an idiot.

'Nah, mate.'

'Sanjeewa Weerasinghe?'

'Don't think so. Dark bloke, kinda shaggy hair.'

'Ah,' smiles Brian. 'Ranjith Madurusinghe.'

'Nah, mate. Not him. Listen, I think we're expected on the field…'

Brian could have gone on bumbling names. Roger Wijesuriya, Sridharan Jeganathan, Don Anurasiri, Roshan Jurangpathy. Nah, mate. Brian, you moron. Not them.

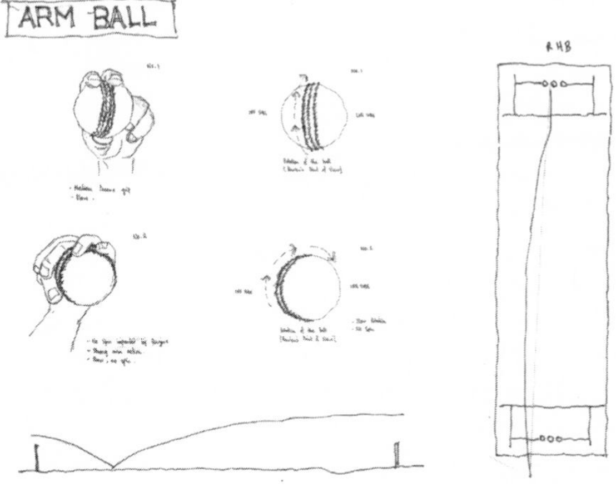

Legends

The Legends Nightclub and Bar is at the top of Empire City, central Colombo's most overpopulated shopping mall. To reach the top requires braving seven escalators or sharing a sweltering lift with thirty-two armpits. We opt for the former. I observe the Em-Cee Boys gazing over railings at the tops of dresses. This baseball cap-and-chain wearing subculture is the fungus of Colombo's malls. They are mostly harmless, unless of course you are under thirty and possess breasts.

The last escalator is the least crowded, but I still find the journey nerve-wracking. Decades ago I read about a child in Maharagama whose foot was shredded by the teeth of one of these moving staircases. The thought still makes me shudder.

The Legends sign above the entrance is unlit. The club is filled with afternoon sunlight and scurrying workmen in plain clothes. The walls are plastered with posters bearing the logo of a tea company, the same one seen on the front of our cricketers' shirts. Danila is trotting in high heels, hair loose, directing young boys in ties. It was Ari's idea to meet her.

She sees both of us and there is a smile. 'Hi. Hi.' She gives us both a delicate handshake. 'Crazy day, no? They've pushed the event to tomorrow. Going mad. Give me a second. I'll come.' The smile vanishes as fast as it appears, causing one to question its authenticity.

We sit at the bar and I gaze upon fine vodkas, gins, whiskies and rums hanging upside down, glistening like the pipes of a grand organ. It is then that I realise that my favourite colour is Mendis Double Distilled mixed with ginger beer, a colour somewhere between sunset and gold.

Jonny boasts of his drug use as if he is privy to some sort of divine enlightenment. How can XTC or LMD or whatever these children take compete with alcohol, a drug refined over the centuries by all the great civilisations?

'Take it easy, Wije,' says Ari, reading my face. 'Two bitter lemons, please.'

'I'll have water,' I say to the giraffe-like bartender. He looks at me an instant too long.

'Today you are doing the talking,' I say to Ari as we lean back and look upon the club's leather-clad interior. Couches where who knows what debauchery takes place. I have seen how Ari's Melissa and her friends dress on a night out.

'Of course,' says Ari, doffing his silly cap. 'Leave it to me, Putha.'

'Excuse me, sir,' says the bartender. 'Are you related to Garfield?'

I narrow my eyes at the giraffe. Ari breaks the pause.

'Yes. Yes. Garfield is his son.'

'You have the same face cut,' says the barman. 'Garfie played bass for Apple Rain after Joe died. Good fellow. How is he?'

I sip my water hoping this overgrown horse will shut up. But he doesn't.

'I heard he got a break in Switzerland with Capricorn. There money is good, ah.'

I begin picturing the bartender's giraffe head impaled on a cocktail skewer marinated in single malt whisky when Danila comes over. 'Come, let's sit.'

She is wearing a short skirt and a saffron blouse that curves with her figure.

'Tell Garfield that Manilal said hi.'

'Of course,' says Ari, as we take the couch by the window.

'We are playing well, no?' says Danila.

'Only at home,' says Ari. 'Let's see how we do in England.'

'You're not at the Cricket Board?' I ask, pretending I am unaware of the scandal draped across the pages of last year's *Leader* that had forced her out of the cricket board.

'I'm back in advertising.' She fishes a card out of her handbag and places it before us. Her title and the three letters that describe the firm are meaningless to me, but I presume it is a good position, which allows one to order around young boys in ties.

'I'm also not with that bastard,' she says, fingering a cigarette. Had the whole town suddenly taken up smoking?

'Which fine gentleman do you refer to?' I realise to my dismay that Bogart is back in Ari's voice box. 'The ex-president of the SLBCC or Pradeep Sivanathan Mathew?'

Danila glares at me and I do not know where to look, so I let my gaze fall.

'Are you looking at my…'

Ari chuckles and I feel blood rush to my ears. 'No. Are you mad?'

'Why not?' asks Danila, arching her back and looking down at her cleavage. 'They're perfectly worth looking at.'

I feel blood rush elsewhere.

Ari coughs. 'I am sure many men have fallen for your…charms, Danila. Or should I call you Shirali?'

'Excuse me?'

'Are you not Shirali Fernando? Former lover of Pradeep?'

She leans back, less like a lady taking offence, more like a rat snake about to strike. She keeps her eyes on us as she calls one of her minions and with a cupped fist orders a glass of wine. Then she doubles over in laughter.

'You're serious?' The glass is placed and another cigarette is lit.

'We know that you met him in Melbourne in 1989. We know that…'

'My God. You are serious. Uncle, can I ask you? Do I look stupid to you?'

Ari stops his monologue, I almost stop breathing.

'If you knew how much I hated that bitch.' She calls out to the bar. 'Upendra. Where the hell is the band, men? Call that bloody Manilal.'

She leans forward, smiles at me, and points at Ari. 'He goes.'

'What do you mean?' splutters a flabbergasted Ari.

'I'm sorry, Mr Byrd. I'm not discussing my personal life with you.'

'It's OK, Ari,' I say. 'Let me take this.'

Ari walks off cursing and sits at the bar. I resist the urge to punch the air like Tim Henman.

Hand on Knee

Ageing has many drawbacks. Not least the proximity of death and the visibility of decay. But also, in the eyes of the world, you cease to be a sexual being. Children are repulsed at the thought of their parents at it. Nauseated by the very act that spawned them.

We are all as old as our eyes and slightly older than our teeth. Everyone has blood running through their veins. Sheila and I have enjoyed a full and rewarding sex life. We don't have to dress like prostitutes to advertise it.

Why should we deny and suppress our desires while the young are allowed to drape theirs across our faces? If a twenty-eight-year-old puts her hand on my knee, she is being warm and endearing; if I do the same I become a rapist. And that is why the young have power. Because they are desirable and we are not.

She tells me she 'dated' eight Sri Lankan cricketers since 1990 but only 'went out' with two. I must ask Ari's daughters to decipher these terms for me. She tells me she broke off with the president of the SLBCC because he slept with his servants. She speaks of her lovers without shame, perhaps believing she is being refreshingly honest.

This I find insulting. Though I am unsure how to feel about the hand on my knee.

Danila Guneratne

She joined the three-letter-named agency straight after her A-levels. She went to Bishops College and liked to party.

She worked on the SLBCC account as a junior executive, long before World Cups and multi-million rupee deals. The Cricket Board may not have paid as much as her other client, Anchor Milk, but it brought prestige, a rich social life and the occasional overseas trip. She was promoted twice and in '95, the client offered her a job at the SLBCC.

'Was that when you began your relationship with the MD?' I ask as politely as I can.

'No. That was after Pradeep left me.'

Ari calls out to us from the bar. Tells us he is departing. We wave him off. Thankfully there is a table between his line of vision and the hand on my knee.

'Aiyo. Change the music, men. Kenny G is bit G, no. Play that blues CD I bought.'

The man behind the bar executes Danila's bidding. A ballad sung by a lady who sounds half asleep floats through the ceiling speakers. Danila lowers her eyelids and sings along to the chorus.

'I love this song.'

'Sounds to me like she's taken drugs.'

'She probably has. Listen to how sad she sounds. Listen to this song enough times, Uncle, and it will be your friend.'

The hand removes itself as she tells me that a certain top order batsman kisses like a goldfish. That a certain bowler is a bit too quick between the covers. That the vice captain took her to Kandalama Hotel before and after his marriage.

'Do you know she never let Pradeep have sex with her? Some virginity pact with God. Then she blamed him for straying. He worshipped her. Said she was the only one who believed in him.'

Danila's first meeting with Pradeep was during the 1992 test against Australia played in Sri Lanka. Mathew had been recalled to the side and Danila was between boyfriends.

'I picked him up,' smiles Danila. 'Believe me, Uncle, that's something I hardly ever have to do.' She tilts her head, blows smoke and flashes her eyes. I believe her.

'I told him, "Pradeep, keep me away from that Ravi de Mel." He smiled and asked me why I was hiding. So I told him.'

She had been drunk at a previous function, had sat on de Mel's knee, but had ended the night kissing one of the Aussie batsmen. 'Men are like Montessori babas in a sandpit. If one picks up a toy, everyone wants to play with it.'

Pradeep kept his arm around Danila when his fast-bowling nemesis approached. During the evening, he complained about Shirali and how she didn't like his friends.

'"What friends?"' I asked, "Charith?" He laughed and told me that he hung out with gangsters. I thought he was trying to impress me.'

The Aussie batsman approached, hoping for a replay of the previous night.

As did each of Sri Lanka's top order. But Danila stuck by her date.

'He would have to be the first cricketer not to try and feel me up on the first night.'

The match was going well and Sri Lanka looked on the brink of an improbable victory. Pradeep said his girlfriend had told him to choose between his friends and her.

'Who were the friends?'

'I never got to meet any of them,' says Danila, not without sadness.

They had an 'on again, off again' for two years, her longest relationship to date, aside from her recent broken engagement. While Shirali was away in Washington, they became weekend lovers, committed but not exclusive.

'Why did Shirali leave him?'

She blushes and shrugs and tells me. 'She caught him with me.'

'He never got over it,' says Danila. 'Even when he was with me, he was with her.'

The tea company client arrives and she has to be excused. But she asks me one more question and it is the only time during the entire conversation that I feel I am speaking to the real Danila.

'Last time you said he was dead. Is he?'

I tell her I am no longer sure.

Middle of the Bat

You may remember that I pinned my classified ad to the Bloomfield noticeboard sometime back. And that it resulted in Ari and me being banned from the club.

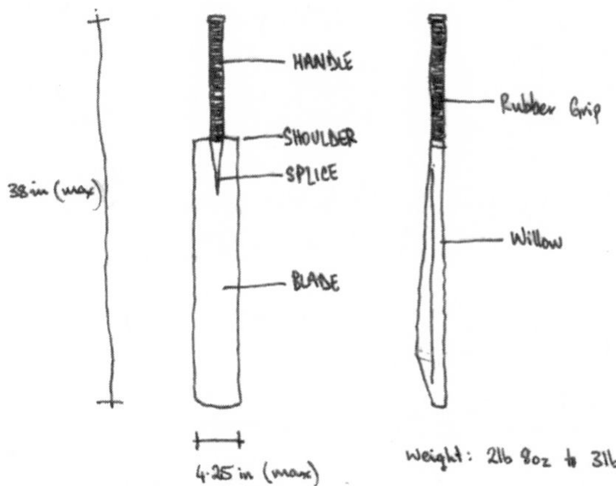

Before it was presumably torn down, the advert yielded one response. The GLOB, stalwart of Sri Lankan cricket for the last decade, still a part of the side despite being past his use-by date. The man who invited me to his first wedding, but not to his second.

While I am walking down to the shop to buy cigarettes I'm startled by a green Jaguar tooting its horn as it pulls up by my side. The window rolls down and the GLOB, wearing a suit and sunglasses, offers me a ride. He has been at a function at Mount Lavinia Hotel. The urchins on the street stare at this famous man sharing a car with the drunk from 17/5.

We drive down to the railway tracks, sit in the car and ignore the ocean. I smoke, he talks. He asks me how the hunt for Mathew is going. I tell him it is going OK. It is then that he tells me about the middle of the bat, about how Pradeep made him and how Pradeep almost broke him.

'He played with me in the A-team in '88, I think. He only told me to take a 2 feet stance. To forget about footwork, to hit on the up. To hit anything that was in the zone.' He pronounces zone to rhyme with lawn.

The other coaches told the GLOB to get to the pitch, to get in line, play along the ground, play with a straight bat. Pradeep told him to swing for the coconut trees beyond the stands.

Every bat has its sweet spot, a cherry at the centre, buried within the blade's meat. If the ball hits this area it stays hit. One can judge the batsman's form and class by how well he middles the ball. Diffident, unskilled batsmen allow the ball to hit the blade anywhere from the shoulder to the toe, resulting in edges that reach the cupped hands of waiting fieldsmen.

'I could never middle the ball when I faced Pradeep,' says the GLOB. 'Even in the nets, even if I was in good nick. I could never judge his bowling. I wasn't the only one.'

The GLOB is not a textbook batsman. He hits with an angled blade, aided by powerful forearms and a terrific eye. On his day he was indestructible.

'When I face him, I lose my confidence. He spins it both ways, same action. Can't judge the bounce or the turn. I faced one over in a Mercantile match. I couldn't see the ball at all.'

The GLOB describes that over from Mathew as the worst of his career. He missed every ball and was dismissed soon after. He suffered months of bad form and was dropped from the national squad.

'Why did Bloomfield get upset when I asked about him?'

'Mr Karuna, you have to understand, cricketers are jealous. Few places in the team and everyone wants them. If you have talent, like me for instance, you have to be humble. Especially to the seniors. No one likes an arrogant panditha bugger.'

When bowling in the nets, in boisterous tones Mathew had offered the Skipper hundred rupees for every ball he hit. The whole team looked on in horror as their leader was humiliated at the hands of a twenty-three-year-old upstart.

Each googly, undercutter and darter eluded the bat, many connecting with the Skipper's stumps. Each was accompanied by taunts from the bowler.

'He was saying "Come on, old man, where is your batting?" How can you say that to the Skipper?'

Mathew was not included in the 1987 tour of Pakistan, despite being the best spinner in the country. Many believe his display in the nets was to blame.

'I know it was a shame,' says the GLOB as he drops me at my doorstep. 'But even I was glad to see him go. It helped my confidence not to face him.'

'Any idea where he is?'

'I think he jumped immigration in New Zealand. If you find him, let me know, would be nice to see the bugger. Now I think I could face him.'

From the way he says it, he doesn't appear completely certain.

Dehiwela Zoo

Writing has become difficult. Perhaps there is too much to say. I no longer know what is true. And I no longer have a bottle to help me focus my gaze. Of course I see advantages. There are no more aches, my piss is yellow and my shit is brown and not vice versa. I don't need the cane any more, though I still carry one. I have even acquired a pot-belly, the true sign of Sri Lankan prosperity.

These days, life is what happens in between my smoke breaks. I have escalated to eight a day. Not bad, not good either. I have a love story that I do not understand. A cloak-and-dagger tale that makes no sense. Whither cricket? Whither genius?

Sheila brings me photos of my grandson playing football in a London backyard belonging to the ex-wife of my ex-son. Garfield is now playing with a rocker band and attempting to reconcile with his family. He is still wanted by immigration in Geneva. How he got past customs in London I can only guess. If he is caught, he will be deported and doomed to give guitar lessons in Rawatawatte. And that will be that.

Ari is upset that Danila did not trust him. 'I brought up five girls single-handedly for three years. Who does she think she is? Personal life. Hmph.'

Ari's TV has remained in my room since my illness, a permanent donation. My room is neat as it always is when I am not writing. Except for the stains of crow shit on my permanently open windows. Brian is on the screen previewing the upcoming test vs England at the Oval.

'Wije. I thought this was our project.'

'You're jealous because the young lady prefers me.'

'Why do you get the girl and I get the dwarf?'

'I think you mean midget.'

The phone rings.

'Can we meet tomorrow?'

'Is this…'

'Don't say my name on the phone.'

'I don't think this is tapped.'

'Every phone in every town is tapped.'

'Tomorrow is OK. Where?'

'The zoo.'

'In Dehiwela?'

'Where else?'

Click.

'That was the nuisance caller?'

'How did you know?'

'Elementary, mon ami. You only look on edge when you're talking to women. I could hear that it was a man or a gruff woman, so naturally I deduce… *très bien*?'

'I'm confused. Are you Sherlock or Poirot?'

'That is not the question. The question is why you are talking about Dehiwela with our prank caller.'

I take a deep breath and I spill the beans. Ari is silent for a long time.

'Is this a true story or are you making it up?'

'When I write about it, I'll make stuff up. Why would I lie to you?'

'Let me follow you.'

'You're too old to play cat and mouse. I will tell Kuga you are my partner. But only if you take me to the midget.'

'Don't talk crap. You know I can't do that.'

'Why not?'

'You don't know this character. He's mad.'

'But you're OK to steal from him?'

'Borrow. Anyway, forget it. I think you're making this up.'

'Too bad. You'd look distinguished in a blindfold.'

* * *

Asia Cup 1988. That was when I was sure.

Sure of what?

That Pradeepan was a god. That he commanded the earth and the air like Hanuman.

Like a monkey?

It was a simple set-up. India would lose to Sri Lanka. Pakistan would lose to India. Pakistan and India would hammer big run rates against Bangladesh and then get into the final. Pakistan would win. Tit for tat.

You're saying '88 Asia Cup was fixed?

Listen, will you. India went to plan. Pakis were supposed to beat SL in a close game. They couldn't score enough runs so Lanka won. Luckily I didn't bet on that one.

Sri Lanka was supposed to throw the game?

Mad? Only good teams throw matches. Sri Lanka were crap, but Malik and Shoaib couldn't score off Mathew. He sent down five maidens. That cost them the match.

You fixed matches? Or just put bets?

I have been on both sides of every fence you can think of.

People like you destroy the game.

Bullshit. I have saved it. In '88, Sri Lanka played like Bangladesh and Bangladesh played like Denmark. Where the contest? We make Sri Lanka pull off an upset, arouse a bit of interest, make the Bangladesh games about the run rate. We made every game in that tournament dramatic. We are for the game, not against it.

How much money did you make?

I do OK. But I don't do it for money. I do it for the cricket. Upsets are good for the game. Like West Indies vs Kenya at the World Cup.

You did that?

Why? Did you put money on that? We don't do impossible upsets that will attract attention. If Holland beats Pakistan, that's not us. We work only with professionals. Like South Africa.

So the Cronje rumours are true?

When I fix it, you don't even know it's been fixed. If I was smart, I would've got into tennis or snooker. Easier to fix one guy. Cricket is too complicated.

Can't fix everyone?

That's the beauty of it. Unfixed player changes the script and then battles the fixed player. Bad for business, but a treat to watch.

Is that what Pradeep did?

His performance got Sri Lanka into the final.

Which Sri Lanka lost.

Of course. That I made sure. Pradeepan took four wickets that match. But Lanka still lost.

So you bribed Sri Lankans for the finals?

No, I just weakened their best players.

With what?

The usual. Booze and whores. It's hard to take diving catches when you're hungover and have pulled a muscle trying to score a 69.

* * *

At the zoo, the animals are as shabby as the people looking at them. This was once the largest and finest menagerie in all of South Asia. Alas, the zoo's great Burgher superintendent migrated along with most of our good ideas to Singapore. Now they have the best zoo in Asia, and Dehiwela is a half-dismantled prison filled with emaciated giraffes and black panthers that look like cartoon pink ones.

Even on a Wednesday, there are crowds. And even though the price of admission is less than half a pack of cigarettes, I'm sure that vast quantities of money flow into this place and go into building enclosures for biped mammals who wear white sarongs and drive Pajeros.

Daniel called me that morning and said to wait by the flamingos. It is only after passing cages of sleeping wolves that I realise they are at the entrance.

I struggle to understand why the boys can't just pick me up from home. When I arrive at the flamingo pool, Sudu and Chooti are hot and bothered.

'What the hell, Uncle? Now almost 12. Come quick,' says the dark one, sweat forming a moustache above his lips.

Daniel is in the van and in a foul mood. 'Next time we are not waiting, ah?' A blindfold and a bumpy ride later I am on the terrace of a lane I do not know, where all the houses have unsolvable fractions on their gates.

'Heard that Uncle was late,' says Kuga. 'Don't be late. Can be very dangerous.'

He is wearing sunglasses and a tie. His moustache has been trimmed to a Clark Gable and his sideburns extend at sharp angles. There is also something different about his home which I am unable to fathom, and then it hits me.

It is the portraits at the entrance and on the walls of his office. Last time they were of a smiling Ms 2ndGeneration in her blue sari. Today they feature the Leader of the Opposition Mr NeverWas in a green shirt.

Mr OldSchoolTie, president in the 1980s, said that under the new constitution, the only thing a president couldn't do was turn a man into a woman and a woman into a man. These days even that is a plane ride to Bangkok away.

* * *

I took Pradeepan to my brothel in Sharjah in '88.

You own an Arab brothel?

I invest wherever business is good.

Did you fix Sharjah?

Sharjah is where things started. Suddenly there's twenty one-day games back to back. I knew clients with too much money, I knew players with too little. Simple economics.

Was the brothel part of Pradeep's payment?

That was to make him a man.

And the English lessons?

A man who is afraid of women will never be a man. A Sri Lankan without English has many doors closed to him.

Did he play well on the tour?

He was reserve. They don't let Tamils become permanent members of the side.

That is nonsense.

I told him that being Tamil, he needed to be ten times as good. And to do that he would have to work and understand who he was.

Our greatest bowler is a Tamil.

Murali is not our greatest bowler. But yes, you are right.

Why have you got UNP pictures on your walls?

I support the opposition.

But I remember last week…

You remember wrong.

When Mathew was out of the side from '89 to '92, what was he doing?

He was with me, training. Recovering from his injuries.

From his fight?

Fight?

With skinheads in Melbourne.

You have done homework. No. Pradeepan was developing carpal tunnel from all the variations in his bowling. I got down a physio from Australia to help him. I hired a fitness trainer. I helped develop his deliveries.

You're not the first to claim that.

That Nelson bastard collected 20 per cent of Pradeepan's Bloomfield salary till I put a stop to it.

Newton. What happened to his coach and physio?

Whatmore and Kontouri. I got them jobs at the SLBCC.

I don't accept that there is race discrimination in Sri Lankan cricket.

There is every sort of discrimination everywhere in this country.

What happened to his girlfriend?

That bitch? If I knew she would be like that I would never have set them up.

You did that as well?

I don't appreciate your tone, Karuna. What do I gain out of lying to you?

What do you gain out of telling me the truth?

It might help you find him. And I would like you to find him.

What if I don't?

Let me rephrase. I expect you to find him.

What if I publish everything you've told me in the *Daily News*?

They wouldn't print it.

Why not?

Because, I'm pretty sure they already know.

* * *

From the terrace I can see how well paved this nameless road is. How well kept the gardens are. How every house has a Sudu and a Chooti lookalike standing at the gate. I ask Daniel who the neighbours are. He says he cannot say. I say I'm sure I don't know them. He says he's sure that I do. Right then, a neighbour comes out, a bearded man with a familiar face. He picks up the morning papers off his veranda and waves.

'No movies, Rohana?' shouts Daniel.

'I'll send,' calls the man.

Daniel looks at me while Kuga gets off the phone. 'Any film that man can get. Even before Hollywood. He has original *Godfather 4*. Film hasn't even been made.'

'Rohana who?'

'Please don't ask dirty questions.'

* * *

That Shirali was a curse. Every project I got for Pradeepan, she would reject.

Project?

Ads, tours. I could've made him a superstar.

Sri Lankan cricketers didn't do ads those days.

What about Aravinda and Keells sausages? Who do you think set that up?

Really?

I had Gold Leaf and Lion beer willing to pay big bucks. Where? That bitch said no, no?

She didn't approve of tobacco and booze.

She didn't approve of anything. She even tried to get him back with his old coach.

You said you put them together. I heard a different story.

What?

About a beauty contest and a fight with skinheads.

No one mentioned me in your story?

I'm afraid not.

Are you sure? Karuna, I have photos of every famous cricketer with one of my girls. I have video recordings of Lanka's seniormost cabinet minister grunting over a Russian tart like a baboon. I have organised complex operations for the government, the opposition and the LTTE. Sometimes at the same time.

Impressive.

You think I can't fix a beauty contest and a bar fight?

* * *

Later in the afternoon, a cricket match is organised between the Sudu and Chooti lookalikes of each house. It is then that I realise they are all wearing the same clothes. White shirts worn tails out and black cotton slacks. It is then that I realise that these are uniforms. One of them has a gun tucked into his belt; in fact, all of them do.

The air smells of fresh flowers and trees, with the occasional whiff of something frying. I recognise the rumbling beyond the tall trees whose names I do not know. It is water, moving down an incline. Peeping between trees I see turrets of cool grey stone, overlapping tiles and varnished railings.

Kuga has to take a phone call and I have to contend with Daniel who is now more than a little tipsy. 'OK. OK. Mr Karuna. I will give you one name. That is all. But don't tell Kuga Anna.'

'Kuga Anna? Aren't you older than him?'

'Doesn't matter.'

He tells me most of these houses were designed in the 1950s by architect Geoffrey Bawa, that none of them face each other, though some share balconies. That the road is shaped like a spiral and a famous river runs around it like a moat on a conveyor belt.

I hear the cuckoo clock, hung next to the portrait in the next room. It makes the koha sound fifteen times.

'Is that a twenty-four-hour cuckoo clock?'

'Upali Wijegunawardena.'

'What about him?'

'See that house with the helipad?'

I follow his jewelled arm and the finger on the end of it. Wijegunawardena, magnate, political prince and owner of several publications I had been fired from, went missing in 1983.

'I thought they found the plane and the body.'

Daniel winks at me.

'They did. That house near the maara tree? Parakrama Ekanayake.'

'The hijacker?'

Parakrama Ekanayake was proof of the lengths Sri Lankans would go to get a visa. In June 1982, estranged from his Italian wife and young son by immigration, Ekanayake threatened to blow up an Alitalia Boeing 747 en route to Tokyo with 'the most sophisticated bombs manufactured in Italy' unless his demands were met. They were. He returned to Sri Lanka, a folk hero to some, with his wife and son and ransom, while Italian and Sri Lankan authorities argued over who would arrest him.

'Far back there, below the hill is Rudi Solheim.'

'Who?'

'Importer of Dutch hoffman, Malali chocolate and Colombian charlie.'

'What?'

'You don't want to know, Uncle.'

'Why does every house have bodyguards? No one can find this place anyway.'

'Bodyguards,' laughs Daniel. 'Those are no bodyguards.'

'Then?'

He winks again and walks off.

* * *

I set up the meeting with Alvin Rowe and Laurence Kallicharran.

The great West Indians?

Those days all the West Indians were great. Even the ones who couldn't make Lloyd's team. Collis King. Franklyn Stephenson. Sylvester Clarke.

What was the meeting about?

A second Sri Lankan rebel tour of South Africa.

I heard the first one was a disaster.

That's because we didn't have the players. In '91, not only did we have the players, almost all were willing to do it.

You mean…

Don't ask names. Pradeepan got me fifteen signatures of some of the leading players in the country. Kallicharran was liaising with the South African Cricket Board, SACB.

What was the catch?

The two rebel West Indian tours of South Africa not only made huge money, they provided some great cricket. Rowe thought if he could get a hungry Sri Lankan team, it would pave the way for another West Indian tour.

How much money?

More than any of those guys would've seen. Pradeepan could've looked after his father, married Shirali and retired. Sri Lankan cricket had no future for him.

So?

Mandela was released the day we started negotiations. Who knew apartheid would end? By the time we had all the signatures, South Africa were being welcomed back. In vain.

Didn't SLBCC punish the organisers?

I had fifteen signatures. If they touched Mathew I would've sent them to the newspapers. I was even able to negotiate Mathew back into the side.

Was the 1992 Aussie test fixed?

That, Uncle, is a very long story.

* * *

Days later Ari brought me a copy of the *Sunday Leader*, a sensational tabloid, the only paper with the balls to take shots at the government. Many feared that the government would one day take shots at them. That Sunday there was a double-page spread outlining connections between prominent politicians and the criminal underworld.

Cheques signed by the president and members of cabinet for vast sums to the likes of Soththi Upali, Baddagana Sanjeewa and Nawala Nihal. Mentioned in the article is a kasippu mudalali called Kalu Daniel and a betting tycoon called Kuga Anna. Unfortunately there are no photographs.

* * *

I was called in for special ops in '93. I didn't see much of Pradeepan.

Did he have something with a girl called Danila?

After Shirali, there were a lot of women. I was happy for the fellow.

What kind of special ops?

Special ops that got me arrested. I didn't get to see Pradeepan's '94 season for Bloomfield.

I saw it. My. He was lethal in the final against SSC. Demon fast.

Did you follow his African tour?

I didn't know he toured Africa. I thought his last tour was against New Zealand in '95.

Zimbabwe, South Africa and then New Zealand. And then he vanished.

When were you released?

Who said I was released?

I didn't know prisons came with driveways and TVs and laser discs.

There is a lot, Mr Karuna, that you don't know.

Matthews

We sent Jabir with our ID cards and he returned empty-handed, cursing the post office staff. 'Dumb bloody lazy bloody buffaloes. Two hours I had to wait, Uncle. Then this ugly woman tells me to see this smelly man, then they go for tea break, then they tell me they can't hand over the parcels.'

I am sent to the third floor where my chit is signed by a large yawn wrapped in a sari, then I go to the first floor where twelve grotesques surround my parcel and make me fill out seven identical forms. I resist the compulsion to break my walking stick across someone's nose, and take a seat with other seething customers. We watch burly bureaucrats sign papers, which they paste onto other papers and put into crumpled files. They then disappear for a tea break at 11 and return at 12 to say the postmaster is bath kanawa. Eating rice. We wait a further hour till he finishes.

In the West, the term 'going postal' refers to alienated postal workers turning up to work with machine guns and opening fire on random customers. In Sri Lanka, it would not surprise me if one day the reverse occurred. In the absence of a gun, I use the only weapon I have a licence for, my foul mouth. I call the postmaster a donkey, refer to the staff as mules and threaten to write to every paper in the land. They hand over my parcels without opening them.

I lean on my walking stick and wait for Jabir to U-turn. He pulls up to the kerb grinning. 'See, I told you, Wije sir. I went and watched a blue film at the Ruby while you were inside.'

Back at Ari's house, we sit at the dining table and stare at the square parcels. 'They could be bombs,' says Ari, a little too hopefully.

'Who would want to bomb us?'

'Maybe Uncle Kuga.'

'If I was him, I'd drop napalm on the parcel office.'

I claw at the cellotape. Ari tears the brown wrapping. On top is a hardcover book with our friend in his straw hat holding a microphone and smirking at the camera. *Graham Snow: Middle of the Bat*. We compare books and grin. Both our books are signed, but Ari's has the inscription:

To the wise Ari Byrd,
I owe you my career.
Your friend, Graham

Page ix is the acknowledgements page. 'This book could not have been written without...'

The list is twenty-seven names long; it contains the names of a few great cricketers, an Indian film star, a British novelist and seven commentators. It also contains the names 'Ariyaratne Byrd' high up and 'W.G. Karunasena' around the middle.

'See, see. My name is above Kapil Dev,' coos Ari.

'It's alphabetical, Putha.'

Ari counts the names. 'At least we made Graham's squad.'

'Of what?'

'Of brilliant cricketing minds that have inspired him.'

'It looks like a list of people he's stolen ideas from. He must be scared that we'll sue.'

Ari's parcel contains a manuscript. He frowns at it, then his eyes widen.

'I say. You know what this is? An original draft of the Duckworth–Lewis with scribbles by Tony Duckworth and Frank Lewis themselves.'

He reads the accompanying note and chuckles. 'Graham found it in an ICC wastepaper basket. Ade pukka! Finally I can understand it.'

My box contains two more books. *Sport is War* by Simon Marqusee, about the West Indian rebel team of the 1980s, signed by Kallicharran, Rowe, Rice and Croft. I gasp and smell the fresh pages. The other book is a hardcover biography, *The Great Anton Rose* by Booth Beckmann. This book is not autographed, though there is a bookmark sticking from its last pages. On it in a familiar scrawl:

To the other great W.G.,

You may find this interesting.

Graham

I open at the marked page and find an index which includes the following:

Matthews, Craig, 59, 72–73

Matthews, Greg, 32, 59, 111, 16–173

Matthews, Jimmy, 8

Matthews, Pradeep, 17, 98, 122–137, 212, 258, 290–297, 320

I begin flipping pages.

I Declare

A captain will declare an innings closed if he believes his side has enough runs on the board, if he wants to give his bowlers more time to bowl out the opposition, or if a player he doesn't like very much is about to break a record.

When Anton Rose declared 117 runs behind in the Robert Mugabe XI vs Sri Lanka in 1994, it was not a sporting gesture to force a result. It was to deny a Sri Lankan spinner from getting 10 wickets. And it was because he knew torrential rains were expected the next day.

The 1994 Zimbabwe test series is not remembered at all. Every match was either rain affected or deathly dull. Neither team wanted to lose and be branded the worst in the world. So everyone from the groundsmen to the selectors to the players played it safe.

Those who were on that tour remember it for a string of brilliant individual performances from Rose and Lankan spinner Pradeep Mathew.

'Like only two players were playing cricket on that tour,' remembers Reggie Ranwala, Sri Lanka's trumpet tooting cheerleader.

The Sri Lankans played the last test in black armbands to commemorate the death of Minister Tyronne Cooray, long-time patron of Sri Lankan cricket. The Minister, builder of stadiums and burner of libraries, was killed by a suicide bomber in Colombo.

The RM XI declared at 270 for 9, having slumped from 232 for 2. Mathew was brought on late and his figures were a remarkable 9 for 8. One more wicket would have given him the best ever first-class figures, beating H. Verity's 1932 feat of 10 for 10.

Rose hit the ball into the air to where Sajeewa Liyanage stood, awaiting the unlikelihood of such a lapse in Rose's concentration. While the ball dangled in the air, Rose glared at the bowler, then at the umpire, and yelled, 'We declare! We declare!' The Zimbabweans walked off the pitch and Liyanage bungled the catch. Mathew didn't get his record.

Saving Private Jonny

On TV, the sign held by the English crowd says, 'Forget Private Ryan. Save Sri Lanka.' Ari and Jonny laugh, I do not understand the joke. They explain it to me and I do not think it is funny.

Jonny's place is beginning to look more homely. No more cardboard boxes spilling over into furniture. Masks, ornaments, wooden carvings and handlooms decorate the drawing room.

Outside the May monsoon arrives four months late and appears to be making up in ferocity what it lacked in punctuality. We used to have defined monsoon seasons. Now it just rains when it feels like it. Maybe there is something to this warming of the globe business.

'You been shopping, Jonny boy?' asks Ari.

'Just been enjoying my retirement.'

'At Barefoot?'

The High Commission had been generous with their severance package. Jonny is thinking of buying land in the hill country once the dust has settled.

'You been to Diyatalawa, WeeGee? It's better than New Zealand.'

'I lived in Badulla for almost five years.'

'What? Didn't know they played cricket in the tea fields.'

'Those days I used to follow boxing.'

I wasn't a sportswriter in those days. I was a newlywed. Sheila and I honeymooned in the hills and stayed there. The *Observer* was looking for a journalist to assist the plantation correspondent; she was escaping Kotahena and I was fleeing Kurunegala. The views from our bungalow were magical and the climate was cool. Though reporting on tea auctions and earth slips was as mundane as it got.

I would travel to Kandy at my own expense to watch rugby games and boxing matches. Over the years I became a fan of both. Muhammad Ali had just been stripped of his title and had his licence revoked for refusing to fight in Vietnam. Like the rest of the world I was stirred by his stance. 'No Viet Cong ever called me nigger.'

My freelance article 'The Golden Age of Ceylon Boxing', covering the present but also harking back to the 1950s, was more a hobby piece to while away the hours between hill gazing, love making and transcribing plantation labour negotiations. I did not expect it to win me Ceylon Sportswriter of the Year in 1969.

'Diyatalawa is a beautiful place,' I say. 'Are foreigners allowed to buy land?'

Jonny taps a wooden elephant with a curved trunk freshly purchased from Paradise Road and winks. I am glad the colour has returned to his cheeks and the twinkle to his eye.

Our drinks coasters show etchings of the topless women of Sigiriya. Jonny sips Scotch while Ari and I drink tea. I pretend this is no longer an issue, even though it very much is.

Outside, the thunder sounds like the cracking open of a thousand skulls. Rain beats down on our roof, drowning out the commentary on

TV. We are playing a one-off test against England. The home team are batting and have just crossed 400.

Growing up, I never thought I'd befriend an Englishman. Or if I did, I didn't think he'd be a Geordie with a penchant for sports and decorating rooms.

'How's the Twelve Steps, WeeGee?'

'I've stayed clean, but I hate it.'

'No, you don't.'

'I can get through the day, but is that a good thing?'

'Shall we change the subject?' asks Ari.

'No, Ari,' says Jonny. 'We should talk about it.'

'Stop putting that stuff into his head, Jonny. Look at me. I stopped after the '96 World Cup. I haven't relapsed.'

'That's because you don't have psychological baggage. WeeGee has got over his physical withdrawal, but he's still tied to it emotionally.'

Outside the late monsoon is still hammering away at Jonny's roof.

'Can we get back to watching this boring match?' I say.

'I'm serious, WeeGee. You thought about getting counselling?'

Jonny is getting on my nerves.

'Discuss with a quack why I shat in my bed when I was two? Whether my ayah tickled my balls when I was three? Fine. Sign me up.'

'Don't be a twat. What about those letters to your brothers?'

He is now using my nerves as a trampoline.

'Ari, can you tell this bugger to shut up?'

'He's right, Wije, you should make your peace.'

'Then why don't you leave me in peace?' I say, a tad too loudly.

There is silence. Lightning flashes like a broken tubelight. I glare at my friends and they look away. And then there is a terrible pounding on the door.

'Arinawa dora! This is police.'

'What the fuck...' says Jonny with widening eyes.

'You wait,' says Ari. 'Wije, come. Let's go talk.'

We open the door to find six raincoated police officers with batons. Outside, there is a crowd with umbrellas peeping over the wall. At the gate is a fat man in a sarong, holding two boys by the scruffs of their necks. The boys are crying and the man is screaming. 'Where's that fucking suddha?'

The policemen barge past us.

'Move, Uncle.'

The road is filled with police vehicles. Before we know what's what,

Jonny is being pushed forward in handcuffs. And that's when the men with cameras arrive. The walk from Jonny's gate to the road can be done in ten seconds at a leisurely pace. This time it takes as many minutes.

Projectiles of invective and venomous curses are hurled by the crowd. The policemen hold back the mob, but are powerless to prevent the snapping of cameras.

'Call my lawyer. Call him,' pleads Jonny.

We can do nothing except look on in horror.

Squirrels and Rats

Two similar problems. Two very different solutions.

Ever since the sparrows vanished from de Saram Road, squirrels have taken their place, scurrying into our homes and helping themselves to fruit. Kusuma and Sheila position a stool under the araliya tree and place a tray of nuts upon it. They convert a broken clock into a makeshift bird bath. As the man of the house I should be helping, but I have typing to do. They sit on the veranda and coo at the bushy tails helping themselves to my beer snacks. 'Aney darling, sweet, no?' says Sheila.

Rats have been enjoying free dinners from our kitchen bin. Every other evening we hear Kusuma's shrieks as a well-fed pig-rat escapes into the pantry. We respond with carpenters who mesh-wire the windows and lay poison behind the cooker and rat-traps in the cupboards. Three days later, when the kitchen starts to smell of corpses, I am called to locate and dispose of twitching bodies.

It is while scraping bloodied fur wrapped in tail and innards into rubbish bags that I spy three squirrels fighting over my manyokka crisps. I realise that humans respond to squirrels and rats on a primal level. One makes us want to squeeze cheeks and go aney, the other makes our skin curl.

Sheila and Kusuma tell me that rats are disease-carrying vermin and that squirrels are nature's little gatherers. But these are not true reasons. We post-justify our prejudice. We respond to rats with revulsion as we do to certain people, without any idea why. We gravitate towards humans with bushier tails for reasons we cannot fathom. Punchipala may get away with murder, while my friend Jonny may be falsely accused of it.

Ari plays me a spool of an Indian batsman complaining to the umpire that the crowd is shining mirrors at his eyes. The umpire's response is clear and his voice is somewhat familiar. 'Play on. This is not Calcutta.' The sound quality breaks up and we hear a young Sri Lankan voice insisting that the umpire apologise to the batsman. Ari claims the voice belongs to Pradeep Mathew. I am sceptical. We hear the Skipper's voice asking the bowler to shut up. The spool is marked 'Indya test seris 85'.

Pradeep Mathew was perhaps more rat than squirrel. Not so much the polecat beast that roams our roof, but more akin to the grey kitchen mouse that no one fears, but no one wants to touch. The world mistook his shyness for contempt and misinterpreted his passion as belligerence.

There have been many times in my life when I have wished I was more of a squirrel. These days I'm glad I'm not.

Match Over

England reach 445 and Sri Lanka lose Atapattu and Jayawardena before the day is done. The lawyer tells us that it's match over. Jonny is being charged with six counts of sexual assault and will be held indefinitely till the High Commission responds.

The lawyer tells us that sometimes the police will negotiate with the High Commission and for the right price could be convinced to drop the charges, provided the culprit leaves the country. Embassies usually comply, depending on the severity of the crime and the potential for embarrassment.

The lawyer speaks like a law book.

'In light of the fact that the British High Commission relinquished a substantial sum of unemployment compensation to our client, it is doubtful they will part with more funds.'

'Can't you pay off the cops with the severance money?'

'Mr Karunasena, this is no longer merely about money. If so, it would be already settled. But six different victims, claiming mental and physical trauma. The allegations are serious. Only diplomatic pressure could save him.'

'But he is innocent.'

'Of course. But there is the record to consider.'

'What record?'

He tells me Jonny has been deported from Thailand and Indonesia for possession of marijuana. That records have been suppressed till recently. He tells me of a strong nationalist lobby, rallying against foreigners who buy land in Sri Lanka and turn slices of our coast and slivers of our hills into holiday homes and boutique hotels. Jonny's case will help the 'Suddhas go home' brigade.

Many of them are spiritual descendants of Sinhala Buddhist leader Anagarika Dharmapala, who at the turn of the century stated without irony to a crowd at Mattakkuliya that 'an effigy of a white man should be made of plantain stems, dressed in trousers and placed before each house and beaten in the presence of children'.

I put the phone down and share the news with Ari. Ari reaches for the Scotch.

This time it is I who does the restraining.

'What the hell…'

'Just one, Wije. To calm the nerves.'

'If you have one, I will have ten.'

'I'll only have one.'

'I'll only have ten.'

He snorts and lets me put the bottle away.

'OK. OK. Take it away. Come, let's sit.'

Ari cups his hands and prepares for a speech.

'Wije, I have something shocking to tell you.'

'Haven't we had enough shocks for the day?'

The Yorkshireman is on Jonny's TV and is comparing Sri Lanka's bowling to an 'Ilford 2nd XI'. Ari turns it off and looks me in the face.

'I'm afraid to say that Jonny…is a homosexual.'

I try not to smile.

Ari's Plan

I love Sheila more than she knows. I love her shrieking voice, her penguin-like waddle, her olive skin, her flopsy boobs and her boundless kindness. I loved her on that bus to Kotahena. Asleep on my shoulder on that train to Badulla. In the back of that taxi cradling baby Garfield. For the years she put up with me. For the years she left me alone.

But when I see Danila Guneratne in a short skirt, my loins are kindled. Desire from my groin spreads to my limbs. If she offered herself to me, there would be little hesitation.

Men have no control over what quickens their pulses or hardens their pricks. We do not know when or where lust will strike and we are powerless to its tyranny. We build religions and elaborate social laws to stifle these appetites. Not all of them succeed.

Jonny has been my friend since Sri Lanka won test status, since the '82 soccer World Cup. Ari and I have never known him to be anything other than gentle and generous.

'Wije. Who knows what goes through a man's head when the lights are out? How can we know?'

'He's not a paedophile, Ari.'

'The boys were aged between fourteen and nineteen.'

'Don't lie.'

'That's what the police said.'

'Have you told Manouri?'

'Are you mad? She would ban me from associating with him.'

'I suggest we tell no one.'

'I agree. But what do we do?'

'We must talk to the families.'

'The victims?'

'Don't call them that.'

'Saying what?'

'This was consensual sex. He must've paid them. They must've come willingly. He's not a rapist. Let's convince them. Maybe even offer some money.'

'There is no such thing as consensual sex with a fourteen-year-old.'

'OK. Tell me your plan?'

'My plan,' says Ari, 'is for you to talk to your Kuga.'

Willey

Peter Willey, international umpire and former England batsman, was involved in two infamous commentary moments. Neither is apocryphal. When he caught Dennis Lillee off the bowling of Graham Dilley, the scorebook read 'Lillee ct Willey b Dilley'. When he faced Michael Holding in 1976, commentary legend Brian Johnston innocently uttered the words, 'The bowler's Holding, the batsman's Willey.'

Wiggling My Ears

I can move my ears without touching them. I discovered this skill in the playground as a child. I don't know how I do it. I just empty my mind, flex my scalp muscles and wiggle like a rabbit.

It is my party trick, though the last time I went for a party was when Ronald Reagan was in office.

According to Reggie Ranwala, Mathew was triple-jointed. He could reach behind his right hip and remove his sweater with his left hand. He could open a bottle of Fanta with two bent fingers and a thumb. He could touch his elbow with his middle finger. Without these deformities, the floater, the skidder and the double bounce ball would not exist.

Sri Lanka produces freaks. Our jungles have been graced by white elephants, golden frogs and blue leopards, though I possibly made that last one up. Our towns are blessed with men who can hang from hooks, women who walk on fire and midgets who record cricket matches.

Aluminium Bat

In the 1978 Ashes, Dennis Lillee used an aluminium bat at a time when nothing in the rule book stipulated the bat had to be made from wood. Opposing captain Mike Brearley complained that the ball was going out of shape. To which Lillee retorted, 'Then maybe you should change the f****** ball.'

Maiden

An over in which no runs are scored. The phrase 'bowling a maiden over' remains one of cricket's most overused and unfunniest puns.

Newspapers

The bail hearing is set for two weeks. Only relatives and lawyers are allowed to see the prisoner. Ari and I spend days staring into space. We no longer talk of innocence, only of friendship. The offence carries a twenty-five-year sentence.

Sheila brings in the tea and the papers. She knows very little. 'Look at these bakamoonas. Face like a papol. I thought Sri Lanka won the test match.'

'But Newcastle lost to Arsenal,' says Ari, the quick thinker.

'Now y'all are following football, is it?' She appears in a good mood. I ignore her and share the Sunday papers with Ari. I take the sports, Ari takes the news, Sheila takes the classifieds.

My paper is still gloating over Sri Lanka's historic win and talks of us becoming world test champions by the year 2000. There is an announcement of the building of a ground in Dambulla to mark the five-year death anniversary of Minister Tyronne Cooray, patron saint of Sri Lankan cricket.

Sheila giggles. 'Look at these people. "Attractive Educated Buddhist Govigama Female, looking for foreign gentleman, 45+, working in Canada/USA/Australia. No fools please."'

'When I fall in love, it will be for visa,' croons Ari.

'"35 years. Good looks. Tamil Virgin bride seeks same. Dentists preferred."' Sheila laughs. 'She has a hope and a half.'

'You're looking for brides for Garfield?'

'No. Just. Garfy is together again with Adriana. Little Jimi is talking now.'

I'd like to think our son named my grandson after the great Jim Laker, though somehow I doubt it.

'It says here that powercuts are going to start again,' says Ari. 'Maybe they will replay our documentary.'

The print quality of our papers has improved in inverse proportion to the quality of the writing. Sportswriting these days is a string of clichés and spelling mistakes. I note with amusement that Newton has started a column on the women's cricket World Cup. It is as unreadable as that sport is unwatchable. I put down the paper and sip some tea.

Right then Sheila and Ari say 'My God' at the same time. Her shriek and his croak are almost harmonised. I thought these things only happen in those bad films I used to not watch at the New Olympia. Being the Thomian gentleman and all, Ari lets Sheila speak first.

'Dulcie has died.' Sheila explains that Dulcie was her classmate who got married to Bunchy and then got divorced and then worked in a shop at Vilasitha and then married the boss and then went to Zambia and came back with an accent and three children.

We nod sympathetically.

'She was married to your Elmo Tawfeeq's wife's cousin.'

I let her hand me the paper and I let my gaze fall upon it.

'Shall we go for the funeral, Wije?' she asks.

'Why would I go for Elmo's cousin's wife's funeral? I wouldn't even go to Elmo's.'

'I'm going to go with Manouri,' grunts Sheila.

She gathers the tea tray and departs.

Ari places his paper in my lap, just as something else catches my eye: **Political thug dies in prison**.

I ignore this and look at Sheila's obituary. Ari snorts in annoyance as his paper falls to my feet.

'Are you blind, Wije? Listen to this.'

While he reads his article, I do not take my eyes off the obituary column.

> Government sources reveal that I.E. Kugarajah, aka 'Kuga', convicted LTTE collaborator linked to the deaths of Brigadier Clancy Kobbekaduwa and Minister Lalith Dissanayake, died while serving the fifth year of a life sentence. In 1996 the LTTE attempted unsuccessfully to negotiate terms for his release. Cause of death is still unknown. (Reuters)

I stare at my friend, realizing that all three of us have been excited over different things.

'That wasn't in the obituaries,' says Ari.

'No, it wasn't.'

Right then the phone rings. I know that it will be the owner of a white van long before I pick it up.

Unsung

The same part of our heart that warms to the underdog should spare some affection for the unsung hero. The defender who assists the goal scorer. The stock bowler who props up the wicket taker. The nightwatchman who scores nothing and saves the game.

I have a favourite unsung hero and it is not P.S. Mathew. Neither is it M.J.M. Laffir, World Billiards Champion 1973, who lived in poverty and died in obscurity. It is another forgotten Lankan sportsman. His name is Kumar Anandan.

Before his death in 1984, attempting to swim the English Channel, V.S.K. Anandan held world records for:

- Swimming the Palk Strait in 51 hours (1971)
- Twist Dancing for 128 hours (1978)
- Balancing on one foot for 33 hours (1979)
- Treading Water for 80 hours (1981)
- Walking non-stop for 159 hours (1981)

159 hours non-stop walking amounts to 296 miles covered over six days. If Mathew's story adds years to my life, I will one day tell Anandan's as well. Sheila brings in my shirts, washed and ironed. She sees the last sentence and strokes my hair. 'Careful, Gamini,' she says. 'One donkey at a time.'

Obituary

Sivanathan, Sivali (1927–1998)
Wife of the late Muhundan. Loving mother of Sabi and Pradeepan. Beloved grandmother of Ram, Raj and Rakil. Sister of Mathew, Shashi and Thangu. Cortège for Borella Kanatte leaves 4.30 from 31 Daham Mawatha, Kadalana, Moratuwa. No flowers.

That was what had caught my attention, though I have to admit, Ari's was the bigger find. He looks pleased that he finally has my attention and follows me to the phone. When I pick it up it is not the voice I expect.

'Kuga wants you to go to the funeral.'

'Whose?'

'Pradeep's mother's. The address is…'

'I have it. It's in the papers.'

'Kuga asked me to make you write it down.'

Even the underworld has its sticklers. I let Kalu Daniel spell each syllable even though my hand goes nowhere near a pen.

'After the funeral, you are to report to Fort Railway Station tomorrow morning at 8.'

'Is Kuga dead?'

Click.

Traffic

'You are mad,' says Ari in Jabir's trishaw. 'What are you planning on doing?'

'Observing. What else?'

'Observing for what? Wije, you were the one who told me not to get carried away with being a detective.'

Just past the Katubedda market, the traffic slows down to 12 metres an hour. Then around Tower Cinema, it grinds to a halt. I used to spend some mornings at the 10.30 show, drinking in the dark amid panting couples, planning my day's articles. The movies were mostly Sinhala soft porn with titles like *Bala Kaamaya* (Power Lust), *Mamath Gaaniyak* (I Am Woman) and the rape–revenge saga *Agey Vairaya* (Her Fury) and its seven sequels.

Ari believes this is the reason I have no appreciation of good cinema. Jabir gets out of his three-wheeler and surveys the column of metal boxes shining in the heat.

'Bloody cops. Must be some election rally. Wije sir, Ari sir. You didn't bring any bombs, no?'

Ari says he left his at home and I ponder that in precisely fifteen minutes schools will open and we will be flooded by impatient white vans.

'It seems they have found bombs in Vihara Maha Devi Park,' says Jabir.

'Can't take New Galle Road?' asks Ari.

'I think that's where the rally is.'

The traffic starts to move. By the time we reach the junction, the police have stopped the security check and are waving us through.

'If Pradeep Mathew is alive, would he go to the funeral of his only surviving parent?'

'I doubt.'

'So why are we going?'

'Because tomorrow I meet Kuga.'

'Kuga is dead.'

'I don't think so.'

The white cloth draped over power poles tells us we are close to the funeral house. We ask Jabir to wait nearby as we get down; he says he wants to come in for some funeral rice. Cheap steel chairs line the pavement. We follow them and the direction of the chatter.

'Ari,' I say. 'The only way I can ask him to do something for Jonny is if I do something for him.'

My friend smiles. 'Why didn't you say so? Come, let's go observe.'

Funeral House

The first priority is to enter unobserved. This is not difficult for two old men at the funeral of an old lady. We blend in deftly, especially since I talked Ari out of wearing any headgear. Like the rest of the garden's population, we are clad in white. Ari's shirt is ironed and tucked into his belt. I wear an open-necked kurta. It bounces off my newly acquired belly.

Sri Lankans generally have their wakes at home. They usually begin as solemn affairs with early visitors walking past the brass lamp with its flickering wicks, bowing at the open casket and sitting outside on metal chairs, condoling with relatives. Once the body has cooled and crowds have arrived, tongues loosen and gossip ensues.

The maliciousness of this gossip is directly proportional to the distance from the casket and the bereaved. Ari and I take seats behind a herd of old ladies in white saris. Their conversation drops in volume at our approach. They are of the age where fat is beginning to turn into skin.

I exaggerate my dependency on my cane. Ari wears his sister's hearing aid and pretends to adjust it. They decide we are harmless and continue their chatter. Like most women whose husbands have slid into senility, they no longer take men very seriously.

'The son is not coming?'

'I heard he is in Australia.'

'I heard New Zealand.'

'I heard he was dead.'

'No. No. He married a Sinhalese.'

'That's even worse.'

'What was his job? Didn't study even.'

'Some sports something.'

A servant girl holds a tray of drinks to us. The choice is between Necto and Lanka Lime. One is red, one is green. Both taste like food colouring. We take one each and survey the rest of the crowd. They are mostly dark and Tamil-looking. The men are dark and moustached and the women coffee coloured and pottu-ed.

I recognise no one.

'First must serve the ladies,' says one of the witches, giving us a sideways glance. We continue to act docile and they continue to stir their cauldron.

'Now daughter will get bakery.'

'Aiyo, quality is bad now. That day I bought some patties. Hopeless.'

'The breudher was superb when Muhundan was alive.'

'The son was at Muhundan's funeral I remember. With some pretty girl.'

'I remember. Here. Isn't that the same girl?'

'That one? Are you mad? Actually might be. Looks similar.'

'She is some size, no?'

'That is not her, men.'

'Why not. Look at the face.'

We follow the direction of their attention and see Danila Guneratne with Charith Silva and a few minor cricketers whom we recognise. They surge as a unit towards the entrance that we avoided. Danila's walk is bow-legged and duck-like and utterly captivating. Greeting them is Sabi Amirthalingam and a tall thickset man who is probably her husband. We hide our faces behind our drinks as she does a head-count of the room.

The women's gossip turns to Sivali Sivanathan's eldest brother and some child he fathered.

'My hearing aid is picking up interesting things on that side,' says Ari, getting up to leave. 'And maybe you should talk to your girlfriend in private.'

'Go, men. Here. Don't let that sister see you,' I whisper. One of the quieter ladies notices Ari's departure.

The cricket party exit past the lamp and take seats around the middle of the garden. The enclosure is packed to capacity and noisy. The house is as small as my cottage in Mount; the balcony over our heads and the staircase leading to it look like recent additions. Danila spies me, smiles and walks over. The ladies in white fall silent.

The lamp is usually lit as soon as the body enters the house. In the distance I see only three of the eight wicks flickering.

'Hello, Uncle,' she says. 'I thought I might see you here.'

'You know the family?'

'I've met them, but I was never introduced.'

Danila wears jeans and a white blouse and has her hair in a bun. She spies the aunties staring at her and gives them an icy smile.

'How's the writing?'

'Very good. Do you think he'll turn up?'

'Isn't that why we're here?'

'Did you know a man called Kuga?'

'Is there something I can do for you?'

The question is not directed at me, but at the quiet old lady who has been staring at us for some time. It is not quite loud enough to cause a scene, but it is loud.

'Aunty, if you want to eavesdrop, why don't you sit here?' she says, motioning to Ari's vacant chair.

'Who wants to eavesdrop on you?' says the fattest of the lot.

'I don't know. Jobless gossips...'

'Has no one taught you how to talk?' asks the greyest.

'I wasn't speaking to you, Aunty. Unlike you I have manners.'

The aunties get up and leave muttering. I am offended and delighted by this disrespect to elders. Their seats are filled immediately by a family of seven.

'Sorry, Uncle. I hate these hags who stare at my clothes. Just because they don't know how to dress. You think we can smoke here?'

I shake my head and watch the aunties cast angry glances at us as they take seats at the corner of the garden. Danila ignores my advice and lights a smoke. Everyone nearby pretends not to notice. Then one by one they begin lighting up. Including the father of the family.

'They said you came for the father's funeral?'

'That wasn't me. He took that other bitch.'

'Shirali?'

'No. Michelle. That Burgher model slut. He was having something with her. We broke up the day his father died. He came back, of course. As usual.'

She tells me that Muhundan Sivanathan's stroke drained the family of its finances. The mother was too proud to accept money from the son-in-law she had shunned, so she pestered Pradeep.

'He didn't make much money. Used to go on and on about it. He said the only way to make money in this country is to cheat.'

She had never heard of a Lucky or a Newton or a Gokul. Though she had heard enough about Shirali.

'High Commissioner's daughter,' she says, not without bitterness. 'Men are such bloody class whores. She used to buy him clothes, let him drive her jeep. He wanted to get back with her. Even when we were together, he made that clear.'

I spy two bodybuilders in white shirts worn tails out who stand out in this sea of elderly. I fancy that they might be Sudu and Chooti, but when they sit down it is clear from their faces that they are not.

'Thing is, he was sweet. Kind, treated me with respect. Didn't just try and get me into bed. We didn't even sleep together at first, just talked.'

'About what?'

'He was worried about letting down his family. He felt he didn't have a future in cricket. He was worried that he was losing his talent.'

'What did the other cricketers say about him?'

'How should I know?'

'You know other cricketers, no?'

'I'm not as fast as you think, Uncle.'

'I am a reformed drunk. I don't judge.'

'Just after school, when I first joined advertising, I used to take the bus home. All sorts of freaks would rub themselves on me. Can't walk on the road without some pervert saying stuff. Then I got myself a boyfriend in office and made him drive me home. Might as well choose which man rubs against you, that's what I think.'

If only the aunties could hear her now. A few more families from the neighbourhood straggle inside.

'I am not like those Burgher sluts. They just cling to ministers' sons. I don't go with anyone. There are too many psychos in this town. I know a girl who had acid thrown on her breasts. Another was stabbed in a salon.'

'How long were you together?'

'I don't know if we were ever together. He assumed I had other lovers. I did till I met him. Then I stopped.'

'Why?'

'Hoping he might notice.'

'Did he?'

'He basically just did what he liked.'

Pradeep told Danila that to win back Shirali, he would even give up cricket.

'Shirali was fat, she had a boru accent, she couldn't even dance. Apparently, she was a virgin. Most rich girls are as shallow as baby pools. This one was shallower than the foot tray.'

The crowd thins out and I spy Ari pretending to be asleep next to the herd of old ladies. Or perhaps he is actually sleeping.

'Pradeep said she believed in him. Encouraged him. Said that I never did. What was I to do? I hate watching cricket. It's so boring.'

'So you didn't believe in him.'

'Maybe I didn't. But I helped him.'

She says he was a gentleman who never gossiped about other players, even though everyone slandered him. That he never sucked up to anyone, even though it cost him his place. That he was honest, even though he knew the truth hurt.

'He said that everyone should choose their life partner. And not settle for someone. He said he was a chooser and I was a settler. It was the nastiest thing anyone's ever said to me.'

As the funeral crowd thins, Danila tells me how Pradeep was terrified of being a failure, how he could sulk for weeks on end and how she once found a girl's panties and a sackful of money in his cricket bag.

'Where was the money from?'

'He never said.'

'Did he practise a lot? Play for different leagues?'

She shakes her head.

'Only when he felt like it. When I knew him, he was out of the side. I think he had given up on cricket and was just doing it because he had nothing else. He thought only Shirali could show him what to do with his life.'

'Did he mention someone called Kugarajah?'

She scratches at her painted nails and eyes me.

'How do you know him?'

'Read about him in the papers.'

'Never met him.'

'Did they fall out?'

'I don't think they were ever friends.'

A second wave of visitors descends upon the garden, mainly men and women in office garb. Some faces are familiar, though having lived in Colombo over thirty years, I find most faces are familiar. We may be a capital city, but our circles of association and our attitudes are very much small-town.

'Oh my God. What the hell is he doing here?'

I think Danila is talking about Ari, who has now woken up and is adjusting his hearing aid. But then I see an Elvis-haired man in suit and sunglasses. It is Jayantha Punchipala, former fiancé of the lovely lady at my side.

'If he makes a scene, I'm leaving.'

I put my hand on her shoulder and give it a squeeze. 'Don't worry.'

The MD goes over to the big men in white and has a word. Then he heads towards Sabi Amirthalingam with a smile on his face. The new lady of the house does not return his grin.

'Why did you put up with a man who was obsessed with someone else?'

'Jayantha?'

'No. Pradeep.'

'Oh. Who knows? When you're young, you do dumb things.'

'You could have had any man you wanted.'

She looks at me squarely and speaks without irony. 'I have. Except one.'

The MD and Sabi are in deep discussion. The mood appears to be cordial.

Ari is glaring at me with a look I cannot read.

'He was a nice guy. Good guys are rare. Didn't matter that he was moody, immature and foolish. I promised myself I'd marry for l ove. Never for money or to be respectable. It's one promise I intend to keep.'

He left for the 1995 New Zealand tour saying that he was retiring from cricket and that he was going to try and find Shirali in Australia and see if they had a chance.

'We had a huge fight. He said that no one can choose who they love. If he could choose me he would. Crap like that. He said if he ever returned he'd marry me, but he didn't plan on returning. Bastard.'

The discussion between the sister and the former MD grows more animated and appears anything but cordial. Voices are raised.

'Will you kindly leave my mother's house?' says Sabi, limbs flailing. Her husband and a few able-bodied Tamil men arrive on the scene and look ready for action. The former MD says something inaudible.

'I told you once. Kindly leave or I will call the police. Indrajith! Call the minister.'

The two men in white T-shirts rise along with another man who I recognise as the finance director of the SLBCC. They have a word in the ear with the former MD who nods at Sabi and says something else that is inaudible. They rise to leave. Sabi then spies Ari with his hearing aid.

'This one. He's also with that Kugarajah. All of you get out! Leave us in peace.'

Ari fumbles his hearing aid into his satchel and stumbles out of the gate mouthing the words 'Let's go'. Sabi Amirthalingam née Sivanathan follows Ari's line of sight and lets her glare fall on me.

'There's another one.'

I leave before she unleashes her fury on me, forgetting to say goodbye to Danila.

Shades of Brown

I am watching football with Jonny. This is a long time before allegations and excreta in pools. He is cursing people from Manchester, a city just a few hours' drive from his own. I ask him what the difference between a Geordie and a Manc is and he starts explaining the accents, both of which I find equally incomprehensible.

I ask him how many accents his little island has and he demonstrates through famous sportsmen. He begins in Scotland with Kenny Dalglish, takes me through the North East, via Messrs Boycott, Trueman and Clough. Then we visit Atherton's Manchester, the Midlands courtesy of Mansell, and end up in the east of London with Phil Tufnell.

By the time he takes me to Wales via the great Gareth Edwards, my stomach aches from laughter. But I am also amazed. One island, three nations, countless accents, but one united race. The race of Britons, united long enough to rule the world, at least for a while.

As much as Keegan hates Ferguson, he doesn't refer to him as belonging to a different species. But sadly in Sri Lanka, that is exactly what we do. It is race and religion first, country last.

'OK then. Explain the differences between Sinhalese and Tamils,' asks Jonny.

I am stumped.

I could start with the stereotypes. Sinhalese are lazy, gullible bullies. Tamils are shrewd, organised brown-nosers. Tamils have moustaches and chalk on their foreheads. Sinhalese are less dark, though not as fair as Muslims or Burghers.

The Sinhala language is sing-songy, Tamil is more guttural. Tamil names end in consonants, Sinhalese in vowels. Tamils are Hindu, Sinhalese are Buddhist. Tamils mispronounce the word baaldiya. Sinhalese eat kavum and don't like people getting ahead unless it is them.

All this tells you nothing. I can introduce you to a fair-skinned Tamil who speaks perfect Sinhala and follows the teachings of Christ and his Mother. Or take you to Tamil places that end in vowels where you may visit a Sinhalese doctor named Kariyawasam.

Sri Lanka is filled with many shades of brown. Not unlike the stuff that ended up in Jonny's pool. It is not so much the colours as the ideas that these colours spawn that I find objectionable. The united super-race of Britons may have started it when they, among other things, segregated our cricket clubs. Though it is perhaps unfair and inaccurate to lay the blame for our racial problems on the streets of Downing or the palaces of Buckingham. Despite the existence of a Sinhalese Sports Club, a Tamil Union, a Moors SC, a Burgher Recreation Club and a perversely christened Nondescripts Cricket Club, cricket as a sport refuses to be segregated. Clubs grab talent regardless of vowels or consonants or moustaches or chalk. So much for divide and conquer.

By the 1950s, we begin to develop our own dangerous ideas without any foreign assistance. The idea that the nation belongs to the Sinhala. Or that the Tamil deserves a separate state. Ideas that have clashed and exploded for the last thirty years. Perhaps one day they will be replaced by an idea of Sri Lankan-ness that welcomes all shades of brown. Though I suspect that my generation will have to die to give birth to it.

India got independence a year before us. They are larger, more diverse and more excitable than us Ceylonese, but still embrace the idea of India above the idea of being Bengali or Sikh or Muslim, something we have been incapable of doing. We are smaller in every way, including being smaller minded.

If I had to explain it, I would adopt the approach of a famous divide and conquer man, Mr Rudyard Kipling. Sinhalese are sloth bears. Lethargic, cuddly creatures of modest brains who break things if riled. Tamils are carrion crows. Resourceful creatures, resilient and peaceful unless provoked. Forget this nonsense of lions and tigers, neither of which have lived in Sri Lanka for over a millennium.

But then I look closely at the shades of brown and I see interlocking patterns. The Tamil Zion is called Eelam which derives from the same Sanskrit word as Hela, the Sinhala word for sovereignty. Men from both races gobble rice and acquire bellies at middle age. Women of both races oil their hair and spread malicious gossip. Both races can be equally feudal, equally cruel and equally capable of turning on their own. Both can be proud to the point of stupidity.

Explain the differences between Sinhalese and Tamils? I cannot. The truth is, whatever differences there may be, they are not large enough to burn down libraries, blow up banks, or send children onto minefields. They are not significant enough to waste hundreds of months firing millions of bullets into thousands of bodies.

Fort Station

At 8 o'clock on a Monday, Fort Station is not a place to be in, though I struggle to think of any time of any day of any week when this is not the case. The corners of each weekend clutter it with tired people and their sweaty suitcases, travelling to and from the outstations. Each night it becomes a homeless shelter where beggars come to lie down and dogs come to urinate.

I have black-and-white pictures of Colombo's Fort and its railway station taken circa 1890, after the British took down the cannons and lined the Dutch buildings with trees. Horse carriages and bullock carts trot the sepia streets. It could easily have been the gardens of Kensington or the boulevards of Sunset.

Today buildings built from the coffers of the Dutch East India Company are splattered with moss and have signs advertising pirated CDs hanging from them like millstones. The nearby Pettah market is clustered like a ghetto and emanates loud heat and baked noise.

I stand at the station entrance, beneath the statue of Henry Olcott, dodging the waves of commuters and ignoring the flies and the dirty children with their palms out. The walls of the station are in need of paint, and aside from a yawning ticket guard and a newspaper-reading security guard, I spy no staff.

'Let's go.'

It is neither Sudu nor Chooti, but Kalu Daniel. He is well dressed in cheap clothing. Like an office peon whose wife works in a laundry. His wavy hair is parted and combed. He is clean-shaven.

'Why so dressed up?'

'Come. Come,' says Daniel, pushing me into the streams of people.

Today the blindfold is tighter. It is not an airline sleeping mask, but a black cotton rag that feels cool against my skin. I do not recognise the driver. The van moves a few hundred metres and stops.

'Is Daniel your real name?' I ask after ten minutes of silence.

'Shut up.'

'In the papers it says your name is Daniel Fonseka.'

'I'm not going to ask you again.'

'Because that's a Sinhala name and I don't think you're Sinhala.'

'I don't like hitting old men. But if necessary I will do it.'

Then I hear a noise. It is a noise that I feel; it vibrates the van and the air around us and is followed by distant shrieks and screams. Daniel asks the driver to start the engine. The bumpy ride takes place in silence. But for once I hear things outside. The rumbling of the river. Louder than the splutter of a tractor, lower than the growl of a tank. I ask for a cigarette and my request is denied.

When the van takes the now familiar turns, I hear the sound of helicopter blades. I hear another sound, but decipher it I cannot, perhaps a Bawa-designed hovercraft. The blindfold does not come off till I'm up the stairs, through the corridor and seated on the cane chair.

The room is transformed. The TV and its speakers have disappeared. The table is a mess of files and papers. In the corner, Sudu and Chooti are feeding documents into an electric shredder. Kuga is duct-taping some boxes. Everyone is dressed in suits.

On the wall by the window the smiling picture of the Leader of the Opposition has been replaced. Now there is a solemn picture of a man a shade fairer than Kuga, but with a thicker moustache. None other than the Thalaiver, the Tiger General himself.

'You've had another important visitor I see.'

Kuga looks up at me and then at the photo. 'Ado Daniel, take this down, men! What are y'all doing?'

Kalu Daniel is pouring a Tennessee whisky that shares his surname. He looks annoyed at being interrupted and casts me a grimace.

'Who is that?' I ask, pointing to the painting of what looks like a Tamil film star bearing a scimitar.

'Kalinga Maga. The greatest king of Sri Lanka. Demonised by your Sinhala historians. There were many great Tamil kings. The last king of Kandy…'

'Who was a paranoid tyrant.'

'Ellara. The Marcus Aurelius of our nation.'

'Killed by a minister's son from the south.'

'You are a humorous character, Karunasena. But today is not the day, unless you would like to be slapped.'

Kuga finishes the last of his taping and gets up off his knees.

'Come, Mr Karuna. Let's go to the balcony.' To the other three he barks, 'I'll be done in half an hour. When I come back, this room must be cleared.'

The three of them glare at me as if it is my fault.

* * *

Do you recall mosquitoes being such a problem in the 80s? Or the 70s?

Malaria. DDT…

No. I mean in Colombo. Didn't you just put your fan on and sleep?

Those days I could sleep anywhere after putting a shot. Fan or no fan.

Today everyone has to light coils, put mats, spray sprays.

Where are you packing and going?

Two large companies came up with a plan to breed mosquitoes along the canals of Colombo in 1986. That was my first freelance assignment.

The papers say…

Today mosquito coils are the second largest selling consumer item in this country, next to cigarettes.

Is the government handing you over to the LTTE?

Let's just say my position is now...what is the word?

Redundant.

Untenable. Redundant? Mr Karuna. Sri Lanka will always need men like me. I will just be replaced.

So fixing matches and running brothels isn't your main source of income.

I went to university in Sussex. I did my masters in Toronto. I lost two cousins in '83. I joined because I had to. When you are young, those things are easy to identify.

Why have you called me?

If you find Pradeepan, I want you to give him this letter.

Will this letter get me killed?

Please see that he gets it.

He wasn't at his mother's funeral, chances are I will never see him.

I think you will.

* * *

Ari's sister's hearing aid was a Siemens Intuit 64, as white and cumbersome as the good lady herself. Patsy Holsinger née Byrd stopped using it after her sister-in-law Manouri took her to a faith healer in Moratuwa who cured her of a chronic ear infection. The same charlatan they tried to inflict on me.

Ari borrowed it to eavesdrop on his daughters' conversations, though Stephanie, Melissa and even little Aruni were aware of their father's efforts. Manouri would warn them whenever Ari began pressing the unwieldy white receiver to the wall. One day he told me with delight that all his daughters were virgins who had friends who were boys, but who knew their limits. I remember trying not to smile and being told off.

In return for not wearing headgear, Ari had insisted on taking the hearing aid. I let him even though I could see no point. The contraption was eleven years old and amplified every sound it picked up. In a crowded place like a funeral house, it would be impossible to distinguish any specific conversation with any degree of clarity.

Ari, the gadget man himself, tells me that I am deeply wrong. He shows me old photographs he stole on his way to the Sivanathan bathroom.

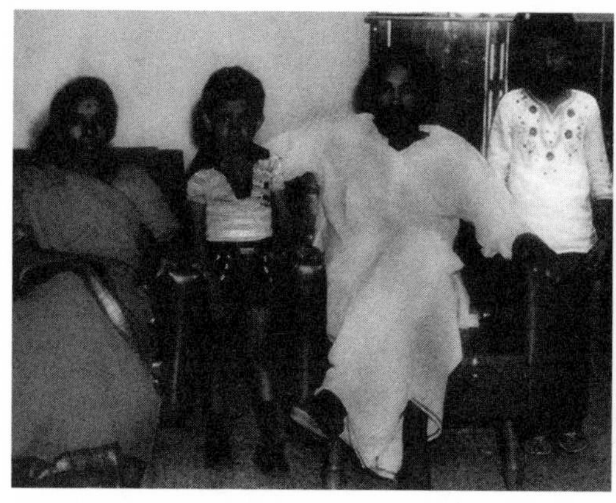

'You stole photos?'

'Good for your book, no?'

'How?'

'I just grabbed the photo album off the piano, took it into the toilet and took a few. There were extras.'

They are shots of a boy that Ari swears is Pradeep Mathew. In a cot, with family, in a junior cricket team. The handful Ari grabbed evidently came from the beginning of the album. I reserve my judgement on both the boy in the photos and my pious friend's kleptomania.

This friend you want me to help. Is he political?

Only when it comes to football. That was a joke.

These days, it's hard with foreigners. I will do what I can, but can't promise.

Are you leaving the island?

What else do you need to know about Pradeepan?

He said he was leaving to find Shirali.

Who said that?

Danila.

The Cricket Board bicycle? Pradeepan took that woman for a ride.

She says she loved him.

For me he was a brother. After the Indian People Killing Force came in, I had to take a break. Orders from Thalaiver. I was doing my best work then. I lost my brothers Kutti and Jegan in the Welikada Prison massacre. I watched my friend Thileepan starve to death, dreaming of Eelam.

How long was your break?

Five years before Eelam War 2 began. So during '89's failed revolution, while Sinhalese were slaughtering each other on the roads, I was fixing cricket matches.

Danila said you and Pradeep fell out.

We weren't on good terms at the end, but that's what families are like. Even though I was supporting the Sivanathans, helping his talent, getting him contracts.

Why?

He was my brother. Like the hundreds of Tamil brothers I had lost. I wanted to help him.

Why weren't you on good terms?

He didn't like the assignments.

Assignments?

A few wides, here and there. Costs a few runs, earns thousands.

You realise I will write about this?

You realise no one will publish if you mention my name? Not this government nor the next. Guaranteed.

You fixed local games also?

Had to. They were so bloody boring. All our buggers scoring centuries for the selectors. I only made them interesting.

How did you fix 1992?

It was a simple job. I only had to fix the last day.

The day our batting collapsed?

Yes.

How many players did you tap?

Just one.

The captain?

Who needed him, men? I had my boy.

Pradeep took eight wickets in that game.

You don't need a ball or a bat to fix a game. There are so many things you can use.

Like whores?

Like kadale.

* * *

When the MD walked in, he said, 'My deepest sympathies, Mrs Amirthalingam.' She asked him how he knew her mother and he replied that he knew her brother well. Then Sabi said something Ari couldn't hear because the ladies were jabbering about the rude girl flirting with the old man. Then Sabi raised her voice and asked the MD to leave.

Then the MD said her brother stole half a million New Zealand dollars. Then Sabi asked them again to leave and her husband came to the rescue. The MD said that he knew her brother was not dead and that he would find him. Sabi's husband said he was calling the Minister of Agriculture. To which the MD said, 'Tell Jeyaraj I said hi,' and left.

This bit is all according to Ari. Not unlike how this whole book is all according to me.

* * *

It's easy being a soldier. They tell you who your enemy is and all you have to do is aim and shoot.

I think it's slightly more difficult than that.

In my line of work it's never clear who your enemy is. I had no problems with my first assignments. Most of the names ended in vowels. I didn't do it for money. Then the names changed. Amirthalingam. Ponnambalam. Tiruchelvam. I asked myself what I was doing it for. You get older. You realise.

Only then you realised? What about when you were recruiting children, using suicide bombers?

Children? Really? The US army and the British armed forces recruit at sixteen. From schools. And train them to go to the third world and shoot at someone's mother. You think Tamil parents who wake their children at 5 to study would want them to run around jungles with guns? But after the government has raped and slaughtered those parents, I defy any fourteen-year-old to not pick up a weapon.

Suicide bombing is a cowardly…

Cowardly? Cowardly is when the US sit in an ocean 75 miles from Baghdad and fire smart missiles into the town. Those missiles aren't very smart. They hit hospitals, schools, shopping malls. With suicide bombing you look into the eyes of the man you kill. You don't flatten a city to punish a handful.

But you're killing your younger generation. And you're not getting international sympathy.

Fuck the international sympathy. The Japs used kamikazes and there was honour in committing hara-kiri for your country. Alfred Lord Tennyson wrote the 'Charge of the Light Brigade'. 'Into the valley of death, rode the 600, blah, blah.' In the Crimean War walking into certain death was heroic. Not for our Eelam war? Fucking bullshit.

So why did you leave the LTTE?

No one leaves the LTTE. The Thalaiver runs this country by default. He decides who is elected, who lives. He is no longer a terrorist, he is a multinational CEO. Our Leader has outlasted the Dynasty. He has outlasted the UNP. He will never die.

What if the Sri Lankan government wins the war?

The LTTE have a de facto state. We even get our own diesel shipped from Norway. The Sri Lankan army will not win till they hold the head of the Thalaiver, blood dripping, in front of parliament.

You're reading too much poetry.

This war will not end. But I have to make my living.

This war will continue for as long as it turns a profit.

That's bullshit. People think it's bravery that wins wars. It's not. It's cruelty. But even that's not enough. You need to be cunning.

All our governments have been cruel and cunning.

Not enough. To win wars you need to carpet-bomb civilians. And to get away with carpet-bombing civilians. Believe me, the second part is tougher than the first.

What about negotiation?

Nagasaki. Hiroshima. Gulf. Gaza. Carpet-bomb and then sell the carpet bomb. I'm bored of this. I invited you to talk about cricket.

Cricket then. Was Pradeep happy to fix matches?

He was an honest Tamil boy. He didn't like it, but what to do? After the rebel South Africa tour failed, he really didn't have much choice.

Father's illness?

He was the highest wicket taker in the Asia Cup, but no one took notice, because they believed the matches were fixed. I told him if he was going to suffer the consequences, he might as well do the crime.

How many matches?

After '92, all of them. Not that he didn't let me down.

He let you down?

I would lose money and threaten to break his fingers.

Did you?

Mad? We are not barbarians like the Indians. There they threaten the players' children. He was my thambi. Like a little brother. If he had stayed I would've got him into the World Cup squad. He would have been a superstar. I still can. He's only thirty-four.

Now with Murali, no chance.

Anything is possible. How do you think Murali is still playing?

You haven't seen Mathew since you were…since you moved here?

I called after the father died. Said he didn't need my money. I told him Tamils should stick together. He didn't care.

The papers say you are dead.

That's how you gain residence in Chelvanayagam Road.

That's what this street is called? Don't make me laugh.

This house is named Janathamangalam. Number 56/19. The great man himself stayed here.

So this is a jail?

Oh no. Jails are places where they don't let you watch cricket.

Really?

Unless you have contacts. I watched every match of the 1995 New Zealand tour from the Welikada Prison, but I'm special. Pradeepan didn't play a single game.

That friend I told you about…

The foreigner?

Yes. Could you do one other small thing for him?

Computer Printout

It is the last I would see of Kuga or Emmanuel or Rajah or whoever he has decided to be. Ari, worried sick about Jonny, is too preoccupied to accuse me of making things up when I report the conversation with Kuga.

I call up my old journo acquaintances looking for reassurance. Rajpal Senanayake of the *Times* has never heard of Kuga, neither has Sonali Sirimanne, the *Leader* writer who exposed former President Mr Benevolent Dictator's dealings with underworld thug Soththi Upali. Rajeeve Ayub of *Virakesari* remembers a man called Emmanuel who ran casinos in Mutwal. Only Dalton Athas, a young war reporter, remembers the name I.E. Kugarajah from a list of Colombo-based LTTE collaborators.

I reopen the letter I am to deliver to the phantom I am chasing. It is a computer printout in the style of Kuga's other notes and made about as much sense.

Pradeepan
Hope you are well.
I have your final payment from Anandan.
I regret your actions. But I miss your friendship.
Please reply
iek@hotmail.com

Danila calls up, skips small talk and asks why we were kicked out of the funeral. 'Are you working for Kugarajah?'

'We're not.'

There is hesitation.

'One day, '92 or '93, I think. Pradeep wanted me to pick him up from hospital. He had a broken finger and a black eye. It wasn't a cricket injury.'

'That's when he was out for an entire season?'

'He wouldn't tell me how he got it.'

'So?'

'He stayed in bed for weeks. Complained of headaches. In his sleep he would say this name.'

I notice Ari coming down my driveway huffing with intent. 'Danila, can I call you back?'

'When I asked him he said Kuga was the reason he wanted to leave Sri Lankan cricket.'

'Why?'

'Be careful, Uncle. These are dangerous people.'

She cuts the line right when Ari enters my room panting.

'Let's go. Jonny's being moved.'

The Lissa

The Aussies claim ownership of the flipper, invented by Clarrie Grimmet in the 1930s. Ari and I do not dispute this. Grimmet snapped his fingers along the ball's axis and made it skid off the pitch, keep low and, more often than not, connect with the wicket.

Mathew upped the ante by developing a ball that skidded and changed direction. He used it against tailenders in the 1989 Australia series and picked up 3 wickets. Walking back after a skidding googly toppled his bails, pace bowler Merv Rackemann spat in the direction of the bowler, 'You been sticking your dick into the seam, mate?'

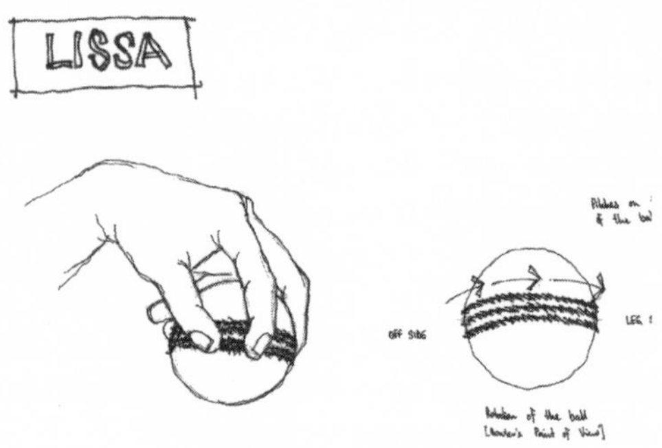

Mathew dismissed Rackemann, Alderman and Lawson with googly flippers in Melbourne in 1989. Ari believes it is probable that somewhere in the grounds Shane Warne witnessed this feat and spent the next few years attempting to emulate it. That therefore it is correct to say that Pradeep Mathew indirectly revived the flipper.

I reply that if three tailenders fall in the outback and there is no one to hear them, then no sound is made. And to attempt to convince an audience ten years later that such a sound existed is an exercise in foolishness.

Bombs

The drive to the Hokandara Remand Camp in Ari's Capri takes over three hours. We get lost several times. After Kadawatha, the roads pass through paddy fields and bewildering wilderness. The road itself is cruel, inflicting torture on the Capri's creaking chassis. After three weeks in Welikada Maximum Security, Jonny has been moved to this prison camp reserved for the aged, the infirm and the white collar. I wonder how kind they are to the white skin.

We listen to the Sri Lanka Broadcasting Corporation, SLBC, and do not speak. It is the only station the Capri will pick up and Ari prefers it that way. This afternoon, a middle-aged lady is talking about Duke Ellington's visit to Colombo. As we enter through a barbed wire fence, a rare bootleg of the Duke's performance at the Galle Face Hotel crackles through Ari's tiny speaker.

The place looks like a rundown retirement home. It is not an unpleasant place, but it is eerie. The gravel that crunches under our tyres is brick coloured and stretches through checkpoints towards the open camp. A red dryness hangs in the air we breathe. The mini-fan clipped to the top of the rearview mirror is powerless to prevent our shirts from sticking to our backs.

Policemen walk dogs along the barbed wire while stray cats pick at abandoned rubbish bags outside. We have to show our identity cards to four different policemen with clipboards before we are allowed to park. Prisoners wear white shirts and shorts, and are herded from one asbestos building to another. It looks like a village school, but is as noisy as several construction sites. Beyond the vegetable fields, we see an empty quarry.

A guard with a rifle leads us into a visitors' hall. The room is empty except for a long wooden table and an assortment of metal chairs. Here we sit and wait.

He wears a white shirt and white shorts and limps in on crutches. He has strawberry patches on his arms and has lost a visible amount of weight. He coughs as he is seated at the other end of the table. There are no handcuffs to remove.

'Can I have a cigarette?' His voice is coloured by the phlegm in his throat; his face is colourless.

'Are you OK, Jonny?' asks Ari.

'Welikada was worse than Bangkok. But this place looks all right.'

'What happened?' I ask, pointing at the crutches.

Jonny looks away. 'Six to a cell. You know how much I love company. They put me with the drug addicts, not with the psychos, thank God. One of them tried it. Told him he wasn't my type. He wouldn't listen. I broke his nose. He broke my hip. I heal easily though.'

Two guards gaze out at the permanent summer sky; the one with the gun watches me.

'This is a bizarre place. They've got everything. They make things out of coconuts over that way; here they're making soaps, over there leather goods. They've got welding, masonry, carpentry. Pity they don't get me to work.'

'How come?'

'I shouldn't be here. This is a place for good behaviour prisoners. I haven't even been sentenced.'

'How's the case?'

'The work I have to do is sit in the TV room and look after the TV.'

We both laugh. 'Perfect job for you.'

'Thought my lawyer pulled some strings, but he's a useless fucking twat. It's a strange TV. Got this laser disc player.'

I silently thank Kuga, wherever he may be.

'Laser disc?' asks Ari.

'Laser disc, my friend. State-of-the-art model. Doesn't have cable though.'

He talks about Newcastle United and how they've sacked coach Kenny Dalglish and replaced him with Dutch hero Ruud Gullit.

'Last season we were thirteenth. Two seasons ago we come second and now this. Bloody Scotsmen can never coach Geordies.'

'And Dutchmen can?'

'Let's see. New season. *Tabula rasa*.'

He asks me how the writing and the not-drinking is going. I tell him I may have stumbled on the most amazing cricket story ever not told. Ari tells him about the midget's spools, I keep the Kuga story to myself. Jonny smiles and chain-smokes.

'Basically, if the High Commission pulls out, I'm screwed. I could get twenty years.'

'Will the High Commission pull out?'

He tells us he spent six weeks in Thailand before the High Commission lifted a finger. It has now been three months.

'That time it was possession of marijuana. They treated it as a misdemeanour. This time…'

He begins shivering, his mouth inverts like a stroke victim's, and he breaks into a sob. The guards look away, the man with the gun keeps his eyes on me. 'Ten more minutes,' he says.

'Ari. Adolf and Eva's last meal. We discussed this.'

'Jonny, are you mad? We'll win the case.'

'I can't wait that long. You said you knew how to get it.'

'You can live here. This isn't a bad place.'

'They could send me to Welikada and throw away the key. I'm too old for this crap.'

Ari shakes his head. Jonny wipes his eyes and straightens up.

'I didn't do what they said I did. You know that.'

'We know,' I say.

'You don't. But I'm telling you. I didn't.'

'We know. We know,' I say, somewhat helplessly.

'The locals don't like suddhas building palaces in this paradise.'

'Don't be stupid.'

'I admit. There are bad foreigners. Who sleep with children. Who give visas for sexual favours. Who bring guns and drugs here. But that's not me. Well…maybe the drugs.'

We both laugh, it is better than crying.

'I was helping the country. That's why I built my homes. This land is beautiful, but you fuckers will destroy it.'

We remain silent.

'When I clashed with the hunters in Udawalawe, the police advised me to leave the area. Me! Not them. Everywhere you go in this country, there are hunters. Can't believe I lasted here this long.'

'We will prove you're innocent.'

'Ari, mate. I sleep with boys. And sodomy is a crime here, so if they want to get me, they can.'

'They're not going to get you,' I say, not looking at Ari.

'I don't do fourteen-year-olds. Whoever says so is a liar.'

'So we'll fight it.'

'What are you going to do? Write to the papers?' Jonny sneers. 'You may think this place is fine, but I'm not spending another month here.'

I pull a paper out of my pocket. 'Here. I brought you a present.'

For the first time that afternoon Jonny laughs his raucous, head-thrown-back laugh. It is glorious to see. He hands the paper to Ari, who joins in the chuckles.

'Saqlain Mushtaq Mohammad Asif Iqbal Sikander Bakht. That's seven. I believe we have a new champion,' I say.

'I feel like Gary Sobers after Lara got 375,' says drama queen Ari, the former Seamless Paki champ.

The guard grabs the paper and inspects it. 'Visit over,' he says.

'There's one fucker around here that I will kill,' says Jonny through gritted teeth. He pushes the guard, who raises his baton. Ari uses his schoolmaster voice and calms proceedings. 'Putha, put that away. Let us say goodbye to our friend.'

We are too far down the table to even shake his hand.

'We will get you out of here, Jonny,' says Ari.

'Chin up, Jonny. You need to be fit for when Shearer and sexy football win Toon the league.'

He laughs and nods and pushes an envelope across the table. 'I don't trust these cunts. Will you post this for me? It's for me Mam.'

'What about brothers or sisters?' asks Ari.

The guards put on the cuffs and lead him away.

'They can all get fucked,' he shouts. 'Ari. Adolf and Eva. You promised.'

We drive back without speaking. Then we get stuck in traffic in Kiribathgoda.

'You know Newcastle is fifteenth in the league,' I say. 'They might even get relegated.'

'You been following them?'

'Ever since he got arrested.'

'Me too.'

'What's Adolf and Eva?'

'You know. You were there.'

'Was I drunk?'

'Probably.'

'I can't remember.'

Ari puts on the radio and curses the traffic.

'It's what the LTTE wear around their necks. And I'm not getting it for him.'

The drunken conversation returns to me. Something about agreeing to euthanise each other if the case ever arose. But I don't remember cyanide ever being discussed.

'This is breaking news. Yesterday's bomb blast in Fort Station is now officially Sri Lanka's worst terrorist attack since the 1995 Central Bank bombing.'

I try to turn up the radio and the knob comes off in my hand.

'What the hell are you doing?' shouts Ari, who grabs it from me and replaces it. The volume jumps several hundred decibels.

'At present 247 are dead and a further 187 injured. Police Search and Defuse Operations also unearthed hidden explosives at Vihara Maha Devi Park and Dehiwela Zoo…'

The knob comes off again in Ari's hand and the deafening news announcer is silenced. It takes traffic three hours to clear and we are unable to fix the radio.

Sri Jayawardenapura Kotte

What's the capital of Sri Lanka? What's our national sport? Neither answer begins with C.

Volleyball is our national sport, even though less than 4 per cent of the population play it. My friend Renganathan reckons that elle, a native form of softball, was our national sport at independence till the Sports Minister fell out with the Elle Federation in the 1970s and conferred that status to volleyball. Renga also reckons that Dirk Welham was the best batsman he'd ever seen.

Sri Jayawardenapura Kotte was made administrative capital in the 1980s, possibly because it housed the parliament, or more probably because it contained the then president's surname. It remains the capital today, which means the majority of Sri Lankans would answer the question that opens this chapter incorrectly.

Kugarajah uses fancy words like genocide and gamesmanship and genius. I wish I had the courage to tell him that just because you say something is something doesn't mean that it is. And just because you want something to be something doesn't mean that it will be.

Kadale

When kadale is boiled and tempered with onion and chilli it becomes more than just a serving of chickpeas. It transforms into a high-protein snack, perfect for both athletes and drunkards.

I make a decision not to get depressed about Jonny. Garfield has been out of touch for three weeks since leaving his wife for the I've-lost-count time. Sheila's good mood has evaporated and she plods through the house, imploring me to do something. As if I possess a global tracking device.

These are the possible scenarios:

A. Jonny is a child molester and will rot for his sins.
B. Jonny is a child molester who the High Commission will rescue and provide counselling for.
C. Jonny is an innocent homosexual who will rot for someone else's agenda.
D. Jonny is an innocent homosexual who will be set free.

I decide to avoid depression, because while C is the most likely, D is not an impossibility. There is little I can do to influence the outcome. Worry for me is like drink. If I start I may be unable to stop.

So I drink tea and hammer at my Jinadasa. But while I write about Charith and Reggie and Danila and defused bombs, my thoughts return to Jonny and his Mam. Ari does not let me read the letter and insists we post it straightaway. 'It is a man's private confession, it is not for our eyes.' Pious bugger.

They can all get fucked. That's what Jonny said about his brothers and sisters. It is a sentiment I know well.

In other news, Jabir, Ari and the midget have a severe falling-out. Uncle Neiris accuses Ari of stealing spools, Ari accuses Uncle Neiris of taping over them. The midget chases Ari away with a mammoty and says he will curse Ari's family.

Jabir takes Ari's side and is also banished. They are told if they reveal the location of the bunker their tongues will rot in their mouths. I am in Ari's room, looking up the archives of Mathew's last tours, when the two of them storm in, flustered and flabbergasted, and begin debating whether the old man's curse has any power.

'I'm not scared of that fool,' says Ari.

'If he can lay curses to keep the Aussies and Windies away, what can't he do?'

'You daredevils are shivering over a midget with a squeaky voice?' I say. 'Pathetic.'

'You didn't see him, Wije,' says Ari.

'Ade, what are those?' asks Jabir, the colour draining from his face.

'Those are…some…his things,' Ari stammers.

Jabir picks up the box and glares like an enraged skeleton. 'You said you returned them all.'

'I must've forgotten.'

'Very bad, Ari,' I say, starting to laugh. But Jabir is not amused.

He pushes past Ari carrying the box and storms through the archway. 'Because of you I will also get cursed.'

'Shall I come with you?' calls Ari.

'Don't ever come anywhere with me,' shouts Jabir.

I look at my friend and smile and shake my head. 'Too much you are.'

He winks at me and grabs my cane. 'Doesn't bother me, kid. He didn't get the real merchandise.'

Then Bogart Holmes reaches behind the TV, fishes out a spool and plops it into his machine, and we sit back and listen. Ari has spent the last five months going through three decades of gobbledygook, a far more tedious task than documenting unreliable memories. In between birdcalls, unintelligible small talk, crowd cheers and unedited stretches of ball hitting bat, he has unearthed a few gems.

We hear a prominent Sri Lankan batsman boasting in the comfort of the dressing room that he only does his best when there's a car offered for the Man of the Match. The said batsman has won over forty such awards in his career.

We hear an Australian wicketkeeper describe a young Pakistani's girlfriend in the most obscene language. There is no retaliation, due either to the Pakistani's sage-like patience or his ignorance of English. Having known a few Pakistanis, I favour the latter.

And then there is this:

What do you mean you can't bat?

Stomach hurting.

You also. Roshan also can't bat. Here. We can't fuck this.

[Roar of crowd]

Marvan? What the hell. Here. You have to pad up now.

Isn't there a doctor?

What doctor? You think this is Nawasiri?

I recognise both voices as belonging to two of our World Cup heroes. It's hard not to.

Bloody fool. What was that shot?
Aney Aiye. Don't be angry. Stomach.
You also have loose motion? This is like an emergency room. What the hell did you eat?
I think it was that kadale.
I also ate the kadale.
Don't talk crap. I also ate the kadale.
You didn't eat like us.
Roshan ate half the bowl.
Who brought kadale into the dressing room yesterday? I will murder you. Was it that thambi bugger?
Clipper-clipper-clipper.

The spool ends there. I examine the cover, knowing exactly what I will spy there. It is a cover that Jabir has forgotten to take, or one that Ari has decided to keep for himself.

It reads: 'Test/one Day Matchs, 1987–1992 (NewZe, Indiya, Paki, Aussi).'

The Creature

The creature returns at the most inconvenient of moments, right when I am telling my wife that we cannot go anywhere for Christmas. She has been spending more of her time at the Mount Lavinia Ladies' Charity Circle. Chinniah the dentist is taking his wife to New York, Mrs Livera is visiting friends in Bangalore, even old Mrs Bodiyabaduge is being taken to Hill Country with her children.

I tell her I have lots to write. She hands me an ekel broomstick before she storms out. I am back on household chores. 'Remember when you were writing your poetry to me? Said you would take me to Paris. Leave alone Paris, even Negombo beach will do. I will seriously find myself a rich lover.'

That threat crops up twice every decade. There was a time when it would fill me with terror. These days, if the candidate was suitable, I might even welcome it.

The creature arrives when I'm sweeping the sand from my car-less driveway. I feel my hands turn to jelly and I cannot stop coughing. Kusuma, who has been watching me from the veranda, brings me a glass of water. I hand her back the broom, but she shakes her head. 'Nona told me not to help you.'

The creature sits at the bottom of my stomach and blows bubbles up through my throat into my skull. The creature is more cat than monkey. It wraps its tail around my spine and blows idly into my head. It is not pleasant.

Will the curse of drink never leave me? When I couldn't write, I drank in desperation. When I wrote well, I drank in celebration. I drank when I was bored and alone. I drank when I was surrounded by loved ones. I drank on the hilltops of Badulla, in the backyards of Kurunegala and in the verandas of Colombo. I drank when I was an angry young man, a petulant father, and a sad old bastard.

I have done things I cannot remember and things I opt to forget. Let me make this clear. This is not my autobiography. Which is why I have gone through over 200 pages without mentioning ________________.

Or ________________.

Or even ____________________.

I have before me a story and I need the strength to finish it. I have no bottle or friendly Geordie to guide me. Is it a coincidence that my crate of Flowery Broken Orange Fanning Special runs out a week after Jonny is imprisoned? Thank God there is no God. Because to believe in him would be to acknowledge that he doesn't like me much.

I put away the broom and lie down on my haansi putuwa and watch Hansie Cronje, on Ari's TV, setting the field like a finicky host against our openers in the blistering Sharjah heat. I close my eyes and dream of Jonny.

Again we are in the pavilion of the SSC. Jonny is wearing white and has the creature on his lap. At first I refuse to sit next to him.

'Relax, WeeGee. It's harmless.'

Before us Hansie Cronje is setting the field like a finicky host.

'I think I've seen this game before.'

'Every game has been played a million times before. Even yours and mine.'

Allan Donald runs in like an albino demon and Sanath swings and misses. Next to me Jonny is stroking the creature like mafia dons stroke cats. Though the animal looks more monkey than cat. It falls asleep.

'It's Christmas, WeeGee.'

'Don't you start.'

'Are you going to make a list and check it twice?'

I wake up with a jolt and decide to do exactly that.

Holiday Plans

Since joining the Mount Lavinia gossip circle, Sheila wears more make-up and prettier dresses. She refers to Kusuma not as our servant, but as our domestic, and she has stopped talking to me about Garfield. Perhaps she has acquired that lover after all.

I am waiting for her on the veranda. She steps out of the afternoon sun carrying a flowery umbrella and a plastic bag of groceries. She avoids my eye.

'We will leave for Badulla on the 15th. We will spend a week there. On the 22nd we will arrive in Kurunegala. We will spend Christmas there and New Year in Dambulla.'

She inspects the swept driveway with suspicion. 'How are we travelling?'

'Ari will lend us his Ford.'

'That wreck won't even get us down a hill.'

'It is serviced and ready.'

'We will break our necks.'

Kusuma brings in the tea and Sheila sits next to me on the ledge. No more Orange Pekoe. This is third-rate factory floor dust, packaged by the name on the cricketers' shirts and sold to us hapless locals. I do not let this depress me.

'Money?'

'I have a bit of the documentary money left. It will be more than enough.'

'Where will we stay?'

'Ossie's son is running the plantation. He says we can stay there. Ossie might come.'

Ossie, a retired planter from Diyatalawa, is one of our oldest friends from our Badulla days.

'What about Kurunegala?'

'We can stay with my sister.'

'What about…'

'I plan on meeting Loku, Maddhu and Bala. I will speak with them.'

Sheila puts her umbrella down, kneels before me, wraps her arms around me and kisses me full on the mouth.

'Not here, men. Kusuma will see.'

'Who cares?' says Sheila, planting kisses on my cheeks and forehead. I dart my eyes to the sides of their sockets and see Kusuma holding an empty tray. She is indeed looking, but she is also smiling.

God in His Tavern

It matters little if God exists. Because even if he does, I guarantee he is not in his heaven, but in his tavern. He is probably exhausted from creation and is enjoying a nice long pint of Lion Lager or polishing off an eternal cup of Old Reserve. Enjoying a well-earned thirty-millennium nap. His bit is done and sorting itself out is now the universe's problem.

We do not have a loving Christian God or a vengeful Islamic God or a non-existent Buddhist one or even a multiple Hindu one. We have an indifferent invisible one. He has done his shift, filled his timesheet and is off for the weekend.

I write to Loku apologising for what I said to his wife. I write to Maddhu saying sorry for the damage to his property. I write to Bala promising to repay him. I write and tell Garfield that I miss him. I tell each of them a white lie. That I am dying and need to see them. Sheila posts all four letters.

Then I make the list. It has ten items on it. I pin it to the wall I stare at and stare at it some more. I hear noises outside. I take down the list and cross out Item 7: Become a cricket umpire. I gaze at Item 3: Write Mathew. I underline this.

I carry my cane and walk outside. The afternoon sun is descending and the light is copper. The trees glisten and a breeze from Mount Lavinia beach catches what's left of my hair.

On the road the Marzooq boys are arguing a run-out with the beach boys.

'He was on the line.'

'On the line is out.'

'Mad. On the line is in.'

I walk up to the shirtless monkeys and their squabbles. The batting team is costumed in sweat-drenched T-shirts. I smile kindly at the batsman. 'Sorry, Mufadel. On the line is out.'

'See, I told you,' sneers the beach boy.

I stand in the shade behind the wicket and look upon the boys staring at me. 'From now I am your umpire. New batsman, please.'

'Last man, have chance,' says the dejected batsman. I nod.

The fielders slowly return to their corners and the Marzooq boy hands the bat to his younger cousin. The boy steps up the crease and takes guard.

'Middle and off, sir?'

I watch the sun streak through the clouds onto this wide pavement.

I watch the cars avoid de Saram Road, for fear of disrupting the game. I tell the boy there is no such thing and give him a middle guard. I wait till the batsman is ready and I instruct the beach boy to bowl. God is indeed in his tavern and he may have just ordered another round.

Three Names

I dig up my scrapbooks to find out where I have seen this bearded man. The bearded man who lives next door to Kuga, who records my documentaries on laser disc, who has a copy of *Godfather 4*, who answers to the name Rohana.

Recent Sri Lankan history does recall a bearded Rohana. The leader of the university Marxists who staged an abortive revolution in 1971, ran an unsuccessful election campaign in '82 and then held the island by its throat during the late 1980s. Rohana Wijeweera, bespectacled, bearded and bereted, resembling Ernesto Guevara, if Che had been dark, short-sighted and ugly.

This is not the Rohana I seek.

When I find the scrapbook entry and view the picture I know I have made no mistake. It is a picture of Rohana Vindana Kumara, twenty-one-year-old naval officer, famous – notorious – for attempting to kill an Indian prime minister.

It was our JFK-in-Dallas moment, political assassination live on camera while the whole nation watched. Rajiv Gandhi was here to sign a peace accord with Sri Lanka, pledging to send ground forces to crush the LTTE, the very rebels his own mother had armed. Straight off the plane, Gandhi is walked past soldiers in white, standing to attention. And then, without warning, an arm of dissent is raised from the sea of conformity and a bearded naval officer brings his rifle butt down on the premier's head.

Our assassin differed from his American counterpart in two ways: (a) He missed his shot. (b) He got caught. The accord led to the IPKF, Indian Peace Keeping Force, raping and burning their way through the north and east. It would be several years before a Sri Lankan successfully took out a Gandhi.

Thenmuli Rajaratnam, the photograph of whose severed head was published by *TimesWeek*, was sent by the LTTE to avenge the presence of the IPKF, known later – not unfairly – as the Innocent People Killing Force. This suicide bomber was unique among assassins for (a) being a woman and (b) not having a middle name.

In fact many assassins are known by three names. John Wilkes Booth. Lee Harvey Oswald. James Earl Ray. Mark David Chapman. I'm sure there are more.

Side note. Sri Lanka's most dependable pace bowler has not three, but six names. One of the wittier Sri Lankan banners of recent times had the caption, 'Sri Lanka will win faster than you can say Warnakulasuriya Patabendige Ushantha Joseph Chaminda Vaas.'

The article on Rohana Vindana Kumara appeared in the *Sunday Times* a year after the would-be assassin's release from prison and described a disappointed man living in a Nawala shanty, filled with audio cassettes and mistakes.

The article described a lone patriot, unaffiliated to any hate group. Who spent four years in prison where some treated him as a hero. While he was there, his brothers were relieved of their government jobs and his family of their Navy-sponsored house. He was courted by pro-Sinhala expats and promised jobs and trips abroad when he was released. Nothing of the sort materialised.

> I saw the Peace Accord as something that would destroy our country. When the entire nation was against it, the leaders went ahead. I felt I had to do something to disrupt it. When I decided to hit the Prime Minister, I knew I could be killed but I was prepared to make that sacrifice.
>
> Rohana Vindana Kumara
> Quoted in the *Sunday Times* 16/03/97

How did a failed assassin with a middle name, a dead magnate and a convicted hijacker end up living on a road with no power poles? What does this have to do with Pradeep Sivanathan Mathew? Answers I believe I have.

Sledging

Sledging refers to on-field verbal abuse, usually meted out by a fielding side to disturb a batsman's concentration. It is called 'gamesmanship' in the same way rugby calls stomping on someone's head 'part of the sport'.

My favourite sledge is from Zimbabwean tail-ender Eddo Brandes when ill-tempered Aussie pacey Glenn McGrath, unable to penetrate the chicken farmer's defence, decides to turn on the belligerence:

McGrath: Oi Eddo. Why are you so fat?
Brandes: 'Cos every time I f*** your wife she gives me a biscuit.

The Aussies are seen as the main exponents of sledging. Indeed, past captains Chappell, Border, Taylor and now Waugh have professed their approval of 'mental disintegration'. But sledging is by no means exclusive to these canary yellow foul-mouths.

Pakistanis sing, chant, argue, swear and soliloquise in raw Urdu right in the batsman's face and nothing can be done. To the untrained ear, even a love song in Urdu can sound like a threat to rape one's mother. Yet it is impossible to bring accusations against a tongue you don't understand. A fact the Pakis are well aware of.

Monolingual New Zealanders would combat this by stringing Maori place names together in aggressive, haka-like phrasing:

Wasim Afridi (at first slip): 'Behen Chod. Gadha. Tattai Chooso.'
Nathan Parore (Kiwi batsman): 'Tamaranui-waipukarau. Rangatekeinelson.'
Afridi: 'Teri Ma kutti. Is this batsman? Gandu.'
Parore: 'Urupukapuka-whakatane. Ekatahuna-ugly cunt.'

A recording of this was found on a spool titled 'Janalinco Trigular 97'. Sri Lankans never talked back, an attribute encouraged by coaches like the GenCY and enjoyed by the Afridis and McGraths of this world. Veteran street fighter Mustaq Miandad once sledged a Lankan opening batsman to tears and for the rest of the tour nicknamed him 'boo-hoo cry-baba'. The batsman averaged 11 in that tournament and never played again.

Another batsman upset by sledging was a pudgy little Anandian who was one day to become the captain. It was on the 1989 Australia tour. The lad had taken verbals from Hughes and Rackemann and had retaliated with a few swear words that drew chuckles from the fielding side due to bad pronunciation.

'He came to our room fully upset,' says Charith. 'Then Pradeep advised us both.'

He told them to ignore the GenCY, but not to just swear and get upset.

'He said to analyse the sledger. Look for weapons. Taylor is battling for his place. Waugh's girlfriend just dumped him. To find the weakness and attack.'

The not-yet captain stopped whining and listened.

'After he became captain, he forgot that Pradeep was the man who gave him that advice.'

Three years later, playing at Hobart's Bellerive Oval, tired of debutant Campbell calling Sri Lanka 'a bunch of useless darkies', Mathew muttered to the bowler from the non-striker's crease, 'Australia may win, but you will be the loser, Campbell. When Lawson is fit, you're out. Enjoy your last moments.'

It was unprecedented for a Sri Lankan to sledge an Aussie on their home turf. But it worked. Campbell did not take another wicket and Ranatunga at the other end helped himself to a brave century. 'After that only, Arjuna even started talking back,' says Reggie.

Former umpire K.T. Ponnadurai tells me that Sri Lanka's test series against Zimbabwe in 1994 was filled with verbal bouts between Mathew and Anton Rose. Uvais Amalean recalls that the suggestion to throw the ball at Kiwi captain Turner in the last game of the tour, in revenge for his unsporting run-out of Samaraweera, was entirely Mathew's idea.

Is it possible that this shy boy, described by sister, lover and friend as 'sweet', 'good' and 'honest', taught our mild-mannered, unassuming Sri Lankans the art of sledging back? As Sri Lanka's greatest sledger once snarled at Aussie umpire Ross Emerson, 'Why not?'

Pioneer

Reggie Ranwala also identifies Pradeep as a Sri Lankan sledging pioneer.

'It was during that '86 Paki tour, Miandad himself.'

After being called a 'rundi ka bacha', left-arm spinner Pradeep Mathew, playing in only his second test, went up to Miandad during the drinks interval and said, 'Old man. Every boundary you can hit from me, I give you hundred rupees.'

'I was on the field with the flag,' says Reggie. 'I heard.'

Miandad whacked Mathew for three fours and shouted, 'Hey kid. three hundred rupees. Give to your mother. Tell her I am coming.' The next ball was an undercutter. Miandad, going for a fourth boundary, mistimed and was stumped by an eager de Alwis. Mathew pulled out his wallet, extracted some rupees and said, 'Give to your wife.'

The umpires instructed Miandad to leave the field; the Skipper asked Mathew to behave. As Miandad was walking back to the pavilion, Reggie Ranwala muttered, 'Got three hundred rupees, boss?' and was chased into the stand by the great Paki batsman, bat aloft. The crowd did not stop hooting Miandad for the rest of the tour.

Prodigal Son

It is January 1999 and Sri Lanka is playing a triangular in Australia again. I have not fared well on the resolutions I made before taking Sheila to the hills. Item 9 on the list was to give up smoking. I lasted from January 1 to January 5. I have now downgraded from Gold Leaf to Bristol, hoping that a drop in quality may reduce quantity.

I have been writing regularly. I eat three meals, drink nothing stronger than ginger tea or the occasional Portello. There is money in my bank. A lot to be happy about, though I am not.

My study is a mess of scrapbooks and *Wisden Almanacks*, all belonging to Ari. I begin writing at midnight. I hunch over my Jinadasa, one table lamp blazing yellow over my handwritten notes. All my interviews, thoughts, stats and unbelievables. The moon is outside and the wall that I stare at is before me again. I listen to the cats, the dogs and the man down the road who beats his wife. To the occasional bus spilling down Galle Road.

I punch the keys till 6 a.m., some nights more than others. Then I walk along Mount Lavinia beach and watch crows. When the sun comes up I buy cigarettes and bread. Four slices and a dhal curry later, I begin my second innings while the sun comes up. This time pen to paper till I fall asleep.

I doze for most of the afternoon and dream a lot; more on that later. I wake for sunset and if Sheila is in a good mood, we take a walk. These days I have been taking my walks alone.

I received this from my son three days ago.

Centraal Hotel
11 Vanderstraaten
Amsterdam
13/1/99

Thaathi
Didn't know you wrote letters. I've been touring Europe with Alice Dali, our lead singer is Janek Easdale formerly of Dramarama. I'm exhausted and doing OK.

You are probably bored or drunk or unable to finish your masterpiece for Wisden. There were years when I wished for your attention. But you have missed your bus.

I'm 24, twice divorced with a ten-month-old son who lives in London. I'm also a damn fine bass player. Now I am touring Europe, making money. We'll make a record soon, it will be a hit.

I appreciate your sentiments. Maybe you're feeling your age. But there are a lot of things I remember. Forcing a young boy to play cricket. Caning him at 14 for not bowling straight. I am still waiting for that apology.

When I played on Variety Fare with Apple Rain, did you watch? When I said I wanted to be a sound engineer, what did you do? You laughed.

None of this matters. I will succeed, not for you, but for myself, for my son Jimi, who I will love and encourage no matter how different he is from me. You say you want to 'put the past behind and to move forward'. Bullshit. You're old and no one listens to you. So now you write to me, wanting me to come home and listen to you go on about cricket.

I have my own life. If you want my forgiveness, you can have it. But you can keep your guilt. That you have earned.

Garfield S. Karunasena

A month ago I wrote trying to find a way back into my son's heart. I find that slowly, painfully and wordlessly, that gate has closed. Item 1 on my list ends in failure.

Item 2 was to give Sheila a holiday. Item 4 was to make peace with my brothers. The results were, as they say, mixed.

Ari's Ford Capri circles the hills of Nuwara Eliya well. It is with a heavy hand that Ari gives us the keys. 'Be careful with the steering, Wije. Sheila, make sure he doesn't sit on the clutch.'

Sheila makes me drive slowly in the evening fog and it takes us eight hours to reach Culloden Tea Estate, home of Ossie's son Newsie, assistant planter. The journey winds through mountains and passes waterfalls and is worth taking slowly. Along the way we play cassettes of Boney M, ABBA, Jim Reeves and Shakin' Stevens. Sheila does not like The Meat Loaf.

The house has nine rooms with high ceilings and is painted in shades of cream. The boy is pleasant, a moderate cricket fan, unmarried and probably bedding his tea pluckers. He has three servants to cook and tend the bungalow, and two cows in the backyard named Ranil and Chandrika.

We meet at mealtimes and exchange pleasantries and stay out of each other's way. The gardens are filled with roses and carrots and all around are mountains of tea.

We have spent many long weekends here with Newsie's parents and their planter friends, playing cricket on the lawns, listening to salsa jazz, drinking beer at the club, eating hoppers and venison in the garden. Sheila and I walk the hills, holding hands under trees where we used to make love. It is a good start.

The drive to my hometown Kurunegala is tiring and I am afraid. Sheila squeezes my arm and says she is proud of me. As we pass through Kandy, I tell her about the story I have uncovered, about this boy and what a talent he is. I omit details of spools and blindfolds. She tells me it sounds like a lovely story, but that she prefers Barbara Cartland.

We get into an argument over Garfield as we enter Kurunegala. I'm too busy defending myself against allegations of being a monster to notice the roads of my childhood or the parks of my youth. The caning incident frequently comes up. My defence is what it has always been. I do not remember.

I remember how Garfield became the U-13 A-team star fielder because of my weekend coaching. How he took 4–17 vs D.S. Senanayake after I had taught him the googly. If Garfield had no talent, I wouldn't care. But he was too good to end up a B-team reserve by the end of the season. I remember threatening him with a cane, I do not remember using it.

By the time we reach Bala's I am in a bad mood and hope this will not set the tone for the rest of our stay. We are welcomed by Bala's youngest, given tea and shown our rooms. 'Thaathi and Ammi will be back in the evening.' I have three hours to lie down and look back without anger.

Loku thinks I am a drunkard, Maddhu thinks I should have married a Sinhalese, Bala thinks I stole his inheritance. Akka did not approve of me till she was born again and then I became her pet leper. There are allegations that I once got drunk and insulted Loku's wife, but you know my response to this.

I pay Bala what he thinks I owe him, give Maddhu a bottle of Scotch. The atmosphere is cordial, my nieces and nephews are friendly, and by the time we all depart for Christmas lunch at Loku's, the thawing of the ice has begun. We discuss children, our official story being that Garfield is in London, studying engineering.

'I say, what engineering, ah?' asks Maddhu.

'Civil,' says Sheila and everyone oohs and aahs.

Sheila is delightful and the wives invite her to the kitchen to help with the preparation. When a bottle of Scotch is opened and I refuse, saying I have given up, there are raised eyebrows followed by softening postures.

Maddhu, Bala and Akka's husband discuss which government should be blamed for which catastrophe and I play the good listener. Loku does not speak.

Lunch goes off well and by the time we are having our fruit salad and ice cream, Loku is talking about cricket and I am generously holding my tongue. My cheeks have grown numb from the smiling. We are about to finish tea, about to begin the choreographed ritual, about to say goodbye four times, once while seated, once standing, once at the door, once again at the car.

I could have held a 0–0 draw. But at the ninetieth minute, I concede a penalty.

Loku, now lubricated and shed of his airs, talks about how he embraces all religions, how he has friends who are Muslim and Hindu and even Christian. This is as historic as the fall of apartheid. Akka and her husband smile and accept the olive branch.

'We are all God's children after all.'

'Sheila, you are a…?' asks Maddhu's wife, a staunch temple sil maaniya.

'I am a Methodist,' says Sheila in her sweetest voice. 'But my sisters are Buddhist.' She then gathers the cups and saucers.

'Don't be silly,' says Loku's wife and grabs the tray, blushing. If it were just about Sheila, I think the draw would have held.

Right then I feel the creature crawling around my spine. The slinky cat monkey is awake and is thirsty and would settle for a cigarette. I refrained all day. Even while Bala was puffing his Benson in my face. Ignore it and it will go away. Last over. Almost there.

'Wije is a…?' asks Bala's wife, a gossip, seeing a sliver of an opportunity for some drama. I smile and give my cup to Sheila. She looks at me as if I am an infant about to throw my food on the floor.

'You are also a Methodist?' asks Loku. He is trying to make it sound like an innocent question. The creature claws at my neck and I take a deep breath.

'No, he's not,' says Sheila, hiding her terror behind a smile.

I look at the people who have slandered, ignored and distrusted me my whole life. I think about white lies and paths of least resistance. Then I think, ah, what the hell.

'Loku Aiya. I don't actually…believe in religion.'

'Which…religion?'

'All religion. It's all the same.' I pause and arch my eyebrow. 'It's all nonsense.'

I will not give you a blow-by-blow. I cannot be bothered. The discussion rages for the next one and a half hours and ends with Loku calling me a drunk and me calling him a fool. Everyone hugs Sheila as I drag her from the house into Ari's Capri. No one looks me in the eye or says goodbye.

Umpire Sir

Back home in Mount Lavinia, the street kids call me whenever they are playing cricket. I umpire their games at least twice a week, even though it interferes with my sleeping schedule. Not only is it fun watching their unorthodox, swashbuckling cricket from close up, it is also good to have one's word respected and never questioned. There are no disputes and everyone calls me Umpire Sir.

I inspect the tennis ball after every over, I adjudge 'any wicket' run-outs, I even offer street cricket something it never receives: accurate LBW decisions. The games are absorbing. The talent varies from chuckers whose balls bounce thrice to a batsman who can hit sixers at will. Sometimes a mother sends a girl with a tray of Sunquick. Sometimes the game goes to the last ball. At no time do I ever think of anything else.

Item 4 on my list was to make peace with my family. Item 9 was to become a cricket umpire. I am hoping that one success can cancel out a failure.

Captain's XI vs Skipper's XI

Elmo Tawfeeq is a competent writer who is fond of clichés and never criticises Sri Lanka. As a result, he was once regularly taken on tour with the national team. I try not to despise him as much as everyone else does. He has made a career of writing glowing tributes to whoever happened to be the captain at the time.

He once told me that Pradeep would never play for Sri Lanka.

Elmo had been put in charge of filming an AV for some SLBCC dinner dance, a tribute to the great captains of Sri Lanka. Footage for the AV was gathered from the match that preceded the dinner dance: Captain's XI vs Skipper's XI.

'I only wrote and directed it.'

This took place many years before my own documentary, so I could only nod and look impressed.

'We had to ask players who the best captain of Sri Lanka was. These pups hadn't heard of Gunasekera or Tissera or Tennekoon. All said either the Skipper or the Captain.'

While Sri Lanka has had eight test captains to date, only the Skipper in the 1980s and the Captain in the 1990s held sway for any length of time.

'I interviewed whole team. Then caught this Mathew chap. On camera and all, after one of their practices. I asked "How would you compare captaincy styles between the Skipper and the Captain?"'

Mathew stroked his chin, and after careful deliberation replied, 'I believe it is a subtle distinction. The Skipper is a prick. The Captain is a cunt.'

And then he walked off.

Elmo laughed louder than me. 'Trust me, Karuna. That boy will never play for Sri Lanka again.'

As with most of Elmo's cricketing analysis, this was proved wrong.

Gentlemen vs Players

In cricket's class-conscious days, the rich played for love and called themselves amateurs; the working class played for money and were known disparagingly as professionals. The aristocrats considered themselves custodians of the game's spirit. The working stiffs pocketed cheques and called the amateurs Mr.

The annual game between them was called Gentlemen vs Players. The assumption was that anyone who played sport for anything other than romance could not be called a Gentleman. This idea died when the annual Gentlemen vs Players encounter was abolished in 1962 and every first-class cricketer turned professional. When the meaning of the word amateur changed from gentleman dabbler to lazy incompetent.

Today no one hides the fact that they are mercenary, all they argue about is the price. And no one associated with cricket dares call themselves a gentleman, even in jest.

Umpire Hora

23 January 1999. Ari has squabbled with one of his daughters and is watching the match at my place. It is a poya morning, and I have wrapped up the previous night's writing early so I can be fresh for the game.

Last week, after three successive losses, Sri Lanka pulled off a miraculous win against Australia. Perhaps the renaissance of the World Champions had begun just in time for the World Cup.

'These beggars won't get past the first round,' snarls Ari.

'Why you're so negative? Look how they played last game.'

Poya days are dry days; the one day of the month when Sri Lankans are free to drink and there's cricket on TV, they ban the sale of liquor. This used to be a great cause of chagrin for me. Not any more.

'I mean, are these bowlers?' laments Ari.

Stewart and Knight blaze to 60 in 10 overs. Ranatunga changes Pramodya and brings on Charith Silva.

'You are to blame for this fool being back in the side.'

I blush. 'Guilty, your lordship.'

The papers are the same they've been for the last fifteen years. Death count on the front page, cricket score on the back. The government had captured a boat and killed seventeen Tigers, Lara had scored 132 against Pakistan.

In Venezuela a man called Chavez had been elected president. I bumped into old man Bandara at the cigarette kade this morning. He told me this man was the new Che Guevara. Old man Bandara used to be known as Comrade Banda in the days of Keuneman and Soysa. He once sold me a Sinhala translation of Trotsky that he spent five years writing.

'What do you think of this Chavez?' I ask Ari. 'Comrade Banda thinks he's another Castro.'

'Bullshit,' says Ari. 'All these Latin bastards are funded by the CIA. Or they are assassinated. This bugger won't last.'

Stewart falls, then Hick comes and bashes Murali for two fours. This match feels just as pointless as I do.

'But it will come back to them. You watch,' says Ari. 'The US are due for another Pearl Harbor soon.'

I scour the rest of the morning's papers.

'Here. King Hussein of Jordan died.'

'Big deal,' says Ari. 'That bugger gave his arse to the West.'

'You're in a good mood, no?'

'Arabs need a bugger like Nasser. There was a leader. All these fellows now, even that Arafat…'

I stop listening to Ari and seconds later he stops talking. It is the 18th over; the commentators are West Indian great Malcolm Holding, and our friend and yours, Graham Snow.

'No ball called from square leg. Now hang on, what's this about?'

Snow stutters. 'No ball called from square leg.'

'I believe it's coming back to haunt Murali,' says Holding in his Jamaican growl. 'Umpire Emerson points to the elbow. Looks like trouble.'

'I knew this would bloody happen,' says Ari.

We watch Ross Emerson no-ball Murali from square leg for the third time.

'Captain Ranatunga wants to speak with both umpires,' says Graham.

'This could have very, very serious ramifications,' says Holding.

And then there is finger wagging. The last time I saw this kind of defiance was in '87, when Englishman Mike Gatting took on Pakistani umpire Shakoor Rana. The incident resulted in an exchange of expletives and the souring of relations. England has not toured Pakistan since.

This is even uglier. We have a man fatter and angrier than Gatting himself, dressed in gaudy blue, folded rag hanging from his circular waist, visor glinting, leaning forward and shoving finger into face. His opponent makes the fat man look athletic. Emerson lifts a weak hand and cuts a pear-shaped figure, wrong-footed by his own deeds.

I have never felt prouder of Arjuna. Not when he scored 52 in the inaugural test. Not even when he lifted the Cup in '96.

Ari and I fall back into discussion. I tell him ICC tests reveal that Murali's action is unusual and supple, but not that it is illegal. Ari says that Murali chucks his top-spinner and his so-called doosra. We remember how our last argument on this subject ended and we keep our tones even.

Ranatunga bowls Murali from the Emerson end, an act of brazenness that makes my heart melt. He insists the umpire stand up to the stumps, rendering him incapable of judging the elbow straightening. A Sri Lankan standing up to an Australian in Australia and winning. It is glorious.

'This is disgraceful,' says Ari. 'The umpire's word is law. Arjuna can't bully him like that.'

Twenty years ago I might have agreed with him. Back then I believed in the glory of the West and in our own savagery. No longer. We spent centuries making the white man rich and then bowing to his pleases and thank yous. The tragedy is, we still do it, even though we wear different costumes and hold different titles.

Everywhere, that is, except in cricket. A Sachin is worth a thousand Kirstens; a Wasim, a thousand Caddicks. Us brown folk play the game better and we should no longer apologise for our quirks; in fact, we should celebrate them, and, if necessary, defend them.

'Wije, you're like a bloody Paki. This is not a race thing. Australia has helped our cricket. They gave us tours throughout the 1980s. Where do you think Whatmore is from?'

'Don't talk cock, men. Murali has bowled everywhere. Only in Australia, he is a chucker. Only when we are winning.'

Emerson, now a cowering shell of a man, miscounts the over, signals 6 when it should be 4, and mutters something to Ranatunga who snarls back, 'Why not? I am in charge here. Why not?'

The stump mic is turned off.

None of this prevents England from blasting 302 for 3. As the TIC and one of the Chappells are interviewed by Harry Bole during the break, Ari says one thing that I do not find stupid. 'Whatever you say, Wije, I believe Ranatunga just saved Murali's career. You heard the commentators, no? The world will be scared to take us on.'

'They should be.'

'If only Pradeep had a captain like this to defend him,' says Ari, 'who knows what would've happened?'

It turns out to be one of the greatest games of them all. Not just because of the morning's drama. Many had been seeing Sri Lanka as a beleaguered team of has-beens who could no longer compete. Maybe this is our turning point, the moment where we recapture the spirit of 1996.

Jayawardena's century cancels out Graham Hick's. Sanath, Hashan and the Captain shine; Kalu, Marvan and Vaas fail. We are left with Chandana and Mahanama, 34 runs and 4 overs from the finish.

I realise that when it comes down to it, our cricket retains the passion of the street. The West respects law, but questions authority. It is us who bow down to lawmakers even as we disregard laws. Today we reverse that. We dare to call the umpire a hora.

We are now infused with the spirit. If our boys could defy the odds here, perhaps we have a shot at retaining the World Cup. The spirit pushes our bodies towards the screen. I am rubbing my hands over my thighs, Ari is pacing the room. Even he does not mind when Mahanama cheats.

Darren Gough steams in for a probable run-out and our man Roshan runs into him and pretends it was an accident. The Yorkshireman screams obscenities at the batsman and is centimetres away from butting his head. England captain Stewart shoulder-charges Mahanama and is unrepentant. This is not Lord's or the MCC. This is urchin cricket played on the streets of Mariyakade or de Saram Road. The Poms are finally playing it Lankan style.

The match goes down to the wire. 2 balls from the end, with 1 wicket to spare, who scores the winning runs, the highest winning score in one-day history? Who else? Mr Muttiah Murali, the man most sinned against, the second greatest bowler Sri Lanka has ever produced.

Crackers go off on the street. Ari and I shake hands and grin. God is in his tavern even though I am not. And then the phone rings and I answer it. I put down the receiver and ask Ari to switch off the TV. A voice has just told me that Jonny has been shot.

Close of Play

'You do well to love cricket, because it is more free from anything sordid, anything dishonourable than any game in the world.'

Lord Harris, England captain (1880–84),
Ambassador to India (1890–93)

Every Possible Glenn

They found the note in his shirt pocket. It was shown to us, but kept as evidence. The handwriting was his, as was, presumably, the browny-red blood smear on the paper.

> Cricket Season Is Over
> Bye Mam. Bye Joseph.
> Bye Ari. Bye W.G.
> No More Running. No More Bombs.
> No More Shit in my pool. No more bloody Hunters.
> I saw the greatest game of them all.
> 67. 17 years past 50.
> 17 more than I needed or wanted.
> Enough is enough. You are getting Greedy.
> Act your old age.
> Relax – this won't hurt.
>
> J
>
> PS. Saqlain Mushtaq Mohammad Zahid Fazal Asif Iqbal Sikander Bakht.
> That's nine. Next time we meet, drinks on you.

'I should've given him the cyanide,' says Ari, lip quivering, placing books into boxes in Jonny's home. It is days later and we have both kept our upper lips stiff, at least in public anyway, though I have secretly wept three times. The lawyer says that unless valuables are cleared and shipped before the authorities notice, the state will assume control of all assets.

Last week, the High Commission withdrew its appeal over the arrest. The Supreme Court refused extradition. Jonny was to be tried in Sri Lanka and if convicted imprisoned here as a sex offender.

'Who is Joseph?' I ask, looking at the giant TV that had enthralled us for many years, now in a cardboard box. The appliances are to be sold to pay the legal fees. The house would be seized under new legislation banning the bequeathing of Sri Lankan property by foreign residents. All that is left are the books and the souvenirs.

'There is a lot we'll never know about Jonny,' says Ari. 'We may find a diary.'

'If we do, we burn it.'

'Will we read it first?'

Whatever we didn't keep, we would ship to Mrs Margaret Gilhooley of South Shields, Tyneside. Though we knew most valuables would fall prey to customs vultures.

Maybe after seeing the country he loved outplay the country he had fled, he thought it was as good as it got. Or maybe it was the very rational fear of prison, of no sunshine and no cricket.

'Newcastle is bottom of the table. That Gullit's sexy football is not working,' I say, putting away his CDs. 'Maybe this was just as well.' My upper lip has stopped quivering.

Right after the Emerson game, Sri Lanka resumed its losing streak. Ranatunga remained unrepentant and emerged a folk hero as the world's press played the politics cautiously. Ross Emerson was sent on stress leave; I doubt he will return.

Why eight bullets were used when two would have sufficed is unlikely to provoke an enquiry. The *Observer* dedicated three paragraphs to **English sex offender dies while in custody**. And seven pages to the fallout from the Ranatunga–Emerson clash.

It is on the third day that I find the cupboard under the stairs. In it is a pettagama, an ebony chest with carving. It is too heavy for us to move, but we both know what it contains. We apply the smallest from a bundle of keys the lawyer gave us. It opens immediately.

I look to Ari. 'What do we do?'

He does not answer me, but walks down the hall with a smile. As I open up the chest and marvel at its treasure, the cupboard's cobwebs make me cough. I put a handkerchief to my lips and point my pen-torch along the open pettagama. Ari wanders in with two ice-filled glasses; I recognise them from the expensive crockery pile.

'What the hell are you doing?'

He smiles. 'Buggered if I am going to let these fall into the hands of some sarong johnnie at customs. Will you have the Chivas or a single malt Glenlivet?'

'Single malt. But just one.'

'Just one,' says Ari, his face taking on a solemn look.

'Just for Jonny.'

'For Jonny.'

Neither of us are fond of Scotch. The shots, Ari's first in three years, my first in seventeen months, thirteen days and eight hours, are so stiff that they bring tears to our eyes. Tears that do not stop flowing.

Jonny's funeral is well attended by many Europeans who we do not know. An Irish lady called Morag introduces herself as the cultural secretary; she offers to help us ship his belongings.

It takes us seven days to put Jonny's life into boxes. Morag brings in two workmen to do the heavy lifting. We tell no one about the pettagama in the cupboard under the stairs. The day before we are to hand over the keys is the 1999 World Series final. Of course Sri Lanka did not make it; we lost five of our remaining six games. I suggest, Ari agrees.

'For Jonny.'

'For Newcastle.'

'Ah?'

'They're playing Spurs in an FA Cup quarter on the same night.'

'So?'

'They never disconnected Jonny's cable. He's paid a year in advance.'

Ari laughs. 'Typical. But you must promise. After tonight we give everything away and do not touch it again.'

'Scout's honour.'

And so it is that we spend that Saturday flipping between games, sipping every possible Glen. We mix Glenlivet with Glenfiddich, Glenburgie with Glenmorangie, GlennHoddle with GlennMcGrath.

As Aspirilla equalises for Newcastle, we talk about what we didn't find among Jonny's belongings. No letters, no photos, no bills, no diaries. Either the lawyers have taken everything or he had nothing to hide.

We tell our wives we are staying over and drink till we collapse. We drink a million toasts to our friend, to Bolgoda, to the mighty Geordies, to the losing Englishmen. Each toast tasting sweeter than the last. And then, silently sprawled in separate rooms, we shed a few more tears.

The next morning Ari keeps his word. The rest of the bottles are donated to Manouri's Easter Raffle, all except one. The Johnny Walker Silver Label Arrack that I had seen in one place before and had abstained from tasting. I find it while stumbling to the toilet at 4 a.m., slip it into my bag, and go back to sleep. This is one of those many drunken stupidities that I may choose not to remember.

If I Met Mathew

What would I do? Ask for an autograph? Present him with my book? Ask him what he thinks of the current side? Ask him if he ever won Shirali back? Ask if the stories about kadale and South Africa were true?

If I am fortunate to ever meet him, the only thing I would want to do is shake his hand, bow my head, and say, 'Thank you.'

Horse Thieves

The day after the Emerson game the *Island* publishes a record of criminals who had been deported to Australia in the last century. Each has an unfamiliar first name, but a famous last one.

Patrick Emerson, Horse Thief (1788)
Robert Hair, Debtor (1792)
John Taylor, Manslaughter (1777)
Mervyn Chappell, Horse Thief (1844)
William Warne, Horse Thief, Murder (1821)
Joseph McGrath, Assault, Debtor (1833)
Thomas Martyn, Highway Robbery (1811)
Samuel Healy, Rapist (1842)
Edwin McDermott, Murder, Rape, Horse Thief (1799)
Francis Reiffel, Robber, Rapist (1852)
Stuart Law, Horse Thief (1823)

The article is written by my good friend T.M.K. Clementine and titled 'Cheating is in Australia's Blood'. I find it quite amusing, but Ari does not.

'Wije, sometimes I am ashamed to be a Lankan. As if our ancestors were any better.'

'It's a joke, Uncle.'

'What is a joke is that they are now changing the rules to accommodate the bending of the elbow.'

'Exactly, Putha. They have scientifically proven that even the McDermotts and the Reiffels bend. If 5 degrees is illegal, everyone is illegal.'

'How can you change a rule book because of one bowler?'

'If you can't change rules, Lillee will still be using the aluminium bat.'

'That's completely different, Wije.'

'Anyway, the whites have been writing the rules for centuries. It's time we added ours.'

'But not like this.'

'Everywhere else you are innocent till proven guilty. Murali shouldn't have to prove his innocence. ICC should prove his guilt.'

Ari grunts and walks out with his newspaper. Unlike Ranatunga, he does not stop at the boundary.

Reggie Ranwala

The *Sunday Observer* reruns the ad. Don't ask me why, I haven't paid them a red cent extra. It is a mistake, a bank error in my favour, proof perhaps that the tide is turning. Almost two years after I stopped running it, it appears out of nowhere and I get a further barrage of calls.

Most respondents tell me about the Asgiriya test or about the Sharjah performance or about how he won Bloomfield the Cup in '93. I mention names like Kuga, Newton and Shirali and get no reaction. I tell most of them that they do not have any information that I am willing to pay for, but they are welcome to drop in at my house for a tea and a chat. That usually scares them off.

With Reggie Ranwala, I agree to travel all the way to Panadura at my expense. That is not because he remembers me winning Ceylon Sportswriter of the Year four times. I tell him it was twice, but he insists it was four times. Not because of this, but because of one thing he says just as I am about to cut the line. 'Mr Karunasena. I don't know where Pradeep Mathew is. But I can tell you how he took NZ$278,000 from Sri Lanka cricket.'

Beer and Pie

Craig Turner took over the captaincy from Martin Crowe in the mid-90s. Crowe was New Zealand's greatest batsman. He would have stood toe to toe with any of the Laras or Tendulkars of his era, had he not been painted by his country's media as a 'tall poppy' and a 'tortured genius'.

Crowe was an Aucklander who drank fine wine in fine restaurants with his fine wife and appeared in women's magazines modelling Armani. Despite his batting prowess and leading New Zealand's Young Guns to an unlikely World Cup semi-final in 1992, he fell out of favour with management and the public and was replaced by that lad of lads, Craig Turner.

Perhaps aware of his journeyman talents, and that his scruffy hair and hook nose were unlikely to win him Armani contracts, Turner famously said in a press conference, 'Crowe is a wine-and-cheese man, I'm more of a beer-and-pie man.' The press were pleased to see a good ole Kiwi bloke at the helm of New Zealand sport. Many were sick of those poofs from Auckland.

Turner was captain when Sri Lanka toured in 1995. He led the sledging against the tourists and was so flabbergasted at Murali's action that he mimicked it on the field to the roar of the crowd.

Early on in the tour, Turner hurled the ball at shaky opener Duleep Samaraweera who, well in his crease, leapt in the air to avoid it. The ball hit the stumps, TV replays revealing that both Samaraweera's feet were off the ground and that therefore, technically, he was out. Sri Lankan supporters, expecting Turner to call back the batsman, booed and hooted when he didn't.

The one-day series went to New Zealand, who won the first two games. At Eden Park, in the last game of the tour, with Sri Lanka in command, Turner came out to bat. The first ball from Gamage he defended. Aravinda de Silva raced in from cover and hurled it at Turner's chest.

'I was there when Pradeep suggested it to the seniors,' says Reggie, pouring me a lager. 'They all thought it was a great idea. Even the Captain.'

An over later, Turner pushed out to mid-off, where Pushpakumara sped in and threw the ball at Turner's head. Beer-and-pie language followed and even though Turner managed to get 30, he never got away from the hurl of missiles, each done with a massive grin, much to the crowd's delight and the Kiwi captain's chagrin.

'Pradeep said he would personally give his gratuity cheque to whoever ran out Turner that way. Pukka fellow, no?'

Mathew didn't play on that tour, not even a practice game. The series was not only Sri Lanka's first victorious overseas tour, it was also Pradeep Mathew's last public appearance.

Ari's Blasphemy

'1996 was luck. We beat crap teams like Zimbabwe, Kenya and England, then beat India and the Aussies. We avoided the in-form teams. Most of our games were at home. We have never been able to string together six consecutive wins outside of Sri Lanka, either before or since.'

I advise Ari not to voice that in public. He might get buriyani shoved into his eyes.

Rules

Rules are many things, but arbiters of fairness they are not. At most they provide a little shape, dispense a little meaning, and put a young boy in Karachi and an old man in Wollongong on the same page.

Rules separate Rugby Union from Rugby League from American football. In my opinion, only one of them is worth staying up for. Hint: not the ones that use shoulder pads.

Rules are responsible for why some racket sports draw crowds and others draw yawns. Follow this logic:

- In table tennis, you switch service every 5 points and race to 21.
- In badminton, you fight for service. Only service can grant you points.
- In tennis, four units of 15 constitute a game. Games accumulate into sets.

The very design of a game establishes opportunities for drama. A tiebreaker, the racket sport's devil dance of one-upmanship, occurs once in a set of TT (at the end), but may occur several times in a game of tennis. In badminton, it can potentially occur with every point.

Rules explain why TT is considered boring; tennis, entertaining; and badminton, tedious. It has nothing to do with ping-pong vs ball vs shuttle.

Rules explain why Andre Agassi dates supermodels. Rules explain why World Badminton Champion Peter Rasmussen and World TT Champion Jan-Ove Waldner do not have perfumes named after them.

New Zealand rugby cricket and basketball teams are respectively called the All Blacks, the Black Caps and the Tall Blacks. The New Zealand badminton team call themselves the Black Cocks. (This is not a joke, look it up.)

When asked why by the press, the NZ badminton chief shrugged and replied that in fifteen years of holding that post, he had never seen a journalist. Since the rebranding, he has seen over twenty. As the Americanos would say, go and figure.

Sunset

'I know you're drinking again.'

It is a crow-filled morning. I am at the tail end of my day's writing, readying myself for my afternoon slumber.

'What rot are you talking? I haven't touched the stuff since…I can't remember.'

'You think I don't know why you shower at six in the morning and gargle Listerine three times a day? You think I'm a ponytail Chinaman?'

'Because I'm hygienic, I must be boozing? Aney, get out, men.'

'I have lived with you for thirty-five years. When have you ever been hygienic? You stayed off it for a year. What happened?'

'My friend Jonny died.'

'Gamini, I will give you a slap.'

'OK. It's all my fault. I'm weak.'

She sits down and strokes the back of my neck. I look down at my Jinadasa and punch some keys.

'I have to write, Sheila.'

I think I prefer it when she is shouting and throwing things. Then I can beat her with logic and wit.

'This last year has been very tough for me, Sheila. How can you understand?'

The slap is sudden and it rattles my dentures.

'I don't understand? Who has to explain to your brothers? Who has to bring up your son? Who has to wait till you write your big masterpiece? You're the mad man who doesn't understand.'

I hold my cheek and retort, 'Has anyone seen me drinking? Has anyone found a bottle in this house?'

Sheila looks across my desk, picks up one of Ari's drawings and frowns at it.

'Gamini. Lie to yourself if you like. I know why you work in the middle of the night. Why you take the route past the rubbish on your morning walks. Why you are suddenly washing your own teacups.'

I close my typewriter, knowing that there will be no more work for the day.

'Ari is Sherlock. Now you are Miss Marple? After all I have gone through, this is the accusation? And you physically abuse an innocent man. A drop has not even touched my…'

'Ari told Manouri that y'all got drunk at that Jonny's house.'

The bloody fool. I cannot help that his testicles reside in his wife's handbag. I will deny till I die.

'He got drunk. I drank tea. Sheila, I'm writing my cricket book. I have no time for booze.'

She holds both my hands in her lap and leans forward. I avert my face, feigning indignation and offence, half-expecting another slap.

'If you want, keep lying,' she says. 'I just want one thing from you.'

'Then will you let me go?'

'Of course. I want us to sit and discuss this. You and me. One hour. No typewriters.'

'When?'

'Today sunset. Right after your nap. The only time of day that you are sober. We'll go to the beach. No one will shout. No one will throw things. If we are to let you drink yourself to death, let us at least have discussed it like adults beforehand.'

'I'm sober now.' Deny till you die. 'We can go for a walk now.'

She places a kiss on my cheek and smiles. 'Maybe you will need to think about what you're going to say to me.' She clears the cups from my desk. 'I'll see you at 5.30.'

The Level

There is a theory that drunks are plagued by thirsty ghosts who wander purgatory seeking earthly delights. Of course it is an absolve-myself-of-responsibility theory and that is probably why I like it. When alcoholics and depressives refer to demons, this is perhaps what they believe.

It is unnerving to think that the dead walk among us and are invisible, particularly if you are a curvaceous young girl about to take a bath. But it is as likely an explanation as any, if you believe in a soul, which even godless W.G. Karunasena does. When we feel despair, it is a thousand-year-old spirit cursing in our ear; when we feel craving it is a drunk apparition coaxing our tongue.

I take a bottle of Mendis Double Distilled to Reggie's Panadura residence. It is as much to coax his tongue as it is to steady mine. His home is built on a plot of land that would be considered spacious in Colombo, except that it is bisected by an ugly wall. Two postboxes sit in opposition to each other on painted gates. R.O.B. Ranwala and A.R.L. Ranwala.

Both gates have Beware of Dog signs, though only one house appears to have canines. I approach A.R.L. because it is closest and watch as three parayas rush to the gate, barking loud enough to wake the neighbours, which is what happens. An old watcher calls out. 'Lionel mahattaya or Reggie mahattaya?'

'Reggie.'

'This side.'

The wall goes through the house. On brother Lionel's side, a second floor is being added. The dogs return to running through bamboo scaffolding. Brother Reggie's does not appear to have been renovated in decades.

He comes to the gate wearing a Sri Lanka cricket shirt and a Sri Lanka cricket hat and a green sarong. His eyes light up at the bottle of Mendis.

'I have seen you somewhere before.'

'I write for *Sportstar*,' I say, handing over the bottle. I decline to mention that it was three articles, three years ago.

'Ah. You must know Rajesh Singh.'

'Why not? Raj is a good friend of mine. How do you know him?'

'He was same batch as my good friend Dilip Vengsarkar.'

'What? You know Vengsarkar?'

'Vengsarkar's wife and my wife are second cousins.'

'Gurusinha is married to my aunty's niece.'

He leads me through small rooms with red floors and too much furniture. We enter a dark room at the end of the house.

'Ah. So must've seen you at the matches.' He scrutinises the mess of typefaces on the Mendis bottle as if he is choosing a fine wine. 'Even if I am plastered, I always remember faces.'

When he opens the curtains, I see the room is larger than I first thought. It resembles a gift shop in a Nugegoda mall selling only Sri Lankan cricket paraphernalia. In the corner, hanging in an open almirah, is every Sri Lankan cricket shirt from 1985's canary yellow/sailor blue number to today's multi-coloured, tea logo-branded monstrosity.

Photographs are not framed, but pasted with cellotape on walls. Each features Reggie, with his papare trumpet, a different style of Sri Lankan T-shirt and the same moustache, with his arm around Kapil, Imran, Wasim, Arjuna, Shane, Gower, Viv, Hadlee, Aravinda, Tyson, Trueman.

'You know Graham Snow?'

'Why not?'

'He dedicated his latest book to me and my friend.'

'I have lot of books, but don't get to read, no time. Every time I start, I fall asleep. You want cricket books? My friend Elmo Tawfeeq has a tha-dang library.'

If only he'd use it, I think.

'My friend Newton Rodrigo, you must be knowing, women's team coach, also was a journalist...'

I nod.

'He gave me this.'

I look in fury at my own copy of *The Art of Cricket*. I flip open the pages.

'It is autographed by Bradman himself.'

I turn to the title page. *Best Wishes Donald Bradman*

'That bloody bastard. Can I use your phone?'

'For what?'

I tell him I'm going to call Newton and scream at him for lending my book out. Reggie's face changes. 'No. No. You take your book. No need to call.' He tries to distract me with autographed bats, balls, pads and gloves, and then pours me a drink. It works.

White sunlight illuminates grubby walls. Next to a pile of video cassettes is a large TV, dusty, with duty-free sticker still intact. In the background a Sinhala station plays Gunadasa Kapuge. The red floors are unpolished and cluttered with souvenirs. Anything concave has been turned into an ashtray.

Batsmen describe it as getting your eye in, American sportswriters refer to being 'in the zone', but that doesn't quite explain it. I drink to attain a level. The level is the point where your thoughts are clear, your body is relaxed and your manner has charm. The optimum before the returns diminish and you turn into a beast.

When I was young, two drinks would get me to the level and I would stop. Those days are long gone. For a long time my level was a half-bottle and anything more would relieve me of my dignity. Then it was two-thirds of a bottle, then it became one and a quarter. As the quantity increased I would move from Distilled to Old to Blue Label to gal.

But then the level would waver, my clarity would become fleeting, unpredictable, my charm would dwindle, my control would vanish. And that's when I would hurl insults like that caged monkey at Dehiwela Zoo who would hurl faeces at visitors.

When Reggie hands me the drink, I think about the level and I tell myself it will be two drinks. The first shot is devastating, my tongue goes into shock and my eyes start tearing. It will be difficult to make it to two. I will keep filling his glass and topping mine with shandy. I shall use the arrack to give me clarity, but I will not let it control me. So that one day perhaps I may drink with impunity and without symptoms.

'So, Reggie malli. Tell me about the 278,000.'

Last Man / No Chance

Every time before I step out to umpire, both captains – the tallest Marzooq boy and the nastiest beach boy – go over the rules with me. Houses are out. Windows are minus 6. The mango tree and beyond is 4 and 6. There are no back runs and the batting side will provide a wicketkeeper.

These rules are subject to fluctuation depending on the number and calibre of players. It is I who insist on clarifying the rules before the toss and on marking the score in my notebook.

The most fascinating debate is over the not-out batsman. Do we, like in real cricket, deny him batting when he runs out of partners? Or do we let him play on, the innings ending only when every single player has been dismissed?

On Sri Lanka's streets and playgrounds, this is known as last man/ no chance vs last man/have chance. No chance means he doesn't bat, have chance means he does. No chance means that there is no hope if the side lets you down. Have chance means that it is possible for one player to single-handedly deliver victory. I know which one I prefer.

Flight and Drift

Flight is how long the ball hangs in the air. Drift is the trajectory it takes from fingers to pitch. Mastery of these two elements is what makes a great spin bowler. Everything else is frills.

The strategy for grappling with a spinner is to use your feet, get to the pitch of the ball and smother it before it deceives you. Good flight makes a ball appear closer than it is. Good drift makes a batsman commit to a shot he may not be able to play. Take away flight and drift and you're just a slow bowler who turns the ball. Insert these ingredients and you become a magician.

In Zimbabwe in 1994, at the twilight of his career, having mastered flight, drift and when to use which, Mathew bowled an assortment of some of the most unusual deliveries ever invented. He was no-balled for a ball that flew some 20 feet skywards before bouncing on the wickets. The ball was deemed illegal for, as the umpire put it, 'hanging in the air too long'.

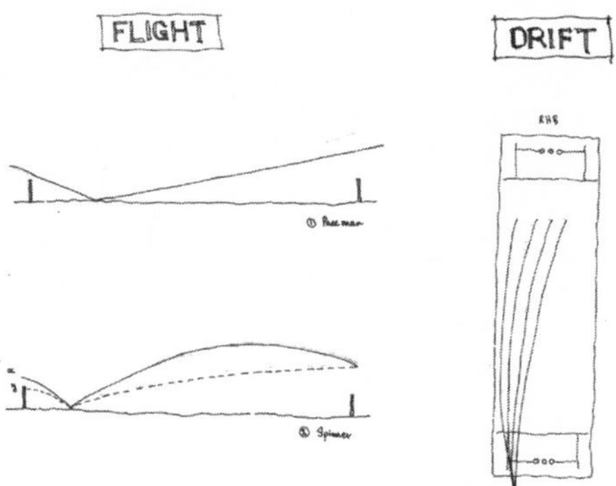

Hacks Toffees

In the end I only had three drinks and Reggie had the rest. He is babbling like a baby as we walk to the Panadura bus stop. I should have left when he started drooling into his lap. Instead I stayed till his emotional age plummeted from teenager to toddler. I told him to pull himself together. On the way, I buy six Hacks toffees, which I consume two at a time.

'Hiding from your wife, ah?' he says, wiping his tears. 'My wife also complains. I tell her my car, my petrol.'

The petrol is burning a hole in my stomach; I cannot wait to go home and pass out. Sleep is the best antidote to pain. It serves to combat hunger, sometimes even life. I pull him back when he almost walks into the path of a Lanka Ashok Leyland truck, its name revealing its multinational origins.

Zebra crossings in Sri Lanka are not directives but optional suggestions which motorists ignore. Traffic lights may some day go the same way.

'Mr Karuna, I can't walk all that way, I'm a bit cut. Do you have that payment?'

'Will three do it?'

'Three hundred?' He frowns.

'Thou.'

He grins and hugs me and burps a vat of arrack breath into my nostrils.

'Anything more you want to know about Mathew or Sana or Arjuna, you call me.'

I hand him the notes and get on the 101 bus. I fall asleep and wake up in Fort.

Soorial Tests

It takes me a few moments to realise that the word Reggie keeps repeating is surreal. He pronounces it 'soori-al' as one would pronounce Sooriyarachchi or the Sanskrit word for sun.

'Maara soorial those African tests, ah. They say it was the devil winds that blew down from Mount Nyanga and that's the reason.'

'Mount what?' I begin to regret allowing Reggie the rest of the bottle.

'There was something soorial about all those matches.'

'Like what?'

He reaches under his bed and pulls out a shoebox; he holds it away from me and rummages.

'There. Your man Mathew, shaved head and all, you should've seen.'

He tells me about a ball that hung suspended in the winds, about flippers that changed direction, and no-balls that bounced twice. I tell him that I have with my own eyes seen the floater, the lissa and the double bounce.

'There.' He hands me a photo. Even with the angle lopsided, the photo blurred and the photographer's finger in the top left corner, I can recognise Heath Streak bowling to Nuwan Kalpage. I can also see that each fielder including the wicketkeeper is on the leg side.

'That was the wind, ammapa. African winds. Even if the batsman hits to the off, ball goes to leg.'

He tells me that the wind was so strong that Haturusinghe reverse-swept three sixers. That at one point there were six sets of brothers on the field at once. From the bowling side there were two Flowers, two Strangs, two Rennies and two Whittles. Ranatunga and Samaraweera who were batting both asked their brothers to run for them. I make a note to look this up.

He tells me that the Sri Lankans had to bowl into the jaws of that haunted wind from Mount Nyanga that favoured the home side.

'You're talking about the wind?'

'The wind only. It followed our bowlers around. Whichever end we bowled from, the wind was against us.'

'Right.'

'Ammapa.'

'What about Zimba?'

'When they bowled, the wind was behind them. Always.'

When I looked up the 1994 Zimbabwe series in our archives, I found no mention of brothers or of partisan winds, only that it was one of the dullest series of all time, between two weak sides, which yielded three drawn tests and three washed-out one-dayers. Reggie Ranwala begs to differ.

'You must look at the subtle Nuwan-Zoysas.'

'You mean subtle nuances.'

'That's what I said.'

When he tells me that in the third test, all four innings were played in one day, I shake my head.

'Of course. We scored 280 and were out third day morning. Then they were out for 97 in 23 overs. We were out for 62 in 17. They began second innings. All in one day.'

'They won?'

'No. They thattu-ed for two days. Rose played a beautiful 144. They ended at 230 for 7.'

SL won the first one-dayer, Zimba won the second. The other games were destroyed by gales and rains long before the 20th over, so even Duckworth and Lewis could be of no help. As if the weather gods themselves did not wish to resolve the 'who is the crappiest test nation' tournament.

According to Reggie four wickets fell in a Mathew over, but he was not credited with any of them.

First ball to Flower, Pradeep slipped on the crease and crashed into the stumps, accidentally running out non-striker Brandes. Second ball was a top spinner, whose rosy revolutions attracted two African bees. Waller, swiping at the insects, accidentally knocked the ball he just defended and was adjudged out hit the ball twice.

'Reggie. Give me that bottle.'

Fourth ball, Gurusinha at short leg appealed when Goodwin passed him the ball and the umpire delivered a verdict of out handled ball. Mathew geared up to bowl the fifth delivery and was left waiting for thirteen minutes, while last man Olonga, suffering from what turned out to be cholera, was unable to put on his pads while emptying his bowels of water. The Captain appealed for time out and it was given.

'Reggie, I'm off.'

'Ammapa. Allistruetruetrue.'

'You have been very helpful. Let's meet up again. Definitely.'

'I'llwalkyoutobus…' says Reggie. 'I tell how Zimbabwean People's Revolutionary Army, who blew up planes in the 1970s, designed bomb like a cricket ball and gave it to the umpires…'

I stop listening to him and I only think of what he told me before the Mendis took effect.

'If the police hadn't caught, opening batsman and keeper would be exploded. Ammapa.'

Ammapa roughly translates to 'I swear on my mother'. I felt sorry for the poor old lady. Wherever she is, she must be sneezing a lot. Or coughing.

Cheating

'In the 1970s, some top US company invented a ticket dispenser that was impossible to fraud,' says Reggie Ranwala. 'One of our buggers cracked it, no?' There is pride in his voice.

The GenCY was involved in the administration of Sri Lankan cricket for most of the 1980s. The GenCY had captained Royal, represented Cambridge and played three seasons for Middlesex. He had served at various times as coach, manager, selector and treasurer.

'Sir would always say, "You are gentlemen first, sportsmen second,"' recalls Charith Silva. As a result, Lankans never appealed for a bump ball, never reacted to sledging, and always walked when dismissed.

The GenCY's rival for the control of the Board of Control was the Minister.

The Minister had done much for Sri Lankan cricket. He had built stadiums, brought in outstation players and set up coaching clinics. He hoped to rise up party ranks on the wave of cricket. And he knew you couldn't rise to the top by being a gentleman.

The Minister insisted that Sri Lanka play tough and win by whatever means necessary. In his biography, Pakistani prince Imran Khan claims that Sri Lanka's home test victory against his side in '86 was the result of a directive by the Minister to local umpires to deliver a victory at any cost. Kapil Dev had voiced a similar opinion a year earlier.

'Our man would never cheat,' says Charith, shaking his head. 'Pradeep would never bowl at the footmarks. Or appeal if he thought it's not out.'

Bowling at the footmarks isn't cheating; wilfully scuffing the pitch to create them, as some subcontinental leg spinners have been known to, is.

'Mathew was the only one who listened to Manager,' says Reggie, referring to the GenCY. 'Other fellows did what the Minister said.'

In sports, politics and everything else, Sri Lankans tend to veer between jungle law and Victorian morality. Ari, for instance, litters, drives drunk, jumps queues, bribes policemen, but refuses to cheat at Monopoly, Omi or 304.

Picking the Seam

The ball has a shiny side and a rough side. One offers less air resistance and causes the ball to move in the air and off the ground. While it is legal to shine one side, it is illegal to disfigure the other.

Many great and not-so-great bowlers have been accused of tampering with the ball. These include the Pakistani fire-breathing demons, whose reverse-swinging yorkers were questioned by opposition captains who had no answer to them.

Before a game in Sharjah, Ravi de Mel announced in a team meeting that he did not believe ball tampering was illegal and that he was going to pick the seam. The GenCY, whose influence was already on the wane, tendered his resignation with immediate effect. Everyone else was strangely silent.

'I also don't think it is wrong,' says Charith Silva.

'Did you ever pick the seam?' I ask.

'Everyone picks the seam. It's like polishing the ball. It's an art.'

'Did you do it?'

'Are you mad? Get caught and I'm finished. I don't have a rich father like Ravi de Mel.'

In three one-dayers in 1993, Ravi de Mel bowled 17 wides and uncountable full tosses and gave away over 150 runs in less than 20 overs. The ball swung, seamed, reverse-swung and reverse-seamed, and failed to go anywhere near the batsman. Even the Minister was unable to save de Mel's career.

'Damn good for the bugger,' chuckles Reggie. 'Thought he could be Wasim Akram. In the end he runs in like Waqar and bowls like Inzamam. Got hammered.'

Proving that even when cheating, one must possess a quotient of talent and skill.

Who's the Daddy?

Failure is an orphan, success has many fathers. If we could do a paternity test on the 1996 World Cup, whose seed would triumph? The Captain who scored the winning runs? The interim committee that was ousted a week later? The coach who would storm out in a year? The Minister who was killed two years before?

Or was it the man who wrote to the ICC demanding cricket reforms for Sri Lanka? The man who showed every time he came on to bowl that Sri Lankans could be as good as anyone else. Who on certain days at certain moments could even prove beyond doubt that we were better.

Who encouraged the GLOB to hit over the top and advised the dark spinner from Kandy not to change his action. The man who taught the Captain to sledge. The man who disappeared 207 days before that final in Lahore.

Stuff that No One Reads

There are many interesting things Kuga tells me. Here are just a smattering of sound bytes.

He tells me that the majority of his employees are Sinhala. His ID forger had been fired by the Ratnapura Grama Sevaka just before completing five years, a ruse to avoid paying gratuity. Workers are then re-hired while management pockets the bonus. The soon-to-be-unemployed civil servant stole ten thousand sheets, the camera and the laminating machine. 'My suicide bombers may not have been reliable. But they all had authentic Sri Lankan IDs,' says Kuga, patting down his stubble.

He tells me his couriers are all Sinhala and move around during heavy monsoon. 'When it's raining no one stops you at checkpoints. Best time to move explosives around.'

He gives me a list of eleven names, enough for a cricket team, though none of them are cricketers. Richard, Ranjan, Lalith, Tyronne, Prema, Rajiv, Gamini, Neelan, Vijaya, Clancy, Denzil.

'Six of those kills were my operation,' says I.E. Kugarajah, the man with three mobile phones. 'But I won't tell you which.'

He tells me that *The Godfather* is his favourite film.

'Do you know what the best line from it is?' he asks, picking at his newly grown goatee. Kuga, despite looking well into his forties, is a man who has not stopped experimenting with facial hair.

As you know, I am no cinema buff, but *The Godfather* is one of those films, like *Casablanca*, that Ari quotes ad nauseam.

'What about that famous line? Here is an offer no one will be able to say no to.'

'No,' he smiles. 'It is…'

'Luca Vaasy is doing something with the fisheries?'

'No, it's…'

'Why you no respect…'

'NO.'

'No need to shout so. Tell.'

'A lawyer with a briefcase can steal more than hundred men with guns.'

'I haven't heard that one.'

The first payment he gave Pradeep at Sharjah had the boy staring at his National Savings Bank passbook. 'I said, 'Pradeepan, what you're staring at?' He said, "The comma." He said he'd never seen a comma in his account balance before.' Kuga's laugh is so loud that you are forced to smile or risk being accused of contempt.

I tell him I do not think I will get the chance to deliver his note; he says he is sure I will. 'You must stop looking so hard. One of my clients was a kalay bowler. Couldn't hit the stumps to save his life. I got Sobers down to coach, he said to aim wide. When the fellow tried to bowl wide, it hit the wickets.'

'What happened to him?'

'He didn't work out for me. My point is, if you stop looking for something, it turns up.'

He tells me that he has letters between ministers and Tigers, that he can hire men to hurl elephant dung on me, but that I am not worth the cost of such services. He tells me many things I do not know what to do with. Here are just thirteen of them:

1. That the Jaffna of his childhood was the most beautiful place on earth.
2. That he invaded the pitch in 1975 during an SL vs Aus World Cup game at the Oval, carrying an Eelam flag.
3. That he lost more relatives in the 1977 anti-Tamil riots than he did in 1983.
4. That he was a founding member of Eelam Revolution Organisation of Students in Wandsworth in 1978.
5. That it matters not whether you believe the Tamils were only brought here in 1823. Or whether you accept that they've been here since King Ellara Cholan's reign in 100 BCE. They are now here to stay.
6. That most Sri Lankan Tamils and many Muslims would fail Lord Tebbit's famous cricket test.
7. That the Burghers told to 'burgher off' in the 1960s by the Sinhala Only policy were the island's first example of ethnic cleansing and its biggest cultural loss.
8. That ministers who laugh loudly, cry openly, bomb civilians and burn libraries deserve to die.
9. That he trained with Palestinians in Beirut in 1979 and several Tamil recruits died during that training.
10. That Buddhist priests have no business carrying handguns.
11. That many Sri Lankan geniuses have been Tamil. Anandan, Sathasivam, Mathew, Kadirgamar, Ediriweerasingham and the Thalaiver himself.
12. That everything has a price. And that a Sri Lankan victory is far more expensive than a Sri Lankan defeat.
13. That Satyagraha does not work.

It is while sitting in his garden, enjoying the Geoffrey Bawa-designed view, that I ask, not for the first time, why he is telling me all this. He never replies, but breaks into more stories, stories that it would not be in his interest to tell me. It is while thumbing through his bookshelves that the answer comes to me. Kuga likes the idea of his story being written, though he would not like it to be read. And he speaks to me only because I am someone who specialises in writing stuff that no one reads.

Isso Vade

On sinking sand, under thatched cabana, on foam mattress, gazing at sea foam, we are sipping thambili through straws and arguing about isso vade. To our left, on a tree-lined crag, Mount Lavinia Hotel and its ballrooms and pools turn on their lights. To our right, in a crumbling Fort, Colombo's World Trade Centre and its village of towers switch off theirs.

The sun changes colour behind a cloud, like a lady behind a screen, discarding amber shawl for tangerine blanket. And my beloved wife and I argue about isso vade.

Three prawns fried in chilli on a thick wafer, as orange and as intoxicating as the setting sun before us. 'Very nice for your cirrhosis. Chilli, oil, salt. How many drinks you're planning on having tonight?'

'I don't have cirrhosis.'

'How do you know? Now one month you have been drinking horen. Now wants to eat isso vade.'

'Sheila, I thought we weren't here to fight. I will drink carefully till my b…'

'Your book. Your book. How much longer? This is just an excuse…'

'I think I might walk back…'

'I brought you some cake. It is just butter cake, but it is good.'

It is several flights of stairs down from an isso vade, but I accept the peace offering.

'Why did you start drinking again?'

'My book is almost finished. I need to finish it soon. Then promise I will give up. I will go to your prayer meetings, therapy sessions. I will do yoga and stand on my head. But for the next few weeks. Just till after the World Cup.'

'The World Cup? That finishes in bloo…blooming June. You'll be dead by then.' Her mouth turns down and her eyes water. 'I'm sorry. Please, Gamini. No isso vade.'

She dabs her soggy eyes with her hanky as I sip more wretched thambili and put butter cake in my mouth. She gets her way and I get the guilt. Women are such cunning creatures.

'Garfield sent a CD of his songs. He is cutting a record in Germany, it seems.'

'How is the music?'

'Hopeless. All noise. There is one song that is nice. Something about poison. He might come for a visit with little Jimi.'

'No wife?'

'Gamini, don't start.'

The sun yawns and the beach fills with noise. Boys chase kites and girls around the palms. Children get thrown by the waves. Soon night will descend and battered prawns will be ordered in the beachside restaurants and hora couples will search for dark corners of sand to sit on. I will read my notes, watch some TV and prepare for my writing.

'I'm going to ask one thing,' she says. 'Do you want to live to see your grandson? Or do you want to leave me?'

If ever there was a loaded question.

'I want to finish what I started.'

'How long will that take?'

'As long as it takes.'

'You're a child, Gamini. Look at Ari. I don't see any difference. He's the same old Ari. He used to drink more than you. Now occasionally has a wine. Why can't you…'

'Be more like Ari? Let's go to Arpico and buy a raincoat.'

'I'll give you to the end of the month. Finish whatever you have to finish. But every day we meet here for sunset.'

I look around at the descending shadows and the emptying beach and realise this sea breeze is good for me. As is the lady sharing my mattress as long as she isn't crying or screaming.

'How many will you have a day?'

'I can't count drinks when I'm working.'

'How many?'

'From seven to five, no? So one every two hours. About six?'

'Two.'

'Two won't even get me out of bed.'

'Two, Gamini.'

'Three.'

'OK. Three.'

Like we are bargaining with a beach hawker over the price of a shawl. We spy a dark woman dragging batiks across the fluffy sand.

'There's a saasthara woman. I'm going to ask our fortune.'

I recognise the midget's concubine by her walk. She drags her bundle of rags as if it were a bag full of plastic bottles. She appears to be looking for something other than customers. I am unable to stop Sheila from clapping.

'Don't, men. She might curse us.'

'Don't be silly, Gamini. Why would she curse us?'

'Not today, men. Please.'

'Is she a prostitute?'

'I think she is.'

'How do you know?'

'Call her if you want.'

Sheila waves the dark woman away. 'Epa.' The saasthara woman stops and stares at me for a very long time. It is over ten years since I spoke with her, though I have seen her now and again near the Tyronne Cooray. She turns and drags her bags towards de Saram Road.

'Are you sure you don't know that woman, Gamini?'

'We should do another trip soon.'

'Aney please, shall we? I enjoyed that trip to Badulla, Gamini. I never said thank you.'

'It was a disaster.'

'Yes, but Badulla was lovely. I remembered the good old days. I did my flower arrangements, you were writing your poetry. What happened to your poetry?'

'I burned it.'

'Don't lie, men. I'm sure it's buried in that room of yours.'

'If you find the poems after I'm gone, please don't publish them. Only publish my book.'

'When are you planning on going?'

'No plan as such. After I finish the book, let's see.'

'I thought you were giving up after your book.'

'I am.'

'You must promise me that you will, Gamini.'

I take her hand. I nod.

'Remember the first film you took me to?'

'Charlton Heston at the Savoy?'

'What Charlton? Freddie Silva.'

'Go, men.'

'Of course. You told me he was the Sri Lankan Jerry Lewis.'

'I never did.'

'That's when you were trying to be intellectual to impress me.'

'I never tried to do anything.'

'Except steal me from my boyfriend.'

We giggle like the teenagers we once were. Sheila squeezes my hand.

'You're friends with him now?'

'I wouldn't say friends.'

'Why he visited you?'

'That's just to show off. I think it still bothers him that you stayed with me.'

'Can't believe that I did,' she says and plants a kiss on my cheek.

A waiter comes over and tries his best not to be rude. 'Uncle. This seat. Foreigners only.'

'Let's go, Gamini,' says Sheila.

'Are you mad? We are sitting here. After we are gone, you can give to your foreigners along with your arse.'

'No need to insult.'

'You are the one insulting. I will write to the papers. We have lived here for twenty years, we can't have a…'

The manager sees us, dashes over, dismisses the waiter, and heaps apology on apology. 'Mr Karunasena. I didn't see you. Sorry. That boy is new.'

'You've instructed him to only serve foreigners?' asks Sheila.

'No. No. Just to keep out the…'

'The what?'

The manager insists that we stay for dinner and that it is on the house.

Sheila cannot stop smiling. There are, after all, some perks to having worked as a journalist in Sri Lanka.

Saasthara

I manage to shelve despair long enough to keep writing. I hold my level at four drinks over ten hours and cut down to ten cigarettes. Every evening we greet the sunset. If it is raining, we sit inside and do jigsaws.

Sheila and I talk about other people's children and friends who have died. She tells me that I can stop eating Hacks and hiding empty bottles. I do not tell her that my bodyaches have returned and that my appetite has faded. That the typing hurts my fingers.

Ari tells me that Sheila is worried and if I'm going to keep drinking I should go for a check-up. I let him read my first few chapters and he is reasonably impressed. I tell him that is why I cannot stop to go for check-ups. He keeps talking, but I stop listening.

Sheila tells me her only regret is that she didn't paint more. I ask what about selling the piano. 'I still give lessons around the neighbourhood. I still get to play every day.'

I ask what about her flower-arranging business that closed down after a year. She tells me that she only regrets the things she didn't do.

I listen to my son's CD. It has a picture of a skeleton staring at a mushroom cloud and is titled *Bring Back the Sun* by Alice Dali. It is unashamedly awful. There is one song called 'Poison on a Tray' where it is just Garfield singing with a box guitar. I have no idea what the song is about, but at least it does not sound like furniture falling down stairs.

The more I write, the less I comprehend. If this were a film, it would end with me tracking down Pradeep, coaching him back to fitness and ushering in his comeback. The final scene would be the World Cup 1999, where Mathew takes the last Australian wicket and Sri Lanka retains the Cup. I have less than three months to make that happen.

I'm beginning to wake up hungover and each hangover brings with it a thin topping of petulance. I try and put on a brave face for my walks with Sheila and hide my irritation when she talks about how proud she is of our son, the abandoner of women.

I feel shame for things I have done to Sheila. Things that I have not smeared these pages with. I do not want my son to become like me.

I see the saasthara woman on her knees in our garden. I call out to her through the window and when I get to the veranda she is at the doorstep holding a sequinned rag.

'The wind blew my cloth,' she says. She shakes the dust from it and ties it over her plaited hair. She gazes through me.

'I have met you, Uncle.'

'Yes. Long time ago. With Uncle Neiris.'

'There are gods in this house.'

It is then that I notice that her features are almost African; maybe she has Kaffir blood. Kaffirs are descendants of Africans, brought here by the Portuguese. Negroid Sri Lankans who are found in villages around Puttalam, just near Lanka's left elbow. I suspect our nation's greatest female sprinter may have Kaffir blood in her. If I'm right, she may win Lanka its first Olympic medal since Duncan White.

'Can I tell Sir's saasthara?'

Her pottu is as red as her betel teeth. Her nose stud is as shiny as her eyes.

'No need saasthara.'

She pulls my hand, but does not look at it. Instead she looks in my eyes. 'You are looking for a Chinaman.'

I pull my hand away.

'You will not find him.'

Sri Lanka Cricket Cap

Sweat slaloms down the many hills on Reggie's shirtless torso. When he lies, he plays with his Sri Lanka cricket cap.

He fiddles with the peak when he tells me that the entire Pakistani U-19 team had grey in their beards. He adjusts the sides and tells me that the Sri Lankan vice captain used to stand at mid-wicket and trade stocks on his mobile phone.

Reggie tells me one story that I choose to believe. It took place in Wellington, in the hotel room of the MD of the SLBCC. Not the current MD, but the then-MD, Jayantha Punchipala, the powerbroker, the man with the iron fist, the man who would inherit Danila after Pradeep abandoned her.

The date was 16 March 1995. Sri Lanka had just won their first overseas test at Napier's McLean Park .

Booze flowed in the then-MD's suite at the Wellington Inter-Continental. Reggie remembers the post-match function filled with every Sri Lankan south of Papua New Guinea. 'Drunken uncles, sexy girls, noisy children, naughty aunties and best of all, unlimited booze,' squeals Reggie.

Unfortunately Wellington noise control cut short the party after 3 a.m., when drunken baila broke the decibel level.

Reggie remembers adjourning with a few other drunks to the then-MD's suite, but not much else. He remembers waking up behind the couch, covered in cushions, curled up next to a pot plant, carpet burn on face, invisible to the rest of the room. He remembers that the morning light was peeping through the blinds and that he felt chilly. Not how or when he came to be lying there. I nod a bit too knowingly.

But he does remember what he heard. And he repeats it with dollops of salt and cartons of spice. I have attempted to paraphrase.

A gruff hungover voice and a quiet, well-rested one:

You little fucking shit. Who the hell do you think you are?

What I'm asking is not unreasonable, considering...

You will leave my room now or I will have you hammered.

Your thuggery may work when you fix elections in Hambantota. But not in clean, green New Zealand. I could walk down to the office of the Dominion, tell them how this tour was financed.

What proof do you have?

None.

Then get the fuck out of my room.

I have names and places and stories. Newspapers are interested in things like that.

You want to be in the side? I will speak with the Captain. No one doubts your talent.

That's not what I want. I want your fee.

My fee. I can give that. But it will be the end of your career.

My career is over. And I have plenty of stories.

Tell your stories, we will sue.

I want you to sign me a cheque for NZ$278,000.

Hello. Is that Sudu? Chooti. Come to my...

Like this one.

It's OK, Chooti. Stay there. I'll call later. Where did you get that?

This is your signature? Why is it on a cheque given to the man who organised the assassination of the Minister?

Which minister?

You know which. I want your salary. And I want the money you skim off each tour. The cream. And the cherry.

You're talking nonsense.

Nonsense that the Dominion will pay me for. Though not as much as you will.

Go fuck your mother.

I will give you a guarantee. One payment only. You will not see or hear of me. What I know dies with me.

Sooner than you think, Putha. I have friends everywhere.

Good thing I don't.

You will never play cricket anywhere ever.

Good. I'm sick of the game.

We are computerising Sri Lanka's records. My brother-in-law's San Francisco firm is doing it. I will erase you. Every wicket you've taken will no longer exist. In ten years no one will remember you.

I'll take that cheque now.

I hope this petty cash is worth it for you. This is peanuts for me.

Thankfully, I am a much simpler man. This better not bounce.

The cheque won't bounce, but you won't get to enjoy it. I'll make sure of that.

Goodbye, Mr MD.

After the door slammed, the then-MD picked up the phone and began screaming abuse into it. Reggie listened as the ranting, raving voice retreated to the other end of the suite and faded onto a balcony overlooking Porirua. Reggie crawled to the door, looked both ways, opened it, and ran.

If my stack of tall stories now resembles the Manhattan skyline, then let this last one be its Empire State. All I will say is this. It took seven drinks for Reggie to relate this story. His shoulders may have slouched, his eyes may have reddened, his moustache may have twitched, his belly may have itched, at times he may have repeated himself and forgotten his place – but not once, not once, I tell you, did he touch his Sri Lanka Cricket cap.

The Floater

A traditional chinaman, but bowled with open chest and a shrug of the shoulders, causing the ball to linger in the air. Ari and Jonny call it the slow-motion delivery. It is the easiest of Mathew's variations to pick; the change in delivery stride is palpable.

'It is energy extraction at its most primal,' says Ari, showing off yet again. 'Mathew momentarily displaces kinetic energy and then guides it towards its trajectory.' Ari scribbles a formula on a napkin and shows it to Jonny. Jonny grabs the napkin, blows his nose on it and hands it back. 'Here. Calculate the viscosity of that.' Ah. The good ole days.

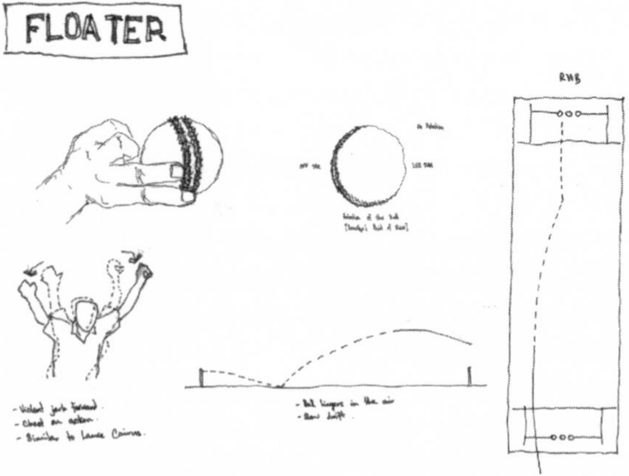

Legacy

Ari comes over to berate me about my boozing.

'I'm just saying, Wije, look at me. I drank for Jonny, then stopped. When you keep your word to yourself, good things happen. Look at last week's Royal–Tho, Ratwatte's Thoras won by…'

'Can we stop with your Thora bullshit?'

'You are looking weak, Wije. Do you realise you are killing yourself?'

If only he knew. That is all I have been thinking about. My death and Charles Darwin and Cary Grant.

I have come across two clippings from my scrapbooks, both from local newspapers, both yellow and faded. If this book gets published I will include both photos on this page, though I do not know how much it costs to have photos in books. But I do not mind bearing the cost for the sake of my reader.

Who is this reader? Who am I writing for? Some days I think I am writing for Pradeep. To preserve his legacy before it is forgotten. To encourage other Pradeeps out there. Other days I feel I am writing for my withered ego. To show Newton, Elmo, Rakwana and all the other pretenders what it is to really write about cricket.

Most times I feel I am writing for Garfield and little Jim Laker, for them to know that there can be greatness in the world and that if they avoid being like me, they may be part of it. Or for Sheila and Ari and Jonny to know that I didn't just waste my time drinking and causing fights.

Picture Darwin. Old, grey, bearded. How you would picture God, the very fellow they claim Darwin tried to replace. Picture Cary Grant. Suave, debonair, dashing. How you would picture James Bond who Grant almost played.

Grant died aged eighty-two, Darwin was seventy-three when he passed on. Why do we remember one as an old man and the other as a dapper fellow? Who is in control of our legacies and is there any way we can influence them? For those of us who are neither movie stars nor scientific visionaries, I fear the answer may be no.

I wish to be remembered on the cover of *TIME* holding aloft my Olympic gold. For the 6 that I hit off the last ball. For the joke I told that everyone laughed at.

But what if I am remembered as the drunk who insulted his sister-in-law? As the coward who hid under the bed when the burglars came? As the man who was always clean bowled first ball?

There are some days, when the sun hits my window and the birds are silent and my fingers hover over the keys like God moving over the water's face, when I feel I am writing a glorious symphony for the whole world to close their eyes to. But sadly those days are too few and too far between.

The Great Anton Rose

Mathew didn't just lose me a job, he also lost me my chance at an extra income. *Kreeda*, a magazine I helped found, was banned by the government because I couldn't resist writing a piece on the Asgiriya test. The magazine was shut down and I made fresh enemies.

Enemies appear to be what Pradeep and I have in common. Pradeep fought with two captains, six coaches, three vice captains and at least one cricket administrator. But according to Charith, Reggie, Amalean and the GLOB, his only true nemesis was Zimbabwean Anton Rose.

Certain cricketers are unlucky to have been born where they were. Astounding talents like Bevan, Slater and McGill would have been national greats had they come from anywhere other than Australia. At present they may be unable to enjoy full international careers due to the cluster of talent that is Australia.

If Pradeep Mathew was one cricketer disadvantaged by the country of his birth, the Zimbabwean Anton Rose was another. The boy from Bulawayo lost his farm and his career to the Mugabe regime. It is another of cricket's tragedies.

Every skill in cricket can be taught, but timing is a gift from God. To know the nanosecond when the willow should be applied to leather to bring forth the sweetest music and the most wondrous stroke. Only a few have that. Sathasivam did, Viv Richards did, and so did the great Anton Rose.

If Mathew was cursed for his race and his temperament, then Rose had a very different curse.

'For each ball, Rose had five or six different shots,' says Amalean. 'Only great players have this. But then after he reached thirty-six, he would hit every ball to the fielder.'

'Rose is the only batsman Pradeep never conquered,' says Charith.

'Others, even if they hammered, he would revenge. Rose could pick every variation.'

Throughout Booth Beckmann's biography Rose cites Pradeep as the bowler he most enjoyed playing against. 'Only one bowler could really challenge me. Mathew from Sri Lanka. But I think I got the better of him.'

Beckmann's book depicts an ambitious man of principle, a perfectionist prone to depression. It is the most candid cricket biography I have read, and it is a scathing attack on Pradeep's perceived gamesmanship and lack of sportsmanship.

'He would never be great, because he was not a good character. He is an example to all youngsters on how to waste talent,' says Rose in Chapter 17.

There is a mythical story of two nineteenth-century planters, one Englishman and one Burgher, who would meet on different Ceylon hills on June's longest day and challenge each other to 5-over games. Each had plantation workers who would field for them. Only the two planters would bat or bowl. Their first game would have been the world's first recorded limited-overs game, had anyone bothered to record it.

Like the Devil and the Wandering Jew meeting in an East End tavern once every century. They would play till sunset and the loser of the most games would treat the victor to dinner and drinks at the local planters' club.

Legend has it that every planters' bungalow from Hatton to Diyatalawa has the score carved into one of its trees. Those who remember the story have no idea where the trees are. I do remember seeing 'England 7–Ceylon 5. Jun '46' carved into a jacaranda tree, though I cannot remember if it was in Maskeliya or Hatton.

Rose was largely responsible for Pradeep Mathew's figures of 0–218. They are the worst figures in cricket history, though even that record no longer appears to exist. I know that Mathew recovered from this thrashing to dismiss Rose in the final test for a duck. And that it was the beginning of a slump that would end Rose's career. And eventually Mathew's.

All my witnesses remember the vicious sledging that went on between them, but no one remembers what caused it. After his wife was attacked in their Harare home, Rose left Zimbabwe and cricket and became an exiled critic of Robert Mugabe. After extorting NZ$278,000, Pradeep Mathew disappeared to somewhere no one knows.

I sometimes conjure up my own mythical match. Played on the fields of Europe and America, from Budapest to Texas, from Berlin to Caracas. Once every ten years, cricket exiles Anton Rose and Pradeep Mathew meet to settle who is the greatest unsung. The fielders who do not bat and bowl are illegal refugees from both their troubled nations. Loser pays for catering.

Mathew bowls, Rose bats. In between unplayable googly and deft leg glance, they sledge each other, though more in the manner of bitter uncles than young hotheads.

'Next year I will play for English counties. After that I will play for England. Where will you be?'

Mathew will trundle in, wave his spider-like limbs and bowl a darter or a boru ball or a double bounce ball, and Rose will be bowled.

Mathew will smile and adjust his headband. 'I will always be on a green field bowling a ball that you will have no answer for.'

The Follow-on

A follow-on is when a team falls woefully short of its opponent and is invited to bat again. It's the winning side sneering, 'Go on. Have another. Bet you still can't catch us.' If the opposing side fails, it is called an innings defeat, the worst possible ignominy for a team playing test cricket.

While the team following on is usually fighting for dear life, the follow-on is also a chance for redemption, to undo the mistakes of the first innings. More often than not, the team following on loses the test. But there have been some spectacular exceptions.

Double Bounce Ball

I saw it on two occasions. And for that I am grateful. At Asgiriya in 1987 and at Kettarama in 1991. It is undoubtedly the strangest ball ever invented. The mystery of mystery balls. A ball that bounces and changes direction *twice*.

A 5 ounce, spherical, leather-bound object made to behave like a pebble skimming water.

Reggie Ranwala says that Pradeep bowled two consecutively against Anton Rose in 1994 and that both were declared no-balls. We have footage of Mercantile Credit vs Sathosa, 1986. Premlal Fernando and Basil Goonatilaka were bowled by double bounce balls.

Newton claims he helped perfect it in 1993 and that there is nothing illegal about a ball that bounces twice. Gokulanath said he knew how to bowl it, though he could not show us.

I remember it in the Bloomfield vs Nomads game 1994, perhaps Mathew's second greatest performance. I was with Ari and Renga. Every over Renga reminded us that the young new batsman was his nephew Marvan Arnold. Short ball outside leg. Arnold pulled at thin air. Ball cut to his off, pitched, bounced into the wicket. Renga swore.

'I've never seen anything like that,' said Ari.

'That's the best ball I've ever seen,' said I.

We turned to Renga.

He scowled and pretended to write in his notepad. 'I've seen better,' he said.

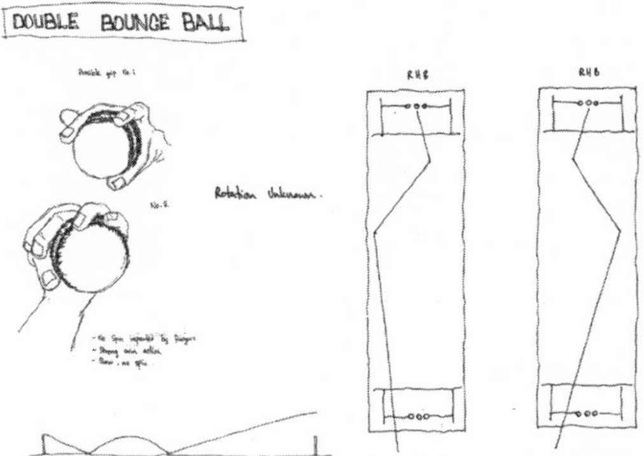

Scorpion Kick

The SSC is festooned in blue.

'They're all here today, mate.'

The man who greets me is Sid Barnes, member of Bradman's Invincibles. He wears a grin and sunglasses and carries two baskets. He was called Suicide Sid because he used to field close without helmet or box. Not because he suffered from bipolar disorder and overdosed on barbiturates in '73.

The stadium is crowded and I see no Jonny, but I do see Ari.

'What are you doing in my dream?' I ask.

'This is not a dream, Putha. This is a hallucination.'

'There is a difference?'

'Dreams are when you sleep. You are in a coma with your eyes open.'

'How did that happen?'

'Two bottles yesterday?'

'My level is five drinks.'

'Why call it a level when you don't stick to it?'

On the field Pakistan is playing Sri Lanka – well, that is what the colours tell me. But while the bowler in green is positively Imran Khan, the batsman appears to be Sri Lanka's current president in a blue sari. There are pictures of her hanging from the rafters.

'Is this a match or a political rally?'

'This is the '99 World Cup final.'

'But they haven't played it yet.'

A tall white man approaches and tries to sell us kadale. I recognise him as I shoo him away.

'Hey, Jack Iverson,' shouts Ari. 'Come back. I'll buy your kadale.'

'You're in the kadale business now?' I ask, but Iverson does not respond.

On the field the score keeps decreasing. It was 400 for 5, now it is 210 for 7. The blues and greens hurt my eyes; there is the noise of papare and cheering everywhere. David Bairstow, honk-nosed ex-England wicketkeeper, sells us sweep tickets. He too does not speak and his tickets all carry the number 5198. And then arrives the bum. 'Got some spare rupees, brother?'

'Jonny?' says Ari.

I see that beneath the grime it is indeed Jonny. We seat him next to us and give him kadale.

'Things aren't going well,' says Jonny, bottom lip quivering.

'You still didn't get to heaven?'

'No, look. England are 33 for 9.'

Minister C.V. Gooneratne is batting in blue. Wasim Akram races in and hits him on the thigh pad. The fielders go up and so does the umpire's finger. Then the umpire runs up to the wicketkeeper and high-fives him.

All the players come and hug the umpire. The batsman storms off in disbelief.

'Ari. WeeGee. I knew he was fourteen.'

'But you said you didn't?'

'Anthony was sixteen. Joseph was fourteen. I knew.'

I look at Ari who looks away. 'There's Ole Neiris. I better be off.'

I see Ari disappear into the crowd though I see no midget.

On the field Pakistan are now batting, though I recognise the batsman as Lalith Dissanayake, the late minister. Vaas's first ball shatters the bat. A shard of it lands on the wicket. The crowd cheers.

'It's not what you think, WeeGee. I loved him.'

'It doesn't matter, Jonny.'

'He loved me. He even visited me in prison.'

'I don't need to know.'

Clear the air passages. We need more oxygen.

Man with glasses and beard looking down. My office ceiling fan turning.

The next batsman is Derek Randall, who is followed by a butcher with a wheelbarrow of pork chops. 'He gets a chop for each boundary he scores!' says a man who may not be Justin Fashanu, the homosexual footballer who hanged himself a year ago.

Unrecognisable faces. Except the angel in the back who is crying.

Lots of voices, none in unison. Don't cry, Sheila. I tried.

Buck Shelford is wearing a headguard and bowling off spin to Ranasinghe Premadasa. On drive. Georgie Best gives chase from mid-wicket and stops a certain boundary. 'Georgie, where did it all go wrong?' shouts someone in the crowd.

Jonny taps me and shows me a fifty rupee note. 'Why is Jimmy Carter in a nilame outfit on the back of our fifty rupee note?' I reply that I do not know but that it is so.

Ambulance doors, white pre-coffin. Two faces, both I recognise and love.

One says, C'mon Wije. Stay with us. The other sobs.

Minister J.R. Athulathmudali gets hit in the unmentionables by an underarm full toss from English aristocrat bully Douglas Jardine. The crowd boos.

Doors. Ceilings. Faces. Voices.

I've lost pulse. Get him to theatre now.

Pradeep Mathew is facing Kerry Packer. Mathew in green, Packer in blue. The ball is skied for a certain 6, when from the stands out jumps a hairy man. It is Colombian goalkeeper Rene Higuita. He runs to the boundary and scorpion-kicks the ball back into play. The crowd goes wild.

Maha Dena Mutta

So now we are back at Nawasiri. Different room, worse view, no AC. Always hot or maybe that's just me. I am hooked up to a fish tank and I have a new term in my vocabulary: renal failure. I could explain to you what it means, but I have bored you enough already.

That last chapter was written in bed by hand on this exercise book where I used to record Colombo Municipality rates. I see I paid them diligently in the 1970s and then let them slide in the 1980s when our taxes went towards rifles and not roads. The government stopped caring, I stopped paying.

The ache in my fingers has travelled past my wrist and has annexed my shoulder. Only if I hold my torso at a precise angle can I prevent the pain from shooting up my side whenever I put pencil to pad. Ari has offered me a solution, a very generous one. He has offered me his daughters.

Each one has volunteered to come on a different day, to record my ramblings and then to faithfully type them. Manouri even made up a roster:

Monday:	Rochelle
Tuesday:	Michelle
Wednesday:	Stephanie
Thursday:	Melissa
Friday:	Aruni
Weekend:	Reading of drafts

If I'm to be under observation for a month, this is a sustainable way of finishing my work. But the chaos of five different hands and five different brains fills me with dread. How do I revise when I know not who typed what? I can barely tell Ari's daughters apart by sight. Manouri came over and provided me with photographs and biographical details and kind assurances that 'The girls are happy to do it, we all enjoy your writing'.

I am touched though I do not say so. Though I'm still nervous about having five different middlemen (who are girls) between me and the page. Then I see a picture of a recent Byrd family trip to Adam's Peak and an idea hits me.

Sri Lankan folklore is littered with as many buffoons as the Sri Lankan parliament. One such character is Maha Dena Mutta, a foolish sage with five dimwitted pupils. The bumbling adventures of this merry troupe involve a goat's head, a boggy marsh and buckets of slapstick. While the tales are somewhat forgettable, the names and physical descriptions of his five pupils are most definitely not.

The shortest is Rabbada Aiya (Toddy Belly), the simplest, Puwak Badilla (Areca Nut Eater), the tallest, Kotu Kithaiya (Stick Figure), the chubbiest, Polbe Moona (Coconut Face), the thinnest, Indikatu Pancha (Tiny Needle). Looking over Manouri's photos and hearing her gossip-laden descriptions of her stepdaughters, the stories of Maha Dena Mutta and his men come to mind. I now have both a system and a method:

Monday.	Rochelle, thirty-four. Always pregnant, talkative. *Rabbada Aiya.*
Tuesday.	Michelle, thirty-two. Fair, hair colour black, should be blonde. *Puwak Badilla.*
Wednesday.	Stephanie, twenty-eight. Hippie, looks like high jumper. *Kotu Kithaiya.*
Thursday.	Melissa, twenty-four. Bit of a number, round face. *Polbe Moona.*
Friday.	Aruni, eighteen. Tiny and sweet. *Indikatu Pancha.*

Done.

Toddy Belly

I'd like you to put RA at the top of all the sheets you type, um… Rochelle. It's a sort of code I have devised to keep my notes in order. This is your third child? Fourth? Those days all the families had six, seven children. Now how to afford? But your husband is doing well. He is an engi…ah grocer. So? People have to eat.
Yes. That's fascinating. Shall we start? Only one hour also, no?

Graham Snow visited me yesterday.

Everyone in the ward is excited and for a day I am more popular than the curly-haired quadruplets born upstairs.

Graham brings me books I cannot hold and VCDs I cannot watch.

'I hear you're finishing your book. Did you read mine?'

'I didn't like your chapter on the '76 summer.'

'Make 'em grovel?'

'It sounded a bit bitter, not like you.'

'You and Ari know how bitter I can get. What are your thoughts for the World Cup? You gave me a good tip last time.'

'Forget Sri Lanka. Bet on Australia.'

The male nurses come into my room at five-minute intervals and pretend to tidy things while grinning at my guest.

'What about Pakistan? South Africa?'

'Forget all. Australia will win this. Maybe even the next.'

'You're all doom and gloom, WeeJay. Cheer up, fella.'

'I'm dying, Graham.'

'Don't be ridiculous. I talked to the doc. He says you'll be right as rain. Now who's sounding bitter?'

'A good captain knows when to declare.'

'Not your innings, mate. Who will I visit to get my World Cup tips for 2003? Now stop talking like an old woman and cheer up, willya? Did I tell you how I met Ross Emerson in the changing rooms…'

Areca Nut Eater

You're not going to take notes, my dear?

You'll just let me speak into this thing and you'll type it. Then?

Oh, on the computer. Yes, that's called typing. No need of a typewriter.

I'd like you to listen though, Michelle. Just in case.

Yes. Very important. Put PB on the top of the page.

Everyone brings me fruit. Bottles of apple juice that will stay unpoured stand in single file next to both my Sportswriter of the Year awards. Ari has had the trophies polished and is currently editing my manuscript. He wants me to sit with his daughters and dream up an ending. Manouri, the stepmother of the fair girl holding this tape recorder, has tried unsuccessfully to sell me religion. I suppose the hospital bed provides the church with most of its customers and I shouldn't blame her for trying. She has after all been very kind to me. There is enough cricket on TV to keep me annoyed. As I see our geriatric team find new and creative ways to mess things up, it is obvious that the vintage of '96 has now turned to vinegar.

Ari's optimism is what sustains me, along with Sheila's love. My doctor is the same pup who diagnosed me many months ago. He does not recognise me, but pretends to. These days I can tell a liar from their eyes, a skill like many I wish I'd had when I was younger.

I urinate through tubes and I shit not at all. Apologies, my dear. I know that I smell and I am grateful you and your sisters come here at all.

Yesterday brought Newton Rodrigo.

When he comes in I begin shivering and require more blankets. Why do I only see him when I'm on my deathbed?

He has shaved his moustache and his hair and wears Gandhi glasses. His head resembles a half-inflated rugby ball with intellectual leanings. He brings a copy of *The Art of Cricket*. I turn to the front page and see: *To Gamini, Best Wishes Donald Bradman*

I giggle.

'Good to see you're in good spirits. How's the Pradeepan book?'

'Almost done, just like me.'

'Why don't you stop being negative and pull through this?'

'OK. I might do that. Thanks. Is your coaching advice this insightful?'

He rises. 'Wije, I just came to give your book. No need to insult.'

'My book did not say *To Gamini* on it.'

'What?'

'Sit, Newton. Tell me more stories about Mathew.'

'What else did you find?'

'That he was brilliant and unlucky.'

'I believe you make your own luck.'

'You would.'

'What's your problem, Wije?'

I look at him with his shirt and his chains and his jiggling car keys. Even the hair on his arms looks groomed. I am aware how repulsive I must look to him.

'When I taught you to write at the *Observer*, did you think we'd end up like this?'

He shrugs and looks at my polished awards.

'You make your own luck.'

'It's a good thing Bradman's still alive.'

'What?'

'You were too proud to admit you'd lost my book. So you went to the extent of getting another signed, rather than apologise to me.'

'You're delirious.'

'I am. But I'm not a hack like you. You think I can't tell when a signature's forged? I know who gulled my book from you.'

'I don't know what you're saying.'

He gets up. 'See you, Wije.'

'You made this entire six-finger thing up just to impress me?'

'Don't blame me because your life is over.'

'Pradeep said you were a racist and an opportunist.'

'Where did you hear that garbage?'

'A man called Kugarajah.'

He shakes his head. 'You will get better if you let go of your anger.'

'Why should I be angry?' I call out.

He stands at the doorway, his shoes and his bald scalp shining.

'Because you wasted your life.'

'And Sheila chose me.'

For a long while he is silent. Then he comes to my bed and whispers, 'If that is all you can boast of after all these years, then you are more pathetic than I thought.'

He leaves and it dawns on me that if I am soon to be dead, then I had better get used to not having the last word.

Sport vs Life

Stephanie, that's a very interesting T-shirt, what is it?

I don't know about all these bands, that you have to ask Garfield, you know he's in a…

Yes. Yes. Just press play on that radio, song number 3. That is our son. Called 'Poison on a Tray'. Not bad, ah?

Yes, yes. Eighteen months old. No, we haven't seen him.

Can you bring me a tea? Have a lot to get through today.

When typing, that's right. KK. Top of every page. Thanks.

My wife asks me why I love sport more than her. More than I do my son and our life together. I tell her then that she is talking nonsense. But perhaps she isn't.

Some people gaze at setting suns, sitting mountains, teenage virgins and their wiggling thighs. I see beauty in free kicks, late cuts, slam dunks, tries from halfway and balls that turn from off to leg.

When the English toured in 1993, their supporters arrived in droves and formed a jolly beer-swilling troupe called the Barmy Army. A T-shirt of theirs read as follows: 'One day you will meet a goal that you'll want to marry and have kids with.'

Anyone who saw Diego Maradona in 1986 will agree that the T-shirt speaks the truth. To be in the right place at the right time and to watch a gifted athlete in full cry is one of life's true pleasures.

In sport, has-beens can step onto a plate and smash a last ball into oblivion. A village can travel to Manchester for a cup tie and topple a giant. Villains, can heroes become.

In 1996, subcontinental flair overcame western precision and the world's nobodies thrashed the world's bullies. Sixty years earlier a black man ridiculed the Nazi race theory with five gold medals in Berlin before Mein Führer's furious eyes.

In real life, justice is rarely poetic and too often invisible. Good sits in a corner, collects a cheque and pays a mortgage. Evil builds empires.

Sport gives us organisms that attack in formation. Like India's spin quartet and the three Ws from the Caribbean. Teams that become superhuman before your very eyes. Like Dalglish's Liverpool, Fitzpatrick's All Blacks and Ranatunga's Lankans.

In real life, if you find yourself chasing 30 runs off 20 balls, you will fall short, even with all your wickets in hand. Real life is lived at 2 runs an over, with a dodgy LBW every decade.

In real life, as Sri Lankan cricket grows sweeter, your wife will grow sourer. The All Blacks may underachieve for two more decades, but your son will disappoint you more. I hope you read this, Garfield. I hope you forgive.

The answer to my wife's question is of course a no. I would go down in a hail of bullets for her and for Garfield many times over. And while Aravinda de Silva has delighted me on many an occasion, I wouldn't even take a blister for him.

But the truth, Sheila, is bigger than both of us, whether it be written on the subway walls or on the belly of a lager lout's T-shirt. In thirty years, the world will not care about how I lived. But in hundred years, Bulgarians will still talk of Letchkov and how he expelled the mighty Germans from the 1994 World Cup with a simple header.

Sport can unite worlds, tear down walls and transcend race, the past, and all probability. Unlike life, sport matters.

Mrs Kolombage

Hi Melissa, how are you?

Right. Put PM on the top of each…

Yes, I know it's the morning, what? It's just a code.

No, don't put MB, yes, I know it's your initials, but my code.

No, I can't explain. Fine. Do what you want.

I asked the nurse to bring me water seventeen minutes ago, but my parched gullet is yet to receive relief. My doctor does the rounds at 8.30, which is still a few hours away. I do not get visitors till well after 10, but today appears to be one of my less unlucky days.

'I thought I recognised your name on the patient board. What is the matter?'

Sari, handbag, circular glasses, circular figure. I had seen her somewhere before.

'Mrs Kolombage. I used to work at ITL with that Rakwana.'

'Hello. How?'

'You here for sugar?'

'Kidney failure.'

'My husband has diabetes. Have to come early or can't catch doctor. Can I get you anything?'

I ask for water and for the curtains to stay drawn.

She chatters about her husband and how she no longer works. Are all women doomed, once the children have left home, to begin prepping their husbands for the grave? Mrs Kolombage makes tea and natters on about Rakwana leaving the media to become a poet.

'You should see the money he made from ITL and SwarnaVision. I only did the books, so I know. If I collected that, even I would retire and write poetry.'

Her skin is the colour of un-drunk coffee and it is darkest around the circles of her eyes. The way she chatters and giggles at her own jokes reminds me of Sheila. I think of things undone and of things that cannot be undone, and in front of this stranger tears begin rolling down my cheeks.

'Mr W.G.? It's OK.' She pats down my uncombed hair.

'Your husband must be waiting.'

'No, he'll be taking tests till noon. It's OK, Mr W.G.'

No stranger has addressed me by my distinguished initials till today.

'Thank you. You are very kind. I'm just a silly old man.'

'But look at how you have used your talent. That documentary was all your doing. All of us could see. Cassim, that girl Danila. All said the script was magic. That Rakwana only messed it up.'

'Thank you, Mrs Kolombage. Your husband must be wondering…'

She starts quoting from the Bible and for some reason it does not irritate me.

'Don't be upset, Mr W.G. You have led a great life.'

'All I have done is make enemies.'

'All great men make enemies. I see your greatness and so does God.'

'I don't believe in God.'

'Doesn't matter. God will believe in you.'

Right then, I believe that if I repent, I will be able to write my book. What a mutt.

Papa, I know I'm just meant to transcribe Uncle Wije's words and not supposed to offer my opinion, but this is classic bargaining behaviour. We studied it in my counselling course, the stages of grief. I can't remember the others, but bargaining was definitely one.

Mrs Kolombage leaves, promising to check in on me. She tells me I must forgive myself. I nod and thank her and wonder why I cannot cry in front of my own wife.

By noon I start shivering and my drip comes out. Blood pours out of me like a million tiny cricket balls. The orderlies wash it away and cover me in blankets. I ask the nurses to keep the radio and TV switched off, and I focus on the revolving fan and dream of Badulla and Bolgoda. I tell myself I do not want to die.

I believed once that I could stave off death by writing. But if I am to accept my place in an indifferent universe, I cannot complain when it treats me indifferently. For me to embrace God after all these years would be hypocrisy of US foreign policy proportions. I can only lie here and hope.

It appears that the bargaining stage has given way to depression. The goal of the therapist should be to lead patient towards acceptance. This should be our goal.

I could call up Garfield and tell him that I like his song. That I am proud that he is a great musician and has bedded more women than me.

I propose that this crude comment be deleted from final draft.

I dreamed two days ago that I was at the SSC and Sir Garfield Sobers led me onto the pitch during an interval and told me the meaning of life.

I remember that it was one sentence that made complete sense in the way things rarely do. I woke up, rang for the nurse and called for a piece of paper and a pen, only to watch it fade from my thoughts.

When the paper arrived at 0.27 SLT, I snatched it and wrote six words on it. Could have. Should have. Did not.

Surprise Visit

Hello Aruni, my Indikatu Pancha.

Don't tell anyone, but you're my favourite of all the Byrd girls.

I prefer girls that are kalu. Your akkis are too sudu, no?

No, are you mad? Of course I am OK. We have so much to write.

No time like present. Let's begin right away.

I have two bits of good news: (a) I am going to live. (b) I have an ending for my story. Yesyesyes. That is indeed correct.

Last night something happened. They told me what it was, but I couldn't understand then, so I don't remember it now. At the time Cassius Clay and Joe Frazier were giving me body shots. Ali delivering one-twos to my left side, Smokin' Joe tenderising my right, just in front of where sweet Aruni is now sitting. These were not quick jabs, but thunderous blows that rattled my ribcage and contorted my spine. 'What's my name, fool?' Ali kept asking. Joe of course just kept silent.

When the doctors came, the boxers vanished. There was much movement and plenty of shouting as I lay writhing while my bruises turned purple. When I awoke there were more tubes pumping life into me, but this time the room was sprinkled with fairy dust. The light was a 4.30 p.m. Attidiya glow and in the background I heard The Meat Loaf doing anything for love. And I felt happy, because for once I knew things would turn out OK.

Then in he walked. His hair had grown long enough to tie in a ponytail. He had a red cricket ball in his hand that he couldn't stop playing with. In his arms was a child. It was none other than Pradeep Mathew himself. Yes. You heard me correctly.

'I got you this from Lord's. It's signed by Richie Benaud.'

'Thank you, son. You don't know how long I've been looking for you.'

'I tried to come earlier.'

'I have written about you. Everyone will know how great you are. You and me will finish this together.'

'I don't know how long we'll be staying. I'd like you to meet my son.'

'Hello, little fellow. Will you be a great man like your father?'

'My son has a present for you.'

Pradeep Mathew's son gave me a picture of a cricketer that he had obviously drawn. To most it would appear as a mess of lines and splotches. But me, I could clearly see a left-handed batsman taking guard.

'I see the boy is talented like his father.'

'I'm glad you wrote what you did.'

'You inspired me to write. The world does not appreciate what an artist you are. Come back to us. You have so much to offer.'

'I will have to think about that. Listen. His mother is waiting. I'll bring her this evening. Now you must get some rest.'

'Shirali? I would love to meet her. I have heard so much.'

Now it seems I have something to live for – something that doesn't come in packs of twelve and isn't measured by the finger-width. Sweet Aruni is trying to interrupt me and I tell her to hold her horses. I can feel nausea as one would see a tidal wave approaching, gathering strength from the horizon. One more paragraph before it hits. Please.

Mark my words, as a writer and a lover of sports. This story shall be finished. It is indeed possible to score a late goal in extra time, to land a knockout at the end of the 12th, to hit a 6 off the final ball. And I, W.G. Karunasena, husband of Sheila, father of Garfield, champion of Pradeep Sivanathan Mathew, am, without doubt, the man to do it.

Follow On

'If I should ever die, God forbid, let this be my epitaph:
The only proof he needed for the existence of God
was music.'

Kurt Vonnegut, Jr, American writer (1922–2007)

Twenty Zero Zero

Mathew prances the palladium
sets it ablaze
Rewrites the rules
erases his name
Performs magic miracles
on the sporting field
Blazes trails
refuses to yield
The mastery and wizardry
the mystery of guile
On occasion he destroyed
with assassin's smile
Unbroken
untamed
unfettered
undiscovered
The genius of Serendib is all but smothered

Som Wardena
© 2000

'Ganga Samaga'
11 Arunella Junction
Madhu River
Balapitiya

Dear Mrs Karunasena,
I received your late husband's manuscript and read it with interest. I too was a great admirer of Pradeep Matthews. You may recall, I directed an award-winning documentary on said bowler. Your husband had a hand in the script.

While there are some interesting points raised in your husband's memoir I feel the style is too rambling, the thesis unclear and the language falls into the informal and the vulgar. I suggest I rewrite this in the form of ethnic prose-poetry, perhaps with some line sketches adorning the page. Through art we will capture the essence of an artisan in a way that anecdote can only hope to.

To undertake this, I will require a 50 per cent advance on my author's fee, plus an agreed-upon royalty on book sales. You may contact my lawyer aritaw@eureka.lk to discuss the business side of this artistic endeavour.

Yours truly,

Som Wardena

BA (Oxon), MA (Harv)
Runner-up, Commonwealth South East Asia Debut Documentary 1999
Shortlist, Gratiaen Prize for Literature, 2000

Twenty Zero One

To conclude the tale of Pradeep Mathew, one must

My good friend W.G., would always say

The night was dark

I'm sorry, Wije, I cannot do this. I wish I could, but I cannot write like you. I don't even know what to say.

It is the year of the space odyssey. I'm sad to say it, old chap, but I was right about many things. Australia took the Cup, even though Paki was the form team. Like I told you, the vintage of '96 has soured. Ranatunga retired and one by one Roshan, Kalu, Pramodya, Hashan all vanished. We now have a decent team, but these days everyone expects them to win all the time. I have a feeling it will never be like '96 ever again.

Didn't I tell you US was due for another Pearl Harbor? Last month some Arabs flew a plane into New York's World Trade Center, thousands killed. They suspect a man with three names. World is now fully in shock even though for us Lankans this is nothing new. US is declaring war on terror. Our Tigers, cunning buggers, are now OK to ceasefire. The sons of the soil are saying the ceasefire allows Tigers to rearm. Some fools are saying to ask America to help get rid of them. I hope I am dead and with you and Jonny long before that ever happens.

We have an OK prime minister, even if he is a Royalist, he seems to have something of a vision. He may be able to pull off a peace deal, but of course all the yakos and sarong johnnies call him a homo and a traitor. Typical Lanka.

I read your book. I think in places it is interesting, but I have to say, in places it is rubbish. You go off the topic a lot and I don't like how you describe me or my girls. If there was so much dust in my room, why did you come in? And you make me sound like a fool, when did I wear a raincoat and a hat? You can't just make things like that up, Wije. I don't like my daughters being in your book. I have asked Sheila to remove that before it is published.

I'm disappointed you didn't use all of my Neiris Uncle stories. It seems that you never believed any of them. I don't believe your Kuga nonsense and I think you should have your fantasies about Danila somewhere else. If Sheila reads she will be upset.

Anyway. What to do now? Sheila asks if I can edit it, but what editing for a fellow like me? I turned seventy last year, had a big party. Now it seems every week there is a funeral around me. Our world is decaying, my friend, soon I may be the only remnant of it.

I'm writing to say I can't help you with your book. And that I miss you, my old friend. Last week Newcastle beat Man United 4–3. It was the best game of football I have seen and I thought of Jonny. They say that boy's father received a share in the Bolgoda property as compensation. He got hold of a minister to bring those charges against Jonny. Now the minister runs Jonny's place as a guest house. I don't know if there was truth to the allegations, though everyone seems to think there was.

Say hello to the old Geordie. I hope you and he are both well and have met Satha, W.G. Grace and Bogart. The great Don Bradman just passed over, so hope you got a book signed. If there is a Bolgoda, then save a haansi putuwa for me.

Your manuscript made me feel sad. I never knew what went on in that head of yours. If I had, I would have told you you were the most brilliant man I knew and it has been a pleasure, sir, to have spent my years with you. And you would have punched me and told me to stop behaving like a little girl.

I cannot forgive myself for making you drink at Jonny's. If there is one thing I regret in all my years it is that.

God bless you and your cockeyed theories.

I miss them all.

Ariyaratne Cletus Byrd

Twenty Zero Three

The Spin Wizard

We have all undoubtedly heard of the dashing and dynamic feats of our grinning assassin, the duke of the doosra, feared the world over, named: Muralitharan, Muttiah Muralitharan. But if I were to say the name Pradeep Mathew, you would frown in perplexed stupor.

A spinner of quixotic wizardry, a bowler of daring and devilish talents, alas, discarded by the national side after ten years of lean service, many saw Pradeep Mathew as Sri Lanka's greatest cricketer who never was. My late good friend Mr W.G. Karunasena, formerly of the *Observer*, was known to have been writing a book about the life of Mathew and his wondrous feats. Alas, Karunasena's untimely death halted its completion. His widow reveals that the book requires heavy editing before it is published.

I met Karunasena once and he told me that Mathew had taken more wickets per game than anyone in history. According to Karuna, had he played a full career of 100 tests and say 300 ODIs, he would have finished with well over 700 and 500 wickets respectively. While I do not acquiesce with my learned friend's fanciful speculations, I must concur that Mathew was indeed a talent worth reckoning with.

I observed this uncut diamond, this rare flower in bloom, in action for Bloomfield on many a moon. By the late 1980s, Mathew was one of the most feared bowlers on the local club circuit, having added a flipper, a darter, a skidder, a floater and the infamous double bounce ball to his varied repertoire of deliveries. But sadly, Mathew's temperament proved erratic, impetuous and dastardly; many accused him of not being a team player.

He did in fact play four tests for Sri Lanka, but was rotated along with the likes of Anurasiri, Wijesuriya, Kalpage, Madurusinghe and de Silva. While Mathew was an effective wicket taker, he could also prove very expensive. This, coupled with his frequent clashes with management over disciplinary issues, resulted in him being sidelined.

With the world praising wunderkinds like Warne, Murali and Saqlain, one wonders what they would have said had Mathew reached his full potential.

© Elmo Tawfeeq, *Daily Views*
11/07/03

Twenty Zero Five

My darling Gamini,

It has taken me years to read it and I am sorry but I don't very much care for it. Ari only suggested that I do this, that I write to you. It feels strange. Sometimes I believe you watch over me, though I never know if you are happy or not.

I did as you asked. We buried you in the coconut grove by the river on the Kurunegala Estate. Bala and Sunila were very helpful and agreed to set aside this plot. I am sitting here at this moment. On the grass by your grave, looking at the land you sold.

I didn't know I made you so unhappy, I didn't know you thought so little of our life. Did you really think it was completely pointless? Did you think I was pointless? You never talked to me. You never listened. For what it's worth, I have memories I will not let you spoil.

Garfield has grown into a man. He has the same spark that you used to have. He has done well for himself and plans on returning to start a business in Sri Lanka. Little Jimi lives with his mother in Geneva, but comes every other year for Christmas. I do not know if I should give them your book.

I write to say that I will always love you and that I will cherish the life that you hated, our life, Gamini. For now it is all that I have.

And to tell you about George. I have not thought of another man since you made me leave Newton all those years ago. George is a widower who comes to our church. He is a retired architect, who lived in England till his wife passed away. We have been a comfort to each other and last Sunday he asked me to marry him.

Garfield says I should 'Go for it'. But I want to ask you. It's hard not having you next to me, I even miss you coughing and swearing in your sleep. What should I do, Gamini? Tell me please. You always knew best, except when it came to yourself.

George has invited me to join him in Egypt. I have always wanted to see the pyramids, but I do not think I will accept this proposal. You wait, Gamini. One of these days I will take that lover like I always said. But I don't think today is that day.

Wherever you are, I hope you are making poetry.
Always yours
Sheila

Twenty Zero Seven

Sri Lanka is once again in a World Cup final against the Aussies. But this time we are getting our arses handed to us.

Crumpled in my bed is a chick I met last week at ClubRB who claims to have met me when I played for Kreb's Square. I never played for Kreb's Square, though I don't think it matters any more. The girl is a decade younger than me and is snoring. Naked flesh peeps through the sheets, but I would much rather watch the match.

Not that I'm really that much into cricket either. I'll watch a World Cup when it comes around, but I can't be arsed sitting through five days of it. I prefer football or motor racing or boxing or women's tennis.

The last two World Cup finals I saw in bars. I was backpacking in Prague when Aussie undid India in '03. I was making deals in Rajasthan when the Aussies hammered Pakistan in '99. If the bastards do it again, they can claim to have conquered the subcontinent over three consecutive World Cups. They can claim to have more than convincingly avenged 1996.

This World Cup has been long-winded and dull, though it did begin with the murder of a coach and with Ireland beating Pakistan. Some say that match was fixed, I am one of them. I have kept track of the tournament as I have had nothing better to do back in Sri Lanka. All my school friends are fat and married with brats, everyone else I would rather avoid.

I have nothing to do and plenty of money to do it with.

The best way to savour the 2007 final, I figured, was from the rooftop suite of Global Towers, with a bottle of vodka, a bagful of white widow and a nineteen-year-old who, till five hours ago, I had not tasted. Great plan, not-so-great execution. Whatserface doesn't stop nattering, her voice is a synth pop song in G#dim. I turn the volume up on the TV as Gilchrist and Hayden bludgeon us out of the game. I swallow gulps of duty-free vodka and stare at the rape of our bowlers – the fearless lion Malinga transformed into a clown in a bad wig.

I have cameo-ed three times in the tall tale you have just climbed. More of a Shyamalan cameo than a Hitchcock one. I have starred under a stage name, the name my father would've preferred me to be known by. My friends, enemies, both my ex-wives and everyone from my childhood know me as Shehan Karunasena. Only my parents refer to me by my first name.

You saw me ask W.G. for money, though he does not mention how drunk he was or that he referred to me as a 'lazy useless fucker' and that is why I left the room. He also did not know that I needed the money for something that wasn't a sound engineering course. There is enough left out of my father's version to write a separate chronicle.

I featured again placing that ridiculous bet on West Indies vs Kenya. I have been depicted as a petulant punk and an ungrateful good-for-nothing. Not completely inaccurate. Though in my opinion the person best matching that description was the man behind the typewriter.

3 overs from the end, Bridgetown's Kensington Park falls into darkness. Outside Colombo's night sky begins to look as fucked-up as Armageddon. The film, not the biblical forecast.

'What the hell's going on?'

Whatserface is wrapping the sheets around her, but I can still see her ripe banana nipples. She is darker than my girlfriend, but less shapely. There is a crease on her cheek from where she has been laying her empty head.

'I think Colombo's under attack.'

She switches channels.

'Oi. That's the World Cup final!'

'Chill out, rock star. I'm just checking.'

The news on RupaVision tells us that LTTE light aircraft are attacking an Air Force base outside Colombo. The army are deploying anti-aircraft tracer bullets to repel the attack. The public is urged to stay inside and away from windows.

'Don't stand there,' says Whatserface. 'The bullets can hit you.'

Below me is Colombo's Marine Drive. Our window faces north and from where I stand I can see the angry ocean as well as the tracer bullets spitting forth from the rooftop of Colombo's tallest building. For a bullet to hit us it would have to have the directional properties of a Pradeep Mathew double bounce ball.

'Can you turn the cricket back on?'

It is 210 for 8 and the match is gone. 3 more overs, 50-odd runs. Duckworth and Lewis have made the difficult impossible, especially without stadium lights on a soggy pitch.

None of the commentators know what the fuck's going on. One says that Sunday is a reserve day and that if the lights don't come back on, we can come back tomorrow. Sinhala commentator Palitha Epasekera emotes that the World Cup finals cannot be decided by Duckworth–Lewis. He urges the Lankan captain to ask for the match to be annulled.

'Aney, you brought your guitar also. Play me one of those Kreb's Square songs. Do you know Cumonova?'

'I never played for Krebs. My band was called Independent Cycle.'

'No.'

'Yes.'

'But you said…'

'So you would sleep with me.'

'Really?'

'Sorry, that slipped out.'

'You're such an arsehole.'

'Are we done?'

'Drop me home now.'

'Not while there's tracer bullets, sweetie. Just chill and let me type. I'll take you home after it's finished.'

'Arsehole.' She pours a vodka and lights a cigarette and makes as much noise as she can doing both.

I finished reading Thaathi's manuscript yesterday afternoon and I have it with me now.

I made a third cameo in it that you may not have noticed. It was at my father's bedside with my son Jimi. Yesterday afternoon, after turning the last page, I found out that my father did not recognise me. And neither, I suppose, did you. I thought that W.G. had blessed me on his deathbed. Now I find out it was not me he was blessing.

The old house has been locked up for over a year. Ammi covered the furniture and fastened the gates before flying off to Rwanda with George. I am coming home to a dust-ridden house that I no longer hate. The sensation is not too dissimilar to that of shagging an old girlfriend.

Ari Uncle is still living next door, though most of his daughters have moved out. Only Aruni the youngest and Stephanie the lesbian remain. Melissa, the first girl to show me her breasts, is married to some dude in Bangalore.

Last week I was in my father's office room, smoking up and not playing my Music Man acoustic. I walked over to Thaathi's shelves and rummaged through crooked shoeboxes stacked amid books that were no longer read. Each was filled with files filled with papers filled with scribbling.

I was seeking W.G.'s poetry: the love songs that had won my mother over, the pastoral odes from the Badulla years. Maybe amid the stuff that Thaathi wanted to set fire to, there was something I could set to music. Instead I find the words 'The Legend of Pradeep Mathew' scrawled in thick correction fluid on the side of a heavy black box. Inside are sheaves of yellowed paper filled with typing, not unlike the crumpled A4s next to my bass, except for the typing bit.

WTF is this? The old man hung out with a terrorist? Told jokes? Stole a girl from a friend? The typed pages took me three days to read. The story, like the man himself, seemed to forget its point. But I read till the end. It was strange to share his warped thoughts and guess at which bits he made up.

The Thaathi I knew was a foul-mouthed, argumentative prick. He has omitted many of his sins, especially that punch-up with Ari Uncle which I would rather not write about. He also doesn't know that I didn't bet on Kenya. That I forged the betting slip and pocketed the seven lakhs. Sara Marzooq, my Muslim princess, spent a quarter of my stolen dowry on shoes in the week that we were married.

I am touched that he has reproduced my letter word for word. I wrote to him a few times after that but never got a reply. I'm glad he omitted that last paragraph, it's not something I'm proud of. I am less glad that he doesn't remember holding his grandson's hand.

The box lies before me now as I type this. The morning sun is heating the hotel windows. I have been up all night, but I am not sleepy. Whatserface has been sent home by taxi. She said goodbye and fuck you very much.

I open the box and out falls a piece of paper I have not seen before. It is in W.G.'s hand and it takes me a moment or two to fathom. When I realise what it is, I do something I have been unable to do since my father's death eight years ago. I stare at my belly and I start to cry.

THINGS TO DO YESTERDAY

1. Garfield peace. X
2. Sheila trip. √
3. Write Mathew.
4. Brothers/Sister. X
5. Free Jonny. X
6. Give up smoking. X
7. Find Mathew.
8. Write for *Wisden*.
9. Become cricket umpire. √
10. Help SL win World Cup.

In school 35 per cent was considered a pass mark. This was to allow mutts from rich families to progress and to prevent classes overcrowding with repeaters. 50 per cent sounds fairer, if you ask me. If you get more things right than you get wrong, you pass. I look at my father's list and the markings beside it. He has got 20 per cent. A failure by any measurement.

I look at it again and realise that it is unfair. Items 5 and 10 are beyond anyone's control. Items 4 and 6 are perhaps real failures and not ones that I can rectify. But the rest, the rest I may be able to mend. If I can do 7, complete 3 and send it to 8, my father's life will be upgraded to a 5/10 pass mark.

Make that 6/10. A credit pass. It is item number 1 and the fact that it is at number 1 that breaks my heart. It is, in my opinion, the first thing he achieved when I finished reading these yellowed pages. And in this matter, unlike in all others, my opinion is the only one that counts.

The Darkening

If you had told me at twenty-one that at thirty-two I'd be a well-off has-been with a ponytail, I might have contemplated an overdose. My mission was to make an album like *Dark Side of the Moon*, play rock in Rio, win a few Oscars and buy an island. Nothing too fanciful.

After I was dumped from Purple Green, I eloped to Europe with a Swiss receptionist called Adriana. In the next few years, I formed a band called Alice Dali, opened for the Scorpions, had a top 40 hit in Luxembourg, failed as a husband again and did some women who weren't married to me.

Of Alice Dali's two albums, one went to number 267 on the US alternative chart. The other was never released. The record label said cheerio, Adriana took the baby and left, and I ended up in Dubai playing jazz with arseholes.

Over the next few years, I had several doses of bad luck and one stroke of outrageous fortune. Its name was The Darkening.

Defying the zeitgeist of morose shoe-gazing, The Darkening had haystacks of hair, lengthy guitar solos and wrote big choruses about cars, bars and guitars. The 80s were due for a revival, and for at least one summer these *lederhosen*-wearing freaks were it.

Their second album featured a ballad called *Poison on a Tray*, a cover of a track by an obscure post-grunge band with a Sri Lankan bass player.

The first cheque I received was more than I'd seen that year playing

Hotel California in a waistcoat for bored Arabs. When it was featured in that teenage show named after a Californian suburb, I received a cheque for more than all the radio royalties in Luxembourg. When it went top 20 in Canada, I found myself richer than my father would've been had he actually placed that bet on Kenya.

Old W.G. made his pension on a lucky wager at sixty-four. His son hit jackpot at thirty-two on what he then thought was his genius. I had hoped it would lead to a publishing deal and a solo album. It would lead to nothing of the sort.

Last year The Darkening split up and *Poison on a Tray* was voted most annoying song of the millennium by that fat git on Radio One.

If I met that twenty-one-year-old now, I'd tell him to practise more and smoke less.

Grandchildren

I get down to the serious business of googling the words Pradeep, Sivanathan and Mathew. I find nothing. I google Pradeep and Mathews with an s. There is an engineer from Kerala who has just had a daughter and is looking for anyone from Sacred Heart College, Villupuram. There is a doctor in Sheffield who authored a paper on spinal injuries.

I type Pradeep, Mathew, Sri, Lanka and Cricket, and find that only two Pradeeps have played for Sri Lanka, an A-team player called Pradeep Hewage and Thaathi's old favourite, Asanka Pradeep Gurusinha. Not much else.

I decide to go to Ari Uncle. He is sitting on a haansi putuwa in his study, watching his grandchildren play video games. He has a smile on his face. 'Come, Shehan, sit.'

'Call me Garfield, Uncle. Too many Shehans in the world.'

'Very good. Very good. Your Thaathi would be happy.'

Ari Uncle carries my father's cane, but walks with more agility and purpose than old W.G. ever did. He wears a banian and his glasses hang from a string around his neck.

'Some of these video games are hena violent. Cutting each other up with hammers and axes and all. No wonder all this violence in the world.'

On the screen two dwarves are attacking three wolves with what look like pitchforks. I decline to tell Ari Uncle that there was violence in the world long before video games.

'Our Jimi also plays these ones. Just a game, no?'

Everyone thinks I named my son after Hendrix or Page or T. Kirk.

W.G. thought it was after Jim Laker, Ammi probably fancies it was after Jim Reeves. I named him after James Jamerson, the finest bass player to walk the earth. Jamerson lived in the shadows of Motown, played uncredited on thirty number 1 pop hits, and died an alcoholic. Now you know everything.

'I of course prefer the car-driving ones. But I'm strange. I prefer test cricket to this 20/20 nonsense. How is the podiyan?'

'Fine. Fine. Wants to be a footballer.'

'Very good. He can play for Germany. That was your father's team.'

'I read the book, Uncle.'

'What book?'

'The Legend of Pradeep Mathew.'

Ari Uncle puts on his glasses and peers at me. I see one lens is cracked and has been cellotaped.

On the TV a fire-spewing dragon enters the frame and the three youngsters scream.

'Shh. Shh. Don't shout,' snaps Ari Uncle.

'Have you read it?'

'Of course. I only told your mother to give you to read. She thought you might be offended.'

'Is any of it true?'

'Some of it. Most of it.'

'There is no record of Pradeep Mathew anywhere.'

'They say his name was erased when the archives were computerised.

'According to Reggie Ranwala. You believe that?'

'Sheh…um, Garfield, that's one of the few parts of the story that I'm sure is true.'

'So he does exist?'

'I saw him with these very eyes,' he says, pointing to his broken specs.

'Then I want to finish it.'

'What?'

'I want to find Mathew and finish the book.'

The youngsters stop their game and look up in shock as their grandfather hugs the long-haired uncle with the tattoo. It's a long time since I've been hugged by anyone. He holds me tight and I do not feel embarrassed. In fact I feel something I have been unable to feel for most of my worthless life.

Copyists

I haven't done much writing before. I tried to steer clear of anything Thaathi clung to. I prefer marijuana to booze, football to cricket, music to words. I do not remember the surname of the cricketer after whom I am named. And it pains me at my deepest level to hear someone describe Meat Loaf as modern opera.

I spent all of 2004 recording demos, putting bands together and calling up labels. I even let another man marry my wife and bring up my son in a city oceans away. Sure it stings, but what kind of father would I be anyway? How different can I be from W.G.? I see my son twice a year and while the moments I spend with him are magic, I have considered caning him for listening to Mariah Carey. Soon he will turn thirteen. Soon he will begin to hate me.

I sit at Barefoot Café listening to jazz amid light rain, squirming birds and locals who act like tourists. I hate everything about Colombo, it's a pseudo city with semi-people living quasi-lives. It is a mess. I despise its lethargy, its stupidity and its pretensions. The only thing I like about Colombo is how it smells during monsoon.

Manilal Simon, my old bandmate in Capricorn, is playing keyboards, still sporting the mullet and the gold chains. Back in the day, Manilal told me to forget about originals and learn jazz. 'Let me tell you, machang. Lankans can imitate, but can we create? We are good craftsmen, I won't say no, but let's not bullshit, we are hopeless at being artists. Learn your instrument, machang, forget about being Bob Dylan.'

Paul Bowles, who lived on a private island off Weligama in the 1950s, once said, 'The Sinhalese are beyond a doubt the least musical people in the world. It would be quite impossible to have less sense of pitch or rhythm.' Not meaning to boast, but I can hear music in rustling leaves, in tractor wheels, in kottu clangs and at certain moments with the right mix of chemicals, I can even smell sound.

I made it my life's mission to prove Mr Bowles wrong, but looking at Manilal playing a cover of a cover to an audience who isn't listening, I think we all may have failed.

Crikipedia

Despite threats of recession, the pound still goes a long way in Sri Lanka. I don't really need to work, but I help out a few friends from the band CrossFire and we do some weddings. It gives me pocket money and a sliver of a social life.

My girlfriend from India visits and notices foundation on my collar. Shouldn't this be lipstick, she giggles. Then she sits on my lap, pins me down, dusts my neck and finds the love bite that I don't remember getting, but do remember trying to mask with cheap make-up. I heed the old man's advice and deny till I die. She tells me to drop dead and departs. So it goes.

I tell my mother I am going to edit the book.

'You think people will be interested?'

'Ammi, it's an important story.'

I do not tell her about the list of things to do yesterday. Maybe I should.

'Be careful about publishing it in Thaathi's name.'

'Otherwise whose name?'

'People used to call home asking about the book. Some threatened to sue if it comes out.'

'Who?'

'Who knows, Putha? Thaathi left debts. I don't know half of what he did. Be careful.'

'Of course.'

'How is your business going?'

'Thought I would do some travel first.'

'How much travel, Putha? Now you are thirty-two. Isn't it time you settled?'

Settle down is what Ammi meant. But she hit the nail on the head. Settling. Settling for whatever limits exist on your present.

'How many times do you want me to get married?'

'Just once.'

'How's George?'

'Good. He heard your song on the radio in Cairo.'

'Not my song any more.'

'Have you thought about asking Adriana about Sri Lanka? Will be good for Jimi.'

'Ammi, she has her own life. So does Jimi.'

'The boy is a Sri Lankan. He should know his country.'

I have no desire to own a woman or be owned by one. I like to have sex with women and to be friends with them. Both of which seem to cease after rings are exchanged. Marriage is two people deciding whose turn it is to be unhappy. I have been there and been unable to do that.

I call her in Geneva, where her husband lectures in something dull and important, and tell her what I am planning.

'I always said you should do writing. Aren't you tired of playing rock star?'

'Maybe.'

'Call when you are.'

'Then you may never hear from me.'

'Your son wants to speak to you. Go chase your father's ghost. Might be good for you.'

She mattered for a while. There was a time when I felt like a corpse every time she left the room. But that fades. Who has not lost his head at the feet of a woman?

I drive Ari Uncle around in his shitty, power steering-less Ford. We go to Malinda Bakers in Moratuwa where I eat a maalu paan made in heaven. The white widow has given me the munchies and I whack three. It is fish and spice cushioned in a hot, hot bun and it is so good it gives me the hiccups.

There is nothing here for us except pastries in cages and crumbs on the floor. The manager, Indrakrishnan Amirthalingam, tells us that his wife's brother died ten years ago, that she never talks about him, and that he would be greatly unhappy if we harassed her. He is a large man and we get his message.

The former Thurstan cricket coach Lucius Nanayakkara died of a heart attack five years ago. The Moratuwa police may have records of the death of a Mr Satyakumar Gokulanath in 1997, but to obtain them I will have to fill out seventeen forms and hand them in on a Thursday between 2 and 4 p.m.

Ari Uncle refuses to take me to Newton Rodrigo, saying that he shamelessly courted my mother right after Thaathi's death. Charith Silva has migrated to Holland and is working as a bowling coach. Uvais Amalean is now CEO of Ceylon Petroleum and is difficult to reach.

Danila Guneratne, accounts director at DDB Colombo, was transferred to New York in 2001. I hope her office wasn't where I think it could have been. She was the one I most wanted to meet.

I dig up articles on TamilNet.com of an operations coordinator, I.E. Kugarajah, aka Kuga, captured by the Sri Lankan forces in '94. I also find references to a South Asian bookie called Emmanuel in Simon Marqusee's rambling book.

I cannot find the midget's ground. Ari Uncle refuses to help me.

'Enough. I cursed your father. I can't have you also cursed.'

I meet Jabir who has traded his cap for a beard and his hair for a belly. He still smiles a lot. 'I will not tell you where, Garfield boss. But you have to find the manhole next to the lamp post, then only you will find the entrance.'

I go from Colombo 7 to Colombo 11. At the P. Sara, I find a manhole and a lamp post. I bend down and heave the lid, straining my spine for the privilege of whiffing sewage. No entrance. I go to SSC, NCC, Bloomfield and R. Premadasa looking for lamp posts and manholes. Finally I end up at the Tyronne Cooray.

No one aside from schoolboys plays cricket here any more. I find out that the lamp post only went up last year and that the manhole has been sealed since the Dutch era. The old man at the rickety scoreboard says he has never heard of anyone called Hewman Neiris Abeytunge. All I find is fallen leaves and swirls of dog shit and the bo tree under which my father claims to have slept.

This time I am the one cursing Ari Uncle.

'Garfield, who said it was the Tyronne Cooray?'

'I've read the book five times. It's obvious.'

'Putha, the obvious things are never worth looking at.'

'So where is the midget?'

'Uncle Neiris died in the tsunami. I don't know where the saasthara woman is.'

'So none of this is true?'

'What are you saying? I can prove.'

'What?'

'I can play you the spools.'

'You still have them?'

'Of course. I just need to find them.'

I resume my search. Cricket is probably the most intricately catalogued subject on the worldwide web aside from porn. I can drum up the scorecard of Bloomfield vs Nomads 1992 at the Tyronne Cooray if I choose to. I do. No mention of Mathew. I get sidetracked by a preview of an India–Pakistan game where the reader comments begin with 'Dravid may struggle against Gul,' and end with 'You goat-fucking paki swine fukkers drink yo ma's urine and cum in your dad's terrorist beard.'

Over my lifetime, yo momma jokes have replaced mother-in-law jokes, Hollywood Arabs have replaced Hollywood Russians, and Indians and Pakistanis have remained incapable of civilised cricketing discourse. Sri Lankans do not behave much better, though not without provocation. I stumble upon www.muralisachucker.com and observe my fellow countrymen using language that makes me blush.

There are evidently people out there more obsessed over this pointless game than my father. I trawl through cricketing chat rooms and in every cockeyed argument I fancy I catch a glimpse of W.G. I wonder if the dead haunt cyberspace, if the old man's soul wafts through internet chat rooms arguing Murali's action with foul-mouthed Aussies for the rest of eternity.

And then, I come across something that makes me spill my tea. I stare at it for as long as I can, exorcizing all thoughts of cyber ghosts, examining the facts as objectively as I can. We know that W.G. was capable of many things. Like fabricating meetings, brainwashing friends, bending truths and hiding behind bottles.

But I put it to you that there is no way on God's green earth or in Satan's purple hell that arrack-swilling, computer-illiterate W.G. Karunasena would ever be capable of uploading a webpage.

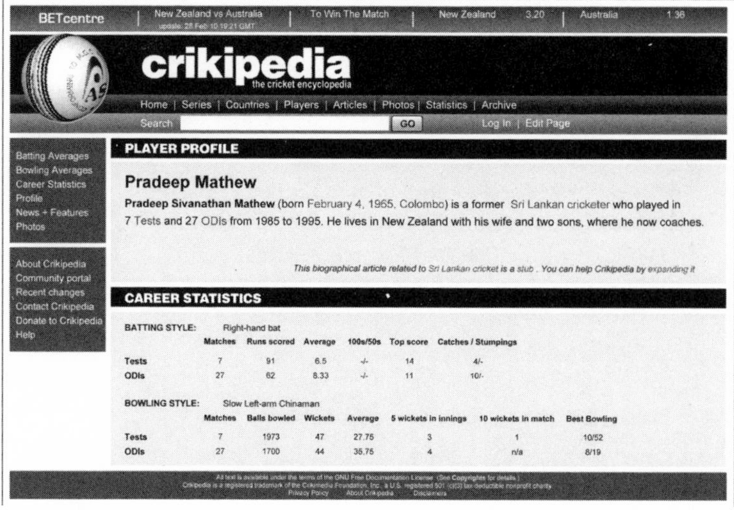

BETcentre | New Zealand vs Australia update: 28 Feb 10 19:21 GMT | To Win The Match | New Zealand 3.20 | Australia 1.36

crikipedia
the cricket encyclopedia

Home | Series | Countries | Players | Articles | Photos | Statistics | Archive

Search GO Log In | Edit Page

Batting Averages
Bowling Averages
Career Statistics
Profile
News + Features
Photos

About Crikipedia
Community portal
Recent changes
Contact Crikipedia
Donate to Crikipedia
Help

PLAYER PROFILE

Pradeep Mathew

Pradeep Sivanathan Mathew (born February 4, 1965, Colombo) is a former Sri Lankan cricketer who played in 7 Tests and 27 ODIs from 1985 to 1995. He lives in New Zealand with his wife and two sons, where he now coaches.

This biographical article related to Sri Lankan cricket is a stub . You can help Crikipedia by expanding it

CAREER STATISTICS

BATTING STYLE: Right-hand bat

	Matches	Runs scored	Average	100s/50s	Top score	Catches / Stumpings
Tests	7	91	6.5	-/-	14	4/-
ODIs	27	62	8.33	-/-	11	10/-

BOWLING STYLE: Slow Left-arm Chinaman

	Matches	Balls bowled	Wickets	Average	5 wickets in innings	10 wickets in match	Best Bowling
Tests	7	1973	47	27.75	3	1	10/52
ODIs	27	1700	44	35.75	4	n/a	8/19

All text is available under the terms of the GNU Free Documentation License (See Copyrights for details.)
Crikipedia is a registered trademark of the Crikimedia Foundation, Inc., a U.S. registered 501 (c)(3) tax-deductible nonprofit charity
Privacy Policy About Crikipedia Disclaimers

Pukekohe

So here I am at the arse-end of the world, breathing the clean green air and counting the money that I'm preparing to bust.

I am in a glass elevator ascending the spine of the Auckland Skytower to the casino at the top. The lift opens and I enter a warmly lit dome. Armies of orientals throw chips at Polynesian dealers, the music of porcelain hitting carpet drowning out the chatter. Unlike W.G. I've never had a weakness for gambling, I just came up here to enjoy the view.

I travel with a backpack, a laptop and lots of pockets. I google Shirali, Fernando, New and Zealand, watch the digital hourglass turn counterclockwise, and then crack up at what I see. Streaks of copper decorating her straightened hair, posing in jeans with two Kiwi lasses on Facebook, looking buxom in a business suit on LinkedIn. Forty-one, married, living in a town called, get this, Pukekohe. I don't know where in the arse of the world that is.

That's a bad pun for Sinhala speakers. The word puka, a Maori word for hill, in Sinhala means backside. On the plane ride through Oceania, I thumbed through my *Hitchhiker's Guide to New Zealand* and looked up New Zealand names that have obscene meanings in my language. I find out the official term for a European New Zealander is Pakeha, Sinhala for fucker. I think I'm going to enjoy my time in Aotearoa.

Under Education, Shirali's online profile says:

- Master's in Finance at Perth (95–98)
- BCom at Monash (86–89)

Under Employment, it says:

- Pukekohe MasterPlumbers ('04 to present) Finance Director
- Manukau City Council (96–03) Finance Manager
- HSBC, Brisbane (94–95) Research Analyst
- Commercial Bank, Colombo (89–92) Business Development Executive

Under Marital Status, it says:

- Married with two kids, Teran and Sabi.

It does not mention her husband's name.

I sit in a motel in Manukau City where I crave a kottu and a joint, but settle for a six-pack of Lion Red and a chicken pie. The plywood walls have a poster of a green lake surrounded by mountains and the varnished bedside table has a Bible in English and Maori. Unlike Thaathi, I'm no non-believer. I go to church whenever there is a woman to drag me there. With the number of sins I have accumulated, it would be foolish not to have the Big Man on my side.

There are two Fernandos in the Pukekohe online directory and one number for Pukekohe MasterPlumbers. I take them down before stumbling upon a website called www.lostrelative.co.nz.

I run a search for Pradeep Sivanathan Mathew and let them take NZ$18.99 off my credit card, but end up with no matches. Unperturbed, I request individual searches for each name and have to wade through pages of disclaimers before I click on OK.

I get a call from a girl who tells me in an accent that is not Kiwi that it will be a further NZ$129.95. I make my voice chocolatey and make her laugh a few times. She tells me free of charge that there are 137 Sivanathans, 1,638 Pradeeps and 154,843 Mathews living in New Zealand. The list stretches from Whangarei to Invercargil. I tell her I'm in Auckland and ask if she's free for a coffee. She laughs for the last time and tells me her call centre is in Chennai.

My passport has been stamped for three months and I wonder if I should not work a detour into this adventure. My *Hitchhiker's Guide* reveals that there is more to these two islands than the sprawling city that I'm caged in. A few days in the Bay of Islands before I start playing detective? A quick ski on those distant mountains before I set out on my quest?

I have heard this voice before, it belongs to an arsehole called Mr Procrastinator Man, a pyjama-wearing, chain-smoking sloth who sits in my skull and tells me to follow my dick, a voice that has plagued me for most of my existence. But this is replaced by Mr Thinker Man, a robe-wearing sage who goes away for long periods only to return with questions but rarely answers.

If Mathew stole the money to woo the love of his life, how did they end up in Pukekohe and why is her surname still Fernando?

The next morning I get the 47 bus on which I am the only passenger. The drive is mostly fields and sheep and sheep and fields and the occasional orchard. I check into the Counties Motor Lodge and take a stroll around the neighbourhood. The roads have no potholes and the people walk barefoot.

I enter a grill where the waiter is Maori and dressed in shorts. He serves me the finest steak I have ever tasted. Two bulls-eye eggs bleeding yolk over the side of a cow. I wash down the medium rare meat with beer, stroke my belly, loosen my ponytail and wonder how long before I start looking like Meat Loaf myself. When it happens, I hope I have the right sense or the right woman to drag me to a barber.

The newspapers are still mourning the All Blacks and another failed World Cup. Even though New Zealand's untimely exit was over a month ago the papers have still dedicated four pages to it.

I hear a scuffle outside and they all pile in, chicks in shorts, guys in skinnies, most are loud, some are drunk. The waiters prepare for the onslaught as the grill fills with young backpackers. Last of all is a blond man with a clipboard, built like a centaur.

'All right, settle down, you lot.' There are a few giggles among the revellers.

'We leave at 1.45. Whoever's last in owes me a beer.'

He points at the pack of girls all wearing similar green T-shirts with the words 'KiwiTour Porn Star' on them.

'Maria, you owe me for last night.' A dark-haired teenager blushes and everyone goes 'ooh'.

Five minutes later the man lays a tray of macaroni cheese and an L&P soda on my table. 'Mind if I join ya, mate?'

I point at the empty chair and nod. He spies the headline on my newspaper. 'National tragedy, eh man?'

I shrug. 'They're still the best in the world.'

'You reckon? What's the point, if you're gonna choke?'

'Should've put Evans at the back and Conrad outside centre, eh?' I say, parroting that day's sports section and the man's inflection.

'McCaw should've gone for the drop goal. You remember when it happened?'

I tell him I only arrived in NZ a few days ago.

'Mate, like somebody'd died.'

'Is that right?' I say, sounding like CrocDundee while trying not to.

'You here on work or...'

The man is bronzed from summers spent driving travellers around these two islands. He has a twinkle in his eye and could clearly chat up anything that moved.

'Bit of a holiday, bit of work. You?'

'My work is a holiday, mate. I got a master's in agricultural economics. Never used it.'

He tells me there is room on his bus and hands me a brochure from his clipboard. He tells me I can buy a North Island pass and hop on and hop off.

'Best way to see New Zealand. We're staying tonight at Pukekohe, then heading to...what's so funny?'

I shake my head.

'If I sign up for a North Island pass, will you drive me to... Pukekohe?'

'As long as you don't mind putting up with this lot.'

I look at the girls in shorts making eyes at this bronzed Lothario and I decide I don't mind.

Gollum

I make an appointment with Pukekohe MasterPlumbers. She meets me in reception and is exactly how I pictured her. Business suit, glasses, hair in a bun. I have nothing against chubby girls, in fact, some are quite juicy in the sack, but if I was a genius chinaman bowler, would I break the law, abandon my career and break the heart of an alleged fox like Danila for this woman? Who knows? Love can wield its club in strange ways.

'Mr Garfield, I'm Shirali Fernando, how can I help?'

She smiles and even though her teeth are not perfect, the smile lights up her eyes and narrows her cheeks.

'Thank you for seeing me, Mrs Fernando. You're Sri Lankan?'

'Yes, I am. How can I help?'

'Actually, it has to do with your husband.'

'Really? Simone said you were from the *NZ Plumbers Journal.*' The smile stays but the eyes lose their shine.

'Not exactly. I went to Hampshire University with your husband.'

'You were with Nalindra?'

'Pradeep.'

'No. I think you've got the wrong person.'

She rises to leave and I do not know what else to say.

'Pradeep Mathew. Cricketer. Played for Sri Lanka. I really have to find him.'

'Pradeep, eh? That's a blast from the past.' She tells me she is busy, but leaves me her business card.

I spend the next day preparing for my first interview. I decide to polish my shoes and comb my hair. Do I do a *HARDtalk* style Twenty Questions or an Oprah-style empathy session?

'My husband's name is Nalindra Fernando. He is a doctor at Good Health Pukekohe. He knows I'm meeting you.'

We meet at McDonald's and it immediately feels more Oprah than *HARDtalk*.

'You don't find the name Pukekohe humorous?'

'Oh yeah. You get used to it. You know the name for white man is…'

I nod. I know.

'So you never heard from Pradeep after your break-up?'

'Mr Garfield, it's a bloody long time ago. Do you remember your first girlfriend?'

'Actually, I do. How did you meet?'

'At some party. A lot of cricketers hit on me. Didn't think I'd date one.'

'Why him?'

'Dunno. He was sweet, I guess. Really moody. Just really didn't give a shit. It's kind of a turn-on, at that age anyway.'

Shirali wears a short skirt and has a plaster on her knee. She speaks in an accent that isn't quite Australian, isn't quite British.

'My mum reckons I did it to piss them off, him being Tamil and all.'

'Did you?'

'Not really. Maybe a little.'

I see a few of the backpacking girls in shorts ordering fries. The bus has anchored in Pukekohe and doesn't leave till tomorrow.

'Did you know of a man called Kugà?'

'No.'

'Emmanuel?'

'You mean Pradeep's cousin?'

'Was he?'

'Real creep. Emmanuel. Pradeep worshipped him. I couldn't stand him.'

'Why?'

'Looked like a real sleaze. Real dodgy.'

'Sorry to be personal, but why did you and Pradeep break up?'

'What did you say your project was?'

'Writing a book on great cricketers.'

'So what do you want with Pradeep?'

She laughs on the last syllable and reveals her imperfect teeth. I notice her boobs are as thick as her arms.

'Did you know his coach?'

'I met one of his coaches.'

'Newton Rodrigo?'

'I can't remember his name.'

'Six fingers?'

'Eh?'

'The coach had six fingers.'

'Don't remember that. He looked like Gollum.'

'Gollum in *Lord of the…*'

'I think. Or did he have a name like Gollum? I can't remember, Mr Garfield. It's like another life ago.'

'So why did you break up?'

'After I nursed Pradeep back from his wrist injury, he started screwing sluts. You want to put that in your book?'

'What sluts?'

'You had all these sluts hanging around the cricketers. Still do. He was having affairs with them.'

'Mrs Fernando, Pradeep never tried to make contact with you?'

'Oh yeah.'

'When?'

'Aw. Ten years ago?'

'And?'

'He came to visit me in Brissy.'

'And?'

'Couldn't recognise him. Shaved head, quite fat, spoke all posh. He said he'd retired from cricket and was rich. I was with Nalindra and I told him we could be friends. He hung around Brissy for a while, then he called me from some bar and told me he was going away.'

'Where?'

'Never said. He was drunk and reading me poems. He used to write me poems, you know?'

She laughs again, I keep silent. She finishes her latte and opens her leather handbag.

'I did manage to find this. Was a few Christmases ago.'

She extracts a postcard of a Maori carving and a beach. The name of the beach, Paihia, closely resembles the Sinhala word for penis.

Hi Shirali

Long time, isn't it? Heard you're leaving Brisbane. Didn't want to lose touch. I'm married and living in New Zealand. Doing a bit of teaching and a bit of coaching. Met some other Sri Lankans here and they say they know your husband. Ubaya and Thilina Manukulasuriya? They told me you have daughters and are doing well. Small world, no? The Wellington Sri Lankan Association is also called USLA. I told the wife about meeting you at USLA and we had a good laugh about it. Remember those crazy nights? She said I should see what you're up to. I've got two sons, Kula and Luke. If this reaches you, email me

at sivan42@clear.co.nz. Hope this finds you well. All the best to your husband and the girls.
Siva

'Oh. That's right. He was calling himself Siva Mathew or something, I think he explained why. Something dodgy to do with immigration.'

I ask her if I can get a copy of this and she says I can keep it.

'He sent it to my Brissy address. By the time I got it and emailed him, the mails kept bouncing back.'

The stamp on the postcard was dated 2006, the postmark was W…A…N…

'What's this?'

'Wanganui.'

'Where is that?'

She points to my *Hitchhiker's Guide to New Zealand* and asks me to hand it over.

Wanganui

I fall asleep on the way there and it is hard to separate what happens from what doesn't. The interior of the KiwiTour bus is graffitied to resemble a forest filled with native New Zealand creatures. Kiwi birds and rams look down upon the lads from Essex pouring beer into jugs stolen from student bars. On my side of the bus, lizards and whales gaze over sleepy Canadians and chattering Chinese girls. Outside the window, open pastures pass us by.

'And on your right, these red trees are called Pohutukawas.'

Jeremy has switched from bus driver to tour guide. I jolt awake and gaze at tree trunks surrounded by flames of crimson. It is late afternoon and most of the frat boys are passed out. A few girls listen to Jeremy's well-rehearsed banter.

'Stu will be serving fish and chips in a bit. Those allergic to fish and chips can try our roadkill possum burger.' Jeremy grins and switches off his mic.

'Ewwww…' chorus the girls.

He takes a seat next to me. 'How's it going, chief?'

'All good.'

He asks me if I want to buy a green T-shirt saying 'KiwiTour Slag', the same one the Eastern European chicks are wearing. I decline politely.

'Fair enough. You hitched?'

'Huh?'

'Married? Girlfriend?'

'Not really.'

'Oh yeah. In which case I can tell you,' he whispers, 'they call this the fuck truck. If you're up for it, there's some fine young cat, up for grabs.'

I smile at him. 'More of a tourist, mate, but always up for some cat.'

'How old are you?'

'Thirty-two.'

'Me too. Tell 'em you're twenty-eight. The three-zero thing freaks some of the little ones out. You want to be the wise big brother, not the dirty uncle like Gregor.'

He points to the tall man with long grey hair wearing a photographer's jacket and chatting to the fat girl from Malaysia.

'He comes here every year. Leaves his wife in Belgium, just to come here and shag the leftovers.'

'Looks like you've analysed this?' I survey the different shades of white flesh, dressed in summer clothes, sporting huge bags.

'Twelve years of truckin' and fuckin', mate. Welcome aboard KiwiTour.'

He gives me the biggest wink I've seen outside of a cartoon.

I decide to spend my nights lying in bed with my laptop, listening to gasps and moans from the neighbouring rooms. Jeremy comes to my room one night, his face warm from beer, his neck filled with lust bites, and with a double-skinned joint in his fist.

'Eh, Garf mate, come out into the porch, bring your speakers.'

We settle on deckchairs overlooking the gorge, laptop on my lap, before us a feast of stars.

'You a bit of a muso, eh?' he says, sparking up the rocket. 'Have a listen to that.'

He plugs his iPod into my speakers and a ghostly ballad soundtracks the view.

'You being a good boy, eh man?'

'Not really. Not in the mood for a shag, I guess.'

'Fair enough. You writing a book?'

'Just a few pages.'

'About New Zealand?'

'About Sri Lanka.'

'Oh. Yeah.'

I notice Jeremy has a thick journal covered in stickers on his lap.

'That your diary?'

'Not really. Just scribble down things. Meet a lot of people in this job. You gonna write something for me?'

'Like what?'

'Whatever. That Bulgarian chick likes you.'

'She's got a boyfriend.'

'They all do.'

'You must have some great stories in that book.'

'Nah, mate. Stories are in here.' He taps his head. 'And down there.' He points to his crotch and chuckles.

He thumbs through the journal, which is filled with photos and stickers and handwriting specimens. 'Have a read of this. Pretty deep shit.'

The quote is written in glittering purple, the caption scribbled in plain black.

I grabbed a pile of dust,
And holding it up,
Foolishly asked for as many birthdays
As the grains of sand.
I forgot to ask
That they be years
Of youth.

Ovid. Metamorph. Luxembourg chick. Kontiki '99. Red.

'I started on Kontiki in Europe before moving to KiwiTour.'

'What's red? Her hair?'

'Red...Oh yeah. She had her pubes dyed red in the shape of a heart. Freaky shit.'

We laugh and I pass the joint.

'I don't think I can fake being a kid for much longer, man.'

He looks at me sternly. 'You shouldn't be faking, mate. If you're faking it, you shouldn't be doing it.'

The KiwiTour pass is valid for eight months and has a hop-on hop-off policy. I hop off at Turangi and hop on an InterCity bus.

My InterCity bus has no graffiti drawings. It is white and bland and strangely soothing. It is also far less packed. There are four grannies, a couple of couples and someone who looks like a nineteenth-century tramp. More sheep and more fields. The soporific effect of gazing at lambs lulls me. Bland towns pass by as I read my father's manuscript for the thirteenth time. Waiouru, Taihape, Marton. I take turns between daydreaming of Pradeep and staring at clouds.

At the turnoff to Wanganui is the town of Bulls, which has recently been through a town-branding campaign. Pun intended. On the Welcome to Bulls sign is a sticker saying 'Incredi-Bull' with a cartoon bull in sunglasses giving the thumbs-up. We stop for lunch in a pie shop which has stickers saying 'Edi-Bull' on its plates.

The shop windows down the street read 'Afforda-Bull'. The library has 'Reada-Bull'; the post office 'Senda-Bull'. Everywhere the cartoon bull in shades thumbs his approval. As the bus pulls out I'm happy to observe graffiti on the Thank You for Visiting Bulls sign. Someone has spray-painted the letters h-i-t at the end of the sentence.

Arriving in Wanganui, we park outside Victoria Avenue. The afternoon sun is not as hot as Colombo's, but is as sharp as a laser and induces headaches.

WangaVegas, my motel, is as tacky as its name and is run by a middle-aged Scottish couple who dress in leather jackets. There are pictures of Elvis and Sinatra and someone called Howard Morrison on the walls. My room has a TV with four channels and a view of a brick wall. The hall leading to the jacuzzi room is lined with slot machines.

The next day, I drive around Wanganui with a map on my lap. The town square is alive with swearing schoolkids. The women wear no make-up, the men wear tracksuit bottoms and no shoes, people in shops are as friendly as Jehovah's Witnesses. There's a nice library, a second-hand tape shop, an old English boarding school and a Maori building with demon midgets carved on maroon rectangular wood. They guard the entrance with eyes as big as rugby balls and tongues that snake around their heads.

On paper, there is nothing wrong with this place. But something less visible than smell hangs in the breeze. I take the drive up Durie Hill through puddles of fallen leaves. I look down from the birdless skies to the shabby cars to the distant river. This is where decent people with nothing to prove come to die.

After three days at Motel WangaVegas, I realise that the silver-haired biker lady's stocky crew-cut husband is actually a woman. Denise and Davina biked down from Kilmarnock in the 1960s. They arrived here via a ferry from Sumatra and decided never to go home. They do not ask me what I am doing in their adopted hometown and they let me borrow their phone book.

In Wanganui, there are zero Sivanathans, five Pradeeps, eight Mathews, eleven Sivas and fifteen Matthews with a double t. It will take time for me to drive around this strange town and park outside unfamiliar letter boxes. It will require preparation to drop in unannounced on thirty-nice strangers and ask them what a double bounce ball is.

I ask the Scottish lesbian biker aunties if they'll give me a good rate on a one-month booking. They give me a generous forty day/forty night discount and are grateful to see me front up with cash.

I retreat to my discounted room with cans of beer and the phone book.

While watching a Ranfurly Shield game on Sky, I make myself one promise. If after forty days and thirty-nine visits I have not found him, I will stop looking. I will go home and write my album and cut my hair and never think about Pradeep or Siva or Mathew ever again.

M.S. Pradeep

I get called curry muncher by glue-sniffing skinheads at Kowhai Park. I avoid conversation with the locals and spend my evenings at empty bars. Each day is measured in crossed-off names. Some days I clear two or three, some days none.

I sit outside houses and look for signs, what signs I don't know. I figure that when I see him I'll know, even though I have little more than blurry photos from several haircuts ago. It takes me a while to get my bearings, to be able to tell these identical streets apart. To tell which neighbourhood houses pensioners and which shelters the methamphetamine addicts.

Having crossed four Pradeeps off my list, I walk into a narrow lane off Anzac Parade. I have saved this, the juiciest lead, for last. This is the only Pradeep with the right initials.

The houses have locks on their gates and the lawns are filled with the carcasses of cars. A pale long-haired man in tight black jeans walks three Rottweilers on a leash. I stay in my car till they pass. The man's face is pierced in four places and his dogs are muzzled.

M.S. Pradeep works at the garage at the bottom of the street. I'm greeted by a pink boy in blue overalls holding a spanner.

'Who you want?'

'Are you Mr Pradeep?'

'Yep.'

'You're Sri Lankan?'

'I'm New Zealand.'

'Your father?'

'He's…' He calls into the house. 'Ma, what country was the sperm donor from?'

A voice shouts from behind the garage.

'Eh?' he shouts back. 'Indonesia?'

The voice shouts something else that neither of us hear.

'Malaysia?'

He looks at me with pale eyes. The only thing Asian about this man-boy is his greasy hair.

'My dad left when I was a kid. He was…'

'Eurasian,' says a blonde woman peeping through the window. She also wears overalls and looks just like the boy. 'He was Eurasian. And don't you call your father names.'

I look at the lad. 'Is your first name Mathew?'

'Nah, mate.' He turns to his mother. 'Well, that's what he was, right? He donated his sperm and fucked off.'

'Mark Stephen Pradeep, you will not disrespect your…'

I leave them to it and walk back to the rent-a-car. I pass an unkempt man in boots and sunglasses sitting on his lawn smoking a roll-up. 'Want some oil?'

'Hash oil?'

'Nah. Engine oil.'

There is a pause. Then he bursts into laughter. 'Me mate Skid will bring a tinny and a cap to your car. It'll cost ya $50.'

He gets up and walks into the house. He comes out with a man in a hood who sits in my passenger seat and empties his pockets into my glove compartment. The man smells of urine and is easy to bargain with. There are three foils, two brown capsules, a lighter with the logo of a political party called McGillicuddy Serious, a carved wooden pipe and some crumpled cigarettes.

I take the pipe and the lighter and just one of the foils and ask him for the shark tooth hanging around his grubby neck. He says it was a gift from his grandfather, but when he sees my money, he hands it over. I sprinkle some cabbage into the pipe and light it up.

Without warning the man puts his hands around my neck, chanting what sounds like a rugby haka. After he ties the shark tooth to my Adam's apple, he rubs his nose on mine, insisting that it is a traditional Maori greeting. Then he takes my money and exits the car.

Matthew Siva

Day eight. It takes longer than I anticipate to pay surprise visits to thirty-nine suspects. Surprise is important. If Pradeep is hiding, he probably doesn't want to be found.

While there are no Sivanathans in the entire Wanganui–Manawatu region, there are a disproportionate number of Sivas, most of whom are clustered around Tuatara Lane, a road that smells of cigarettes and fried food.

At the first house Karalea Siva, mother of seven, directs me to her brother-in-law next door. I meet Malini Siva, Visith Siva and Aaron Siva, all of whom tell me they are unemployed.

Matthew Siva is in his fifties and is related to everyone in the neighbourhood. He wears a singlet over his beer belly and is more belligerent than his cousins. I ask him how come they all have an Asian surname. He scratches his head and asks me if I'm from the dole office.

'I'm looking for an old friend.'

'Our family name is Siva, bro. You got a problem with that?'

'Then why does your cuzzie's letter box say Sivatu?'

The door is slammed.

S.M. Pradeep

Patricia Beatson at Marsellaine Grove has three dogs and has never watched cricket. But her lodger S.M. Pradeep watches it all the time. Her house is painted in rainbow colours. The foundation is violet, the roof is red. The interior starts at blue-green and ends at yellow-orange. She is a retired professor who teaches at the Wanganui Polytechnic.

She describes her lodger as a shy man in his forties who works at the local library. She believes him to be from India or Fiji. She says he is unmarried and obsessed with cricket.

The rainbow house is filled with paintings, mostly figures in garish garments with eyes that follow you around the room. She serves me Dilmah tea while I wait for her lodger to come home.

She tells me she lectured in art till she lost her sight in one eye. Now she lectures in mathematics.

'That's a big switch.'

'Not really. Art is maths. Maths is art.'

She spends all afternoon showing me paintings and talking of numbers. She says that colours have musical frequencies and that if she ever lost the sight in her good eye, she would conjure up paintings through sound.

She speaks with a wonderful lilt and her language is as colourful as her topics. Her tea smells of flowers and tastes like fruit. And when she laughs the whole house sparkles. So when Sanjay Maninda Pradeep turns out to be a geek with a lisp who did not play cricket for Sri Lanka, I do not feel as if I have wasted an afternoon. In fact my thirteenth day was perhaps the one I enjoyed the most.

Peter Plumley Matthew

Adriana calls to say that if I go back to Sri Lanka, she will let me have Jimi for the summer. I tell her my work is not yet done and we get into an argument. She says she is separating from her professor. I ask if she will join us in Sri Lanka over the summer and she says no.

The biker aunties start cooking me breakfast and I start chipping in with groceries. They tell me there is a debate raging over whether Wanganui should be spelled Whanganui. Neo-Nazis have sent hate mail to the *Wanganui Chronicle* over this. We make fun of a TV soap called *Shortland Street* and end up watching a show I do not understand called *Lost*. Denise and Davina still do not ask me where I go during the day, but they offer to pack me sandwiches.

The quest has its moments – not all of it is lawns and picket fences and unhelpful neighbours. I get to take a canoe upriver to a Christian marae called Jerusalem. My oarsman is a Maori with a tattoo on his face, who tells me of pagan worship in the nearby villages. As if on cue, in the ripples before us we see a dead cow surrounded by wasps floating amid the reeds.

Past Ratana we arrive at Jerusalem where Katarina Gray Mathew invites me for a christening. I am given mulled wine and meat baked in an underground pit. We end the evening huddling around a guitar singing sweet songs.

I drive to Gonville and visit three Matthews families, each slightly shabbier than the last and all white-skinned pakehas. After that I decide to visit the local asylum.

'You look like Caine in *Kung Fu*,' says Peter Plumley Matthew gazing at my cloth bag. Peter is at the Lake Lewis Mental Hospital, an institution that was investigated for the liberal use of electro-shock therapy in the 1980s.

Peter Plumley Matthew tells me that Gonville used to be filled with swingers and that it destroyed his seven marriages. He is the most well-mannered person I encounter on my travels. I suppose seven wives is enough to drive any man to an asylum.

He tells me that he will become mayor of Wanganui and ban nuns. That he will napalm the Collegiate School. He tells me that everything in the universe rots, especially the human soul. He doesn't tell me anything about Sri Lankan cricket or about a cricketer who shares his name. On my twenty-first night in Wanganui, Peter Plumley Matthew features in every one of my nightmares.

P.S. Mathew

My final suspect, P.S. Mathew, lives at 93 D Longbeach Drive, Castlecliff.

After this I have no more leads. I may as well hook up with KiwiTour and head for Queenstown and not think for a while. Not think about whether I want to live in Sri Lanka with Adriana.

The fields around Castlecliff are covered in scrub and the streets are sandy. P.S. Mathew's flat is next to a fish and chip shop. I climb the stairs and am almost mauled by a sheepdog. The dog runs past me into the open doorway and disappears into the street. The steps are rose red and the walls are egg white. The door to 93 D is green and has the words Arnie, Coruba, Leander spelled in letters culled from newspapers cellotaped onto it ransom note style.

I knock and the door opens wide. Inside is dark and cluttered. Dark blue sheets with rune symbols block out the afternoon sunshine, shielding the room from the laser-like, headache-inducing heat that I'm still not used to.

A coffee-coloured lady with a slight moustache looks me down. The only light in the room comes from a TV playing a cricket match. It looks like New Zealand vs Bangladesh. The light falls on two Polynesian women dressed in shorts and T-shirts. One is knitting a wall hanging, the other is chopping up green leaves with scissors.

The one before me wears a housecoat that tugs at her sides.

'What do you want?'

'I'm looking for P.S. Mathew.'

'What for?'

'I'm a friend from uni.'

The ladies in the room cackle with laughter.

'What did you do at uni, Coruba? Your PhD?'

'Hey, I know this guy,' says the curly-haired one doing the knitting. 'You used to come to Courtneys on the square.' She turns to the one wearing glasses. 'The curry fella, used to sit by himself, we thought he was gay.'

'Leanne!' says the one who answered the door. 'Don't use that word.'

'Yeah, Leaky,' says Glasses. 'Curry muncher is racialistic. You should say sorry.'

'I didn't say curry muncher,' says Curly. 'I says curry. Hey bro, do you like curry?'

To my ears, curry muncher sounds less like a racial slur and more like a Looney Tunes character.

'Yes, I do. You ladies like cricket?'

I have seen these slappers at the empty bars I've sat at. They wore too much make-up and clothes ten years too tight. Harmless, middle-aged women who thought they were twenty-three. The apartment is a quagmire of wine bottles, plates, chocolate wrappers and cushions. It smells of incense and stale perfume. There is a poster of the Dalai Lama on the wall.

'Nah,' giggles Moustache. 'Leanne wants to sleep with Chris Cairns. Arnie wants to root Adam Parore.'

'Don't be gross, Coruba,' shouts Curly.

'You want to have a smoke?'

Something stops me from crossing the threshold.

'My fella likes cricket,' says Glasses.

'Your fella likes fellas,' says Curly, who gets a cushion thrown in her face.

'So none of you know a P.S. Mathew?' I ask from the doorway.

Moustache answers. 'I'm Sandra Mathew. Everyone calls me Coruba.'

'Do you have a husband, Ms Mathew?'

Her two friends squeal with laughter. On TV, a Kiwi batsman skies a sixer.

'This fella doesn't beat around the bush, does he?' says Curly.

'Yeah, Coruba's got a man,' says Glasses. 'His name's Siva.'

They laugh some more.

'I thought it was Shiva,' says Curly.

I glance at Moustache and feel my pulse quicken.

'Ms Mathew, your husband's name is Siva?'

She blushes while her friends chuckle. 'We named him Shiva last month, 'cos we're all getting into Indian yoga meditation spiritual stuff.'

'Where is your husband?'

Curly and Glasses do not stop laughing.

'Here he is,' says Moustache.

'Come here, Shiva. Where did you go, boy?'

I watch the sheepdog that almost mauled me run into the arms of the woman with the moustache. 'Where you been, Shiva boy?'

The dog starts licking her face.

The Big Man

I park at Castlecliff Beach, roll up what's left of my stash and wait for the sun to set. The beach is nothing short of abysmal. The sand is blacky-brown and the water temperature is a single digit despite it being the height of summer. I sit on the rocks and watch some Maori kids playing touch rugby on the hardened sand. I hear boy racers in the distance revving souped-up Holdens on the open road.

Just like love, karma can wield its club in strange ways. Why have I not been punished for all my cruelty? Why have I not been rewarded for my selfless dedication to my father's cause? Has the Big Man in the sky lost sight of me since I disappeared Down Under?

That would have to be it, I suppose. I've given it my best shot. What more can I do other than head home, clean up the book and try and get it into print? I don't think Lankan publishers are all that picky about books that ramble and have no conclusion.

As the breeze drops I notice the Maori kids doing something curious. They have abandoned their rugby ball and are hammering sticks into the hard black-brown sand. And then from their bag they pull out the two most beautiful things in the universe. A bat and a ball.

I spark my joint and step towards them. If they are not too skilled, I'll ask if I can join, it has been years. There are five kids all in their early teens and they all have bad haircuts. Mullets, skinheads and everything in between. I'll tell them I'm twenty-eight.

Before the first ball, they share a cigarette and eye me with suspicion. I turn and face the ocean and wait for them to begin playing. The tall boy with the mullet bowls quickly, but with little accuracy. The short batsman hammers a full toss to the sea.

'Good one, Corey, ya fucken meat,' says the boy in a hoodie at short leg.

'I reckon that's out, eh?' says the shaven-headed boy at mid-off.

'Get stuffed,' says the shorty with the bat. 'Yous are cheating.'

De Saram Road, Mount Lavinia. A flock of seabirds skim the horizon and a gang of cars whiz past at twice the speed limit.

From the other end, a fair boy with a mullet bowls from a shortened run-up. His first ball causes controversy. His second ball causes more controversy. His third ball makes me drop my smoke. I run towards them, the argument getting clearer as I near.

'That ball is sweet-as,' says Fair Mullet.

'It's a fucken no-ball,' says Hoodie.

'Just 'cos you can't play it.'

'You can't bowl that,' says Shorty the Batsman.

'Fuck off, bro. You're out.'

'Who taught you that?' I ask.

They all look at me.

'Who are you?'

I look at the fair boy with the mullet.

'Bowl that again.'

I pick up the bat from the beach floor and face up. The others sneer at me as the boy runs in to bowl.

He whacks it short outside off. It bounces, spins to leg, bounces again, straightens, and bowls me. It is the ball that bounces and spins twice. I didn't think it existed. I run up to him and I am screaming.

'Who taught you to bowl that?'

They mistake my enthusiasm for aggression. Shorty blocks my way.

'Steady on, bro.'

Hoodie advances, rolling up his sleeves.

'I invented that,' says Fair Mullet.

'Bullshit,' says the quiet, goggle-eyed one I hadn't noticed.

'I did so.'

'Mr Nathan showed us at practice last week.'

I look at Goggle-eye. 'Who's Mr Nathan?'

'He's a curry muncher like you,' says Hoodie and they all laugh.

'What's all this?' The man is scarier than the voice. He is browny-pink, obese, tattooed along his arms and face and wearing leathers. The sort you cross the road to avoid.

'You making trouble, eh, cuzzy?'

I throw aside the bat and walk up to him. 'Are you Mr Nathan?'

For the second time I cause the boys to laugh.

'Not likely, mate.'

'Where can I find Mr Nathan?'

The man regards me as if to gauge if the contents of my pockets are worth a bullet. I take a breath as he unzips his coat and reaches in. He pulls out a wallet and from it extracts a business card. It is then that I notice his crucifix and his collar.

Castlecliff Cricket Club
Free U-13/U-15 Coaching.
Gonville Grounds. Tues/Thurs 4.00 p.m..
Call S. Nathan 06-345-1614.

Mr Siva Nathan teaches maths and science at Wanganui Collegiate School and has done so since 2003, when he moved to Wanganui with his wife and family. The bursar's secretary is chatty without being nosey. She says he coached the 2nd XI for three years, but is no longer involved with school sports.

School is not due to open till February and both the headmaster and the bursar are away. She is unable to give out staff details. I thank her and run to the WangaVegas phone book, now permanently in the back seat of my rent-a-car.

The address I get is 3 College Street, a street I have travelled through many times before. While I drive there, through roads with more traffic lights than cars, I wonder what fresh disappointments await me. I think of my father jabbing his Jinadasa, tanked up on gal arrack. Did he expect his words to lead his son to a green fence and a flowering garden at the bottom of the world?

Two young boys are kicking a football. At the far end of the fence, away from the flowers, there is a wicket painted on the wall. The grass around it is shorn shorter than the rest of the lawn.

Both lads have curly hair and dark complexions. 'Is your dad in?' I ask. As the younger one nods, I pull out the postcard that Shirali Fernando gave me.

'You must be Luke.' He gives me a grin with teeth that have fallen out. The elder one ignores me and kicks the ball against the wall.

'Kula,' I call out. The boy raises his head, frowns at me, and then looks away.

The garden is like the rest of New Zealand. Spacious, empty and safe. The boys keep kicking the ball as I step onto the threshold.

I look to the sky and thank the Big Man for bringing me here. I ring the doorbell and I wait. The air is still and all I hear is the sound of ball hitting foot. Through the glass, I spy coloured shadows dancing like djinns before my eyes. And then slowly, painfully, and wordlessly, it is opened.

Last Over

'We'll only be remembered if we win it.'

Alan Shearer, Newcastle striker (1996–2006)

Twenty Zero Nine

No one wants to touch the fucking thing. Not even Nallathamby Printers in Pamankada. Every bugger I call, when I say I'm Garfield Karunasena, gives me the same reply, 'This is that cricket book, no?' I say yes and that is the end of the chat. I have tried big publishers like Flamingo India, but they refuse to even fart on an unpublished nobody from Colombo.

I have renovated the old house, got a regular gig with a jazz band at Barefoot, and done some weddings with CrossFire for extra cash. Jimi will be coming to stay with me this summer. Adriana, who just got back together with her professor, will not be.

The only local house to read the manuscript was BinPieris Publishers. These guys have put a few Gratiaen Prize winners into print. Their books are printed on good paper, have 'saffron', 'monsoon' or 'frangipani' in every other title, and have fewer spelling mistakes than most. When they agreed to read my manuscript even after hearing who I was, my hopes were high.

Two days ago, Frank Pieris told me they were unable to handle my book at this point in time. I leave to pick up the manuscript that cost me 3,000 bucks in toner and paper. I plan on barging in on Farouq Bin's office to ask what his problem is. If he can publish everyone else's crap, why can't he publish my harmless cricket book?

The office is a cottage in Colpetty and my book has been entrusted to a pixie-like girl behind the counter. 'Mr Karunasena. You've come for your manuscript?'

'No. I've come to speak with Farouq and Frank.'

'They're at a lunch meeting with a client.'

I plant myself on the couch. 'I'll wait. Got anything to read?'

'The meeting is scheduled through the afternoon.'

This girl is cute, but not really my type. I don't usually go for Lolitas.

'Is it, now?'

She frowns. 'Don't you want your manuscript?'

'No. I want to know why those two literary queens, the ones you call boss, why they don't want it.'

She comes out from reception and I see the rest of the pixie. Under her shalwar kameez I imagine a petite body.

'Here is your manuscript,' she says. 'You better take it home.'

'I'm not leaving without speaking to Farouq and Frank.'

She casts a gaze down the hallway and whispers. 'I will call you.'

'Why?'

She casts another glance down the hallway. She reaches behind reception, pulls out an envelope and hands it to me. 'Don't read it here.'

Defiantly, I open it then and there and she goes into paroxysms. She tries to shoo me away. I ignore her and look at the photocopied letter.

I swear very loudly.

The Sri Lanka Board of Control for Cricket
39 Maitland Place
Colombo 7

To whom it may concern
It has come to our notice that a libelous and defamatious book on Sri Lankan cricket may be seeking a publisher. It was written by late sports journalist W.G. Karunasena and is an insult to the administration and players of Sri Lankan cricket.

Karunasena has been known throughout the industry as a shady character, some say he suffered from mental illness in his final years. This book is gutter journalism at its worst and it would be irresponsible to publish and taint our national team who has brought such glory to our nation.

The SLBCC exist to protect and uphold the legacy of Sri Lankan cricket. We will not hesitate to take swift legal action against anyone who chooses to publish this antipatriotic rantings of a drunk.

We trust you will do the correct thing.

Yours faithfully,
Jayantha Punchipala
President SLBCC

She snatches the paper and pushes me. 'Go now. I have your number. I will get them to call you.'

She shoves me through the doorway. 'If you want this published, go.'

I stumble down the driveway, look back at the cottage and spy Farouq and Frank peeping from behind a curtain like two pantomime cats.

Enid Blyton

The call I get is at 8.30 sharp and it is not from Frank or Farouq, but from…

'My name is Enid.'

'Like Blyton.'

'That's funny. I am calling you to advise you on your manuscript.'

'Will BinPieris handle it?'

'Farouq and Frank won't. I advised them to. But they don't want risks. That letter was sent to all the newspapers, printers and booksellers. The Prime Minister's brother is now in charge of the Cricket Board.'

'*You* advised them?'

'Farouq and Frank don't know a ball about books. They keep up the image in *Hi!* magazine. Me and the cover designers only read manuscripts and recommend. We liked your father's book. But we have concerns.'

'What's the point if no one will touch it?'

'We can try international.'

'Yeah right.'

'Cricket non-fiction is a small market. We have boxfuls of Pramodya Dharmasena's biography collecting dust in our storeroom. But true fiction from South Asia on the other hand…'

Her voice changes. She almost sounds human.

'What's true fiction?'

'Are you willing to undertake changes?'

'Changes?'

'Get rid of the unbelievable stories.'

'What unbelievable stories?'

She mentions one.

'That one's true.'

'No, it's not. What about…'

She mentions another one.

'That's true as well.'

'I would prefer more stories like…'

She mentions one of the more believable parts of my father's book.

'That is 100 per cent bullshit.'

'Really?'

'Yes, my dear.'

'I don't believe you.'

'Ditto.'

'Also. Avoid real names. That is what will get you sued.'

'I have to make up a name for every single character?'

'Write the book as fiction, not as a documentary.'

'That's a helluva lot of work.'

'If you want international, Mr Karunasena, you need to work. About the writing style…'

'I can't change my father's…'

'Not his. Yours. You're cribbing his lines. Stop being lazy. And less swearwords please.'

'How old are you, Enid?'

'About half your age.'

'Funny.'

'Another thing. Less about you. More about Pradeep.'

I bite my tongue.

'We do not like your father's racial stereotypes. Tamils are ambitious, Muslims are greedy, Sinhalese are drunk. Please amend these.'

'Who is this "we"? How many of you are there?'

'Editorial decisions are made by three of us. We all have MBAs.'

Enid Blyton is getting on my nerves.

'One more thing. The ending.'

Enid Blyton is using my nerves as a trampoline.

'What about it?' I say as if I am a drunk in a bar wielding a broken bottle.

'To put it bluntly, it sucks.'

'I think you suck.'

'It's lazy.'

'It's poetic. It crystallises the moment of discovery. I want to show that I found him, without revealing what I found.'

'It's a cop-out.'

'I made a promise not to tell.'

'I'm sure it won't be the first promise you've broken.'

'I don't like your tone…'

'Will you write down what happened? Get it to us by Thursday and we shall have a contract ready.'

'A contract for what?'

'I shall be in touch on Thursday. See you later.'

Click.

Mr Siva Nathan

The door opens and the man before me is neither bald nor mulleted nor slit-eyed nor Pinocchio-nosed nor skinny.

'Mr Nathan? Mr Siva Nathan?'

'That's me.'

'I just moved with my wife to Bulls. Was down in Castlecliff on business and I got your card.'

I hand it to him. He nods, obviously having seen it before.

'Was looking for a cricket coach for my ten-year-old. Do you take youngsters of that age?'

'Not really…'

'I also have a thirteen-year-old. He's really keen to play.'

'Right. Come in, will you.'

He calls out. 'Luke, just ten minutes, then homework, OK?'

He is Friar Tuck in a tracksuit. He is stocky with dark hair on the back and sides of his head but none on his crown. The drawing room is blue carpets and green sofas. There is a cat asleep in a basket by the windowsill. Thin light comes through slats from venetian blinds. I see no sporting trophies.

'How long you been in New Zealand, Mr…'

'Garfield Karunasena. Is it that obvious?'

'I've been here a while, I can spot someone fresh off the boat.'

'How many years have you been here?'

'This is the thirteenth.'

'We landed last month. I'm a quantity surveyor.'

'Don't know what quantity you'd be surveying in Castlecliff.'

'The new…Japanese…construction. I was glad to meet you. My boys are cricket crazy, but there's no good coaches in Bulls. I'm Sri Lankan, so cricket's sort of a tradition for us, you know.'

Mr Nathan smiles. 'Kohomada? How? How?'

'Don't tell me?'

'Hard to believe, huh? Everyone here thinks I'm part Maori. Can I get you anything to drink?'

'Just water, thanks. Where in Sri Lanka are you from?'

'Moratuwa.'

I walk towards the window and spy some photos on the sill near the cat. The boys appear in various sizes and guises. I do not recognise Mrs Nathan in the large family photo. She is a tubby woman with short hair and faded skin.

'Your boys bat or bowl?' asks my host, handing me a glass.

'Youngest is a wild pol adi batsman. Older one is a left-arm spinner.'

'Ah really. What type?'

'Chinaman.'

'I also used to bowl that at one time.'

'Did you ever play professionally?'

His accent is curious. It retains its Lankan lilt, but also has a rough chipped quality. Part Maori, part something I cannot identify.

'Bit of club cricket here and there. But never had the temperament.'

'Everyone says that you're a wonderful coach.' I almost tilt my neck and bat my eyelids.

'I'm a much better coach than a player. As a player I never thought about what I was doing. Just did it, you know. When it worked, I rode it. When it didn't, I fell apart. What about you? You play?'

I let myself blush. 'Badly. I prefer to watch.'

'Are you sure you're OK with water? I have an arrack.'

I smile and shrug. 'As long as I'm not intruding on your day.'

He walks over to the decanter by the trolley.

'In Wanganui, things don't really intrude on your day. I'm surprised to see a young guy like you. Most Sri Lankans get bored here and want to go to Auckland or Wellington.'

'You're the only Sri Lankan here?'

'There's eight families on the other side of the river, some have been there for two generations. None of them are talking to each other.'

He chuckles and passes over his drink.

'You don't mix with the other Lankans?'

'They all know me, but I try and keep away. I used to play cricket in Manawatu with some Sri Lankan doctors. Half the time buggers were fighting with each other. I'd avoid Sri Lankans if I was you.'

'Sounds like good advice.'

'Kula, Luke.' He taps on the window and gestures through it. 'Enough now.'

He turns to me. 'My children hate cricket. Older one watches rugby league, the younger likes soccer. What can you do?'

'My ones love it.'

'Best thing you can do as a father is let things happen. Let them do what makes them happy.'

'Kula and Luke.'

'Both named after great men.'

I scratch my head. 'Only great man I know named Luke was Skywalker.'

We both laugh.

'A man called Lucky, my first coach, taught me a lot of things. I didn't always listen to him.'

The arrack stops in my throat.

'Kula was named after Mr Gokulanath, the man who taught me everything I know about cricket. Sadly, both men are no more.'

'I have heard that name...'

'Very strict man. Could spin a ball on water. Taught me all the grips. Told me to think of nothing when I bowled. To empty my head of thoughts.'

'There was a famous coach called Newton Rodrigo. Had six f…'

'Who?'

'Newton Rodrigo.'

'Never heard of him.'

I have to put my glass down. 'Excuse me, could I use your…'

'Sure. Down this way.'

I splash my face with water and glare at my eyes. I look more human on the days that I don't smoke. On the way out I pass an open door. The two boys are seated at desks listening to terrible, terrible Pacific Island hip-hop. I peep in.

The walls are covered with posters of severed limbs with the words Saw on them. The computer screen is bigger than my TV at home and is rigged to what looks like several time bombs. Wires scale the walls like ivy and creep along the floors.

'It was you, Kula. Wasn't it?'

The boy on the larger desk with the larger head of curly hair turns and looks at me. 'What?'

'You put your dad on Crikipedia.'

'Is that why you came?'

'Yes.'

For the first time he smiles. 'Good.'

Back in the sitting room, Mr Nathan is pouring a second shot. 'Come, let's sit in the garden.'

The Kiwi sun glares its lasers into my skull. We sit on a bench and look over the shorn lawn.

'Bring your boys next week. I don't charge, but we encourage parents who can afford it to donate towards equipment and stuff.'

'Sure. What made you coach there?'

'I used to coach at Wanganui Collegiate.'

I nod. 'The old English boarding school?'

'The job pays and the facilities are good and all, but I couldn't stand the kids. Bunch of rich brats. Spoilt. I teach there for the money. I guess that's why we all do things.'

I nod and sip.

'But some of these Maori kids, you should see their talent. Raw talent. Like our guys.'

I nod and sip and nod.

'I have one guy like Joel Garner. Big fella, thundering pace.'

'I saw them playing on the beach. There is an interesting spinner. Fair boy.'

'Ariki. Troublemaker, but he's a quick learner.'

'He was bowling this strange ball. Bounces twice.'

'Oh yes,' he smiles. 'That was a thing my coach Mr Gokulanath invented. You can't bowl it in a match. It's illegal.'

'It's genius. How do you bowl it?'

He gestures to the wicket painted on the fence. 'C'mon. Grab that bat.'

I don't think. I just do what he says. I stand where the fence is. He warns me to watch my shins. And then he runs in.

The Guatemalan

I have seen genius twice in my life. Once was in a garden in provincial New Zealand. The other was on the streets of Covent Garden.

The kid was dark and lanky, almost hunched. He had a weasel face and thick hair. Behind him was a tabla player and an amp. Surrounding him were about a hundred people, all with their jaws on the pavement.

His guitar spoke languages, sang sonnets and hypnotised strangers. The Guatemalan kid could push buttons that I could barely reach. I hated him for having a gift I would never share regardless of how many decades I practised.

I think of the Guatemalan as I watch Siva Nathan bowl. I watch the ball become conscious as it is guided by something other than gravity and wind. I give up trying to hit the deliveries and just marvel at the man's skill. The ball sits in the air for longer than necessary and spins at impossible angles. 'Play late. Watch the ball.' Mr Nathan has barely broken a sweat.

After missing several overs' worth, I finally manage to hit a double bounce ball back to the bowler.

'That's right,' says Mr Nathan. 'Play late. Always play late.'

He holds the ball with his long fingertips and turns it into a gyroscope.

'Don't think about it. Just see it in your head. And push your wrist this way. Simple.'

Simple is one thing it most certainly is not.

As the sun snuggles behind a cloud, we sit under the apple tree and watch cars glide down College Street.

'Why don't you come back to Sri Lanka and coach? These foreign coaches are no good.'

'Last year seventeen murders in Castlecliff. One twelve-year-old boy was knifed in the throat last Christmas. This year none. Not one. All the gang boys play in my teams. Our 1st XI beat the Collegiate seconds.'

'The Collegiate headmaster doesn't mind you training rival clubs?'

He drains his glass and smiles.

'He knows I work harder than half the teachers there. I used to be lazy. Can never understand that. Sri Lankans suddenly become model workers when they go abroad.'

'We have seventeen murders every day in Lanka. And those are the good days. Your country needs you more.'

He shakes his head. 'If I come back and try to do something, there'll be a thousand and one reasons not to and a million and one people to prevent me. In the end nothing will get done. I'll just get frustrated. Trust me. I know the scene.'

'It's not so bad,' I say, as a blue Peugeot pulls into the driveway.

'Here, the air is clean, you can live a good life, do your bit. There you just waste your energy. That's my wife. I think I may have to go.'

I recognise the woman from the photograph, though her skin is glossier in person. She carries a bag of groceries and her tracksuit trousers hang on her chubby waist. She looks sweet and matronly, somewhat of an MILF.

'Meet my wife Danila. Dani, this is Garfield…'

I drop my glass, but luckily it is empty and luckily it bounces off the grass. I squat down and pick it up. When I look up, she is staring at me.

'Garfield Karuna…tilaka.'

'I've seen you somewhere. Where did you work in Colombo?'

'I was mostly in Dubai,' I stammer. 'Thank you, Mr Nathan, for the drinks. I'll be in touch.'

I turn to his wife, who is now frowning. 'No. No. You must stay for tea. Siva, bring some ice cream after you drop the kids.'

'I really have to…' I stammer.

'We don't get to meet many Sri Lankans, no, Siva?'

'The tragedy of our lives,' says her husband, twirling the car keys. 'Luke, Kula. It's almost 4. Come now.'

Siva bundles the two curly-haired lads into the car. The elder one smiles at me this time.

'If you're gone when I'm back, I'll see you Tuesday with your boys, eh?' says Siva, turning the ignition.

I reach into the car, shake his hand, bow my head and say thank you.

'Excuse me,' says Danila, 'I need to make some calls.'

I am served Dilmah tea and Anchor milk and sit in the study as she makes her calls in the living room. The house is messy but nice. The study is filled with files and a small computer. After about fifteen minutes, she joins me. She sits at the computer and types.

'You look a lot like your father. Same face.'

I say nothing.

'Did he finish his book?'

I say nothing.

'Didn't think he would. I never told Siva about his secret biographer.'

'You mean Pradeep?'

'Reggie Ranwala went around telling everyone that Karunasena's book would ruin the SLBCC. You'll have trouble publishing it.'

'I don't intend on publishing.'

She looks at me and winks. 'Your father used to scratch behind his ear when he was lying.'

I stop scratching behind my ear.

'Here we go,' she says looking at her screen. '"Alice Dali. US/Swiss/Sri Lankan Post-Grunge 4-piece. Bass: Garfield Karunasena." Hmm. That picture was such a bad idea.'

I know exactly which picture she is referring to and I nod. 'You got me.'

'And are you going to get us?'

'Can I interview him?'

'No.' She holds my gaze and watches me flinch. 'His sister says the threatening calls have stopped. We have a good life here.'

Danila Guneratne was the one person in the book I most wanted to meet. I expected a femme fatale, not a soccer mom with an evil glare.

'I'll leave all of this out. I'll say I never found him.'

'Can we trust you?'

'I give you my father's word.'

She laughs. I'm not sure if it is out of scorn for my father's word or out of contempt for me.

'I have a note for Pradeep.'

'From whom?'

I fish out the paper I've been carrying with me for almost a year. 'Someone who said he was a friend.'

I have kept this paper in the condom pocket of my wallet. It has tears around the creases, but it is in decent condition.

'Who's it from?'

'A man called Kuga.'

She takes it and does not look at it.

'Do you smoke?'

'Sometimes.'

'Come outside.'

We sit on the porch and she borrows the lighter that I bought from the P. addict in Aromoho.

'Put your ash here,' she says, pointing to a barbecue-like contraption. 'In clean, green New Zealand, there's a separate bin for every type of rubbish.'

'So you're happy here?' I ask. In the warm porch light, caressed by shadows, she begins to resemble the creature my father once described.

'Siva doesn't know I smoke,' she says, staring at the McGillicuddy logo on my lighter. 'Soon I'll give up and he won't have to know.'

'He's a brilliant cricketer.'

She shrugs and eyes me with something resembling menace. 'You won't let us down, will you?'

I watch her spark the lighter, hold its flame to the air and set fire to a note that she hasn't even read. The corner glows orange and then fat flames grope her painted fingers. She drops it. It curls into black powder in the ashtray grille and we watch the flame turn it to dust.

'Everything turned out fine,' she smiles. 'Let's leave it like that. OK?'

Last Man / Have Chance

I spend a month in Unawatuna, editing chapters, chopping down tall stories and changing names. It's a wonderful place to be. Each day I eat crab curry and drink Portello and watch the bay change colour. Enid calls and reminds me of deadlines in her Sergeant Major voice. I have gotten used to her.

The day before I am to leave the beach, forced inside by a monsoon, listening to the wind bow down coconut trees, trying not to think of tsunamis, I pick up my acoustic and play a bass line that I have never heard before. I write a song about a rich kid who goes to nightclubs and shoots at mirror balls. I call it 'The Minister's Son'.

By the end of the week I have seventeen pieces of music I've never heard before. I swallow hard and call OP, guitarist from Independent Cycle, my friend from another lifetime. He agrees to meet me for a beer. I go for a swim after dinner. I float in the warm ocean, gaze at the stars and think of nothing.

'Uncle. You were supposed to be back last week.'

'Enough with the Uncle.'

'I must say you have worked hard.'

'From you that is high praise.'

She laughs, a rare treat indeed. Her laugh is a perfect melody in A major.

'Author's name I have an idea,' says Enid.

'Good. 'Cos I don't.'

'That surname you gave that Danila.'

'When?'

'When you met her and dropped your glass. Maybe drop that dropping the glass bit. Bit Charlie Chaplin, no?'

'Karuna-tilaka?'

'That's the one. With your middle name.'

'Shehan Karunatilaka? Bit common, no?'

'It'll be a good disguise.'

'I hate it.'

'OK. What about title?'

'I emailed you a new list.'

'Really? Let me check.'

I hear a computer keyboard being punched by a pixie girl and outside I hear waves. I imagine a sparse bass under a flanging C#maj7 chord. I have the urge to cut the line and pick up the guitar.

'You know, Garfield. The bits that we left out.'

'So?'

'We should put them back in.'

'Why?'

'The man from Flamingo reckons getting sued will be good for book sales. Free media coverage. Look what the fatwa did for…'

'You called Flamingo India?'

'Flamingo New York. Cricket and the subcontinent are very much in. So are lawsuits and scandals.'

'If we weren't on the phone, Enid, I would kiss you.'

'Can we finalise title? Are these the names you sent?'

She reads out my last night's work. '*The Book That No One Will Read*. Boring… *Revenge of the Chinaman*. Sounds like a Bruce Lee… *Shades of Brown*. What?... *Konde Bandapu Cheena*. No…'

She sighs. 'I don't think we're there yet. Let's keep thinking.'

So that's it then. I have finished something. Hurrah for me. Maybe nothing will happen. Maybe everything will. Maybe this guitar will catch a song. Maybe my son will play in the Royal–Thomian. Maybe the war will end. Maybe we'll get home safely after all.

'Garfield?'

'Can we wrap, Enid? I have a song to write.'

I can feel the melody approaching like a tidal wave gathering strength from the horizon. One more paragraph before it hits.

'Few things. Have you decided on the main character's name?'

'Either Vinothan Karnain.'

'Nope.'

'How about Charlie Jeganathan?'

'Nope.'

'Sanjeewa Amarasinghe?'

'Can't be a Sinhala name, men!'

'Jurangpathy Jeyarajasingham?'

'Sounds stupid.'

'Pradeep Mathew?'

'Who's that?'

'I don't know, I just…'

'Try it.'

Acknowledgements

Aadhil Aziz
Aftab Aziz
Ajit Chittampalam
Amit Varma
Anila Dias Bandaranaike
Anjali Gurusinha
Anton Rose
Anuruddha Fernando
A.R.L. Wijesekera
Arittha Wickremanayake
Ashley Halpe
A.S.H. Smyth
Azhara Aziz
Callum Sutherland
Channa Gunasekera
Charith Senanayake
Charlie Austin
Chula Karunatilaka
Dakshith Wekunagoda
Danushka Samarakone
Dhinesh Manuel
Dominic Sansoni
Ed Smith
Elmo Tawfeeq
Francis Felsinger
Gowri Ponniah
Harini Diyabalanage
Indi Samarajiva
Ishan Seneviratne
Jehan Mendis
Jehan Mubarak
Joe Lenora
Kanchana Warnapala
Kamal Kiriella
Kasun Karunaratne
Kumar Sangakkara
Lawrence Booth
Mahinda Wijesinghe
Malinda Seneviratne
Marcus Berkmann
Michael Ondaatje
Michael Roberts
Mike Marqusee
Nazreen Sansoni
Naren Ratwatte
N.B.D.S. Wijesekera
Paddy Weerasekera
Para Molligoda
Percy Karunatilaka
Prasad Pereira
Rajeeve Bernard
Ralph de Silva
Ranil Abeynaike
Ransley Burrows
Ravi de Mel
Reggie Ranwala
Richard Simon
R.O.B. Wijesekera
Rohan Ponniah
Romesh Dias Bandaranaike
Russell Miranda
Sajith Jayaweera
Sean Amarasekera
Selva Fernando
Shanaka Amarasinghe
Shami Gamage

Sid Dassanayake
Sidin Vadukut
Simon Barnes
S.S. Perera
Thangu Manuel
Tracy Holsinger
Uvais Amalean
Victor Ivan
Wendy Ebenezer
Wijesiri Mathugama
www.cricinfo.com
www.cricketarchive.com
www.youtube.com

Special thanks

Eranga Tennekoon
Michael Meyler
Deshan Tennekoon
Lalith Karunatilaka
Chiki Sarkar
Rimli Borooah
Dan Franklin
Ruwanthie de Chickera

SHEHAN KARUNATILAKA lives and works in Singapore. He has written advertisements, rock songs, travel stories, and bass lines. This is his first novel.

Manufactured by Versa Press on 30 percent postconsumer wastepaper.